I0772732

Black Kids Read Press LLC

https://blackkidsread.org/

© 2024 by Jomo W. Mutegi, Ph.D.

ISBN: 979-8-9866292-4-7 (eBook)
ISBN: 979-8-9866292-3-0 (Hardcover)
ISBN: 979-8-9866292-4-7 (Paperback)

Book design by Black Kids Read Press LLC

Printed in the United States of America / First Printing May 2024

TO IMARI J. MUTEGI

"He who is ruled by his appetite belongs to the enemy."

~ Ptahhotep

Table of Contents

BOOK 3

Prolusion

Dear Reader:

I am Dr. Jomo W. Mutegi. Howvever, you may call me "Professor." That is what Kamau and his friends call me. By profession, I teach at a university and conduct research on how people learn science. I focus specifically on the science learning of African people.

This story that I now share with you is unrelated to my professional work. I was asked by Kamau and his friends to share this story. I should admit here that this is not a task to which I am well-suited. However, you will come to learn, as I have, that Kamau and his friends are very persuasive. They don't hear, "No" when it does not suit them.

How This Began. One of my hobbies is camping. I am nothing like a survivalist, but I enjoy getting out in nature with a backpack and hiking through the woods. In fact, each year I take a special trip where I hike alone for a few days. This is an annual, personal retreat that provides me time and space to reflect. What is interesting is that, to my knowledge, no one outside of my wife and sons knows that I take this trip. Both the location and the time of my trip change from year to year.

One year, not long ago, I was on my retreat alone... or so I thought. It was the evening of the first day. After making camp, I gathered firewood, sorted and stacked it near my fire ring, then went to my tent to read and wait for sunset. It was an exceptionally hot summer day and, as mentioned, I was alone. So, for comfort, I came out of my sweaty, soiled outer clothing, wiped myself clean with a moist cloth, and slipped into fresh skivvies. For the next hour or so, I lay in my tent, reading, on top of my sleeping bag. Once it became too dark to read by nature's light, I decided to put on fresh evening clothes, make dinner, and enjoy the company of my fire.

Jomo W. Mutegi

As I turned and unzipped the doorway of my tent, I looked out to find five young men, sitting on the ground no more than seven feet away and looking right back at me. They sat cross-legged with their hands on their laps. Forming a half circle, they stared at me intently, saying nothing.

As you might imagine, I was scared senseless. How long had they been there? Had they followed me all day? What was their intention? I was convinced that they intended to do me harm. All I could imagine were pictures of my bloodied and beaten corpse all over the newspaper. *It might be days, or possibly weeks, before anyone found me. It could be worse; suppose they beat me, and I lived. I might survive the beating so badly injured that I would need to wait helplessly for relief. How would I get food and water? Wild animals would pick at my dying flesh! My wife would be a wreck.*

I refused to be an easy mark for a bunch of kids. My fear gave way to rage. I was determined that mine would not be the only corpse to be found. I reached back into my tent, grabbed my machete, and leapt forward to confront the group.

Now anyone who has tried to get out of a tent (and mine is a small two-man tent) knows that it cannot be done gracefully, or quickly, especially while holding a machete. So, my "leap" was probably more of a stumble. At any rate, as I exited the opening of my tent, one of them spoke, "Professor, forgive us for sneaking up on you. If you do not mind, we would like to speak with you. May I please introduce myself?"

I was completely taken aback. I didn't know what to think. My heart had been beating almost out of my chest. I am sure I was a sight, standing there dumbly, in my skivvies, holding a machete. But at that moment, I didn't consider how foolish I must have looked. I was too relieved. They're not trying to kill me. But as soon as I felt relief, I felt rage again. How do they know me? Thoughts and emotions raced through me. I must have stood quietly for minutes, trying to make sense of this situation. Why would they stalk me of all people? After a few moments, I realized that I was not as decent as I wanted to be. I had come out my tent mostly undressed.

I then realized that the nature surrounding us was indifferent to my dilemma. Crickets chirped. Leaves rustled as chipmunks scurried about. Wind whistled through trees. It was nature's way of saying, "Everything's okay. We'll let you know when there is a real catastrophe."

I chuckled, mostly at myself, and finally, I answered, "Sure, you can introduce yourself. But first let me get dressed. In the meantime, please give me some privacy. We need a fire." I motioned to the fire ring as I entered my tent to dress.

By the time I returned to the group, the fire was roaring. Maybe the shock of the event caused me to misjudge time. I didn't think I was gone long enough for them to have any fire going at all, let alone a blazing campfire. They were not even tending the fire. They were sitting around it laughing and telling jokes. I came to the circle, sat with the young men, and introduced myself. "Hello! I am Jomo Mutegi. But I imagine you know that. Now, please, tell me who you are."

Kamau smiled broadly at my introduction, and he introduced himself, "Dr. Mutegi, I am Kamau Njama." He then introduced each of the young men that were with him. I shook hands with each in turn. As Kamau concluded, I invited the young men to join me for dinner. They agreed enthusiastically. A little too enthusiastically, as it turned out. They ate all the dinner provisions I had for my entire trip.

As we began cooking, Kamau looked at one of the young men, then motioned to the tree line. He zipped off. Then another young man began what looked like a second fire about thirty feet off in the distance. He appeared to be stacking thick logs in a square configuration, leaving the middle empty. It looked more like a miniature cabin than the start of a fire. After a few moments, he returned to our fire and, without saying a word, pulled a camp shovel from his backpack, took some red-hot coals from our fire, marched off to his new fire, and dumped them into the empty middle of his "little cabin." He repeated this three times. He then added a row of thick kindling across the top of the square structure he had built. This was unlike any campfire I had ever seen. I commented to Kamau, "He'll never get a fire going like that."

Kamau smiled and nodded confidently. "No worries, Professor. If it doesn't work, he can always start again." The young man then stacked another layer of large logs on top of the kindling, and disappeared into the wood. While he was gone, the first young man returned with a dead rabbit hanging from his left hand. He said nothing. He sat down and began skinning it just as plainly as if he were washing his eating utensils.

I looked at Kamau in protest, "I have food for us to eat!"

The young man looked up and replied coolly, "Yes, sir. This is for later." As it turned out, the second fire was a smoker. The young man who had begun the second fire returned with freshly cut evergreen boughs that he used as a cover for the smoker. The freshly killed and skinned rabbit was to be smoked.

Over dinner, Kamau and the young men wasted no time. They jumped right in, telling me the most fantastic story I had ever heard. As they began, Kamau insisted that I take notes on their story. I protested, claiming that I had no notebook with which to record notes. Before my protest was complete, one of the young men offered me a composition book with my name neatly written in it.

According to the young men, they had traveled to a distant planet, met other life forms, fought against an alien race, and returned to earth unscathed! Their story was a great campfire tale. I would have enjoyed it, had they not been so insistent that it was true. I did not believe a word of it. In fact, the more they talked, the more absurd their story became. In time, I began to doubt even their names. Why would these young men stalk me, of all people, create this elaborate fiction, and try to convince me of it? They were a strange mystery. They were all very polite, much more polite than most young people nowadays. They were far more mature than typical young men their age. Certainly, they had all the awkwardness and some of the silliness that came with adolescence. Their voices cracked, and they giggled. Someone would make a reference that was really not funny, and they would giggle. They sometimes teased each other playfully and, of course, they giggled. However, none of them spoke too much. They were very disciplined, so much so that they seemed trained. Although the mood was light, and despite their awkwardness, I felt as though I was in the company of men whose first priority was business.

Yes, these young men were a great mystery, and that night I never came to understand this mystery. But after a while, I did not try. I simply resigned myself to enjoying the entertainment and their company. For the remainder of that night and into the morning, we ate, laughed, sang songs, and told tales.

As dawn began to break, Kamau looked at me and said, "Professor, we have enjoyed your company. Please write and share our story. It is vital to the well-being of our people."

I thought to myself, *The last thing our people need is another grand deception.* I didn't share that thought. It would have been rude. I did, however, protest a third time, "You know I am not an author."

Kamau retorted, "Actually, sir, you are an author. You are a very good author. I have read several of your papers. You make complex ideas easy to understand. It is also clear from your writing that you love Black people."

"Kamau, it is not the same. Those are academic papers. They are written for a completely different audience."

One of the other young men intervened, "Baba, of course we cannot make you write this story. But you should know that you *specifically* were chosen to do this small task. It is not for us. It is for our people. You were chosen by people much wiser and more powerful than us. You were chosen by the Council! Our job is simply to ask you to do this. If you are uncertain about anything that we have shared, please take time to see whether our story is consistent with known facts."

The appeal was very reasonable. It was too reasonable for a young man his age. I nodded towards the young man, "I will consider it."

"That is more than fair," he responded.

Kamau then interjected, "Professor, do you have moist towels that we could use to freshen up?"

"Sure!" I said. I headed towards my tent and climbed in to retrieve a pack of wet wipes. As I returned to share them, the young men were gone. They had vanished just as quickly as they had come. What was most strange was that they left no trace of having been there. I circled the camp area. Their gear was gone. The fire of the smoker had died out. There was not even so much as a footprint indicating their presence. I walked to the edge of the clearing and peered into the wood. I saw no trace of them. I did not hear footsteps. I saw no unnatural movement in the wood. I began to question my own sanity. Had I dreamt or imagined the whole thing? It was weird, and I had no answers.

As I approached my tent to lie down and gather my thoughts, I saw a bundle of leaves just to the left of my tent door. To my complete surprise, it was smoked rabbit meat wrapped in sycamore leaves. I laughed loudly, "Those are some young men!"

After that day, I saw Kamau and his friends many more times. These meetings were never planned by me. However, I have learned to be ready for them. Kamau might show up at any location, at any time, under any circumstance. He is like a living apparition. He might appear to review a draft of this text, to pass a message, or even to provide new information. It has gotten to the point that Kamau's presence is always felt.

This story only came about as a result of his persistence. The next time Kamau visited me was three months after our introduction in the woods. He appeared at my hotel when I was traveling on business. He simply wanted to ask how the story was coming. I had not written a lick. I had not intended to. After this second meeting, however, I began to investigate the viability of his claims.

I have learned that none of his claims can be disproven. None of his claims contradict any known facts. The technology that the young men claim to use is either real, existing technology, or it is viable technology. The method they claim to use for time travel is theoretically validated. The scientist Kamau identified as a pioneer of this work is real. I have spoken with him. In the area of space they claim to have visited, there is a star. In fact, all available evidence suggests that there is an earth-like planet orbiting that star. Even theories about the climate of that planet fit Kamau's description.

So, although their story is a fantastic one and although it sounds far-fetched, there is no available evidence that allows me to disprove or even to discount it. And given what I know of science, technology, Kamau, and his friends, I am inclined to believe them.

Sincerely,
Jomo W. Mutegi, Ph.D.
"The Professor"

BOOK 1

CHAPTER ONE

A Perfect Summer, A Perfect Day

Kamau's Big Opportunity

Kamau ran excitedly to the school gym. It was sixth period study hall, on the last day of school, and he and one other boy had been summoned to the gym to meet with the basketball coach from the neighboring high school. This could only mean one thing, Kamau thought. Coach Salters is going to let me try out for the JV team next year! DuBois High School had an incredibly competitive athletic program, and the boys JV and Varsity Basketball teams were the school's strongest performing teams. Kamau and his teammates had seen Coach Salters at a few of their middle school games this year. The whole team knew that someone was being scouted, but no one knew who. Now, Kamau had some answers.

The other young man was Big Jayven. Big Jayven was a center. He was a six-foot-nine-inch, thickly built eighth grader with very little basketball skill and even less athleticism. But what Kamau and his teammates learned this past year is that a six-foot-nine-inch, eighth grader doesn't need basketball skill or athleticism to make an impact. By contrast, Kamau was a wiry, five-foot-four-inch thinly built eighth grader with average basketball skill and tremendous athleticism. He was the team's point guard.

All year, Kamau's middle school coach, Coach Jenkins, was hounding him to "bring out the best in Jayven." Kamau didn't really know what that meant. When he passed the ball to Jayven in the post, Jayven would drop it. When he dumped the ball to Jayven on a drive, Jayven would drop it. When he lobbed a pass to Jayven from the perimeter, which he only did once, Jayven raised his hands and flapped at it as it went by. With his hands up, Kamau could see Jayven's stomach and back jiggling shamelessly underneath his jersey. Yet, he never spoke ill of Jayven. In fact, they got along very well. Off the court, Kamau befriended Jayven. On the court, Kamau used Jayven for screens, had him set picks for everyone, and forced opponents into his zone on defense. Jayven averaged twelve blocked shots per game and scared the bejesus out of most opponents.

Was that bringing out the best in Jayven? Probably not. Washington Middle School finished the season with a very mediocre record of six wins and five losses, and they finished third in the conference tournament. It was no matter, Kamau finished the year as the leading scorer. No one doubted *his* game.

Jayven and Kamau arrived at the gym and approached Coach Salters, who was standing and talking with Coach Jenkins.

Kamau reached out to shake hands with Coach Jenkins, "Good afternoon, Coach." He made sure to stand straight, project his voice, and look Coach Jenkins in the eye. Kamau's father had conditioned him to make proper greetings.

"Good afternoon, Kamau." Coach Jenkins smiled at him warmly.

Jayven nodded towards Coach Jenkins, "Hey, Coach."

"Jayven," Coach Jenkins replied. "Gentlemen, this is Coach Salters. Coach Salters is the coach of the boys JV and Varsity teams at DuBois High School. I have talked with Coach Salters about your strengths and weaknesses, as I see them. Coach Salters has also watched a few of your games."

Kamau nodded, smiled at Coach Salters, and continued listening. Jayven shuffled his feet slightly, stared at his shoes and uttered, "Hmmm."

Coach Jenkins continued, "Coach Salters, this is Kamau Njama, our point guard, and Jayven Brown, our center."

Kamau reached out to shake hands with Coach Salters, "Pleased to meet you, sir."

Jayven followed Kamau's lead and shook Coach Salters hand saying simply, "Coach."

Coach Salters addressed the boys, "Boys, I will cut right to the chase. You both have a chance of making the JV team next year and possibly making the varsity team by the time you reach tenth grade. But you don't have a *good* chance. You both have potential, but it is going to take a lot of work for you to realize that potential. You will need to put in the work and grow in some key areas."

Coach Salters was a brusque, no-nonsense man. He didn't waste words and had little concern for anyone's feelings. Kamau appreciated his straightforward approach. Jayven was now looking Coach Salters squarely in the eyes. He was all ears.

Coach Salters continued, "Jayven, you have two left hands and ten thumbs.

SECRETS OF THE VANGUARD ORDER

You need to improve your skill with the basketball. You need to work on catching, passing, and shooting, particularly your shooting in the paint. This summer, I want you to spend two hours a day catching, passing, and shooting. Normally, I would not look twice at a kid with your skill level. But you, son, are six-nine. Enough said." Jayven stared at Coach Salters, nodding and grinning.

Coach Salters turned to Kamau, "Kamau, you are a phenomenal athlete. In fact, you are the strongest athlete I have seen in the past fifteen years. Because of that, I am willing to work with you. However, to improve, you will need to work on your skills with the ball as well, especially your shooting and dribbling. Your shooting percentage from the field is thirty-five percent and from the free throw line it's sixty percent. Those numbers are too low. Your goal should be to improve those numbers to seventy percent and ninety percent on a practice court. Then we will see what they look like in competition. But your biggest challenge is learning to manage a game and lead a team. To help with managing a game, Coach Jenkins will give you some film to watch and study over the summer. Learning to lead a team is more difficult."

Kamau was so excited he could hardly contain himself. You wouldn't think he had just been told what a terrible shooter and team leader he was.

Coach Salters handed each of the boys a brochure. "There will be a skill building camp at the Stokely Center this summer. It's a two-week camp. It costs $400.00, and it's well worth it. If you expect to play for me, you will be there." Coach Salters grabbed his valise and walked towards the door. "If you have any questions, reach out to Coach Jenkins." He waived to Coach Jenkins. "Thanks again, Chris! I will see you next Friday." With that, he was gone.

Coach Jenkins smiled at Kamau and Jayven. "Congratulations, gentlemen. Work hard this summer. I look forward to seeing you take your game to the next level."

Kamau and Jayven couldn't stop high-fiving and back slapping one another. Kamau bounced all the way back to study hall. For the last twenty minutes of class, he sat there grinning goofily and hiding his face behind a book. He knew he looked ridiculous, but he didn't care.

Another Win

Just before the bell rang, Kamau's study hall teacher approached and handed him a hall pass, "Mr. Evans wants to see you at the end of sixth period."

Kamau's heart sank, and his grin was wiped clean. "What did I do?" he muttered to himself. The teacher smiled, raising her eyebrows, and walked away.

Mr. Evans was the Dean of Students, and no one ever wanted to see him. Kamau racked his brain trying to recall any mischief he'd been involved in over the past few weeks, but he could think of nothing. When the bell rang, Kamau headed towards the main office, hiding the yellow hall pass. The bounce, the light heart, and the never-ending grin he had just minutes before, were all gone. He walked slowly and solemnly, trying to figure out what he was going to say to his father. The thought of seeing Mr. Evans unnerved him, but the thought of facing his father scared him.

Kamau walked into Mr. Evans office and offered him the hall pass. Ignoring the pass, Mr. Evans looked at Kamau, smiling, "Have a seat, Kamau."

Kamau took a seat and addressed Mr. Evans, "Good afternoon, sir." He was instantly at ease as he thought, *A smile? A smile is good news. I didn't know that Mr. Evans ever gave good news.*

Mr. Evans began, "Kamau, earlier this year you took an eighth and ninth-grade version of the Preliminary Scholastic Aptitude Test, the PSAT 8/9. The Scholastic Aptitude Test, or SAT, is a test that students take, which is used in making college admission and scholarship decisions. Normally, the PSAT 8/9 is voluntary, but our PTA (that stands for Parent Teacher Association) decided to have every eighth-grade student at Washington Middle School take the exam."

Kamau's eyes glazed over as his mind drowned in Mr. Evans' alphabet soup. Mr. Evans continued speaking, but Kamau was no longer listening. Mr. Evans paused, "Do you follow me so far?"

Kamau stammered, "Uuh, I think so, sir. Uuh. So, I took a test?"

Mr. Evans responded eagerly, "Yes. You took a test. And you performed very well on the test. Very well! In fact, you scored in the seventieth percentile of all students taking the test. Now, my understanding is that you intend to attend DuBois High School next year. If that is the case, then you should know that DHS students with high academic potential are encouraged to apply for the Gifted and Talented program. Once in the GT program, you will have the opportunity to take AP courses (that stands for Advanced Placement) and dual enrollment courses. With your score on the PSAT 8/9 and your GPA, you have a very good chance of getting into the GT program."

Kamau's lips were moving, and he looked confused.

Mr. Evans asked, "What part is unclear?"

Kamau wanted to say, "All of it," but he felt that might be disrespectful and didn't want any problems. Instead, he said, "So, you're saying that I took a test, and I did well on the test."

Mr. Evans smiled, "Yes, Kamau. That's right."

Kamau couldn't reconcile getting a seventy percent on a test and having that be a good thing. But he didn't dare ask. That would invite Mr. Evans to give an impromptu math lesson. Instead, he asked, "Have you told my parents?"

SECRETS OF THE VANGUARD ORDER

Mr. Evans knew where this was going, "Not yet. I plan to call them this evening between 4:00 and 4:30 pm. Does that timing work for you?"

Kamau smiled, "That timing is perfect. We eat dinner at five o'clock." Kamau thanked Mr. Evans and left quickly before he had a chance to break into another elaborate explanation.

It was all Kamau could do to keep from running to seventh period. The bounce, the grin, the light heart… they were all back. Kamau thought, *Today is a perfect day. This is going to be a perfect summer!*

A Long Walk Home

At the end of eighth period, when the final bell rang, the school erupted in a frenzy of shouts and cheers. Students flooded the halls and made liberal use of the garbage cans, eighth graders especially. Kamau's section of the hall was abuzz with chatter.

Kevin clapped Kamau on the back and exclaimed loudly, "Yo, Kamau! Word on the street is that you 'bout to be the starting point guard at DuBois next year. Go get 'em my dude!"

Kamau thought wryly, *Well, as usual, word on the streets is wrong.*

But before he could speak up to add some truth to the discussion, Andre added, "Man, with Kamau running the point and Big Jay running the paint, DHS is gon' take state!"

Take state?! Are you kidding, Kamau thought. *We couldn't even…* Kamau's thought was interrupted as Carmen Anderson walked past, smiling flirtatiously at Kamau. "Congratulations, Point God!" She ran her hand along his chest and shoulder as she walked through to her locker, hips swinging to-and-fro like a pendulum. What little cool Kamau had, he lost it. His stupid grin went into overdrive. He felt it stretching the muscles of his face, but he couldn't make it go away. Carmen was one of the finest girls in the school. She was a copper-complexioned beauty that had blossomed into womanhood a bit earlier than the other girls, and everyone knew it.

As the chatter continued, Kamau gave up hope of adding truth to the discussion and got lost in his own thoughts of local high school stardom. He imagined an entire school year of boys congratulating and high fiving him and girls giggling at him, starry-eyed whenever he'd give them attention. His daydream was interrupted by a deep voice, "Yo, Big Man, you ready?"

Kamau turned quickly to see Imani holding a few books and smiling at him. She giggled and said deeply, "You like my man voice?"

Kamau smiled, "Let's go, Sis."

Imani Baharia was Kamau's best friend, and they had literally grown up together. Their parents were close friends. They were born two weeks apart and, since that time, they shared cribs, playpens, toys, and books. They learned to walk and talk at about the same time, and they had too many playdates to count. As they got older, they had both gotten into nasty fights protecting each other. Many of the kids at school thought that Imani was Kamau's twin sister.

As they headed home, Imani commented, "So, you had a big day. I heard, well, everyone has heard, that Coach Salters invited you to play at DuBois next year."

"Well, Coach Salters invited us to try out for the team. But he emphasized that, right now, we are not good enough to be on the team. He wants us to work on improving our basketball skills this summer."

She asked, "How do you feel about that?"

"I feel great about it! He gave me an opportunity, and I'm gon' take it. I am going to work hard this summer, practicing and training. I've already made my daily schedule. The way I look at it, this summer, I will be on a twenty-four-seven grind: physical conditioning, strict diet, film study, skill development." Kamau's voice rose with excitement. "Then next year, when I try out, I am definitely going to make the JV basketball team. There ain't no doubt about that. But my real goal," Kamau lowered his voice, "just between me and you, is to earn a starting position. This summer is about to be perfect. Everything is almost lined up."

"Lined up for what?" Imani asked curiously.

"Lined up for a good year. If I make the team, especially if I start, I am going to be *the* man! But I also need some new gear. I need some new kicks. I need a little bling." Kamau held his thumb and finger close together and squinted when he said *little*. "So, I am working on getting a landscaping job at Gary's Garden Center." Kamau smiled, "I told you – twenty-four-seven grind."

Imani smiled at Kamau with admiration, "Kamau, I am really happy for you!"

"Thanks, Sis!"

After a moment of quiet reflection, Imani's smile faded and she asked hesitantly, "What about your dad? Does he know about the plan?"

Kamau Faces Reality

Kamau clicked his teeth and exhaled forcefully, rolling his eyes, "Not yet. But I plan to tell him tonight." The enthusiasm was gone from Kamau's voice, and suddenly, his confidence was shaken. Kamau's father was a very strict and unreasonable man. Kamau asked Imani, "He has to agree? Right? What father doesn't want his son to work?"

Imani raised her eyebrows, tilted her head, and softly mouthed, "Yeah." But nothing came out. She knew Baba Njama. He was very much like her own father. They were both strong-willed, Black men, filled with paranoid delusions about how the world worked. They saw conspiracies around every corner. Hollywood was out to get us. Homosexuals were out to get us. The fast-food industry was out to get us. Corporations, schools, book publishers, Black churches, white churches, the police, FBI, CIA, politicians—there was no end to the list of organizations that were lined up to destroy Black people. Their fathers' paranoia severely restricted Kamau's and Imani's lives. But Imani also believed that such fathers were harder on their sons than on their daughters.

After a long silence, Imani thought again about Kamau's question, and she talked straight, "Kamau, 'What father doesn't want his son to work?' If any father wouldn't want his son to work, it would be *your* father. It would be *my* father if he had a son. And we wouldn't even know the reason why."

Kamau shook his head. "Yeah. You got that right. Even if they told us, we wouldn't understand." He deepened his voice and began mocking his father. "You see son, the Illuminati came together in the Middle Ages and invented jobs to deprive the peasants of their freedom."

They both laughed. Then Imani, using her man voice, added, "Then when official slavery ended, they introduced job-peasantry slavery and gave it to the Black man. Now you don't want to be a slave, do you?"

When their laughter subsided, Imani stopped walking and grabbed Kamau's arm, "Kamau, you don't need a plan to get past Coach Salters. You need a plan to get past your father. What are you going to do?"

Kamau sighed heavily, "I don't know, Sis. I did get a high score on some test we took, and Mr. Evans said it would help me when I went to DuBois next year. He is supposed to call my parents tonight. So, that's good news, and it might help."

They continued walking and Imani asked, "Why is basketball, new kicks, and a little bling so important to you? You are already a good athlete. You are a strong student. You dress fine. Everybody likes you."

Kamau gave Imani a sideways, disbelieving look. "Really? You think everybody likes me? I am a slightly above average basketball player, a slightly above average student, with average clothes and a few friends. If I weren't here tomorrow, no one would care."

Imani punched Kamau's arm angrily, "Why would you say that?! I would care! Your mother would care! Your sister would care! And your mean father, even he would care!" Still angry, she muttered, "I can't believe you would say something like that!"

Kamau clicked his teeth again and looked down sheepishly, "Yeah, I suppose.

But that's family." His voice dropped, "I just don't feel important to anyone."

Imani nodded in understanding. She knew that Kamau was baring his soul, and she also knew she should handle it with care. They walked for a few minutes in silence. When she broke the silence, she asked, "What was that show Carmen was putting on for you in the hallway?" Imani mocked Carmen with a sultry voice, "Let me rub you with my musty mitts, Point Gaahhd."

Kamau nodded and laughed, "Yes, she was doin' too much, wasn't she? That's not my style."

Imani nodded, "No doubt. You better wash that shirt. You know she got cooties."

Kamau walked Imani to her door, then headed home. They lived in the same small community. There were about three, square blocks where all the families knew each other. Kamau once overheard his father explaining to someone that the Njama's and a group of four other families moved into this neighborhood when it was rundown and overrun with drug activity. Each of those five families fixed up their respective houses and, together, they chased the drug dealers out of the neighborhood. Over time, they pooled their money, and whenever a new house became available, they bought it, chose a family, and invited them to move in. Kamau did not know the exact number of families in the neighborhood. He had never counted, but he knew he was safe in this three, square-block area. It was an oasis of well-maintained homes, beautifully manicured lawns, and clean streets. The neighbors all looked out for one another. Neighborhood toughs knew it was not a safe place to ply their trade, so they did business elsewhere.

The closer Kamau got to his home, the more his heart raced. As he approached the door, he realized that he was light-headed. How would his father respond? Kamau felt sick with worry as he keyed the lock and walked in.

CHAPTER TWO

The Last Dinner

Kamau's Good News

The smell of dinner smacked Kamau as he opened the door. He threw his head back slowly, and his eyes grew wide as the smell of spaghetti sauce and seasoned fish surrounded him. His shoulders dropped. His fear subsided. His mouth watered, and his stomach gurgled. He headed straight for the kitchen. "Momma!" he exclaimed, as he moved to hug her.

Kamau's mother, Ayanna Njama, was a lean, dark complected, attractive woman. All the Njama's were lean, dark complected, attractive people. Despite her lean build and advancing age, she still had the curvaceous, hourglass figure that had caught the eye of her husband many years ago. Unlike many teenagers, Kamau was never ashamed to be seen with his mother. She always looked good. She was very fashionable, but she dressed like a mother. Mothers of some of the kids at school didn't handle aging very well. They thought they could regain youth by removing fabric – short cut skirts, low cut blouses, too tight sweaters. These women looked like hookers, and they embarrassed their kids, especially their sons.

But to Kamau, his mother was nothing like that. In his eyes, his mother was flawless. She could do everything. She was a phenomenal cook. She kept the house spotless. She decorated their home so beautifully that, at times, it felt like they lived in an art museum. She was brilliant. There were very few topics that she couldn't speak about intelligently. Religion, health, politics, history, she seemed to know a good bit about everything. In the rare instances when she didn't know about a topic, she would drive a conversation just by asking insightful questions. She was probably the coolest, most composed woman he had ever seen. He had never seen her lose her patience or her self-control. She had to be borderline perfect. How else would she have survived all these years married to Jabari Njama?

"What's for dinner?" Kamau asked.

Ayanna smiled. She knew Kamau loved her cooking, and his excitement about dinner made her feel good. "Spaghetti, fried whiting, spinach, Caesar salad, and garlic bread."

"Beautiful!" he shouted. Kamau looked at the clock. It was 3:55. His mother didn't say anything about the test. It was still early, so he figured that Mr. Evans had not called yet. "What time will Pops be home?"

"He will be here any minute. Why don't you relax, freshen up, and help Rafiyah prepare the table? Dinner will be ready at five o'clock."

Kamau ran to his room, changed his clothes, and washed his face and hands. He peered in Rafiyah's room. "Good afternoon, Princess Rafiyah."

"Kamau!" Rafiyah stopped her play, ran to Kamau, and gave him a big hug. She had just turned five a few months ago, and she was always excited to see her big brother. "I'm building an airport with Lego blocks. Come build with me Kamau!" She grabbed his hand and tugged on him.

Kamau smiled, "No, sweetie. I'm going to my room. I will come back in a few minutes, and we can set the table for dinner."

Rafiyah, let out a disappointed whine, "Ooookkkkayyy."

Kamau went to his room, shut the door, and calculated how much money he could earn this summer working at Gary's. Over ten weeks of summer, he could earn just under $3,000. "What could I do with $3,000?" he mumbled to himself as he wrote out his list. "Let's see, this will pay for school clothes, school supplies… Oh! Student Activity Fees!" The school was always charging additional fees for things—field trip fees, athletic participation fees, class retreat fees, P.E. uniform fees. If it happened outside of class, there was a fee for it. His dad hated it. He sometimes called the school Fees-R-Us Middle School. He also complained that DuBois would probably be worse. "No worries, Pops. I will cover some of those pesky fees."

Kamau felt proud of his list. Of course, he wouldn't mention the bling. There's no need to distract the old man. Hearing his father at the door, Kamau jumped up, went to get Rafiyah, and headed downstairs.

"Daddy!" Rafiyah sang out as she ran to Jabari, jumped into his arms, and hugged his neck. She hugged him just as she had hugged Kamau. She gave him the same invitation too. "I'm building an airport with Lego blocks. Do you want to help me?"

"Of course, beautiful! I will help right after dinner." Jabari kissed Rafiyah on the forehead and put her down.

SECRETS OF THE VANGUARD ORDER

"Hujambo, Baba?" Kamau asked in Swahili as he approached. His father liked it when Kamau spoke Swahili. But Kamau never really applied himself to learning it, and he only knew a few phrases. This simple greeting meant, "How are you, Father?"

Hearing the greeting, Jabari looked up at his wife as if to ask, "What gives?" She shrugged. Hugging Kamau, Jabari responded, "Sijambo, mwanangu." Jabari knew that, despite his best efforts, Kamau knew very little Swahili. So, he kept his response short and simple. This greeting meant, "I am fine, my son." And with that, Jabari moved to hug Ayanna.

Kamau guided Rafiyah as she set the table. She had a general idea of how to set the table, but she sometimes confused the location of glasses, and the place settings were almost never lined up properly. Kamau didn't care. If the food was in arms' reach, he could handle the rest. But he was asked to help, so he did. These types of details were important to his father, and there was no use in arguing. He stopped periodically to give explanations to Rafiyah, reminding her how it should be done and then letting her do it herself. While they worked, Kamau kept an eye on the clock.

Then it happened. Right at 4:30, the phone rang. His mother answered it. Kamau tried to look disinterested in the call. He squinted his eyes as though checking the alignment of a place setting. At the same time, he strained, trying to hear the phone conversation. He wasn't fooling anyone. Rafiyah asked for help with the serving dishes three times, but he didn't hear her. He just stood there squinting and nudging a plate back and forth.

The phone call ended, and dinner was served at 4:45. Kamau searched his parents' faces, but he could tell nothing. They were both pleasant, but impassive. It was strange. They both had this habit of hiding their true emotions and presenting a neutral face to the world. Kamau once saw them drive a car salesman to frustration as he presented his sales pitch. He joked, cajoled, flattered the Njama's, proclaimed how great the car was, and talked about the high demand for the car. The whole time, Jabari and Ayanna just watched him, listened expressionless, and said nothing. As he went on, the salesman began stuttering, sweating, and growing increasingly uncomfortable. By the end, he almost gave the car away. Even as they signed the paperwork, they were composed and expressionless. Kamau had no such ability. He was eager to hear about this phone call, and it wouldn't have been more obvious if you wrote the word "eager" on his forehead.

Mr. Njama said grace, and as everyone began to eat, he steered the conversation to reports of everyone's day, news from friends and family, and reflections on society. No one said anything about the phone call.

After he began eating, Kamau didn't seem to mind. He had a voracious appetite, and the food was delicious. He had two full servings of everything. After his second serving, he stopped. It was not that he was full, but he didn't want to be seen as greedy, especially not today.

After everyone had eaten their fill, Mrs. Njama went to the kitchen to get dessert. As she stood, she looked at Kamau, "We received a call from Mr. Evans today. But of course, you knew that." She smiled as she walked away.

Mr. Njama picked up where she left off, "Congratulations, Kamau. That is a noteworthy achievement. Your work is paying off." Jabari's affirmation surprised Kamau, and he grew visibly excited.

"Asante, Baba," Kamau said, thanking his father. "I don't understand how seventy percent on a test is a good score."

Mr. Njama explained, "No, Son. A score of seventy percent on a test would mean that you got seventy percent of the answers on the test correct. Your score was at the seventieth *percentile*. That means that your score was higher that seventy percent of the people who took the test."

"Wow." Kamau was shocked and impressed with himself, but he wasn't sure if it was impressive. "Is that pretty good?"

Jabari looked at him intently, searching him. "That depends." He paused. "Is it your *best*?"

Kamau shrugged, "I don't know."

As Ayanna returned with dessert, Kamau blurted out, "I have more good news!" In his excitement and nervousness, he began sloppily spilling his plan. "Coach Salters from DuBois High School came today. He met with me and Big Jayven…"

"Big Jayven and me," Ayanna corrected.

"He met with Big Jayven and me," Kamau continued. "He wants us to try out for the JV team at Dubois next year!"

"That's excellent news, Kamau!" Jabari exclaimed. "Coach Salters is very restrictive about who he allows to try out for the team. So that is a very special invitation."

More affirmation? Kamau was beside himself, and he continued even more excitedly, "He gave me and Big Jayven… uh, Big Jayven and me… some things to work on over the summer, and he wants us to go to a basketball camp. I have the flyer for the camp."

Ayanna flashed a glance at Jabari. Jabari saw her, but he continued looking at Kamau.

Kamau continued, "But don't worry about the cost of the camp. There is a very good chance that I will be getting a landscaping job at Gary's this summer.

I will be able to pay for it."

"You will be able to pay for the camp?" Ayanna asked coolly.

Kamau nodded his head vigorously, "Yeah and…

"Yes," Ayanna corrected.

"Yes, ma'am. Yes, I can pay for camp and school clothes and fees." He blurted out "fees" and grinned stupidly.

Jabari sat for some time, saying nothing. Ayanna quietly ate her dessert. Kamau's grin and his excitement faded with the prolonged silence. He pushed his dessert away and stared blankly at the table.

Rafiyah looked around confused and asked innocently, "Is dinner over?"

A Final Rebellion

Mr. Njama's head turned from Rafiyah. His expressionless face settled squarely on Kamau, and he spoke slowly and deliberately. "Son, we have already made plans for you to attend the Akhet this summer. You will not be able to work at Gary's, and you will not be able to attend Coach Salter's basketball camp."

Kamau's face contorted into a mask of anger, but he remained silent.

Mrs. Njama excused Rafiyah. "Sweetheart, you can go if you would like. Be sure to wash your face and hands before you play."

As Rafiyah stood from the table to be excused, she walked towards Kamau, grabbed his head, and whispered loudly in his ear, "Don't be mad, Kamau. You can have some of my allowance."

As she walked away, Kamau sighed heavily. He opened his reddened eyes. They were beginning to tear. "Why? Why do I have to go? All I want to do is to spend my summer working and training. Is that so bad?" As he spoke, he realized he was not being interrupted, and he grew more confident. As he grew more confident, his voice found more bass and more volume. "I don't cause you any problems. I don't hang out in the streets. I don't use or sell drugs. I have never disgraced you. Why can't I have just one thing that is important to me?"

As Kamau's tone and volume rose, Ayanna feared he would go too far, and she knew that Jabari would bring Kamau and his volume back down. She didn't want to see that, so she interjected, "Kamau, we want you to have and to enjoy every good thing that life has to offer. And we are preparing you for that. Now, the Akhet is a once in a lifetime experience. Most young men will never see this opportunity. You are going to make new friends, probably lifelong friends, and you are going to become a stronger man because of it." Ayanna's tone was soothing. She was nurturing. She dropped her mask of impassivity and allowed Kamau to see and to feel the love she had for him. And it worked.

Kamau protested again, this time with a more moderated tone. "You think I need to go to this Akhet to make friends and to be a stronger, better person?" As he thought about the implications, he grew incensed, and his volume rose again, "I am not bad. I am a good kid!"

Mr. Njama responded, "Yes, Son, you are a good kid. But we are not rearing you to be a kid. We are preparing you to be a man. We want you to be a man that does more than survive in this wretched world. We want you to thrive. To do that, you must be more than a good kid." Mr. Njama showed none of the warmth and nurturing that his wife showed. He was impassive, strictly business.

The conversation was getting to be too much for Kamau. His head was swimming in a sea of thoughts, ideas, rebuttals, protests, and he was so angry, he couldn't sort it all out. He knew there was no use in arguing, but his disappointment and pride drove him on. He could not let it go. "But I am thirteen years old. I am almost fourteen! You can't keep making decisions about my life without talking to me about it!"

It was all Ayanna could do to keep from laughing. *Thirteen years old?* she thought. *Boy, we have clothes older than you.*

Jabari responded, "Kamau, we *can* make decisions about your life without telling you, and we *will* make decisions about your life… without telling you." Mr. Njama was growing weary of the debate. So, he ended it. "Now this conversation is over. Take some time and get yourself together. When you have cleared your head, we can talk more about what your summer will look like."

Kamau sat at the table for a moment, brooding. Ayanna began clearing the dishes.

Kamau stood to walk away, but stopped when he heard Mr. Njama's forceful reprimand, "Excuse me?!"

Kamau looked down at him disrespectfully and muttered, "Can I go?"

Mr. Njama stood, allowing his face to show outrage. He bent close to Kamau, so that his lips rubbed against Kamau's nose when he spoke. "Son, I have given you a good life these past thirteen years. And if you are upset, if you think that you've been dealt a bad hand, if you think life can't get any worse, then you need to be more creative. Because I can certainly make years fourteen, fifteen, sixteen, seventeen, and eighteen more miserable than you can apparently imagine! Are we clear?"

Kamau's eyes were as big as saucers. His head and torso were arched back as he tried to get away from his father's yelling and spitting. He replied, "Yes, sir."

Mr. Njama just stood there, lips to nose, peering into Kamau's eyes.

Kamau's brain, which must have been stunned by Mr. Njama's hot, garlicky breath, finally came alive. Then Kamau asked with a great deal more respectfulness than before, "Sir, may I be excused?"

Hearing these words, Mr. Njama straightened up, stepped back, and replied in the most pleasant voice and with the hint of a smile, "Of course. If you would like, we can talk about the Akhet later this evening."

When Kamau left, Jabari joined Ayanna in the kitchen and helped her to clean the dishes.

She looked at him inquisitively, "Did you know about these pre-pubescent plans?"

"I knew something, but I didn't know Kamau's plan. Coach Salters reached out to me last week. He didn't say anything about the camp, but I could tell that he was feeling me out. He was trying to get an idea of how much we would let JV basketball invade our home. After that conversation, I assumed he was interested in having Kamau on the team. I just heard from Gary this afternoon. He was trying to get an idea of how much we would let that petty, minimum wage job invade our home. I made assumptions there too."

Both Coach Salters and Gary knew the Njamas. In fact, most everyone throughout the city knew the Njamas. Most everyone also knew that the Njamas were weird. Their eating, their dress, their socializing was always a bit outside of the norm. And everything they did seemed overladen with rules and restrictions. It made people uncomfortable. To Kamau, it made life unbearable. At any rate, the Njamas also had a strong reputation throughout the city. They were intelligent, accomplished, and honorable people. And they were not pushovers. They would stand toe to toe with any politician, corporate leader, or any criminal, for that matter. They would stand up against anyone who tried to take advantage of them or their friends, and they would win. If you wanted to get something done, Jabari and Ayanna Njama were powerful allies to have. So, people respected them. This is why Coach Salters and Gary took the time to talk with Jabari Njama before approaching Kamau.

Ayanna smiled and said playfully, "Well if you knew all of this, why didn't you tell Kamau? You know he's almost fourteen! You can't keep making decisions about his life without conferring with him!"

He smiled at her flirtatiously. "That's funny, because I seem to remember that we created his life… and we didn't seek his approval or consult with him in any way."

Ayanna smiled dreamily and purred, "No, we did not!"

Jabari reflected out loud, "Were we that dim as teenagers?"

"I don't think I was, but I am quite certain that you were. There's something about testosterone. It just overrides the reasoning part of the brain."

Jabari nodded his head in agreement. "Yes, it can do that." He breathed a sigh of resignation. "Well, what can you do?"

Ayanna huffed, "Just keep loving them." She gathered herself. "Sir, I believe you have been called in to work. You have an airport to build."

"Yes! I do."

"I'll finish cleaning."

Jabari patted her backside, kissed her proffered cheek, and went upstairs to see Rafiyah. When he peered up the stairs, Rafiyah was looking down at him crying, "Daddy! Kamau is gone!"

An Awkward Dinner (O'Leary)

Amelia fidgeted with her silverware as her eyes darted about. Daphne smiled at her warmly, "Amelia, I just love your earrings. They complement your dress perfectly!"

Amelia giggled slightly through her thin, pursed lips, "Thank you." And she looked away nervously.

Timothy smiled and thought, *How does Dan live with this sour puss?*

Daphne continued her gushing, "You have a gift for accessorizing! You have got to show me how you do it. We should make a day of it." Daphne smiled flirtatiously at Timothy, "How much of these guys' money can we spend in an afternoon?!"

Amelia hummed something incomprehensible through her closed mouth. Daphne gazed at her blankly.

Timothy jumped in, "Well, Daph, don't do too much. You wouldn't want to deprive us the pleasure of spoiling you."

Timothy and Daphne laughed affectionately. And Timothy watched Amelia smile. Or did she have gas? It was hard to tell. Her lips stretched slightly, but they never parted. There was no spark in her eyes. There was no joy. *Yeah, it was probably just gas.*

Just then, Dan returned to the table. Seeing the awkwardness of his wife, he quickly took command. "Thanks for your patience. Tim and Daphne, you are both as good as gold!" He smiled broadly and rubbed Amelia's back. Daniel Silverstein was Senior Vice President of the Biological Technology Division of TechInnoGen, Inc. Within the company, it was known simply as BioTech.

Given Dan's academic and professional background, this position was a tremendous accomplishment, because he was not a high achiever. As a student, he was good but not great. As an intern, he was good but not great. As an entry level researcher, he was good but not great. In fact, at every point in his career trajectory, he was extremely mediocre. Where he excelled was in his ability to advance. And here, he had two special gifts. His first special gift was that he was a social chameleon. He was able to blend seamlessly into any situation. Once there, he knew how to make himself beloved. His second special gift was picking the right people. He knew who to befriend, who to mentor, who to be mentored by, even who to fight. His one failing seemed to be his wife. No one quite understood how or why he picked her. By contrast, his greatest pick was Timothy O'Leary.

They had first met when Timothy was a college student. Timothy was working as a summer research intern with Dr. William Crosby, one of the research coordinators at TechInnoGen. Daniel, who had been vying for a promotion to a position as research coordinator, spent a lot of time around Dr. Crosby's Research Team, especially the interns. He often took them to lunch and asked a lot of questions about the research. He especially gravitated to Timothy, who was very knowledgeable and very friendly. Daniel felt safe with Timothy.

Near the end of that summer, and just a week before the internship would end, Timothy overheard Dr. Crosby having a heated exchange with the senior vice president for R&D. Dr. Crosby was accused of fabricating data for the project on which Timothy was working. This came as a shock to Timothy, as he was familiar with the research and could verify that there was no fabrication. But he was only a college student. No one would believe his word over that of well-established, senior scientists.

Two months after his research internship ended, Timothy heard that Dr. Daniel Silverstein had replicated Dr. Crosby's research and replaced him as research coordinator. Upon hearing this, Timothy went to Dr. Crosby's old office at TechInnoGen with a package. He was told that Dr. Crosby no longer worked at the company, and that his replacement, Dan Silverstein, was unavailable. So, Timothy left a package with Dan's secretary, Marlene. The package was addressed to Dr. Crosby, and it contained copies of the original data from the summer research project. It also contained a note thanking Dr. Crosby for the research opportunity and indicating that Timothy was still in possession of his own copy of this data.

Once he received the package, Dan reached out to Timothy and offered him a position as lead intern the following summer. This is a position that Dan created specifically for Timothy. Once he graduated from college, Dan offered Timothy a position with a starting salary that was forty percent higher than any other offer he had received. From that point on, Dan and Timothy were inseparable. Whenever Dan advanced, he made certain to give Timothy the best position possible, and always under his own supervision. In return, Timothy did excellent work.

Timothy was a brilliant scientist—one of the best. He was a far better scientist than Dan, but this never interfered with their arrangement. Timothy was not self-seeking. He was not envious. He was content to toil away in obscurity. In fact, to many, he was too passive. He was sometimes criticized for not seeking advancement more aggressively. And he may have had good reason for this approach. Marlene once overheard him speaking in hushed tones to Daphne, "This is a difficult business for African Americans. Dan is a good person. He's always taken care of me, and I trust him." Hearing this report from Marlene, Dan was secure in their arrangement.

"Speaking of gold…" Dan smiled confidently across the table and looked squarely at Daphne. "Daphne, you should know that I am on the verge of making you and your husband very wealthy."

Timothy tried to mask his eagerness, "Oh, really Dan?! Well, do tell."

Maybe it was the nasal, whininess of Timothy's voice. Or perhaps it was Dan's repulsive self-importance. Whatever it was, Dan ignored Timothy, the same way an adult ignores a nagging child. "Daphne, TechInnoGen has never had an African American hold the position of senior vice president. But if all goes well…" He looked condescendingly at Timothy, "…and if you play your cards right…" then back to Daphne, "…your husband will be the first to hold that honor."

Daphne smiled, as though impressed and appreciative.

Amelia's face contorted into that gassy smile as she cooed, "Oh, Dan, that is so kind of you."

Dan nodded in agreement. He seemed to approve of himself.

Timothy whined again, "Well thank you, Dan. That is very generous. What's the project? Maybe I can be of help."

Dan chuckled dismissively, "No, Tim, this is a project that I am better off handling alone." He guffawed loudly, "Besides, your promotion is not a gift if you have to work for it."

Amelia grinned smugly as Dan scanned the faces of both Timothy and Daphne. Both of them sat there grinning at Dan. In fact, they were admiring him. Neither of them, it seemed, had even a modicum of self-respect.

Kamau Plans His Escape

After being dismissed from the table, Kamau sat in his room and fumed. His face contorted into a snarl, and wicked thoughts paraded through his mind. *Who does he think he is? What thirteen-year-old needs to get permission to get up from a table? I'm almost fourteen! You can save that for Rafiyah, not for me. I'm not a child! Who does he think I am, getting in my face to talk? Next time I ought to head butt him. What kind of man would try to keep another man from making money? He must be insecure. I'll show him. I don't need his house. I can take care of myself.*

SECRETS OF THE VANGUARD ORDER

Kamau had worked himself into a frenzy. He was angrier now than he had been at the table. But now he had a plan. He made two phone calls. The first call was to his mother's mother, Grandma Charline. Kamau didn't think Grandma Charline liked his father very much. She was always questioning Jabari's heavy-handed ways. Anyway, Grandma Charline seemed a bit confused at first, but Kamau helped her to understand the gravity of the situation. Grandma Charline agreed that Kamau had an "understandable reason for concern" and offered to let Kamau stay with her and Grandpa as long as he needed. They also agreed that Grandma Charline would pick up Kamau Sunday at afternoon from the community center playground. This would give Kamau a day to say goodbye to most of his friends. The second call was to Imani. He would say goodbye to her now.

After getting off the phone with Imani, he walked over to her house, and they met in her backyard. Kamau told her what had happened with his father: how he had ignored Kamau's desire to play basketball; how he laughed at Kamau's prospect for a job; how he belittled Kamau in front of his mother and little sister; and how he threatened to beat Kamau.

She commented, "Kamau, I have never seen you this upset before."

"I just can't take it anymore. I can't take *him* anymore. That's why I'm leaving."

"Leaving?!" She shouted this before she realized what she was doing. Then she moved closer and spoke in softer tones. "Kamau, where are you going to go? Is it that bad that you need to leave?"

"Imani, you know better than anybody how bad it is. Everyone has a cell phone, except me. Everyone goes to parties, except me. Other kids go on dates. I can't go on a date unless he meets the girl, meets her parents, gets a completed application, a five-hundred-word essay, and a background check. I can't watch TV. I can't listen to popular music. Now, I can't even get a job?! No, ma'am. I've made up my mind. I'm leaving Sunday, and I wanted to tell you goodbye."

Imani's voice trembled, "Goodbye? Where are you going? You're leaving *me*?" Imani was in disbelief. She had never imagined any phase of her life without Kamau. As she began to cry, she dabbed tears from the corners of her eyes.

Kamau stared off in the distance, and he said nothing. He was resolved. He refused to look at Imani because he knew he would get emotional, and he didn't want her to see that.

Imani gathered her composure, and they sat in each other's company for fifteen minutes or so. They said nothing. They enjoyed the breeze, and the city sounds that came in early summer.

Imani broke the silence. "Wait here. I have something for you." She ran into the house and returned, pinching a small piece of paper. As she got closer, Kamau could see that it was a 2"x3" photograph. "Keep this," she said.

He nodded. "I will. You know I don't plan to die. I just won't be able to see you as much because I won't be around the corner."

"I know." She hugged him tightly and long. "You better get home before Baba Njama sends out the troops."

Kamau nodded again, "Bye, Sis."

****

Mr. Njama ran to the top of the stairs, picked up Rafiyah and hugged her. "It's okay, sweetheart. It's still early. Kamau may have just gone out for a bit."

Rafiyah rested her head on his shoulders and groaned softly. She wasn't convinced. As a matter of habit, the Njama's never went anywhere without letting each other know where they were going. If their three-block neighborhood was an oasis, the surrounding city was the desert. And it was dangerous to stray too far. Rafiyah was too young to know about all the dangers that lurked outside, but she knew it was strange for Kamau to go somewhere and not tell anyone.

Hearing Rafiyah's cry, Ayanna came to the bottom of the stairs and looked up, "What's wrong?"

"Kamau is gone." Jabari set Rafiyah down, and she grabbed his leg. "I'll call Rafiki. He and I will canvas the neighborhood."

A few moments later, Jabari returned to the kitchen with Rafiyah trailing behind. "Kamau is in Rafiki's backyard with Imani."

Ayanna looked at him but said nothing. She didn't have to speak. Jabari knew what she was thinking. "No, I'll give him a pass this evening. He still needs to get his head together."

The three of them retired to the living room and read. Jabari read a magazine, Ayanna read the newspaper, and Rafiyah read *Daffy Dog Diva*, which was one of her favorite books.

After a time, Kamau stepped through the door to see the Njamas sitting peacefully. The peacefulness had him confused, and it was obvious. His eyes grew large and began darting around the room in search of an explanation, and he braced himself for a tongue lashing. But none came. No one said anything. Mrs. Njama and Rafiyah didn't even look up at him. He stammered, "H-Hello."

Mr. Njama, wearing the hint of a smile, looked at him, nodded, and replied, "Hello." Then he returned to his reading.

As Kamau headed to his room, he began to fume all over again. He thought, *They don't care anything about me! I can't wait to leave this house.* In his mind, he revisited his plan. *There are just two more days. Tomorrow, I will let everything slide. I can't give them any warning.*

SECRETS OF THE VANGUARD ORDER

Kamau spent the rest of the evening in his room. He packed a duffle bag with two changes of clothes, a toothbrush, a small tube of toothpaste, and Imani's picture tucked inside a small envelope. He hid the duffle under his bed, laid down, and turned on the Friday Night Mix Party. He kept the volume low so no one would hear it. The Mix Party, in fact most contemporary hip hop and R&B music, was frowned upon in the Njama household. Within minutes, Kamau had fallen asleep.

Final Goodbyes

The next morning, Kamau woke, dressed, and went downstairs for breakfast. It was Saturday, and on Saturdays, Jabari cooked a big, juicy breakfast. Today's breakfast was spinach and green onion omelets, turkey sausage, waffles, strawberries, and orange juice.

For the Njamas, every meal was an ordeal. It took a lot more work than one might imagine. In this meal for example, the eggs weren't grocery store eggs. They were purchased from a family who lived just three houses down, where they kept a flock of backyard hens. Two families in the neighborhood had hens, and most people got their eggs from these families.

The sausage was homemade. Once a year, Jabari and a few men from the neighborhood purchased 400 pounds of turkey meat from a farm on the outskirts of town. They spent the weekend making sausage.

The waffles were made from scratch with whole wheat flour, and the Njamas only ate the waffles with real maple syrup or with apple butter. They didn't eat maple flavored corn syrups. The strawberries were grown by another family in the neighborhood that had a huge garden in their backyard, and the orange juice was fresh squeezed.

As Kamau approached the breakfast table, he was conflicted. On one hand, the food was intoxicating. Like clockwork, the smell of the food wafted into his nose and hit some magical button in his brain that started his mouth watering. His stomach rumbled with anticipation. Food in this house was unparalleled. It was unrivaled. It was hands down the best, the most addictive substance he had ever encountered. But on the other hand, it was so much work. It was *too* much work. Who in the world wanted to spend their entire weekend making sausage? Don't they have grocery stores for that? Don't you have better things to do with your life? What's worse, much of this unnecessary drudgery fell on Kamau. He had to go around the neighborhood and trick or treat for groceries. Get the eggs from this house. Get the strawberries from another house. Get the meat from a farm. *Who needs it? They should invent one house where you can go to get all your groceries,* he thought wryly. *Oh yeah! That's a great idea. We can call it, 'The Grocery Storehouse'.*

He smiled to himself, amused with his own wit.

Mr. Njama interrupted this internal comedy. "Kamau, if you plan to go out today, you will need to let your mother and me know where you are going."

Kamau, still feeling pleased with himself, replied, "Yes, sir. I apologize for leaving last night without permission. Today, I am planning to see Andre after breakfast. I will be back home for lunch. Then after lunch, I'll be going to the rec center to play basketball." His tone was respectful and showed none of the resentment he felt for having to give an account of his whereabouts. He was even more pleased with himself for having remained respectful.

"Do you want to speak with me today about the Akhet?" Mr. Njama asked.

"No, sir. The decision has been made. I am fine with that." *You can go to town with that Akhet*, Kamau thought. *I won't be there!*

Kamau spent the day with friends just as he had described. He did not tell any of them that he would be leaving. That would be too risky. He didn't want word to get back to his father before he left. Instead, he focused on enjoying this day in the company of friends. He and Andre spent the morning talking about school and the girls at school, clothes and the kinds of clothes that girls wear, cars and which cars get the most girls, sports and how many girls you can get when you play sports, and they also talked about girls. Later that day, he played pick-up games for about three hours. He surprised himself; his game was really good. He thought, *I might become one of the best point guards to ever play for Coach Salters.*

Kamau made sure to be home in time for dinner. He didn't want to cause any disturbance to the routine, that might upset his plan. And dinner? It was a fabulous dinner, and halfway through, he realized it would be his last dinner in this house. After that realization, he went back for seconds. Then, throwing caution to the wind, and at the risk that he might be perceived as a greedy boy, he made sure to get thirds. It was a big heaping plate of thirds. No one said a word. After dinner, he lumbered, potbellied, up to his room, turned his radio on low, and spent the evening thumbing through magazines. He was content, for tomorrow he would be free.

Sunday Morning Visitors

The next morning, Kamau was awakened by his mother at 6:30 a.m. This was unusual. He was never up this early on a weekend, and his parents never woke him up. One of his many responsibilities was to wake himself up, and as far as he was concerned, waking up at 6:30 a.m. was very irresponsible. Someone owed his growing body two more hours of sleep.

Mrs. Njama shook Kamau gently and explained, "Kamau, we need you to get up early today. Two men will be coming to the house to do some work."

SECRETS OF THE VANGUARD ORDER

Kamau turned away from the light and replied groggily, "Okay. I'll be up at 8:30. I'll be out of the way."

She persisted, "Kamau, I don't need you out of the way. I need you to let them in the house."

Trying desperately to hold on to sleep, Kamau negotiated away one hour. "Okay. I'll get up at 7:30."

Kamau felt the covers ripped from his body, and a rush of cold air snatched the last vestiges of sleep from him. "Kamau, wake up!" The stern voice of his father boomed at him. As he turned towards his mother, sunlight seared his eyes to complete the awakening.

Mr. Njama's booming voice continued, "Kamau, your mother and I are taking Rafiyah to church this morning."

"Church?!" Kamau responded in shocked surprise. Among the Blacks throughout the city, the Njamas were notorious for not attending church. It was another one of the many lifestyle practices that had them pegged as weird.

Mr. Njama explained, "Rafiyah was invited to church by one of her friends at school, and she agreed to go. Get cleaned up and come down for breakfast. Later this morning, two men will come to the house. You will let them in. You will see us later this morning."

"Kamau stretched himself and let out a strained, "Yes, sir." As his parents walked away, Kamau climbed out of bed and thought, *Why do they make me suffer like this?*

Breakfast was another culinary delight. Mr. Njama, Mrs. Njama, and Rafiyah were dressed to the nines. They looked like the first family of Black Christendom. Kamau? Not so much. In his frumpy jeans and faded t-shirt, he didn't quite fit this family portrait. But he didn't care. Today was his last day of abuse and bondage, and at 2:00 p.m. he would be free.

With his parents and Rafiyah gone for the morning, Kamau spent his time watching TV. While the television wasn't banned in the Njama household, it was strongly discouraged. Mr. Njama often commented on how television (in fact all media, let him tell it) was responsible for the breakdown of society, especially Black society: broken homes, disrespectful children, immature and emotionally unstable adults, high anxiety, low self-concept, obesity, hyper-consumerism, even hypersexuality.

Really? All of this just from the TV? It seemed a bit far-fetched to Kamau. He didn't need a TV to get excited at the sight of a hot chick. But what did he know? He barely watched it. This TV didn't get turned on more than once every two weeks. He flicked through the channels: cooking show, church service, soap opera, shopping show, church service. *Who even wants to watch this thing?* he thought. *There's nothing on it.* He finally let it settle on a western. But he couldn't seem to get the volume right. It was either too soft for the speaking scenes or too loud for the action scenes. He decided to keep it low and miss some of the dialogue. He didn't want some nosey neighbor telling his folks his own business.

At 8:30 a.m., a van pulled into the driveway. Kamau quickly turned off the TV and peered out the front window. *What kind of company was this?* he thought. *There's no sign on the van. Maybe these are some of the 'community' folks.* Two men approached the house. They were dressed in black cargo pants, grey t-shirts, black boots, and black caps, like the ones they wear in the military. One of the men was dark complected, lean, and held a clipboard. The second was taller, very muscular, and wore a stern look. It looked as though his arm would tear through his sleeve at any moment. The second man carried a small tool bag. *What were they supposed to be fixing?* He couldn't remember.

Kamau didn't trust this situation one bit. There was no signage on the van. There was no lettering on the uniforms. They didn't have name tags, and they wore all black. No one wears all black uniforms. No company sends workers out at 8:30 a.m. on Sunday morning. These definitely weren't professional service workers. It all gave him a very bad feeling.

Kamau's first thought was to refuse the men entrance and to call for help. *Maybe they are friends of my father,* he thought. *I could probably call Baba Rafiki. He will be home.* Then he imagined his father's anger and the chastisement he would receive for disobedience. Kamau cracked the door and left the chain on. "Can I help you?"

The smaller man smiled, "Yes, sir. We are here on a call for Mr. Njama. Is this the right home?"

Kamau was racking his brain trying to get information to help him make a decision. If these men were here to do harm, he shouldn't tell them what house this is. But if they were the workers his father told him about, then he should definitely let them in. He tried to bide time, "What's the purpose of your call?"

The big man looked around furtively, and Kamau noticed. The smaller man gave an overly big smile and replied in an overly kind voice, "We're friends of your father. He gave us a list of things to look at. We're going to take some measurements, leave him some estimates, and we'll be on our way."

It all came clear to Kamau at once. He realized that he didn't know these men. He knew or, at least, recognized everyone from the neighborhood. He had recognized most of the people that his parents interacted with, especially those that came to the house. And why were they dressed alike? If these aren't professional service workers, if they are just some guys helping on a job, they wouldn't come dressed alike. Kamau's heart throbbed in his chest. Now he was scared.

He raised his voice almost to a yell and found bass he didn't know he had, "Go away! I am calling the police." Kamau began to close the door, then hearing a response, he paused.

"No worries, young brother," the smaller man replied in his cheerful, friendly tone. "We can come back when Mr. Njama is home. You are doing the right thing. You keep your house and yourself safe." With that, he turned to leave.

Kamau watched as he turned towards his van and nodded to the larger man. His heart began to beat less vigorously, and he felt a wave of relief overtake him. He began to close the door. Suddenly, he felt an explosion in his head, and he was thrown back into the living room.

CHAPTER THREE

The Check-In

Meeting Smith and Jones

Kamau woke up with a start. He couldn't see. Everything was black. He couldn't move his hands. "Am I dead?" he muttered.

"No, sir, you are not dead."

What in the world?! It was that overly friendly voice. He wondered to himself, *Did the fake fix-it man follow me into the afterlife?*

"Kamau, you got a nasty bump on your head. But don't worry, it will heal."

Kamau's senses were beginning to work for him again. He opened and closed his eyes and realized that he could see. He was wearing a hood. He wriggled around a bit and realized that he could move. But his hands were bound. He also began to feel a throbbing in his forehead.

After a lengthy pause he asked, "How do you know my name?"

"You are Kamau Njama, son of Jabari and Ayanna Njama, oldest brother of Rafiyah Njama. I'm Smith, and this is Jones. Good morning, little brother!"

Little brother?! he thought. Kamau was outraged and confused and relieved all at the same time. *How is he gon' call me 'little brother' after kidnapping and blindfolding me? What in the world are they going to do to me?* But he was alive, and that was a good sign.

Kamau tried to settle his emotions and asked, "Where are you taking me?"

Smith replied cheerfully, "We're going to the Check-In. We have to be there at 0930. And we have two more stops to make."

Kamau had no idea what "The Check-In" was, but he was getting answers. This was another good sign.

He asked, "Why am I blindfolded? Can you take it off?"

"Oh! No, sir." The location of the Check-In is confidential. In fact, all the locations are confidential. It's for your own safety, sir."

Sir? Kamau thought. *Who does this fool think he's talking to. I'm only thirteen years old.*

"What happened to my head?" he asked.

"Well…" Smith gave an embarrassed chuckle, "We had a little mishap. We kicked in the door… and you were standing right in front of it… and you took a strike to the head. But not to worry, we stopped the bleeding and gave you a *fresh* bandage."

He emphasized the word "fresh" as though that were some sort of special accommodation. At this point, Kamau noticed that Jones never spoke. *Is this a gimmick?* he wondered. *Is he supposed to be the quiet enforcer?*

Kamau couldn't figure out what these guys were after. They were friendly. They answered all his questions. They apologized for his bump on the head. He actually began to be worried for them. "You know my father's name. Do you know who he is?"

Jabari Njama was not to be trifled with. When Kamau was very young, about six years old, an old woman was visiting her daughter and son-in-law who happened to live in the Njama's neighborhood. She wanted some coffee one morning so she ventured outside of the neighborhood oasis, which was a bit smaller back then. The immediate neighborhood was so nice and welcoming that the old woman didn't notice how dangerous the surrounding area was. She got her coffee and was headed back to her daughter's house when three hooligans tried to steal her purse. She resisted, and, in short order, one of the delinquents threw a vicious haymaker and knocked her out cold. They made off with the purse, and she lay on the ground for some time before a Good Samaritan came to her aid. The poor old lady suffered third degree burns from the hot coffee, which had spilled in the assault. She also suffered head damage from the blow, and a subsequent walking impairment.

Needless to say, she never came to visit again. Her son-in-law and his two sons found the hooligans and beat them mercilessly. They broke three ribs, a leg, four knuckles in one of the boys' right hand (probably the one who threw the punch), and an eye socket. The son-in-law left them with a simple message, "You straighten up, or I'll kill you." Then he and his sons went home.

This would have been the end of it, except that the three hooligans sold dope for Little Poochie. Within a week, someone drove by the home of the old lady's daughter and fired three rounds into it. No one was hit, but the shooting shook up the whole neighborhood. Many families started talking about relocating, especially those with young children. Other families were talking about going to war, especially the son-in-law whose house was shot up. Over the next three days, the Njama's phone rang non-stop as Jabari worked to keep order in his corner of the world. And there was a constant stream of neighbors in and out of the house. It is from overhearing the conversations of these visitors that Kamau learned the story.

After the fourth day, the phone calls and the traffic stopped. On the morning of the fourth day, Jabari and Rafiki went across town to meet with Little Poochie. Jabari and Rafiki knew Little Poochie. When Jabari had moved into the neighborhood, Little Poochie was just a kid – a low-level pusher that hung out with a drug dealing gang.

At the meeting, Jabari asked pointedly why he gave his boys permission to shoot up the neighborhood. By this time, Little Poochie was not little anymore. He was older, bigger, and now the head of a fairly large operation. Even at this meeting, he was flanked by two bodyguards. He arrogantly told Jabari that the agreement was broken when men from the neighborhood hospitalized his men. It didn't matter to him that they had attacked an old lady. According to Little Poochie, the only thing that mattered was that he was losing money while three dealers were hospitalized.

Jabari asked how much money it would take to make up for his loss? Little Poochie told him $10,000. Jabari offered to meet him at a neutral location later that evening to settle his losses. Two days later, Little Poochie and four of his bodyguards were found dead. Little Poochie had third degree burns all over his face and head. It was believed that his head had been submerged in boiling water. He was also missing both of his hands. Two of the four bodyguards were shot, and the other two were strangled. For a week after the bodies were discovered, the Njamas were not available to speak with neighbors. It was rumored that they had gone away on vacation. Ironically, the Baharias and the family of the old lady took their respective vacations that same week. The local police didn't try too hard to solve the case. They were glad to be rid of a few low-level dealers. No one spoke of Little Poochie again.

Smith answered Kamau's question cheerfully, "Yes sir, we know your father! He is a fine man, a great man. You should be very proud to have him as a father."

At that moment, Kamau didn't feel the rage he normally felt towards his father, and he thought, *My Dad is going to wear you out when he gets you.*

The van came to an abrupt stop, and Kamau heard Smith and Jones get out. This must have been one of the stops Smith had talked about. Minutes later, they returned. Kamau felt something press against his right shoulder. It was another person. No one spoke, but Kamau could hear the muffled groans.

Smith and Jones picked up a third person before finally arriving at the Check-In. Surprisingly, Kamau was not as worried as he had been. With each moment that passed, he grew more confident that his father would find him. With each stop and each new person that Smith and Jones abducted, he knew his father would be more enraged. No, he wasn't worried. He pitied Smith and Jones. They were dead men.

Kamau was ushered off the van, through a grassy outdoor area, and into a cold building. There were more men now, not just Smith and Jones. He heard multiple voices, but he could not determine how many. He was handled roughly and made to stand in position. It seemed as though he was being made to line up. The hood was snatched from Kamau's head. Bright lights blinded him momentarily, and a man with a deep voice commanded, "State your first and last name, Son."

Kamau looked around hopelessly as he waited for his eyes to adjust to the brightness. A huge paw of a hand clasped his back and another voice shouted, "He's talking to you, soldier!"

Kamau stammered in his confusion, "Oh. Uhhh! Kamau Njama?"

The man with the deep voice began to come into focus. "Are you asking *me*, Son? Don't you know your name?"

He could see more clearly now. The man with the deep voice was standing just inches from Kamau's right side. His face wore the same expressionless expression that his father often wore; and his question, wrapped in sarcasm, was just the type of question his father would ask. Kamau responded instinctively, "Yes, sir. My name is Kamau Njama."

"Well, that's grand, Son. It looks like we found your heart. I *must* be the wizard." He quickly snapped over to Kamau's left.

It was just then that Kamau looked around. There was a room full of boys about Kamau's size. They stood in a circle, and all of them wore gold hoods. There were several men, some inside the circle and others outside of it. All were dressed like Smith and Jones.

A man standing behind Kamau snatched the gold hood off the head of the person to Kamau's left. At the same time, the man with the deep voice commanded, "State your first and last name, Son."

This went on, as the man with the deep voice circled the room, commanding each person there. Each hood that was removed revealed a boy that looked to be about the same age as Kamau. As Kamau scanned the circle, he was amazed at the look of each boy. They looked flaccid, frightened, and frail. Most of them were skin and bones. There were a few portly fellows, but even they looked weak. Kamau had never seen himself as weak. He was athletic, very athletic. Even Coach Salters had said so. Did he fit in with this pathetic lot? As he looked at the boys, they were contrasted against the men like Smith and Jones, who were thick faced, barrel-chested men. Their clean-shaven expressions were serious and determined. Kamau was uncertain, confused, and scared. Had he lost hope of his father coming to rescue him? No. He had forgotten it completely.

As he surveyed the room, he saw a hand wave from across the circle. "Hey, Kamau!" Instantly, a tall, thin, and very light complected man was in that kid's face, barking questions and instructions. "Did I give you permission to speak? Are you swatting at a fly? Did I give you permission to swat at my flies? That fly was minding his own business. Why did you terrorize that fly? Apologize! Not to me, Son! To the fly. Give me ten pushups." The poor boy tried to answer, but the minute he uttered any type of sound he was smacked with another question.

As the boy did his pushups, Kamau saw that it was Alton Bailey. Speaking of portly fellows, Alton and Kamau had met in the sixth grade at Washington Middle School. Kamau didn't dislike Alton, but he tried to keep distance from him. Alton was a hanger-on. He always tried to hang out with Kamau, sidling up to him at lunch, in the hallway, after school. Kamau didn't like hanging out with unpopular kids. He had enough problems being from a weird family. He didn't need questionable friends. Despite Kamau's borderline rudeness, Alton was fiercely loyal, always cheerful, always friendly. In his eyes, Kamau Njama could do no wrong.

His loyalty to Kamau went back to their first meeting. When Kamau and Imani were walking home one day, they saw two groups of boys fighting. As they got closer to the action, they saw that it was actually one group of four boys taking turns beating up one pudgy boy. The ringleader, Dorian, had been caught cheating on a test that day, and he had accused the pudgy boy, Alton, of snitching on him. No one believed it, of course. It was no secret that Dorian was not the sharpest pencil in the box. But this was his way of saving face after being embarrassed. As Dorian and his friends beat Alton, there were about eight other boys and girls standing around watching.

The lopsided fight, the kids who gathered to see the spectacle, the whole scene sickened Imani, and she urged Kamau to leave. But Kamau wouldn't leave. Instead, he dropped his books, stepped to the middle of the ruckus, right next to Alton, and squared up against one of the other boys. "What are *you* doing?" Dorian sneered.

"Me?" Kamau replied. "I'm about to beat the brakes off you and your boys."

Dorian protested, "This ain't none of your business, Njama."

Kamau retorted, "Four on one is always my business. If you want me out of it, then you fight this boy fair. Just you and him."

Dorian agreed, and Kamau stepped back to join Imani in the crowd. He wanted to be sure the odds stayed even. Truth is, Alton should have gotten whooped by Dorian. He was already beaten very badly. One eye was swollen shut, his nose was bloodied, and he was tired. But something in him wouldn't let him quit. And he fought. He fought Dorian so hard, and beat him so badly, that Dorian gave up bullying that day. When he was nearly defeated, Alton sat on Dorian and gave him open handed slaps until he apologized for the false accusation. Since that time, Alton has always been eager to offer Kamau whatever help he could.

When Kamau and Imani left, she commented on what a nice thing Kamau had done for "that pudgy boy."

Kamau replied carelessly, "I don't care anything about that pudgy boy. I just wanted to see Dorian get his." The moment he said it, he wished he could take it back. It was one of the few times he saw a look of shame and disappointment pass over Imani's face.

As Alton finished his pushups and stood up, Kamau looked around the circle. He counted nineteen boys, twenty including himself. He also recognized Amari. Amari also went to Washington Middle School. He had played basketball with Kamau just yesterday. Aside from Alton and Amari, Kamau didn't recognize any of the boys.

Amari and Kamau made eye contact, but neither said a thing. Amari looked scared. He was a tough kid, a strong kid, and Kamau had never seen him afraid. Kamau wondered if he himself looked scared to the other boys. As he thought about this, one of the men came up behind Amari with something in his hand. Kamau wanted to warn him, but no words came out. His eyes grew large as the man raised something above Amari's head. Kamau nodded towards Amari vigorously, trying to get him to turn around. Then, all of a sudden, everything went black.

Chocolates for Marlene (O'Leary)

Timothy left his house hurriedly. He wanted to get to work before it got busy and well before Dan arrived. When Daphne asked why he was in such a rush, he ignored her question. Instead, he kissed her quickly and promised to see her that evening.

Once he arrived, Timothy dropped his briefcase in his office, checked himself in the mirror, grabbed two packages, then headed to Dan's office. Marlene greeted him. "Good morning, Timothy!" she sang his name flirtatiously.

He smiled confidently and tried to deepen his voice, losing the nasal whine, "Good morning, Marlene." He stepped back to make a show of examining her, "You are as beautiful as ever!" The truth was she was not beautiful. She was average. She did what she could. She kept a slim figure. She kept her hair styled nicely. She was always well dressed. But she was average. She was a twenty-nine-year-old, white woman who looked like she would turn forty any minute. Timothy kept his fraternization brief and as secretive as possible.

He handed her one of the packages. As she opened the gold foil wrapper and squealed in delight. "Oh, my goodness! This is the absolute best!" It was a small box of expensive Belgian chocolates that sold for over $150 a box. The chocolate was very hard to get in the US. Marlene took one of the chocolates and groaned as she savored it.

Timothy watched her swoon over the chocolates and thought, *I've got her. She's still mine*. Over the years, he had made a study of Marlene. He watched and listened to her closely. He knew her motivations, drives, and desires. But he was careful not to let his work life get messy. He asked coolly, "Is Dan in yet?"

She grinned at him, "No, not yet. He shouldn't be in for another hour."

He looked disappointed. "Hmm. Okay. I thought he might be working early for a few weeks or so. He said he was working on a project that could mean a big move up."

Marlene's eyes got big. "He told you about that?!"

Timothy replied matter-of-factly, "Well, he didn't give me any details. He just said it was a big project that might very well result in a promotion. I wish he had told me. I might be able to help."

Marlene pursed her lips and thought for a moment. She knew that Timothy was the key to any credibility Dan had as a scientist. More important than that, if Dan got a promotion, then so would she. He could not mess this up! Besides, Timothy was fiercely loyal. *Why did he not include Timothy in the planning?* she wondered. Then she spoke, "Well I don't know the details of the project, but I do know this… he is taking the lead on a project that involves SEV Fitzroy. Did you know that it was viable?"

"No! I didn't know!" he replied in shocked amazement.

"Well, it is. It has been viable for just under a year. It completed its first voyage about nine months ago. The second voyage is being planned now. Dan is in charge of the mission."

Timothy's eyes grew large, and his mouth hung open. "That is huge! I don't know how I could help with that. If you think of anything, let me know."

Marlene stood there nodding, "Yeah! It's a big deal." She eyed the file of papers in Timothy's hand. "Is that for Dan?"

Timothy stared blankly. "Oh, I almost forgot." He handed the file to her and absent-mindedly turned to walk away. *Wow!*

As Timothy walked away, he processed what Marlene had shared with him. He was not quite as surprised as he had made out. Space Expeditionary Vessel

SECRETS OF THE VANGUARD ORDER

(SEV) Fitzroy was a project that had been in development for some time. It drew on theoretical ideas of fourth dimensional structures and closed timelike curves to support manned interstellar space travel. Timothy knew all of this. What he did not know was that TechInnoGen had been preparing to launch a mission within the coming months. *Why had Dan kept me out of the loop?* he wondered. *Is he going to cut me off?*

Kamau's Many Tests

Kamau felt himself being pushed and shoved this way and that by a mass of bodies. He couldn't see a thing, and he tried to take slow small steps to avoid hurting himself. But this only made the shoving worse. Someone grabbed his arm and jerked him roughly to the right. They let him go and he stood still. A gruff voice barked, "Take off your shirt."

Was that for me? he thought. Kamau stood there motionless, staring into blackness, unsure of what to do.

The voice barked again, "I'm talking to you Njama. Make it quick."

Kamau pulled his shirt over his head. Instantly, he felt a cold piece of ice pressed against his chest and he flinched.

Again, came the barking, "Stand still, Njama. Who do you think you are? Beyonce? Michael Jackson?"

He wasn't sure if he was supposed to respond. Uncertain, Kamau whimpered weakly, "No?"

"What's the matter with you, boy? Speak up like a man."

He tried more forcefully, "No."

"Then you stand still. This ain't *Soul Train*. We don't want to see you gyrating and dancing about. Take a seat!"

Kamau found himself thrust forcefully back into a chair. His arms were pushed down to the arms of the chair. He heard fabric being pulled and felt his arms being strapped down. He was beginning to panic, *What in the world?!* he thought.

A soothing feminine voice began to speak, "Hold still. This is only going to…"

The woman was interrupted by the barking voice, "Don't you cry, Njama. I *hate* tears!" Kamau felt hot breath against his hood and tried to move his head away.

"Tears are a sign of *weakness*. I *hate* weakness!" The barking voice seemed to growl out the word "hate."

Kamau felt a shooting pain in his arm. They were stabbing him! He cried out, "Stop it! Don't do it!"

"I told you not to cry, Njama. Son, I want you to dig deep and find your cahoonas. Dignify yourself. People are watching."

Kamau felt woozy. The pain subsided. Kamau stopped crying aloud and he listened. *Were people watching?* he thought.

He felt wetness on his arm, and the feminine voice said kindly, "That's it."

Kamau felt a bandage being stuck to his arm, and he thought, *That was a shot. They must have given me a shot.* Initially, he was relieved that he had not been stabbed. Then he began to worry, *What kind of shot did they give me?*

Kamau's hood was snatched off, and he was hit in the face with a blinding light. He closed his eyes to protect them from the light. Kamau heard a small motor snap on. It whirred like a small saw or rotary tool. It was just behind his head. *Are they going to cut me?!* he thought, with his eyes clinched tight. He hunched his shoulders and thrust his head forward, trying to move his head away from the sound of the drill.

The man with the barking voice grabbed his chin, forcing his head upward. "Hold still. You don't want to hurt yourself, Son."

Kamau felt cold steel at the base of his neck, and hair began falling on his back. For a moment he relaxed. *They're cutting my hair.* Anger jerked him alert. *Who told them they could cut my hair?!* Kamau took pride in his high and tight fade. It helped to hide the odd shape of his head. Besides that, Imani once told him that the high and tight made him look handsome. So, he had worn that hairstyle ever since.

Now, however, he felt helpless. He didn't know what was going on and there was nothing he could do to stop it. Big clumps of hair were brushed from Kamau's chest and back. The small bits stuck with him. The hood was pulled roughly back over his head and cinched tight. The straps on his arms were released, and someone pulled Kamau to his feet.

Kamau was given his shirt and told to put it back on. He was marched around, picked up, pushed down, poked, prodded, dressed, and undressed. He couldn't see a thing. The hair made him itch terribly. The barking voice yelled at him constantly. This went on for hours, and he was getting very sleepy.

Finally, Kamau was led to a chair and told to sit down. There was a table in front of the chair. He heard a door slam behind him. He waited for a moment to see if anyone might speak. No one did. Kamau lay his head on the table to rest. Almost instantly, the door opened. The barking voice began again, "Njama, I certainly hope you are not sleepy. Son, sleep is a luxury that you cannot afford." With that, the hood was yanked off Kamau's head. He began to turn to see who was behind him. The barking voice yelled at him, hot breath on his neck, "Eyes front, Njama! This man wants to talk to you."

Just then, a man wearing a white lab coat came into view. A hologram of a stack of cards appeared between them. The man in the white coat made a gesture, and the card on the top of the holographic deck appeared. "What do you see?"

Njama looked at the hologram in amazement. He had never seen a hologram in real life before. The man repeated, "Njama, what do you see?"

Snapping himself alert, Kamau replied, "Two men sitting at a fire."

Without responding, the man appeared to "type" in the air. But there was no keyboard, not even a holographic one. He gestured again, turning over another card, "What do you see?"

"Two witches playing pattycake?"

The barking voice scolded him, "He's asking the questions, Njama! You give answers."

After going through a set of cards, the man in the lab coat gave Kamau a pencil and a multiple-choice test. He put a clock on the table and said, "Answer as many questions as you can in fifteen minutes."

This went on for quite a while. The man in the lab coat gave Kamau a series of tests. He administered one test where wires were attached to Kamau's chest and head, and Kamau was asked a series of questions. He did another test where he told Kamau to read a holographic paragraph, then had him answer questions and spit in a series of vials. Kamau was exhausted by the stress of it all. After a time, he could barely stay awake.

Finally, the man in the lab coat motioned to the man with the barking voice, who then left. The man with the lab coat then began packing his briefcase. The man with the barking voice returned with a woman who was carrying a plate of hot cookies. The man with the briefcase looked at Kamau and asked, "Are you hungry?"

Kamau eyed the cookies greedily. His mouth began to water, and his stomach rumbled. He replied, "Yes."

"You can have this cookie tray now, or you can wait an hour or so for more cookies and a full meal."

Kamau looked at the man, distrustfully. "So, if I eat these cookies now, then I won't be able to eat a full meal later?"

"No, there won't be time."

The options seemed silly to Kamau. *Who wants cookies in place of a meal?* Kamau smirked, "I'll wait."

The man in the lab coat said absent-mindedly, "Oh. I forgot one thing." Then he stepped out of the room. The woman set the cookies down, and together, she and the man with the barking voice left the room after him.

About fifteen minutes later, the barking man returned. He handed Kamau a brown paper bag and spoke normally for the first time, "When I leave the room, take off all your clothes and put them on the table. Put on the clothes that are in the brown bag. While you are dressing, the door will be locked, and you will have privacy. When you are finished, come out and wait with the others."

Kamau was too exhausted to protest, too exhausted to think, too exhausted to try to figure out what was going on. So, without protesting, without thinking, without understanding what was going on, he simply did as he was told. Every article of clothing he needed was in that bag, even underwear, socks, and boots. Every article of clothing was just his size. When he emerged from the room, he was ushered to a large open room, the room where the boys first stood in a circle. For ten minutes, he stood in that room, as there was nowhere to sit. One by one the other boys gathered. Each of them looked confused and exhausted and wore the same exact clothes: black cargo pants, grey T-shirts, black shirts that almost felt like jackets, black socks, and black boots. All the boys were dressed like Smith and Jones.

When all twenty boys had returned, the man with the deep voice stood and commanded, "Eyes front!"

All the men stopped what they were doing and turned to face him. Seeing this, the boys did so too.

He continued, "Baba Thulani, form this rabble into a line."

The man Kamau first knew as Smith stepped forward and began organizing the boys into a straight line. Some of the other men moved to tables arranged in a semicircle around the room. Others stood in line with the boys. Once the line was formed, Smith turned to the man with the deep voice, "Line formed, Baba Ojore."

"Baba Thulani, lead the forlorn to their provisions."

Smith directed one of the boys at the end of the line to move towards the first table. At the first table, the boys each picked up a carryall, four sets of t-shirts, pants, and shirts. At the second table, they picked up socks and underwear. At the third table, they picked up soap, toothpaste, toothbrush, dental floss, and deodorant. This went on until they had visited all the tables and received all provisions. They scrambled to get in line. This time Kamau found himself at the end of the line.

The man with the deep voice stood and commanded again, "Eyes front!" The men snapped to attention, even those behind the tables stopped their work, stood, and faced the man with the deep voice. For the first time, Kamau took notice of this man. He was medium height, slightly shorter than Kamau's father. He was thickly built, broad shouldered, and barrel-chested. Even his legs looked like tree trunks. He was not overly muscular like Jones or one of those celebrity tough guys. This man was a real tough guy. And it was clear to Kamau that he was not to be crossed.

"I am Baba Ojore." He commanded, "Say it with me."

The boys repeated, "Baba Ojore." Their response was soft, uncertain, and out of unison.

"Let's try it again. This time, say it like you care! I am Baba Ojore."

Kamau and the other boys repeated "Baba Ojore." This time, they were louder and more confident.

Baba Ojore continued, "Welcome to the Vanguard Akhet!"

Kamau's head jerked up in surprise. His mouth fell open and his eyes grew wide. It all became clear to him now. *This is the Akhet?* Anger welled up in his chest. *I'm not supposed to be here,* he thought. Then one realization after another hit him. His father was *not* going to come to his rescue. He was *not* going to go live with Grandma Charline. He was *not* going to work at Gary's Greenhouse this summer. He was *not* going to Coach Salter's basketball camp. His eyes narrowed, and he began breathing heavily. He wanted to strike out and hit people and break things. But he didn't dare do that, not with Baba Ojore and Smith and Jones and those other men in the room.

"For the next ten weeks, you will enjoy a fun-filled, all-expense paid vacation at Camp Furaha. You will each have your own personalized sleeping quarters. You will enjoy the best meal accommodations. The Akhet staff will provide you with three square meals a day." As Baba Ojore spoke, his voice was smiling (if that's possible), but his face was stern and expressionless. He stood straight as an arrow, looking up and down the line and making eye contact with each of the boys.

"You will have access to comprehensive recreation facilities, and you will enjoy unlimited recreation opportunities."

Kamau looked down the line and noticed that some of the boys were smiling and nodding agreeably.

Baba Ojore continued, "You will enjoy the challenge of Vanguard games, the camaraderie of Vanguard brotherhood, and the joy of self-discovery that is part of the Vanguard experience." Baba Ojore paused and looked at the boys, "Are there any questions?"

Before he finished uttering the word "questions," he went on, "Very well then. Say goodbye to your mothers and prepare to depart. Baba Thulani, lead the forlorn to the bus."

Kamau wondered what he meant by, "Say goodbye to your mothers." *Were they supposed to call? Write a letter? Maybe this was just a figure of speech.* While Kamau was wondering, Baba Thulani walked by Kamau and commanded, "This way." Following, Kamau led the boys out of a side door. Each boy held a carryall and followed the boy ahead of him. The building exit led the line of boys between two ropes, just like the lines at amusement parks. Kamau walked to the point where the ropes ended. There was Jones, blocking the path to a bus. So, Kamau and the line of boys stopped.

As Kamau stood there, waiting and staring into Jones' broad chest, he noticed Baba Thulani walking towards him accompanied by a woman. It was his mother! Kamau's heart jumped inside of his chest. She had finally stood up to Mr. Njama and was going to put an end to this madness. She would see how hungry and upset Kamau was. She would see how these monsters had butchered his hair and terrorized him, and he would be going home.

As she approached, he began to speak, "Ma, I'm so…"

She interrupted him hurriedly, "Kamau, listen. You are going to face many challenges over the next ten weeks. You have, within you, everything you need to meet those challenges, and you have, around you, everything you need to grow from those challenges. Go, and come back home the man that you were born to be." With that, Ayanna Njama opened her arms.

Kamau moved to hug his mother and to beg her to let him come home, but Baba Thulani stepped between them, "No hugs, Mom. The course is set."

Ayanna Njama stepped back and dropped her mask of impassivity. She let Kamau see all her love, hope, and admiration. "Be strong, Son!"

Kamau's heart sank.

Once she turned, Jones said flatly, "Board the bus."

Dejected, Kamau approached the bus, gripped his carryall, and watched his mother walk towards her car. He reflected that, *She knew this whole time, and she didn't try to help me.* Then Kamau saw a small head in the passenger seat of the car, peering out of the side window. His eyes narrowed, *Is that… It's… Grandma Charline!*

The Bus Ride

One at a time, the boys said their final goodbyes to their mothers and boarded the bus. The goodbyes were brief. There were no hugs. There was no crying. There were no drawn-out speeches. Once on the bus, the boys did not speak. Each boy sat there, staring off into space.

Soon, the bus was loaded, a few of the men got on with the boys, and they were off. As the bus began rolling, Jones walked the aisle and gave each boy a gold hood. "Put these on," he commanded. Kamau was too tired to protest. He put the hood on and fell asleep within minutes.

SECRETS OF THE VANGUARD ORDER

The bus ride was the longest, most boring and strangest bus ride that Kamau had ever experienced. When the ride began, it was 10:30 a.m. He knew it was 10:30 because he had caught a peek at Jones' watch as he was handing out the gold hoods. Kamau was surprised that it was only 10:30. The morning was long and harrowing. It felt like it was much later in the day.

The bus made only four stops that day. Two stops were for bathroom breaks. Both times, the bus pulled up to gas stations and, while the driver refueled, the men hurried the boys into the restrooms in groups of four. The third stop was for food. As part of this "all-expense paid vacation," the staff at Vanguard Akhet provided cold cut sandwiches and apples for lunch. Unless you count the granola bar snacks from the morning and bananas provided in the evening, the Akhet had already reneged on its promise of three, square meals. And to think, Kamau passed on a tray of cookies for this "food." In addition to the food travesty, the boys wore hoods for most of the ride, and no one spoke. Most of the boys either slept or sat quietly, shrouded in darkness and emotional shock.

The fourth stop was at Camp Furaha. Kamau could feel the bus slowing down. It bounced and swayed, and Kamau heard gravel crunching under the weight of heavy tires. Baba Thulani instructed the boys, "Gentlemen, remove your hoods and place them in your carryall. Then head to the shelter to receive the rest of your provisions."

Kamau removed his hood and looked around. There was nothing but wilderness: trees, fields, gravel roads, and an open shelter. It was also getting dark. Kamau thought, *It must be about 7:30.* Back home, if he were out playing, this would be the time that streetlights would be coming on, and he would start heading back to the house.

Camp Furaha

The boys exited the bus and fumbled their way over to the shelter. There were groans and loud yawns as the boys stretched and took in their surroundings. As they huddled together, Baba Thulani gave instructions, "Approach Baba Kojo to receive the rest of your provisions."

When Baba Thulani gestured to Baba Kojo, Kamau shuttered. It was the tall, light-skinned man with the barking voice. And again, he barked, "Organize yourselves!"

As the boys moved towards Baba Kojo, Baba Thulani announced, "There will be no Vanguard provision distributed to a disorganized, unsynchronized, mongrelized, gelatinized, scrum! Now organize yourselves!"

Aside from the words disorganized and organize, Kamau had no idea what Baba Thulani had just said. From the looks of confusion, none of the other boys knew either. But they did know what organize meant. So, clumsily and slowly, they formed a line.

Baba Kojo gestured and barked, "Come receive your provisions."

The first boy approached tentatively. Baba Kojo barked, "Name, Son!"

"Ch-Ch-Chandler Ga-Gardner," the boy stuttered sheepishly.

Baba Kojo's mouth fell open and his eyes widened as he looked at the boy. "You gotta be kidding me," he spoke in disbelief. "You don't know your name, Son?"

Looking down at his shoes, the boy pushed his glasses up his nose and stammered, "Yes, sir. I…"

Baba Kojo interrupted him impatiently, "Are you ashamed of your name, Son?"

Still looking down, the boy began stammering again, "Well no. I…"

By this point, Baba Kojo was in the boy's face. "Didn't your parents give you that name? Haven't you worn that name for these thirteen or fourteen years? Don't all your friends and family know you by that name?" The contrast between Baba Kojo and the boy was stark. There was physical difference, of course. While Baba Kojo was not muscular like Jones, or thickly built like Baba Ojore, he was lean, and solidly built. On the other hand, the boy in line was one of the skinniest boys Kamau had ever seen. He looked like a pool noodle with a melon for a head. But this wasn't the real contrast. The real contrast was in their bearing. Baba Kojo was steely-eyed and determined. His every movement exuded certainty and confidence. The skinny boy seemed scared of his own shadow, uncertain of everything.

Well, he won't be here long, Kamau thought wryly.

Baba Kojo continued, "Let's get your name right, Son." He stepped back, looked at the boy, and barked, "Name."

The boy responded, "Chandler Gardner." This time he responded more quickly and with a bit more volume.

Baba Kojo commanded, "Louder!"

"Chandler Gardner!" came the reply with even more force.

"Be proud of yourself. Say it like you mean it. Name!" Baba Kojo was almost yelling. His voice could be heard echoing in the evening sky.

This time the boy threw his head back and shouted with force, "CHANDLER GARDNER!"

Kamau watched the boy's head wobble as he shouted. The shouting effort seemed to take all the energy that bag of bones had to offer. Kamau thought to himself, *Look at him. Now he's exhausted. Yeah, he definitely won't make it.*

Baba Thulani, who was holding a clipboard announced, "Alton Bailey. Step forward." Alton stepped out of line and approached the front. "You're quarter mates."

Baba Kojo handed Chandler one roll, and he handed Alton two rolls. Alton stammered nervously, "Sir, may I ask a question, sir?"

"Speak, Bailey."

"Sir, what are these rolls?"

Baba Kojo, looked at him blankly, "Those are your personalized sleeping quarters."

Kamau thought to himself, *Okay. So those are tents and sleeping bags.* He was disappointed, but not surprised. *I've got to sleep in a tent for ten weeks? What type of parents do I have?* He watched Jones lead Chandler and Alton up the path. Between the two of them, they were dragging two carryalls, two sleeping bags, and one tent. Alton was wheezing, and his jowls were flapping with every step. Chandler had to stop every few steps and put down some provisions just to push his glasses back up his nose. Kamau chuckled to himself, *Who in the world made these pairings? This is going to be interesting.*

The next boy in line was called forward, Bongani Jekwa. He was quarter mates with Deiondre Everly. Bongani was very different from the other boys. Kamau first noticed him at the Check-In. They also sat across from one another on the bus. When Kamau wasn't wearing his hood, at bathroom breaks and during "meals," he observed Bongani a bit more. Bongani carried himself with confidence, not the confidence of Baba Kojo or Baba Ojore, but with much more confidence than the other boys. He also seemed to be unfazed by the events of the day. He never seemed overwhelmed.

Kamau did not previously take notice of Bongani's quarter mate, Deiondre, until now. In Kamau's estimation, this boy was not right in the head. He looked wild – wild like an animal. It is not that his hair was disheveled; he was shaved just like the rest of them. It was not that his clothes were messy; he wore the same clothes as all the others. It was his eyes. He had a wild, untamed look in his eyes. Kamau thought, *This is a boy to avoid. He looks like trouble.*

Kamau was called next. His quarter mate was a boy named Raymond Hewitt. Kamau took no notice of Raymond up until this point. When his name was called, Raymond bounded to the front of the line, smiled, and nodded at Kamau. Kamau sized him up quickly. Raymond was about the same height and weight as Kamau. He also seemed to have his wits about him. He appeared to be a very friendly boy. Kamau thought that they would get along well.

As each pair of boys received their provisions, they joined the line. This continued until all the boys were paired. Once all the boys were in line, Baba Thulani handed Jones a carryall and a roll, and together, they led the line up the path. Two other men formed a pair in the middle of the line, and Baba Kojo followed the back of the line by himself.

The group walked for about ten minutes. Alton coughed and wheezed the whole way. Kamau thought he was going to pass out. His quarter mate was even worse. Chandler stopped several times and for several reasons—to get a better grip on his bag, to remove a rock from his shoe, to adjust his glasses. Kamau sensed that the real reason behind the stops was that Chandler was weak and tired. The poor boy didn't look like he had done physical labor a day in his life. Jones had no pity on him. Every time he tried to stop, Jones reached back, grabbed him, and dragged him along with a "Keep it moving" or "We're almost there."

The group stopped at the edge of a clearing, and Baba Kojo commanded, "Make camp! You have five minutes!" Kamau wasn't sure how they were supposed to "make camp." He hadn't heard that expression before. He looked towards Raymond, but it was dark now and he couldn't see very much. Seeing a few flashlights, Kamau remembered that he was given a flashlight in his carryall. He and Raymond both took out their flashlights and started unpacking the tent.

In less than two minutes, before Raymond and Kamau could get all the tent parts out of the sack, three tents were fully erected. Unsurprisingly, these tents belonged to the Babas. These tents formed an evenly spaced triangle in the open clearing.

Raymond asked, "Have you ever put together a tent before?"

Kamau answered, "Sure. But not this one. Not in the dark. And certainly not in five minutes."

Raymond explained, "I have never put a tent together at all. So, I will hold the flashlight for *you*." He then pulled out the directions, stretched them on the grass and shone the light on them.

Kamau said, "Forget about that. I need light over here. I need to see what parts we have."

Baba Kojo began circling the boys, announcing how much time they had left. "You have two minutes and thirty seconds remaining. Move quickly!" The other men circulated among the boys but said nothing.

Kamau ignored the time restriction and focused on preparing the poles, sliding them through the sleeves, inserting them in the grommets.

"You have one minute remaining!"

"Can I help?" Raymond asked. He tried to sound calm, but Kamau heard fear and desperation is his voice.

Kamau responded, "Yes, hold the end of this pole steady in this grommet. Our tent is almost done."

"You have thirty seconds!"

Kamau and Raymond finished the first pole and quickly moved to the second. After setting up the second pole, Kamau ran hurriedly around the tent, gathered unused components, and placed them in the tent sack.

"Time!"

Kamau threw the tent sack in the tent and motioned to Raymond to place his carryall and sleeping bag inside. Then both boys climbed inside. They heard Baba Kojo yelling outside, "Son, did I mutter? Did I utter? Did I stutter?" You had five minutes! Your tent is complete. It's sack time. Lights Out!"

Raymond was tickled by the exchange. He leaned an ear in the direction of Baba Kojo and couldn't stop smiling.

From another section of the clearing, they overheard a boy protest, "Baba Kojo, we can't go to bed, our tent won't stand up."

While trotting towards the protesting boy, Baba Kojo said sternly, "I don't care if you have to wrap that tent around your backside like a blanket. It *is* sack time, and you *will* sleep! Are we clear?"

After hearing no response, Kamau and Raymond looked at each other. Baba Kojo barked, more forcefully, "Are we clear?!"

The protesting boy responded, "Yes, sir."

Kamau reflected that he was lying on the ground, in a sleeping bag, in a tent, next to a strange boy, surrounded by other strange boys and men, in an unknown place. Kamau reflected on the events of the day: having his house broken into; having his head busted; being kidnapped, yelled at, poked, and prodded; having his head shaved; being blindfolded and hooded; being snatched away from his mother; and being given ridiculous food. Kamau reflected on his parents' and grandmother's complicity in these events. He felt helpless, abandoned, and alone. And he wept.

BOOK 2

CHAPTER ONE

The Hwamanda Awakening

Courage, the First Virtue

A shrill horn pierced the air, startling Kamau awake. A long note was followed by a series of short alternating low- and high-pitched notes. Kamau searched his mind trying to get his bearings. When he recalled where he was, he felt sickness in his stomach. The long note was played again. And again, it was followed by short alternating low- and high-pitched notes. This pattern was repeated a total of four times. Then the horn stopped.

"Rise and Shine, Vanguardians!" Baba Thulani's voice followed the call of the horn.

Is he smiling and happy? Kamau thought to himself. *What in the world?* Kamau stretched and lay there for a moment, allowing himself to adjust to the reality of his situation.

Baba Thulani continued, "Yes, sir! Today is going to be a great day! A great day!" Raymond slowly padded about the tent, digging through his carryall, looking for clothes. Baba Thulani announced cheerfully, "The day will commence in one minute!"

They could hear other boys outside the tent talking and asking questions. "Everything is wet! Damp clothes, damp boots, damp socks."

Someone left their provisions outside of the tent last night, Kamau thought indifferently. *That dew will get you every time.*

Another boy inquired, "Baba, what time is it? Can we get ten more minutes?"

Kamau couldn't see who asked that question, but experience with his own father and a touch of common sense told him that it was not a good idea. He looked at Raymond and said, "Hurry up and get dressed." The two began getting dressed with a greater sense of urgency.

Their instinct was right. They heard one of the men excoriating the poor, unsuspecting boy who had asked that stupid question. "You must be out of your tree, Little Bird. You will get your backside out of that tent this instant."

Kamau and Raymond glanced at each other and began to move even faster. They heard the sound of nylon rustling and a boy whimpering and shouting for help. But the berating continued, "What *time* is it? It's time for you to face your fears. It's time for you to live with courage. It's time for you to get out here and join your brothers. It's time for work. It's time to soak in the joys of living. It's time to prepare for the arrival of the sun, Little Bird."

Kamau and Raymond wriggled out of their tent. When they emerged, about five or six boys were watching as the boy with the stupid question was being dragged, feet first, out of his tent. "You want ten more minutes? I'll give you ten more minutes. I'll give you ten more minutes of pushups. I'll give you ten more minutes of the Vanguard Chair. I'll give you ten more minutes of the Warriors' Edge. You had better think twice before you speak, Little Bird."

Little Bird stood there weeping, wearing nothing but underpants and socks. By the time he had been dragged from his tent, the rest of the boys had emerged from their tents. Like Kamau, they had gotten the hint.

The men were dressed in black cargo pants, grey T-shirts, and black combat boots. They were alert, clean, and ready to go. The boys were another matter. Although everyone looked better than Little Bird, the boys still looked a mess. Only a few boys were fully dressed. Many had unlaced boots. A few were wearing their full uniform with the Black shirt over the grey T-shirt. One boy wore a black shirt with no T-shirt, and one boy wore his T-shirt backwards. *How did that happen?* Kamau thought. To Kamau's surprise, Chandler and Alton were two of the boys who were fully dressed. *Wow!* he thought. *Well, that's a little miracle.*

Baba Kojo began walking amongst the group. As he looked around, his ears glowed red and a look of disgust took over his face. He rubbed the back of his neck, shook his head and spoke, "Baba Thulani, what is this?"

Baba Thulani replied, "Sir, this is a sloppy, slobby, slovenly kambi. It is beneath our dignity."

Baba Kojo sneered at the kambi then growled at Baba Thulani, "Hmmm. They must learn."

He turned towards the group and commanded, "Vanguardians, look around you. For the moment, ignore the shameful mess you have created in this kambi. Take note of the men that surround you." He paused as the boys looked at one another. "For the next ten weeks, these men will be your brothers, your friends, your teachers, and your confidants. You will shed blood, sweat, and tears with these men." He continued slowly and passionately, "We will work, eat, and enjoy leisure together. For ten weeks, we will fight side by side. We will embolden one another. We will learn together. We will fail together, and we will succeed… together."

As Baba Kojo spoke, Kamau was transfixed on him. For a moment, he had forgotten that he was lost in the wilderness of who knows where. He had forgotten how angry he was at his father, how he had been betrayed by his mother and grandmother. He even forgot about Little Bird, as foolish as he looked standing there in his tidy whities. Baba Kojo's voice was filled with commitment and emotion, and a part of Kamau felt it too.

"This is our Mkhosi. We are Mkhosi Kunye. We are twenty-six strong. We are twenty Vanguardians in training. We are five Mwalimu, and we are one Bausi."

Kamau did not understand or even remember the African terms Baba Kojo used. He wished he had paid more attention when his father was trying to teach him Swahili.

Baba Kojo then commanded, "Vanguardians, introduce yourselves," as he gestured towards Chandler.

Recalling the lesson from the night before, Chandler threw his head back and yelled, "CHANDLER GARDNER, sir." Once again, he was visibly worn out.

The faint trace of a smile passed quickly over Baba Thulani's face.

Baba Kojo nodded and responded, "Okay." He repeated it, "Chandler Gardner." He addressed the group, "Let's welcome him."

Everyone responded in unison, "Welcome, Chandler Gardner." Upon hearing his name, Chandler smiled.

Baba Kojo then gestured to Alton. Alton introduced himself, "Alton Bailey!" Again, Baba Kojo led the Mkhosi in welcoming Alton. Each of the twenty boys, the twenty young Vanguardians in training, gave their names. They learned that Little Bird's name was Charles Hall. After this morning, no one would forget.

Baba Kojo then commanded, "Mwalimu, introduce yourselves."

Baba Thulani stepped forward cheerfully. "Baba Thulani."

Without prompting, the Vanguardians responded, "Welcome, Baba Thulani."

There were five Mwalimu. Kamau already knew the names of two of them: Baba Kojo and Baba Thulani. In the full light of the sun, Kamau noticed that Baba Kojo had three patches of freckles. One patch covered the bridge of his nose and the other two covered the tops of his cheeks. His ears also turned bright red when he was angered.

He learned this morning that Jones' name was actually Baba Abiola. The other two were Baba Kahuthia and Baba Chinua. Baba Chinua was the tallest of the Mwalimu. He had small, ferret-like facial features. His facial expression was not friendly like Baba Thulani, but it wasn't threatening either. He was a thin, unassuming, soft-spoken man. Judging from looks alone, he seemed to be the most approachable of the Mwalimu. So, it came as a surprise when Kamau learned that it was Baba Chinua who so violently dragged Charles "Little Bird" Hall from his tent.

Baba Kahuthia was a stout, brown complexioned man. He was built very much like Baba Ojore, but he was just a shade shorter and not quite as thick. And his presence was not quite as commanding. He must have been a quiet man. Kamau did not recall hearing him speak at all prior to the introductions. Despite his quiet demeanor, it was clear that Baba Kahuthia was not to be taken lightly. Kamau could see in his eyes that he had tremendous resolve and confidence.

These five men comprised a tremendous force. They reminded Kamau of the awe and fear that his own father inspired in others. *Well, this is great*, Kamau thought sarcastically. *I've just exchanged one ruthless taskmaster for five. Probably six. Who is this other man?*

Baba Ojore's Inspection

No sooner had Kamau thought about the Bausi, than Baba Ojore came into view. He seemed to appear out of nowhere. He wore the same black pants and grey t-shirt as the Mwalimu, except the black shirt he wore had a hood on it. As he approached the kambi, the Mwalimu became sterner in their demeanor if that were possible.

Seeing the kambi, Baba Ojore's face transitioned, first from joy, then to disgust, then to confusion. Although everyone could hear him, he spoke as though to himself, slowly and in a tone of shocked disbelief. "What in the name of all that is righteous and just?" Then as if he had a revelation, his head snapped up. "Baba Kojo."

"Yes, sir."

Baba Ojore looked at Baba Kojo as though searching for an explanation, "Your Mkhosi must have been attacked by a band of gypsies last night. Is that what happened?"

Baba Kojo replied curtly, "No, sir."

Baba Ojore looked confused and said flatly, "No gypsies." He was still thinking as he continued to look around. "Baba Thulani."

"Yes, sir." Baba Thulani's smile was gone.

"You must have been attacked by a pack of wild, feral hogs," Baba Ojore explained excitedly. "I've heard there has been a rogue pack of hogs attacking farm animals and vagrants in the city. Did they attack you?"

"No, sir," Baba Thulani replied flatly.

"No hogs." Baba Ojore's excitement faded, his confusion turned to anger, and his voice began to rumble. "Well, Baba Kahuthia, if you were not attacked by gypsies, and you were not attacked by wild, feral hogs, then, in the name of all that is gracious and true, how did evil come into this Mkhosi and cause Isfet? Who caused this mess?"

Before Baba Kahuthia could answer, a quiet, yet confident voice was heard from the edge of the kambi, "We did, sir." It was Deiondre, the wild-eyed boy, who spoke. Kamau noted that he still looked wild-eyed.

"Well, what do we have here?" Baba Ojore walked towards him slowly, even dramatically. As he walked, the Mwalimu stood at attention, their hands at their sides, their heads high, and their eyes staring off blankly into the distance. The Vanguardians in Training fidgeted nervously. Their eyes darted back and forth between Deiondre and Baba Ojore.

Baba Ojore stood just to the left of Deiondre. Deiondre looked blankly into the distance, just like the Mwalimu. Baba Ojore asked, "What's your name, Son?"

"Deiondre Everly, sir."

Baba Ojore smiled briefly, "Well done, Everly. Honesty is a virtue." He then turned, scowled, and his voice while not yelling, still rolled like thunder, "Now let me tell you what is not a virtue. Chaos is not a virtue. And this kambi is rife with chaos. There is no order to the placement of your quarters. There is no grace to the construction of your shelters. There is no care in the disposition of your provisions."

All eyes stared blankly as no one wanted to make eye contact with Baba Ojore. Kamau felt as though the words were vibrating in his chest. Baba Ojore continued, "Helplessness is not a virtue. And this kambi tells me that you are helpless. You cannot properly assemble shelter that is machine crafted and provided to you. You cannot organize yourselves into a suitable defensive arrangement. You cannot protect your provisions from the morning dew!" Baba Ojore's voice jumped up an octave on the last word. He was so upset that Kamau imagined their group to be one of the worst he had ever seen.

Baba Ojore paused and paced to calm himself. He resumed, this time in a normal speaking voice. "Self-deception. Self-deception is not a virtue. Many of your peers, and probably some of you, have been told that you are special…" he mockingly whined the rest of his sentence "…just because you are you."

He resumed, speaking normally, "You have received top marks in school after doing very little work. You have received sports trophies and awards after getting beaten all over the city. You have received accolades, back pats, and attaboys just because…" He again mocked, this time with baby talk "…mommy wants you to feel good. Well, here at the Vanguard Akhet, the Babas love you. And because we love you, we are not going to foster a spirit of self-deception."

He turned to Baba Kahuthia, "Baba step forward, please." He then turned to the Vanguardians. "What color is the shirt that Baba Kahuthia is wearing?"

Albert Dorsey replied, "The shirt is grey, sir."

Baba Ojore asked the group, "By show of hands, how many believe that this shirt is grey?"

Each Vanguardian raised his hand. Kamau noticed that none of the Mwalimu raised their hands.

Baba Ojore turned to Baba Abiola, "Baba Abiola, what color is this shirt."

He answered, "Baba Ojore, the color of this shirt is Vanguard Steel."

Baba Ojore smiled and nodded, then he made eye contact with several Vanguardians as he spoke, "Yeeeessss. The color of this shirt is Vanguard Steel. In it, we harden our resolve, our determination, and our discipline. The color of this shirt is Vanguard Steel. In it, we sharpen our perception, our awareness, and our skill. The color of this shirt is Vanguard Steel."

Some of the Vanguardians nodded in understanding. Kamau actually felt a bit of confidence. His chest and shoulders perked up, and he felt a tinge of pride wearing his Vanguard Steel.

Baba Ojore continued in an unnervingly calm voice and slow cadence, "Now, because we are not going to foster a spirit of self-deception, you must know…" he began speaking very quickly "…that you are not worthy of this Vanguard Steel. You have provided not one inkling of an indication that you are in any way whatsoever prepared to harden your resolve, determination, or discipline. Take off my shirts! You must first show us that you have resolve, determination, and discipline, then maybe we can harden it."

The Vanguardians who were wearing shirts took them off, and Baba Abiola collected them.

Baba Ojore commanded, "Baba Kahuthia, give these Ginks their shirts!"

Baba Kahuthia passed out three pink shirts of the appropriate size to each of the Vanguardians. While he did this, Baba Ojore continued, "Everly, what color are these shirts?"

Deiondre hesitantly responded, "These shirts are pink, sir."

Baba Ojore asked the group, "By show of hands, how many believe that these shirts are pink?"

This time, only half of the Vanguardians raised their hands in agreement. Kamau raised his hand. He knew the answer was not pink, but he didn't know what the answer was, so he thought it safest to stick with the obvious answer.

Baba Ojore turned to Baba Abiola, "Baba Abiola, what color is this shirt."

He answered, "Baba Ojore, the color of this shirt is insignificance."

Baba Ojore quickly agreed, "That's right," he snapped. "These shirts are the color of messy confetti. They are the color of tooth-rotting cotton candy. They are the color of tissue paper used to hide ugly sweaters in cheap, lazy gift bags. The color of these nasty shirts is insignificance." He paused and slowly looked over the Vanguardians. "Now, you must *earn* Vanguard Steel."

With those words, and at that moment, the Vanguardians were made to hate the pink shirts. Kamau cringed as he put his on. While they put on the shirts, Baba Ojore stood in front of Charles Hall, who now looked even more foolish standing there in a pink shirt and tidy whities. "What's your name, boy?"

"Charles Hall, sir," he replied solemnly, with an appropriate measure of shame.

Baba Ojore narrowed his eyes, "Charles Hall if you ever present yourself to this Mkhosi in such a shameful manner again, I will run you to the Never-Mark. I will run you until your ankles swell up to be as thick as your thighs. I will run you to the Ohio state line and then make you run the perimeter! Do you understand me?"

"Yes, sir!"

Baba Ojore commanded, "Dignify yourself!"

Charles "Little Bird" Hall couldn't get into his tent fast enough.

"Baba Kojo, when these boys are no longer Ginks, then I will train them. De-Ginkify these boys! Do it quickly and by any means necessary." Baba Ojore then walked away from the kambi. As he left, he placed his hood on his head. Kamau must have been distracted because he never saw exactly where Baba Ojore went. He just seemed to fade away.

The Mwalimu all looked at Baba Kojo. Some looked angry. Baba Thulani, who looked uneasy, asked, "How do we de-Ginkify these boys?"

Baba Kojo's face was a mask of fury. He turned slowly from Thulani, looked over the sea of pink shirts, and growled out a long one-word response, "Pain."

An Old Friend (O'Leary)

As Timothy stepped through the glass entry doors and looked around, he noted that Coordination Center Two was surprisingly quiet. It was only about a quarter of the capacity one would typically find for a project that was nearing release.

Seeing him enter, Anand Devi approached with a broad and genuine smile, "Welcome, my friend! I heard you were looking for me."

Anand, a clean-cut, slight built man, was one of nine research coordinators in NanoTech Division. He didn't report to Timothy, but the two had worked on projects together in the past, and they had a very good relationship. When they first met, Anand was a lab specialist who had just arrived in the US. He had a wife and three small children, very little money, no extended family, and no social support. Even the Indian Affinity Group, which comprised the majority of the research workforce at TechInnoGen, seemed to ignore him. To make matters worse, his English was very poor and many of the whites, which comprised the majority of the administrative workforce, avoided him. So, he had no support. But he was an insanely hard worker and a very good scientist. Seeing this, Timothy reached out to him.

Timothy and Daphne visited Anand's home and met his wife, Kuyili, and their children. They both liked Kuyili. She was fiery! The Devis were living in a rundown, drug-infested slum. Timothy helped them to get out of the lease, and Daphne helped them to find a modest home in a safe neighborhood. She also helped Kuyili to get the children enrolled in school. Anand had no car. Initially, he took public transportation, but he was mugged twice. So, he started taking a cab, which he could not afford. Timothy helped him to get a driver's license and purchase a car. Timothy had seen many internationals come to the US for school or work, but he had never seen any as isolated or as destitute as Anand. One afternoon over lunch, Timothy asked Anand why he had no support.

The story Anand told was horrific. He told Timothy about his upbringing in abject poverty. As a child, he lived in a box on the side of the road. He began working at six years old, cleaning out latrines. His father was an alcoholic and took the little money Anand earned to buy cheap liquor. When he turned eight, Anand left home and wandered the streets as a beggar. He was ten when he met Kuyili. A group of three drunk men were beating her in the back of a garment factory, and they were about to take advantage of her. He ran at them with a heavy metal pole. As he swung the heavy pole, trying to fight the men, they were humored by his bravery. They forgot about Kuyili, and she ran away. Once the novelty of Anand's bravery wore off, the men took the pole and beat Anand. In his drunkenness, one of the men tripped and hit his head on a concrete step. Seeing this, the other two ran off.

Kuyili had been watching from a nearby hiding place. When the men were gone, she came back and tended to Anand. After a few days, when he was mostly healed, Anand and Kuyili agreed to take care of each other. They would each be family for the other. They also vowed that they would no longer be poor. From that day, they began working and saving. They cleaned latrines and sewers, removed the bodies of dead animals, scavenged for recyclable trash, anything that would earn them money. They both took classes, learning to read and write whenever they could. Over time, they had saved enough to rent a shabby apartment. They continued working and saving. Soon, they were able to buy and resell little trinkets and food. And they continued to work and save. By the time they were old enough to marry, they had saved enough to open a small shop. Money was scarce, so they lived in the back of the shop. In addition to taking care of their growing family, they used the money earned from the shop to put Anand through college. Soon after he completed college, they moved to the US.

Hearing his history, Timothy understood Anand and his situation much better. Both he and Kuyili were estranged from their families as young children, so they had no extended family of which to speak. Both were Dalits, or Untouchables. This is why many in the Indian Affinity Group seemed to ignore Anand. Timothy recalled that the concept of Varna in Hindu is thousands of years old. It organized Indian people into four groups: Brahmins (the class of priests), Kshatriyas (the class of rulers and warriors), Vaishyas (the class of artisans, merchants, and farmers) and Shudras (the class of laborers). But ancient Hindu texts make no mention of Dalits (the class of impure or untouchable people). This is a concept introduced by the British in the 1900s. It helped them to divide and control the Indian people.

Poor Anand, Timothy thought. *Here, he is thousands of miles from India and decades from British colonialism, but the British still have him divided from his own people. And his white co-workers won't even speak to him because his English is a little rough.* From that point on, Timothy looked out for Anand and supported him in his career. In return, Anand had been a faithful friend.

"Anand! You *are* the one!" Timothy greeted him with a firm handshake and hug. "I appreciate you taking time to chat."

"Of course. It's no problem."

As they walked to Anand's glass-walled office, Timothy got straight to the point, "Anand, I have a project coming up and I want your NanoTech research group on it. Before I reach out to your associate vice president, I want to be sure your schedule is clear and that you are interested."

Anand was very agreeable, "Of course, I'll always work with you. But we have a project ongoing. When does your project start?"

"Anand, I am planning ahead. The start time is flexible. It can start in one day, one month, or one year. When do you think you will complete the current project?"

Anand hesitated, "I don't know. This is very big project. We don't have specific timeframe."

"Very big?" Wearing a look of surprise, Timothy turned and surveyed Coordination Center Two. "It doesn't look very big. You only have a handful of people working."

"Yes. We are working earlier than normal," Anand replied.

Timothy pressed him, "Project coordination takes place two to three months before release… four months tops. How much earlier could you be working?"

Anand seemed a bit uneasy. "This is different kind of project."

"Hmmm." Timothy seemed to be thinking. "Is it a product release? Maybe we could make an outside estimate of the time."

Although this project was highly secretive, and he had signed a non-disclosure agreement, Anand trusted Timothy completely. He stood to close the door, and he spoke with his back to the room so no one could see his mouth moving. "This is not a product release. We are managing the launch of the SEV Fitzroy. We will also serve as the command center during the exploration. This project could last up to a year. We are scheduled to launch in just over six months. We can talk more later?"

Timothy worked to keep his face impassive. He nodded and replied, "Yes. Thank you."

Anand opened the door, and they shook hands as Timothy left. "Thanks, Anand. Give my best to Kuyili. Hug and kiss the kids for me."

The Morning Run (Day One)

Baba Thulani walked to the edge of the path and commanded the group, "Guard… Colummmmmn Two!"

Confused, the boys meandered about, each contributing to what he believed was being asked of them. The Mwalimu quietly provided instructions and guidance to the group. Within moments, they formed a column of two in front of Baba Thulani.

Baba Kojo stepped to the front and addressed the group, "Bahari laini haifanyi mabaharia stadi." He looked at the Ginks and repeated it, "Bahari laini haifanyi mabaharia stadi." Then he commanded, "Say it with me!" He repeated the phrases slowly, and the Ginks fumbled through it. Baba Kojo paced up and down the column as he continued to speak, "Vanguardians are men of virtue. Our first virtue is courage. We do not fear rough seas. We know that rough seas make us stronger. Do not fear the trials of the Akhet. These trials will make us stronger. Do not fear the pain you will experience. The pain that you will experience, will let you know that you are growing stronger in both your bodies and your mind."

The Ginks said nothing. Baba Kojo turned to face the front of the column, "Baba Thulani!"

Baba Thulani announced, "To the Three-Mark." He turned and began to run. The column of boys ran behind him. Babas Kojo and Abiola ran to the left of the column. Babas Kahuthia and Chinua ran to the right of the column. The Mwalimu were evenly spaced along the length of the column.

Kamau and Raymond ran side by side. There were two pairs of boys between them and Baba Thulani: Deiondre and Bongani were first, Amari and his quarter mate Carl were second, followed by Kamau and Raymond. One of the first things that Kamau noticed was that the t-shirts the Mwalimu wore, the Vanguard Steel, had a quote on the back:

I have freed thousands of slaves and could have freed
thousands more if only they had known they were slaves.
- Harriett Tubman

Over the course of the run, Kamau read that quote several times. It confused him. How could slaves not *know* they were enslaved? About five minutes into the run, commotion was heard from the middle of the line. Some of the boys were not keeping pace, and the Mwalimu ordered the boys to, "Hold the line!" and "Keep the line tight."

This went on for a few minutes until, finally, Baba Chinua shouted, "Stragglers! Fall Out!"

Baba Abiola slowed his pace and commanded, "Tighten the line!"

Kamau looked back as best he could, but it was hard to keep pace and also look back. After a time, there was a turn and the path curved so completely that the group was running back in the direction it had come. When this happened, Kamau could see the back of the column on the path behind him. There was no longer one column. There was one column up to Kamau and Raymond. Between them and the next pair, there was a space big enough to drive a car through. After that pair, there was a space twice as big, followed by a small mob.

Kamau didn't have any idea how far they were running, but he knew he had never run this far before. It seemed that they would never stop. The path had changed from gravel to asphalt shortly after they had begun running, and his feet hurt with every step. He struggled to breathe and noticed that Raymond was panting very hard as well. To make matters worse, the Mwalimu repeated the Swahili phrase, "Bahari laini haifanyi mabaharia stadi" throughout the run and made the Ginks repeat it. Kamau had no idea what it meant, but about halfway through the run, he could repeat it without help.

As they continued, Kamau realized the path was shaped like a large snake. At each curve there was a small stone obelisk, about two feet high. After the second turn, Kamau was able to see the remainder of the line much better. It didn't have the large gaps, and it looked more like a line, but it was not straight. Most of the boys ran slightly to the outside of the man in front of them, so the line began to look like a "V."

As they approached the third obelisk, Kamau breathed a sigh of relief, and five of the first six boys began to stop, thinking they had reached the end. Only Deiondre kept pace with Baba Thulani who made the third turn at the obelisk and continued running.

Seeing them slow, Baba Abiola encouraged them, "We are not there yet. Keep it moving." Don't count the obelisk, read the marks. Kamau, Raymond, Amari, Carl, and Bongani picked up the pace and reformed the line.

About five minutes after the third turn, Kamau again saw the stragglers. There were five boys: Chandler, Alton, and three other pudgy boys. Chandler and the three pudgy boys had given up all pretense of a run, and they simply walked. Not Alton. Alton was determined. The problem was, he couldn't run. He was shuffling so slowly that the other stragglers' walking pace matched his shuffle. That was the last time Kamau would see the stragglers on that run.

The remainder of the run was torture. Kamau's lungs burned, his chest heaved, and he struggled to get air. His feet stung as they slapped the pavement, sending shooting pain up through his shins and to his knees. He had a sharp, piercing sensation in the side of his stomach. His lower back ached. It could not hold his body upright. He desperately needed to sit down.

Eventually, they reached the obelisk with "Three-Mark" engraved on the pyramid-shaped top. Baba Thulani smacked the obelisk and, instead of turning to continue on the path, he ran straight onto a second path that veered left. All the boys followed suit. As he followed the others onto the second path, Kamau saw that it was a straight path. Baba Thulani picked up the pace. He encouraged them, "Run hard! Finish strong!" Baba Thulani sprinted up the path, returning to Camp Furaha.

When Kamau finished the run, he collapsed of exhaustion. His face lay in the dirt and gravel of the path. He was not alone. Most of the boys fell out in the same way. Baba Abiola chastised them, "Get up! You will not show your weakness! Stand on your feet like men."

Kamau stood and limped around. Baba Abiola made the boys stretch while they waited on the stragglers to return. After a time, Baba Abiola walked away from the boys, and the boys complained of their aches and pains. They described the various injuries they believed they had incurred. And soon, they were discussing and laughing about the mishaps of the run: the gaps in the line, the false stop, and of course, the stragglers.

Deiondre commented off-handedly, "I'm sore all over. I like it."

Kamau looked at him and thought, *That boy is not right in the head.*

SECRETS OF THE VANGUARD ORDER

After ten minutes or so, the stragglers returned, coughing and wheezing. Baba Chinua would not let them stretch or sit to rest. He said, "You Ginks rested during the run." He then pulled a stopwatch from beneath his shirt and announced the time. "Ginks, you finished this run in forty-seven minutes, twelve seconds."

Baba Abiola shook his head and sighed in disappointment.

Baba Chinua continued, and the longer he spoke the louder and more emphatically he yelled, "You will not be Vanguardians until you run the Three-Mark in a respectable time. You will not get out of those faggoty pink blouses until you run the Three-Mark in a respectable time. You will not leave this Akhet and see your mommy until you run the Three-Mark in a respectable time." He paused to calm himself down. He continued in a normal speaking voice. "Every Vanguardian runs the Three-Mark in twenty-four minutes or less."

Chandler's eyes grew wide. He wheezed, and a look of distress took over his face.

The boys were made to form a column of two, and they walked back to the kambi. As they walked, Babas Thulani and Kojo led the column. Babas Abiola, Chinua, and Kahuthia made sure the boys kept the line straight and tight. The Mwalimu had noticed that the line flared out like a "V." They called this a goose line.

Baba Kahuthia spoke with a thick Cajun accent, "We don't run goose lines. We are smarter than geese. Geese need to see the leader. We don't need to see the leader; we are one unit. Whether that unit be a Squad, a Mkhosi, or an Ibutho, we are one unit. You watch the head of the man in front of you and nothing else. Follow his head. Study his head. You should know every pimple on that man's head. You should know the number of hairs on the back of that man's head. You should know the size of each follicle that holds a hair on the back of that man's head!"

Some of the boys snickered quietly at Baba Kahuthia's accent and his insistence that they focus on the man in front of them. He continued, "We hold the line. At all costs, we hold the line. If a line is weakened, we are leaving an opening for evil. If a line is broken, we are inviting the enemy to come in and destroy us. You should never be more than an arms-length away from the man in front of you. At all costs, hold the line."

On the walk back to the kambi, they worked at keeping the line straight and tight.

Put 'em Up and Take 'em Down

Once they returned, Baba Kojo had each man return to his tent. He explained some of the factors to consider when deciding how to organize a camp and where to position the entry of a shelter. Weather, terrain, defense, and size of the camp were some of the factors he described. He had the boys disassemble their tents and relocate the rolled packs so that the camp could be arranged in an orderly way.

With the camp arranged, Baba Kojo had the boys gather around him at his tent location. Like the other men, Baba Kojo's tent was rolled neatly and stuffed in its sack ready to be assembled. The boys' tents were also stuffed in their sacks, for the most part, but they certainly were not neat. He began, "We assemble the tent in four steps. Step number one, unroll the tent." Baba Kojo quickly removed his tent from its sack and unrolled it like you might roll a bowling ball. He then unfolded it so that it laid flat.

He paused to look at the boys. "Step number two, stake the tent." Baba Kojo returned to his sack and removed a handful of stakes. He circled the tent, running stakes through loops at the edges and corners of the tent, stretching the tent as he went. Some of the boys nodded, whispering to their quarter mates. This was a step that many of them had missed.

Again, Baba Kojo paused and surveyed the Mkhosi. He continued, "Step number three, extend the poles." Baba Kojo removed two poles from his sack and extended them. He ran one pole through a sleeve and inserted the end into a grommet at the corner. He repeated this with the second pole.

Baba Kojo stood and, without pausing, said, "Step number four, raise the tent." He took the end of one pole and bent it upwards. The tent began to stand. He continued bending it upward until he could place the end of that pole into a grommet. He repeated this with the other pole, and his tent took shape. "Are there any questions?"

No one responded, and Baba Kojo looked at Baba Thulani. Baba Thulani smiled. Baba Kojo then nodded to Baba Chinua. Baba Chinua took his stopwatch in hand and commanded, "To your tents." Once all the boys were standing near their tents, he commanded, "Put 'em up!"

The boys began assembling their tents. Kamau and Raymond worked seamlessly together. Without conversing, they each had an intuitive sense of how to complement each other's work. While Kamau unrolled the tent, Raymond extended the poles. While Kamau staked the tent, Raymond ran the poles in the sleeves and inserted the ends in the grommets. They each grabbed a pole and raised the tent together. They were the first two finished. When they had finished, they stood and watched the others. Deiondre and Bongani were the next to finish. They finished almost immediately after Kamau and Raymond.

The other boys had a much more difficult time. Some of the boys lost stakes.

Some had difficulty extending the poles. A few argued between themselves as to which step should be next. Chandler and Alton were the third group to finish. It took them about twice as long to finish as Kamau and Raymond. Kamau noticed that, despite their physical challenges, Chandler and Alton worked well together.

One tent at a time, the rest of the boys in the Mkhosi finished the task. Each pair stopped to admire their work and then turned to watch the others. After the last tent was assembled, Baba Chinua announced, "Time! fifteen minutes, forty-three seconds." He snapped at Raymond, "Hewitt, how long did it take you to assemble your tent?"

Raymond replied nervously, "Uh… About th… th… three minutes or so? Sir?"

Baba Chinua gave Raymond a piercing stare, "I'm asking the questions, Hewitt. Now how long did it take you to assemble your tent?"

Raymond gathered himself and responded more assertively, "Three minutes, sir."

Baba Chinua replied curtly, "No!" He then turned to the others. "Does anyone know how long it took Hewitt and Njama to assemble their tent?"

Most of the boys stood quietly, not daring to speak. But Kamau noticed Charles "Little Bird" Hall. For some strange reason, Charles Hall seemed to be itching to open his mouth. He was fidgeting and just dying to draw attention to himself. Kamau snickered in his head and thought to himself, *Don't do it Little Bird. Didn't that pie hole cause you enough trouble this morning?*

Baba Chinua must have noticed Little Bird's anxiousness. He walked up to him, aimed his piercing stare right at Hall and snapped, "Hall? Are you able to improve upon the silence?"

Poor Charles was cowed into good reason. His shoulders slumped. He looked down and muttered, "No, sir."

Baba Chinua cocked his head and bent over slightly to look directly into Hall's eyes, "Say it like a man, Hall! There are no doormats in this group!"

Charles stood erect and responded with a bit more bass and volume, "No, sir."

Baba Chinua growled, "Good."

As much as Kamau enjoyed a good show, he was glad that Charles saved himself from further embarrassment. After a lengthy silence, Kamau finally spoke, "Baba Chinua, it took Hewitt and Njama fifteen minutes, forty-three seconds to assemble their tent."

Baba Thulani nodded and smiled. Baba Chinua spoke to the group, but he addressed Raymond, "Hewitt, does the horse's nose criticize the horse's tail for arriving late?"

"No, sir!"

Baba Chinua continued, "No, it does not. We are one unit. We are one Mkhosi. And right now, this Mkhosi is too slow. Every Vanguardian assembles a prefabricated tent in three minutes or less. Today you will work on it." After a pause he took his stopwatch in hand and commanded, "Take 'em down!"

The boys disassembled their tents. Most did so haphazardly and sloppily. Poles weren't collapsed, stakes were unaccounted for, and tents weren't rolled tightly. Over half the tents would not fit into the sacks. Baba Kojo went through another demonstration. This time, he gave four steps for disassembling a tent. It took twelve minutes, thirty-two seconds for the last tent to be properly disassembled and stuffed away.

After explaining to the boys that a Vanguardian was expected to disassemble a tent in ninety seconds or less, Baba Chinua again commanded the boys to, "Put 'em up!" Once the tents were assembled, he commanded them to, "Take 'em down!" Baba Chinua continued with this drill for hours, and with each assembly and disassembly, he reported the time.

Kamau didn't know how many times they assembled and disassembled the tents. But the novelty of the exercise had worn off quickly, and he grew irritated after assembling the tent five times. After assembling the tent eight times, he began to hate the boys who still couldn't get it. In his mind, Kamau called them tent stragglers. The Mwalimu worked patiently with tent stragglers, giving them tips on how to work more quickly, how to work together, how to keep track of the tent materials. *Why couldn't these fools get it?! It's not rocket science. It's a tent!* His hatred for these boys grew. They were responsible for this drudgery and waste of time.

After assembling the tents twelve times, his hatred turned to Raymond because he was so pathetically cheerful and friendly. That boy wanted to grin about as much as Charles Hall wanted to talk. Soon after, his hatred turned to the Mwalimu because they wouldn't let it go. *No one sleeps in tents. We have houses for sleeping. Three minutes? Thirty minutes? Thirty days? Who made up these times? And who cares? Why am I still doing this drill when I obviously know how to put up a tent?* And of course, he hated his father all over again, the one person responsible for sending him to this wretched place, surrounded by these wretched people, and engaged in this wretched waste of time.

With each repetition, "Put "em up! Take 'em down!" his hatred grew. He withdrew within himself, and his animosity became apparent to those around him. Where the other boys became fatigued, Kamau became enraged.

No, Kamau didn't know how many times they assembled and disassembled the tents. He lost count after seventeen.

SECRETS OF THE VANGUARD ORDER

When, finally, the boys were able to complete the assembly in under three minutes and the disassembly in under ninety seconds, Baba Chinua announced, "Task Complete!" Many of the boys cheered and high-fived one another. Kamau rolled his eyes. He was too disgusted to find pleasure in that moment.

Seeing the boys' excitement, Baba Kojo addressed the group. "You feel accomplished. That is good. Accomplishment is essential. But in the midst of accomplishment, it is important to have perspective. Remember, Vanguardians do not foster a spirit of self-deception." The Mkhosi was quiet as the boys listened. "In these past few hours, you learned to assemble a tent. It is a tent that you did not make. It was made for you. It is a tent that you did not buy. It was purchased for you. Now, if one day you should find yourself homeless, and someone, in their generosity, should give you a tent, you would be slightly less helpless on that day than you were yesterday."

The Mkhosi was visibly deflated, and Kamau laughed in his head, *Ha ha ha. That's right Baba! Tell 'em.*

Baba Kojo continued, "Today's accomplishment is one step, but it is a small step. It is a long way from self-determination. One day soon, you will make primitive shelter. You will build simple homes, like log cabins, huts, or yurts. You will build elaborate modern homes. You will build commercial buildings. And you will establish multi-million-dollar companies that specialize in the construction trades."

When he finished, Baba Thulani commanded, "Guard... Colluuuumn. Two!" A column formed quickly in front of Baba Thulani.

As Kamau stood in formation next to Raymond, Baba Chinua approached and spoke to him directly in low tones, "You are angry that the drill took so long."

You got that right, Kamau thought sardonically.

"The entire Mkhosi missed breakfast because of the time we spent on that drill."

Yeah! thought Kamau. *I forgot about breakfast.*

Baba Chinua spoke matter-of-factly. "All of this is your fault, Njama."

Though he said nothing, Kamau looked at Baba Chinua in stark surprise and disbelief, his mouth gaping. *My fault?* he thought. *How could it be my fault?*

Baba Chinua continued, "You could have helped your brothers. But you did not. You knew how to assemble a tent when you arrived last night. In fact, you assembled your tent in the dark. Yet today, for nearly four hours, you watched them struggle and didn't lift a finger to help." Baba Chinua's tone was calm and dispassionate as though he were reporting the news. He was not accusatory. He did not belittle Kamau. He simply stated the facts. Those facts were enough. Kamau felt small. The wry arrogance and hatred he had bathed in for the past few hours began to dry, and he felt shame.

Baba Thulani led the boys to lunch. The second half of the day was just as difficult as the first. They were served a very mediocre lunch. It was better than the cold sandwiches they had eaten on the bus ride, but not much better. They were not permitted to speak during lunch, and they ate hurriedly.

Murdered by Monotony

After lunch, they did PT for sixty minutes or so. Although it was short, by comparison to other activities, it was brutal. They did an exercise feverishly for forty-five seconds, only to be teased by a fifteen-second break before starting the next exercise. This went on for thirty minutes. After thirty minutes, they were allowed a four-minute water break. Then they did it again for another thirty minutes. It made the morning run to the Three-Mark seem easy by comparison. The stragglers couldn't "walk" through the exercises. Chandler Gardner lost his lunch. *Too bad*, Kamau thought. *That skinny boy needed it.*

After the exercises, they spent three to four hours doing drills. They were taught "the Vanguard way" to "fall in" to columns of two, four, and five; stand at attention; stand at ease; stand at parade rest; march; turn while standing; turn while marching; salute; rest; and form a shield. It was a miserable experience. The sun beat down on the boys. The bugs bit at any exposed skin. Kamau's legs and back ached. His feet, which had been sore since the morning run, continued to throb, especially his left foot. He would have given anything for a chair or even a chance to kneel. But it was not allowed. If they tried to shade their eyes or shoo a fly, if they moved in any way that was not commanded by the drill leader, they were chastised by the Mwalimu. As bad as all of this was, the very worst part was the boredom. The drills were repetitive. They were mind-numbing. Kamau felt he was being murdered by monotony.

Dinner was as mediocre as lunch. Again, the boys were not permitted to speak. Following dinner, each boy was given a copy of the *Autobiography of Malcolm X*. They read the first three chapters that evening. Although most of the boys had heard of Malcolm X and were familiar with his story, few had actually read the book. As they read, the Mwalimu stopped frequently to explain the context of the story. Whenever the book referred to a particular place, they pulled out maps to show it. When the book referenced particular songs or singers, they played audio recordings. They also used photographs and other writings and encouraged the boys to stop and think as they read.

Kamau had never read a book this way before, using so many references. It helped him to understand the book much better. And he would have enjoyed it if he could have stayed awake. But the events of the day had exhausted him. He was sore and tired in his body, mind, and spirit. Aside from lunch and dinner, the reading was the only chance the boys had gotten all day to sit, and it was the first time, except for the silent meals, that the Mwalimu weren't yelling at them. Many boys would have slept through the book if it were not for the Mwalimu keeping everyone awake.

After reading, the boys took showers. Baba Kojo gave them instruction in showering "the Vanguard way." According to Baba Chinua, each boy was expected to complete his shower in four minutes or less.

Following the showers, Baba Kojo assembled the Mkhosi in the middle of the courtyard. He explained to the boys that one of the most important features of the Akhet is that it helped men to better understand themselves. To help support this self-discovery, each boy was given a composition book. The boys were instructed to take thirty minutes to write a reflection on their experience of that day. They were told to reflect on any aspect of the experience that they wanted.

When he opened his composition book, Kamau found three photographs taped to the inside front cover: Mrs. Njama, Grandma Charline, and Imani. When Kamau saw the pictures, his first feeling was excitement. Then his heart sank as he was reminded of the betrayal of his mother and Grandma Charline. He moved the pictures to the back of the book so he wouldn't have to see them. As he moved the pictures, he noticed that the picture of Imani was the one she had given him when they last spoke. Kamau had hidden the picture in the duffle bag he was going to use to run away. This meant that, somehow, his mother had found the duffle bag. There was also a good chance she had known Kamau's plan all along.

As Kamau lay in his tent on his sleeping bag writing, he fell asleep. He was startled awake to the sound of Baba Thulani announcing, "Lights out!" He folded his composition book, climbed into his bag, and continued to sleep.

Kamau's Suffering

Improvement (Day Two)

As soon as he had begun to sleep, Kamau was startled awake by the horn with its alternating long and short tones. Kamau was sickened by the ugliness of the sound made by the horn. "Rise and Shine, Vanguardians!" Baba Thulani's voice pierced the morning air.

"It can't be morning already," Kamau said.

As he began crawling out of his sleeping back, Raymond replied, "It is."

Kamau was stung by the chilly morning air as it drifted into his sleeping bag. He pulled his bag tightly around his shoulders and rolled away from Raymond.

Raymond, who was already out of his bag and getting dressed, said, "Remember Little Bird from yesterday."

Kamau's eyes widened. He forgot his aversion to chilly morning air and quickly dressed.

Baba Thulani continued, "Yes, sir! Today is going to be a great day! A great day!"

Kamau and Raymond were the third pair of boys to assemble. When they emerged from their tent, Deiondre and Bongani were already outside waiting, smiling at Kamau and Raymond smugly. To Kamau's surprise, Alton and Chandler were also outside. *Why are those two so eager?* he thought.

Urging the others on, Baba Thulani announced, "The day will commence in one minute."

As the others emerged one by one, Kamau began to feel sick. He thought about the day before, his feet that were still sore, the pain of the morning run, the constant yelling of the Mwalimu's, the hours upon hours spent repeating the same simple activities, the heat of the day, the bugs, the terrible food. Today, he would have to do it all over again. And these disgusting pink shirts… Yesterday's activities were so torturous that he had forgotten how much he hated the pink shirts. Well, now he remembered.

Today, no one was late. The men were as clean today as they were yesterday. The boys also looked much better. Aside from the weariness and the Gink shirts they wore, the boys were squared away.

As the Ginks spoke quietly among themselves, Baba Ojore appeared and approached the kambi. Kamau didn't see where he came from, but it didn't matter. *Okay, good!* he thought. *We've got the kambi organized, and we learned our drill commands. Maybe now, we can get our Vanguard Steel shirts back and begin learning.* There was a low murmur among the Mkhosi as other boys shared the same ideas.

Baba Thulani silenced the boys with a drill command, "Guard… colluuuumn. Five!"

Without saying a word, Baba Ojore inspected the boys. The boys knew that they should not move. Their heads remained fixed forward. However, in their nervousness, they did not keep their eyes from darting about. They tried to watch the Mwalimu, Baba Ojore, and each other. And Baba Ojore noticed. He turned to inspect the kambi. After looking about, Baba Ojore asked, "Where is Charles Hall?"

Charles replied, "Here, sir."

Baba Ojore looked him over and smiled slightly. He moved away and stood just to the left of another boy. "What's your name, Son?"

"Kamal Ofori, sir." From what Kamau could tell, Kamal was a good kid. He was always near the head of the pack, but never the leader. He also avoided mistakes. He made sure not to draw attention to himself.

"Ofori," Baba Ojore repeated. "Let me hear The Creed." He extended the word creed, which seemed to suggest it had significance.

Kamal answered plainly, "Baba Ojore, we did not learn The Creed." This was a gamble as neither Kamal nor any of the boys knew what creed Baba Ojore was referencing. But it was a reasonable gamble. Would he really be asking about the Apostle's Creed or any other such nonsense?

Kamau noticed that Kamal did not hem and haw. He answered confidently and without hesitation. It was becoming clear that the Mwalimu and Baba Ojore valued straight-talk.

Baba Ojore, stepped back to address the Mkhosi. "Baba Kojo, these Ginks are much improved. The kambi is respectable. They are all appropriately dressed." With that comment, he looked squarely at Charles Hall. Charles dropped his eyes in embarrassment. "They have the appearance of an organized unit." He paused. "But they are still Ginks. They have wandering eyes. They look weary and worn. And they are purposeless. They don't even know The Creed." He said the last sentence slowly, pronounced each word deliberately, and again extended the word creed. He then snapped as he walked away, "Keep working."

Baba Kojo replied, "Yes, sir!"

Kamau's hopes of getting out of the pink shirt were gone. *What difference does it make?* he thought. *Shirts won't make this experience any better.*

Mti wa Umoja

Baba Thulani announced, "We will begin the day at Mti wa Umoja." He then formed the group into a column of two and began walking up the path.

Kamau knew that "Umoja" was unity. He thought that "Wa" might be an article or a preposition like "of" or "for" or "with," but he wasn't sure. He did not know what "Mti" was. Just as he began to wish, for a second time, that he had paid more attention when his parents had tried to teach him Swahili, his cynicism took command of his thoughts, *What difference does it make?*

They arrived at a courtyard, in the middle of which was a circular stone wall about waist high. The wall had two openings. Inside the circular wall was a small stand of trees. There was one very large tree at the very center of the enclosure created by the stone wall. Baba Abiola instructed the boys to each grab a glass carboy and fill it with water. He gestured to a structure outside of the wall, which had glass jugs and an old-fashioned hand pump.

Most of the boys had never seen a hand pump before, and they were uncertain as to how it worked. One of the boys, Carl Lofton, stepped up cheerfully and interjected with a heavy southern drawl, "I got you." He went to the pump and raised the handle as high as he could, then he lowered it. The metal handle creaked loudly, and nothing came out. He did it again, and there was more creaking, but still no water.

"Are you sure you know how to work that thing?" Charles asked playfully.

"Sure!" Carl smiled broadly, "You can't get water with just one pump. My grandpa used to say, 'Success is like an old well pump, you have to pump a long time before you get water. But don't stop, because if you do, you got to start all over again!'"

Carl kept smiling, pumping, and joking with the other boys. He reminded Kamau of Raymond. In fact, he could have been Raymond's country cousin. They were both very friendly and outgoing, and neither seemed to be bothered by the tortures they faced. When water finally started to flow, Carl hollered with a hoot, "Da'it is!"

Each boy and man filled his carboy and joined Baba Abiola by forming a circle around the big tree. Carl joined the group last, bouncing and smiling the whole time. When he arrived, Baba Kahuthia began speaking in his thick Cajun accent. "Gentlemen, the ceremony we are about to perform is how we start every day at the Akhet. We should have started day-one here as well, but you weren't ready."

Baba Kahuthia's tone was very different. There was no yelling, no commanding. He spoke in a low conversational voice, very deliberately, and the raspy, huskiness of his voice was mesmerizing. "The large tree at the center of this courtyard," he gestured, "this tree, is called the Unity Tree. It is a symbol of our brotherhood, of our bond, and of our unity. It is also a symbol of the unity that we share with those liberating Afrikans who came before us, who paved the way for us so that we could be here today: our fathers and mothers, our grandfathers and grandmothers, and, for some of us, our great grandfathers and our great grandmothers. It is also a symbol of the unity that we share with those liberating Afrikans who have now entered the ancestral realm. The spirit that possessed them lives on today in us. Finally, this Unity Tree is a symbol of the unity we share with those who are yet to be. We live for them, we train for them, we fight for them and, ultimately, we will die for them. We who are here today are one unit. We are one Mkhosi. Our unity ensures it. But we also enjoy a larger unity—the unity of our people. And we are one people. Our people are more numerous than the stars in the sky. Our people are more eternal than time. We are a mighty people. Our unity ensures it."

Baba Kahuthia paused, and no one stirred. He stood there broad-shouldered and barrel-chested as though he was waiting for the fires of Hades. Every boy in the Mkhosi mirrored that look, including Wild-Eyed Deiondre, Little Bird Hall, skinny Chandler, happy Carl, even Kamau who momentarily set aside his wry sarcasm. It would have been a bad idea for a gypsy or pack of wild, feral hogs to stumble into that courtyard at that moment.

After a while, Baba Kahuthia continued, "The ceremony is called the Watering of the Unity Tree. We refer to it as Mti wa Umoja, which in Kiswahili means tree of unity. Mti wa Umoja. Say it with me."

The Mkhosi replied in unison, "Mti wa Umoja."

"Mti wa Umoja. The Watering of the Unity Tree. We begin by seeking permission from the eldest member of the gathering to begin. Baba Kojo, may we begin?

Baba Kojo replied, "Yes."

"We who are gathered here affirm the unity that we share with one another, that we share with our forebearers, that we share with our ancestors, and that we share with the unborn. The tree of Afrikan unity must be watered by the blood, sweat, and tears of our enemies and of Vanguardians."

Baba Kahuthia then grabbed his carboy and explained, "The speaker will be the first to go. He will share an affirmation with the Mkhosi. He will then take his gallon of water and water the Unity Tree. As he waters the tree, all those gathered who accept his affirmation say, 'Ashe.' After he has watered the tree, he will return to his place in the circle. The man to the speaker's left will go next." He gestured to Baba Abiola, who stood to his left. "We will continue moving clockwise around the circle until all have gone. The speaker will then conclude by leading those assembled in a recitation of the Vanguardian Creed. Are there any questions?"

Charles Hall fidgeted nervously. It was killing him to remain silent. Baba Kahuthia addressed him, "Charles, you were invited to speak, so you may speak freely. But do not speak carelessly."

Charles responded, "Baba Kahuthia, what is an affirmation?"

"Thank you Charles, for the thoughtfulness of your question. An affirmation is a statement, sometimes a reminder, that we use to encourage or motivate ourselves or one another. Make sure that you believe your affirmation to be true. We do not lie, especially in the Mti wa Umoja. Charles, does that satisfy your question?"

"Yes, sir."

Baba Kahuthia began to step forward, but he was interrupted by Charles Hall, "Baba Kahuthia?"

"He responded patiently, "Yes, Charles?"

Charles Hall spoke nervously, "Baba Kahuthia, we don't know the Vanguardian Creed. What should we say?"

"No Charles Hall, you don't know The Creed. So just fumble along today. Follow the lead of the Mwalimu. By tomorrow, you will know The Creed." He paused, "Are there any other questions?" There was silence as Baba Kahuthia made eye contact with each of the boys. As there were no questions, he stepped forward with his carboy and gave his affirmation while watering the tree, "Vanguardians make daily sacrifices for our people."

The Mkhosi responded, "Ashe" and he returned to the circle.

The ceremony continued, and every Mwalimu and every boy gave his affirmation. Throughout the ceremony, Kamau felt a sense of calm. The sickness he had felt at the thought of the pain he would experience that day was gone. Instead, he felt a connection to the other boys and the Mwalimu. By hearing everyone's affirmations, Kamau grew to know them better. This would be the last bit of peace that Kamau would experience on day two.

SECRETS OF THE VANGUARD ORDER

Isolation

When the ceremony was complete, Baba Thulani organized the Mkhosi for the morning run, and the stragglers were ordered to the back of the column. This morning's run was far worse than the first. Kamau could barely run. His feet were in tremendous pain, and he could think of little else. It seemed that Baba Thulani ran faster than yesterday. And when the Mwalimu weren't making the Ginks repeat the Swahili phrase, they were yelling at the boys, telling them to "Keep pace!" and "Hold the line!"

The stragglers seemed to be doing better. Although they got behind, they never got lost around the bends. Today, none of them were walking. All of them shuffled with Alton. At the end of the run, Baba Chinua ordered the Mkhosi into a column of five and announced, "The stragglers finished this run in thirty-nine minutes, twenty-one seconds."

Baba Abiola called out, "Echols, how long did it take *you* to complete the run?"

Danny Echols was not one of the stragglers. He finished the run with the first group. He and his quarter mate, Gerard Winford, were the fifth pair in the column. He answered, "Baba Abiola, I don't know, sir. There was no time announced when we finished, but we were about four or five minutes ahead of the stragglers."

Kamau shook his head slightly and thought, *This won't be good.* He noticed Bongani peering at Danny disdainfully.

Baba Abiola gave him a stern stare, "Chaki! Give me five! On my count."

Danny stood there with his mouth agape, confused and uncertain. Gerard whispered to him, "Pushups." Danny lay down to do pushups. The other boys stood at attention.

For a long moment, Baba Abiola looked at the Mkhosi as if waiting for something. Suddenly he exploded, "You have got to be kidding me! Are you a bunch of old women waiting around for bingo cards? I think not. Are we not one unit? Why is this man on the ground alone? Is he your brother? Join him! Motivate him!"

Quickly, the entire Mkhosi was face down in the gravel and grass. Baba Abiola announced, "Begin." As the boys began doing pushups, Baba Abiola forgot to count. Kamau had done four when Baba Abiola finally counted, "One!"

Shortly after the one-count, some boys paused, uncertain as to what they should do. Kamau and a few other boys kept doing pushups. Charles Hall stood up. *Don't do it, Little Bird*, Kamau begged in his thoughts.

Baba Abiola was enraged, "What are you doing, Little Bird?! Is there a fire?

Are we being attacked by a rabid bear? Why are you not on your face? Why are you not doing pushups?"

Stupidly, Charles Hall responded, "Sir, you said do five, sir. I did five."

Baba Abiola, leaned into Charles Hall, their noses touching, and he screamed violently, "Why are you standing when every other Gink and Mwalimu in this Mkhosi is in the plank position? Are you better than them?"

Charles Hall tried to respond, "N…," but he was cut off.

"No, you are not! Did I command 'Give me five! On Little Bird's count'? No, I did not." Baba Abiola began answering his own questions, which probably saved Charles Hall from getting himself beaten. "Have you been taught how to count 'the Vanguard way'? No, you have not!" Baba Abiola brought his volume down to a normal yell. "Little Bird, you had better close your mouth so you can learn."

Charles Hall opened his mouth and began to protest, "Baba Abi…"

Before he could say any more, Kamau jumped to his feet, covered Charles' mouth, and whispered through clenched teeth, "Get down and be quiet." Together, they got down in the plank position.

Baba Abiola commanded, "Start in the up position. Begin."

The boys and three of the Mwalimu continued to do pushups while Baba Abiola counted. It turned out that Baba Abiola gave one count every time the boys completed four pushups. So "Give me five!" actually meant doing twenty pushups. Between counts, Baba Kojo gave instructions. He talked about the concept of unity. He emphasized that the group was only as strong as the weakest man and only as fast as the slowest man.

After completing the "five" pushups, Baba Abiola commanded the group to stand at attention. He then called out, "Jekwa, how long did it take *you* to complete the run?"

Bongani Jekwa finished with the first group. He and his quarter mate, Wild-Eyed Deiondre, were first in the column. He responded, "Baba Abiola, we finished this run in thirty-nine minutes, twenty-one seconds."

Baba Abiola continued, "Hewitt, how fast are you expected to complete this run?"

Raymond responded, "Baba Abiola, every Vanguardian is expected to complete this run in twenty-four minutes or less."

This began the tortures of the second day. Before lunch, they spent hours learning the Vanguard Creed, and with every error, they did pushups. They learned that the morning horn was called the Hwamanda. And with every error in the pronunciation of the name, they did pushups. They learned to make the sound of the morning call. And with every error in mimicking the morning call, they did pushups.

After lunch, they did PT. Then they were drilled for hours, and with every misstep, they did pushups. They learned that the uniforms they wore were Battle Dress Uniforms. They learned the names of each part of the uniform, and with every error, they did pushups. After dinner, they read more of the *Autobiography of Malcolm X*, and throughout the reading "in celebration of Malcolm's strength," they did pushups. There was no doubt in Kamau's mind that he had done thousands of pushups. It was impossible to count.

After showering and before falling asleep on his journal, Kamau thought back on the horrors of the day. While the running, the PT, his throbbing foot, the heat, and the pushups were torture enough, Kamau's greatest torture was that he seemed to be the only one bothered. The others were starting to accept this abuse. They complained less. They complied more eagerly. Sure, he would go along a bit to keep from suffering more abuse, but he wouldn't like it. *These sheep!* he thought derisively. It seemed that, now, he was alone in his hatred and misery. Yes, he alone hated the Akhet. He alone was miserable here.

Kamau's Kerfuffle (Day Three)

Day three began with the sound of the morning horn and Baba Thulani's cheerful announcement of how great the day would be. Kamau awoke with the same misery he had felt the night before. He ignored Raymond, despite his morning pleasantries. Kamau moved slowly and was the last boy to report to Morning Call. After performing the Mti wa Umoja, the Mkhosi ran. Kamau began the run as normal, in the third position with Raymond, but all he could think about was the pain in his foot. Every step was excruciating, and giving up the will to continue, he fell out of line and joined the stragglers. Uncertain as to what he should do, Raymond joined him.

"Kamau, is everything all right? You usually run much stronger?" Raymond asked pleasantly.

"Mind your business, boy!" Kamau snapped bitterly.

Raymond was stunned, and he continued running in silence. Over the next few minutes, Kamau and Raymond observed the stragglers saying things like, "run strong" and "no pain," in order to encourage one another.

A few of them gave these same motivations to Kamau and Raymond. Raymond, being good natured, returned the encouragement. Kamau, on the other hand, either sneered, rolled his eyes, or ignored them altogether.

Irritated by the apparent joy of the stragglers, Kamau soon gave up all pretense of running. He watched contentedly as the stragglers went on without him, and he walked the greater portion of the run. The Mwalimu took notice of this, but none of them said anything.

The lead group finished the run in well under twenty-four minutes. The stragglers finished in just over thirty-three minutes. Kamau finished dead last in fifty minutes, fifteen seconds. He strolled to the finish and he couldn't have appeared more indifferent. Several of the boys, Deiondre chief among them, looked at him disdainfully. Kamau could not have cared less. In fact, he had hoped, no, he had wished that Deiondre would start something. He would be the perfect punching bag for Kamau to vent his frustration.

Baba Chinua went through the drill of announcing the time and ensuring that everyone knew that the group had finished in fifty minutes, fifteen seconds. When asked, a few of the boys took ownership of the slow time, but not one of them accepted it. Not even the stragglers accepted Kamau's slow time as their own. Kamau was willfully lazy. He purposefully made no effort.

Throughout this charade, Kamau stood in formation indifferent to what was happening. Baba Kojo made the entire Mkhosi do pushups "to motivate them" to work harder. They continued to do pushups while Baba Kojo recited motivational poems. He would pause after each poem, for a minute or so, to ask one or two boys to explain what they believed portions of the poems meant. Then they would return to the pushups.

There was mild grumbling after the third poem. After the fourth poem, a few boys noticed that Kamau was not doing all the pushups. He was resting. This is when many of the boys began to dislike Kamau. Here they were being punished for his laziness, and he didn't have the decency to take his own punishment. After the sixth poem, the boys of the Mkhosi were livid. Kamau was resting even more. By now, all the boys saw it. The Mwalimu must have seen it, but they said nothing.

Kamau knew how they felt. He could sense it. But he didn't care. He was full of venom. He didn't care one bit about any of these boys or this Akhet. He was begging for an opportunity to pounce on someone.

Baba Kojo recited the seventh poem and began the eighth poem. It seemed he knew *all* poems. He could go on forever. While many of the boys were fed up, after the eighth poem, Deiondre was the one who spoke. "Baba Kojo, may I have permission to speak freely?"

Baba Kojo responded, "Speak, Everly."

Deiondre's voice remained controlled, but his eyes were wild with rage— wilder than usual. "The members of this Mkhosi are giving Njama our best. But he is giving us his worst. We cannot have unity with someone who does not want to unify!" Although he began with a controlled tone, it had grown defiant by the end.

Kamau knew Deiondre was right. But he ignored Deiondre's words. Stepping out of formation, Kamau looked squarely at Deiondre and smirked. And before Baba Kojo could respond, Kamau said, "Don't get your panties in a knot."

Losing his composure, Deiondre bellowed, "Panties?!" as he lunged towards Kamau.

Deiondre's right hand was cocked, ready to explode into Kamau's jaw. As he lunged, Kamau smiled deviously and said to himself, *Oh yes! Come get it.* He waited for Deiondre to get within striking distance. As Deiondre began to swing, Kamau took one step back and pulled his head back to avoid the blow. Deiondre missed. As he missed, Kamau stepped forward and thrust his right hand upward, grabbing Deiondre's throat. Kamau continued his forward movement, stepping just behind Deiondre and kneeling, using his weight to force Deiondre to the ground.

Deiondre gagged. Between Kamau's choking grip on his neck and the hard landing knocking the wind out of him, he struggled to breathe. As he heard Deiondre gag, Kamau felt blows all over his back and head and ribs. Several of the other boys had jumped on him soon after Deiondre attacked. Kamau knew the Mwalimu would break it up soon. So, he ignored those blows as best he could and went to town beating Deiondre at the bottom of that pile.

Within moments, the Mwalimu had gotten the boys off of Kamau. Raymond, Carl, and Alton pulled Kamau off of Deiondre. In under fifteen seconds, he unloaded six days of frustration, and he unloaded it on that smug, wild-eyed boy. *I wonder if he's still 'sore all over'?* Kamau thought gleefully. *I wonder if he still 'likes it'?* Yes, Kamau felt good.

Surprisingly, the Mwalimu did not seem very angry. They ordered everyone back into formation, then promised to provide the entire Mkhosi with instruction in conflict resolution. Kamau took this to mean more pushups interspersed with lectures. Baba Thulani ordered the Mkhosi into a column of two. Baba Kahuthia and Baba Kojo pulled Deiondre and Kamau out of the column, and Baba Thulani led the rest of the Mkhosi to breakfast.

Babas Kahuthia and Kojo asked Kamau and Deiondre if they wanted to say anything to one another. Neither boy said anything. Baba Kahuthia responded, "No one can make you apologize. All that would do is make you a liar. When you are ready to apologize, *if* you are ready to apologize, you simply need to summon your manhood, put your pride aside, and do it."

Baba Kojo added, "We don't mind aggression. As a matter of fact, we like it. God gave us testosterone for a reason. God gave us musculature, strong bones, and agility for a reason. What we do mind is behavior that is destructive to our unity. Do you understand?"

Both boys responded simultaneously, "Yes, sir."

Baba Kojo left with Deiondre. They walked in the direction of the gathering hall. Baba Kahuthia stayed with Kamau. Once they were alone, Baba Kahuthia walked, leading Kamau to a shaded area, and asked, "Kamau, do you feel better now?"

Kamau was startled. The Mwalimu never referred to the boys by their first names. He also didn't know what Baba Kahuthia meant by, "Do you feel better now?" So, he responded, "I don't understand, sir."

Baba Kahuthia clarified, "Son, you are angry. You have a lot of pent-up hostility. You *wanted* to fight. You wanted to release some of the anger you have been working to control these past few days. So, do you feel better? Or do you have more to get out?"

Kamau was stunned. *How did he know? How could he know how I felt?* Kamau thought for a moment, then he responded. "Sir, I do feel better. But I also have more to get out."

Gesturing for Kamau to have a seat on a nearby stone, Baba Kahuthia also sat and said, "Kamau, tell me what has angered you most these past three days."

Before speaking, Kamau took a moment to think. Could he trust Baba Kahuthia? Should he give an honest answer, or might it be used to cause him more punishment later? Kamau had a feeling that this conversation was not part of the typical Akhet. There was no hard physical labor, no yelling, no mental gymnastics, no excessive repetition. He decided to trust Baba Kahuthia. He started slowly stating the thing that angered him most. "Well first, I don't want to be here. I wanted to do two things this summer: work to earn money and train so that I could have a better chance to make the JV basketball team in high school next fall."

Baba Kahuthia nodded and listened patiently, "I see."

Kamau continued, "My parents… probably my father, sent me here without telling me. He completely ignored *my* wishes and what *I* wanted to do. I just… sometimes I just don't like him very much, and everything about this place reminds me of him. He angers me, and everything about this place angers me."

Baba Kahuthia asked, "When you say everything, do you really mean many things?"

Kamau seemed frustrated, "I don't know. The food is terrible, but I can't say it angers me. The things we do…" He stopped himself.

Baba Kahuthia smiled, "You can speak freely, whatever is said under the shade tree will remain under the shade tree."

Kamau continued, "The drills and exercises are stupid… kind of…"

Baba Kahuthia encouraged him, "Talk straight!"

Kamau began to talk straight, "…they're stupid. But they don't anger me. I am not fond of some of the boys. I am not saying I dislike them; I just don't care anything about them. But they don't anger me."

Baba Kahuthia asked, "So is it safe to say that the primary thing that angers you is that you are here?"

Kamau thought for a moment, "Yes, I would say so."

Baba Kahuthia said, "Thank you, Kamau. I have enjoyed our conversation." He then stood to leave.

Kamau asked in surprise, "Is that it? Aren't you going to punish me? Aren't you going to tell me what to do?"

Baba Kahuthia looked at Kamau curiously. "First of all, unless you make amends, your brothers in the Mkhosi are going to give all the punishment you can handle. Second of all, you just said that your father makes you angry and ignores your wishes and what you want. So why would I take it upon myself to make decisions for you? Why would I tell you what to do?"

Frustrated, Kamau asked, "Instead of telling me what to do, would you please tell me what you would do?"

Baba Kahuthia said flatly, "No. I will not. What I would do is irrelevant. I am not in your situation. You are. And you need to learn how to live the life that was given to you. Don't be lazy. Don't try to get someone else to live it for you."

Baba Kahuthia paused and watched Kamau take in these words. Then he asked, "Now, I can help you think through your current dilemma. Would you like that?"

Kamau answered quickly, "Yes, Baba. Please!"

Baba Kahuthia looked at Kamau and asked, "What are your options?"

Kamau's face grew sad, and he asked, "Are you saying I don't have any options?"

Baba Kahuthia remained patient, "Kamau, I am not *saying* anything. I am trying to help you think through your situation. This is not a rhetorical question. Now, what are your options?"

Kamau was dejected, "I don't have any?"

Baba Kahuthia responded curtly, "Everyone always has options. Remember that. Now, can you convince your parents to come get you, to take you home?

"No. They wouldn't do that."

"How about your grandparents?"

"Tsk." Kamau shook his head, "Not likely."

"Okay. So, asking someone to come get you is not a good option." Baba Kahuthia said, "If you left the campground, could you find your way home?"

Kamau, shook his head, "I don't know where we are. I wouldn't know where to go."

Baba Kahuthia said, "Okay. So, running off is not a good option."

Kamau stopped this line of reasoning. "I can't go anywhere. I have nowhere to go. How can I make this Akhet work for me?"

Baba Kahuthia stared at Kamau as though looking deep within him. He then said, "Kamau, you are probably in physical pain right now. Your chest, your back, your ankles, these are all sore. You're hungry. It's getting hot. You have mosquito bites that are irritating you."

Kamau responded excitedly, "Yes! How did you know?"

Baba Kahuthia smiled, "We all know it. We are here with you. We run with you. We drill with you. We do those motivational and instructional pushups with you. But that's not the point. The point is that life gives us pain. That is inevitable. But you are giving yourself something far worse. You are turning your pain into suffering. When you do thousands of pushups, your chest and shoulders and arms will be sore. That is pain. But if you dwell on the pain, wallow in self-pity, think 'woe is me, and hate the source of the pain, then that pain will become suffering. Pain is inevitable. But we don't have to suffer. You don't have to suffer. Let it go. Just, let it go."

Kamau sat in quiet thought for several minutes. Was he really bothered by the pain? It couldn't be. Kamau had planned a fun-filled summer of pain. The training he had planned for himself would be painful. Landscaping forty hours a week or more would be painful. No. He was not afraid of pain. Could he avoid pain if he never endured the physical hardship of PT or sports? No. Exercise is painful, but so is the sickness that comes when you don't exercise. Training is painful, but so is the defeat that comes when you aren't good enough to compete. He smiled knowingly and thought, *Yes, pain is inevitable.*

Baba Kahuthia had been watching Kamau. He broke the silence, "Now you understand." Kamau nodded.

Baba Kahuthia added, "Later today, we are going to teach you how to function with pain."

"Just me?" Kamau asked.

"No, Kamau. You are part of a group. This is a lesson that is taught to the entire group. This is a lesson that would be taught whether *you* were in pain or not, whether you were *suffering* or not, whether you were *here* or not." Kamau felt a tinge of shame for his self-centered thinking.

Baba Kahuthia motioned for them to walk, "Let's rejoin the Mkhosi." As they stood to walk, Kamau took one step, and suddenly, he collapsed.

The Stolen Satchel (O'Leary)

Timothy and Marlene joked with one another as Marlene made suggestions for Timothy's next project team. They both overheard Dan finishing his phone call in the next office. "Yes sweetheart, I understand." Dan tried to be patient.

Meanwhile, Marlene crossed off another potential team member. "He's good when he's sober, which is rare."

Timothy nodded, and just as he was about to speak, they heard Dan snap. "Look, Amelia! It's work and it needs to get done!" Seeing his audience, he lowered his voice, "Now you get yourself together and be a supportive wife, or I will send you *back* to your father! If he's so perfect, let him marry you!"

He slammed the phone into the receiver, took a deep breath, then looked up at Timothy and Marlene, smiling. "All right then. Are you ready, Tim?"

Without commentary on the apparent argument, Tim replied, "Yes, sir."

About a week ago, Dan had invited Timothy to dinner, but he was vague as to the reason. He had simply said he wanted a better understanding of plant biocommunication. Dan often relied on Timothy's expertise, and usually, Timothy was happy to offer it. In preparation for tonight's meeting, Timothy had read a few books on intraspecies plant biocommunication (plants communicating with one another) and interspecies plant biocommunication (plants communicating with other species). He had also prepared a short, five-page summary that reviewed established findings and hypothesized predictions in biocommunications research.

Timothy doubted that Dan would read the summary, but he provided it anyway. As they headed to the lobby, Timothy stopped short, "Oh! I forgot my summary. I'll be right back. Do you mind waiting for me out front?"

"Not at all," Dan responded. "In fact, I'll get my car and wait for you."

"Great." Timothy ran back to his office.

Dan was lost in thought as he walked toward the garage. He couldn't get Amelia out of his head. *She is a stubborn, whiney, bratty woman. And she is making my advancement difficult.* Lost in his thoughts, Dan stepped over a homeless man as he entered the garage. The man wreaked of whiskey and urine. "Spare change for the homeless?" The man held out a cup in Dan's direction.

"Pardon me, sir." Dan muttered as he continued walking. Moments later, Dan heard footsteps behind him and turned to see who it was. It was the homeless man walking towards him. Dan was visibly confused.

The homeless man was Black, tall, and lean. He spoke forcefully and indignantly, "Sir?! Do I look like a sir? Do I smmmellll like a sir?" His hand emerged from under his soiled coat, holding a handgun. He pointed it squarely at Dan, "Break yourself, fool."

Dan was speechless, paralyzed by shock and fear. He had never been robbed before. He had never had a gun pointed at him before. The homeless man reached out and snatched Dan's briefcase. "Thanks to you, I'm gone be a 'sir' today."

Dan stood there, staring at the homeless man. He noticed that the man had scruffy facial hair, but it was all black. He had smooth, young-looking skin. After a brief moment, the homeless man sneered at Dan, "This is where you run. Take your sorry self on home and be glad I ain't kill you." He then kicked Dan in his backside, shoving him towards his car.

Nurse Zuri

Baba Kahuthia rushed to help Kamau to his feet. As Kamau walked, he limped very badly. He could put almost no weight on his left foot. Baba Kahuthia helped him walk and asked, "What's happening? Did you hurt your leg in the scuffle?"

Kamau replied, "I don't know. My foot's been hurting since day one, but not this bad."

Baba Kahuthia said, "We want to be sure it's not broken or fractured. We had better head to the infirmary."

Kamau waited alone in the infirmary. While he waited, he recited the Vanguard Creed in his head. Baba Kahuthia returned, followed by the nurse and Baba Ojore. The nurse was beautiful. In fact, she wasn't just beautiful, she was paralyzingly beautiful. To Kamau's eyes, she was perfect. She was slender with voluptuous hips and a generous endowment of breasts. She was perfectly proportioned. Her neck was perfectly sized to hold her perfectly shaped head, which was topped with flawless locks. As if her mere presence was not enough of a weapon, she smiled. Kamau was struck in catatonic awe.

Baba Kahuthia stifled his laughter and pressed his lips together to contain his smile. "Njama, Mama Zuri is the nurse here at Camp Furaha. She wants to speak to you, Son." Kamau did not respond. He seemed to forget that Baba Kahuthia and Baba Ojore were even there. Baba Kahuthia and Baba Ojore looked at each other and smiled knowingly.

Baba Kahuthia slapped Kamau's arm and said sharply, "Njama!" This seemed to break the trance as Kamau stirred in his seat. He leaned and whispered in Kamau's ear, "Close your mouth, Son. Dignify yourself!"

Kamau straightened, and his eyes became alert. Mama Zuri gestured for Kamau to stand on a platform. Kamau stood and watched as a robotic arm swung about him. There was a low whirring sound, and his body was engulfed in various lights. As Nurse Zuri read a computer screen, Kamau looked on. The screen displayed pages of information about Kamau. It showed his birthdate, blood type, height, blood pressure, oxygen levels, and many more metrics with strange symbols that he didn't know how to read. His head jerked towards Baba Kahuthia, "How can it know this?"

Not waiting for a reply, Mama Zuri spoke to Kamau, "Kamau, please tell me what's going on with your foot." Kamau explained the pain he had been having, when it began, and how it escalated just moments ago.

Helping him down from the platform, Mama Zuri removed Kamau's boots to inspect his feet. When she removed his left sock, it was stained with a large bloody ring. She held his foot by the ankle and inspected it. "It's not broken, but I am certain that you are experiencing great pain." She left and returned with a metal pan. She placed Kamau's feet in the pan and soaked them in a warm solution.

While Kamau's feet soaked, Mama Zuri, Baba Ojore, and Baba Kahuthia moved to the next room to speak. She spoke with the same Cajun accent that Baba Kahuthia had, only hers was not as thick. "It's just blisters. He will be fine. But he does need a larger pair of boots. The boots he has are too small. Boys at this age grow so fast, it is nothing for them to have a growth spurt and wake up to clothes or shoes that are too small. I'll clean his wounds, give him some thicker socks and new boots, give him some moleskin, and teach him how to apply it."

Baba Ojore asked, "Mama Zuri, when will he be ready to resume training activities?"

She smiled, "Well, it would be nice if he could take the remainder of the day to rest from all physical activity. However, I know how committed you men are. If he does continue to train, it won't kill him. In fact, after we apply the moleskin, and give him new shoes and socks, his feet probably won't even hurt."

The three returned to Kamau, and Mama Zuri explained to Kamau that he had blisters. She explained what they would do to treat the blisters and when he could expect them to heal completely. She said that she wanted to see him again in two days to check his progress. This news got him grinning.

Kamau's joy was short lived as Baba Ojore addressed him sharply. "Njama, did I give you permission to bleed in my sock?"

Kamau was shocked that he was being reprimanded for blisters. But he kept his composure, "No, Baba Ojore."

"Do you know that socks cost money, that washing socks takes time, that blood stains are very difficult to get out?" Kamau hesitated. Baba Ojore snapped, "Do you know this?!"

Kamau answered quickly, "Yes, Baba."

Baba Ojore growled, "Hmmmm. Well, as I see it, you owe me for two socks. You only stained one, but we are not peg-legged pirates. We need two. One sock is *useless* being alone." He spat out the word "useless" and continued, "Tomorrow at morning call, you will pay me the price of twenty push-ups for one pair of useless socks." Baba Ojore, then turned and left. Suppressing a smile, Nurse Zuri left behind him.

Kamau decided to continue with the training. His foot was still sore, but with the new boots, socks, and moleskin, it was only a mild irritation. He missed breakfast and joined the Mkhosi as they were reviewing the Vanguard Creed and learning the Vanguard Code of Conduct. That morning, during the Instruction Set, the Ginks learned that the Swahili phrase they memorized was a proverb. The English translation of the proverb was, "Smooth seas do not make skillful sailors."

Throughout the remainder of the day, while doing PT, drills, and other repetitive instruction, the Mwalimu railed about how much Vanguardians loved rough seas, bad weather, broken tools, impossible tasks, lopsided odds, and all other manner of hardship. They each gave dozens of catchy phrases about how Vanguardians overcome no matter how much the odds are against them. They gushed about the joys of becoming stronger amidst hardship. And they talked incessantly about the virtue of courage.

Later in the day, the Mkhosi learned to purify water. They learned the various ways that water might be contaminated with bacteria, viruses, protists, and chemicals. They learned the effect that waterborne contaminants could have on their bodies. They learned four methods for purifying water: boiling, filtering, distilling, and chemical treatment. And they learned the pros and cons of each method. Each boy made a water filter with materials found in the woods. The Mwalimu showed the boys how to test the effectiveness of their filters.

The boys also began VCT (Vanguard Combatives Training). They were given padded suits, helmets, and padded sticks. They formed a circle and, two at a time, members of the Mkhosi took turns fighting each other in the middle of the circle.

Kamau was like a new person. His venom was gone. He accepted that he was not going to leave the Akhet before the end of ten weeks. So, he committed to learning as much as he could, and he strove to be the best Vanguardian at the Akhet. The change in his attitude was noticeable.

After lunch, the Mwalimu had the Mkhosi assembled in Ukumbi wa Kunye. Each boy was given a bowl filled with ice. Baba Kojo began by addressing the Mkhosi. "In life, our enemy will often try to control us in two ways. First, they will try to seduce us with pleasure. Second, they will try to deter us with pain. However, we, who are the tip of the spear... Who are we?"

The Mkhosi responded in an enthusiastic, unified, staccato, "The tip of the spear!"

Baba Kojo continued, "Yes. We, who are the tip of the spear, will not be manipulated or directed by our enemy!"

Baba Chinua shouted "Yebo!" His shout was followed by shouts from several boys in the Mkhosi.

The assembly was highly energetic. It felt more like a Pentecostal revival than instruction. Baba Kojo waited for the cheers to die down. "Today, we will learn to control our response to pain, so that it does not control us. Each of you has a bowl of ice. At your table are pitchers of water. Fill your bowls with water. On my command, you will submerge your left hand into the ice water. Hold it there for as long as you can. When you remove it, use the pages provided at your table to record the length of time you kept your hand submerged and to record your thoughts about the experience. Baba Chinua has placed a timer on the wall. Use this to note your time. Submerge!"

Kamau plunged his hand in the ice water. After ten seconds, his shoulder became numb. Kamau removed his hand after fifteen seconds. When he did this, he rubbed his left hand trying to warm it up.

While the boys wrote, the Mwalimu went round adding ice to the bowls.

Baba Kojo asked several of the boys to describe the experience. Many described Kamau's experience of numbness, some described a burning sensation. They said they removed their hands to stop the pain. "The natural human inclination is to avoid pain, to run from pain. This inclination is so strong that, sometimes, we run from pain even before we experience it. Many of the sensations that we experience as pain, are not really painful." Baba Kojo paused and paced around the room.

Kamau noticed several of the boys seemed to be deep in thought. Kamau, too, took time to consider this idea. Had he ever experienced something as pain that was not really painful?

Baba Kojo continued, "To control our response to pain, we must first control our inclination to run from it. We will not run from our pain. We will study it. We will understand it. We will command it. This time, when you submerge your hands in the water, wait until you feel what you think may be pain, then study the pain. To study the pain, we will ask three questions. First, 'What do you notice in your body right now?' Second, 'How would you describe the sensation?' Third, 'Does everything seem to be working normally?' After you have asked and answered these questions, leave your hand in the ice water for a while. Make sure that when you take it out, you are taking it out because you will it to be so, not because you are running from perceived pain. When you are finished, record your time and your thoughts of the experience. Submerge!"

Kamau tried to study the pain, but he couldn't keep his hand submerged long enough to ask and answer any questions. As boys reported their second times, Baba Kojo noticed a decrease. "Well, it looks like this Mkhosi needs more practice. Submerge!"

Like many of the Vanguard activities, this exercise was repeated for nearly an hour. With each command to submerge, Baba Kojo repeated the same three questions. Unlike the other activities, Kamau was not bothered by it. He could have hated the activity, the monotony, the ridiculousness of it all. But instead, he chose to embrace it as an opportunity. *Think of how much better I could be*, he thought, *in training, in sports, in life, if I had better control of my response to pain.*

Before the day ended, just after the reading of the *Autobiography*, Baba Chinua assembled the Mkhosi around a campfire. He explained to them that, typically, there should be an opportunity for group reflection at the end of each day. This was to be a time that allowed the boys to collectively think about and learn from the activities of the day. It was also intended to allow for the type of socialization that would strengthen the bonds of brotherhood.

During the group reflection, Baba Kojo led the group in a reflection of the proverb, "Bahari laini haifanyi mabaharia stadi." Many of the boys and two of the Mwalimu shared their reflections on the meaning of the proverb and what lessons Vanguardians should take from it.

Kamau also took time to address the Mkhosi. "I want to begin by apologizing to the Mkhosi for my attitude and my behavior. Six days ago, I learned that I was supposed to come here, to the Akhet. I did not want to come, and I acted badly because of it. But there is no excuse for a poor attitude and bad behavior. I am sorry for that. I want to apologize specifically to Alton, Raymond my quarter mate, and the others that I ran with briefly this morning. You extended me friendship and support, and I rejected it. Finally, I apologize to Deiondre for provoking you this morning."

Baba Ojore noticed how mature and polished Kamau's apology was. What he didn't know was that between Kamau's attitude and Jabari Njama's firm hand, Kamau had plenty of practice apologizing. Several of the boys extended Kamau handshakes, fist bumps, and otherwise showed that they accepted his apology. Deiondre did not. Kamau noticed. Bongani, Raymond, the Mwalimu, and several others also noticed. But no one said anything.

Baba Kahuthia introduced the Mkhosi to another ritual, Mduara ya Heshima, which means circle of honor. This ritual was performed at the end of the day. During the ceremony, each member of the Mkhosi was expected to share one thing for which they were grateful. When it was his turn, Kamau indicated that he was grateful for the "rough seas" afforded by the Akhet. He intended to use them to become stronger.

SECRETS OF THE VANGUARD ORDER

VITs (Day Four)

Kamau opened his eyes to blackness. He turned left and saw nothing. He turned right and saw nothing. He stirred and then remembered that he was sleeping in a bag, on the ground, under a tent. Within moments of this realization, the morning horn blared, and Baba Thulani welcomed a new day. For the first time since coming to Camp Furaha, Kamau took the photo of his mother from the back of his composition book. He looked at it lovingly and inserted it and the picture of Imani into the left chest pocket of his BDU.

Kamau crawled out into the cold morning air. When it stung him, he flinched. His flinch made him think about the pain, and he wondered if he could control it. Baba Kojo's voice rang in his head, "What do you notice in your body right now? How would you describe the sensation? Does everything seem to be working normally?" He relaxed his shoulders and studied his reaction to the cold. He realized that the cold was uncomfortable, but not unbearable. He dressed quickly and waited for Raymond. They were the first to report for morning call.

This was Kamau's fourth morning run, but it felt like his first. For the first time since he had arrived at Camp Furaha, he was not filled with hatred. He had given up his fight against the inevitable (he was losing that fight anyway), and he allowed himself to enjoy the challenges of the Akhet. At the start of the run, Kamau leaned forward and spoke to Amari, "Slow the pace a little to keep the line tight. Tell Bongani." He waited until he saw Amari lean forward to speak to Bongani.

Bongani looked over his shoulder. He could not see Kamau, but Kamau saw that he nodded. Kamau then told Raymond to drop back and join the stragglers. Together, Kamau and Raymond allowed the Mkhosi to pass them, and they fell in at the very back of the line, just behind the stragglers. Raymond cast a look of confusion towards Kamau.

Kamau saw this look and was pleased with himself. He then spoke loudly to the stragglers, "Chandler, Alton, Michael, Wayne, and Omowale, good morning, my friends!" He didn't wait for a reply. "Aren't you tired of wearing those nasty pink shirts?!"

The stragglers replied affirmatively and enthusiastically.

Kamau spoke cheerfully, yet with command and force. "Today is our last day of the Pansy Pink!"

Wayne agreed forcefully, "That's right!" Alton and Michael added the bass-laden, "Yeah."

Kamau continued, "Today we run the Three-Mark in under twenty-four!"

Omowale added, "Let's do it. Let's do it!" The pace of the stragglers quickened. Full of pride, Raymond grinned from ear to ear. Baba Chinua observed the entire event and said nothing. He simply kept an eye on the stopwatch.

The run was difficult. Except for Chandler, all the stragglers were large boys, very large boys. Alton and Wayne were better off than the rest. Alton was like a loyal racehorse that would run itself to the death if its rider demanded it. He kept pace out of sheer determination. Wayne was not as pudgy as the rest. He was very muscular, but being young and untrained, he had a layer of baby fat covering up what would one day be a massive frame. He was not accustomed to moving such a large frame, but he had the ability to complete the run and only needed motivation.

Omowale and Michael were another matter. These two boys were truly fat, but they were not as fat as they had been at the start of the Akhet. Although they had made good progress over the past four days, they were still too fat for the run to be easy. They had gotten into the habit of shuffling along slowly. Kamau positioned himself behind Omowale, and he positioned Raymond behind Michael. Whenever either one of these two boys slowed their pace, Kamau and Raymond physically pushed them and gave them encouragement. After the One-Mark, Kamau and Raymond pushed Omowale and Michael at least fifty percent of the time. They ran out of encouraging words and, ultimately, just resorted to "push" or "finish strong."

The stragglers had not kept the line tight with the first group, but they were not too far off. They were much closer than they had ever been. After finishing their run, the boys in the first group ran back to the stragglers to cheer them on. The finish point came into view about twenty-one minutes into the run. They would need to finish in three minutes to reach their goal.

Baba Chinua broke his silence, "Vanguardians! You are lions!" The boys were shocked. They had been called nothing but boys and Ginks since day one. Baba Chinua pointed to the finish. "On the other side of that line stands your enemy. Charge the line and charge the line hard! Show them your strength!" The stragglers were surrounded by the rest of the Mkhosi. Together, the whole group stormed forward, cheering with arms waving in a near sprint to the finish.

Kamau was the last to finish. As he crossed, Baba Chinua announced, "Twenty-three minutes, forty-five." The Mkhosi erupted in cheers.

For the first time at the Akhet, Kamau's mind was clear, and his judgement was not clouded. He had begun to see the structure of the daily Akhet schedule. It was not nearly as random as it initially seemed. Each morning began with the Hwmanda Awakening and the report to morning call. Following that was Mti wa Umoja, then the morning run. After that the Ginks were given personal time, and then breakfast was served. The afternoon included two and one-half hours of instruction just before lunch. After lunch, they had three and one-half hours of instruction, thirty minutes of personal time, then dinner. After dinner, they read, had group reflection, had Mduara ya Heshima, showered, journaled, then slept. The Ginks took turns washing laundry during their personal time.

Today was a good day. After breakfast, the Mkhosi reviewed the Vanguard Creed and the Code of Conduct. They also began learning General Orders. They reviewed their drill commands. Here, the Mkhosi was very good. The Mwalimu gave them obstacles, re-enacted complicating scenarios, and provided all sorts of distractions, but the Mkhosi held strong.

After lunch, they did more Combatives Training. The Mwalimu had them fight again. What was strange about VCT is that the Mwalimu did not provide instruction in how they should fight. They simply shouted encouragements, "Fight hard!" Stand strong!" This was unlike all other instruction at the Akhet. Typically, the Mwalimu were excessive in their instruction: teaching them how to stand, how to stare, how to shower, how to bend over and pick up a stone without "leaving an opening for evil." Why did they not provide instruction during Combatives Training? After VCT, they returned to the Ukumbi wa Kunye to practice pain endurance. The average times began to increase slightly.

Today was also special in another way. After pain endurance practice, and just before their personal time, Baba Kojo assembled the Mkhosi together at the kambi. As the boys waited for instructions from Baba Kojo, Baba Ojore appeared. Without addressing the group, he looked at Baba Kojo and commanded, "Danjuma, disassemble your tent."

Without hesitation, Amari Danjuma responded, "Yes, Baba." He then ran to his tent and removed two carryalls and two rolled bags. He then disassembled the tent and had it stuffed in a sack in under ninety seconds.

Baba Ojore looked at Baba Thulani, "Lofton, you will *not* die of thirst. Construct a filter so that you can have potable water."

Carl Lofton responded, "Yes, Baba." He then ran into the nearby woods.

While Carl was gone, Baba Ojore turned to the Mkhosi and commanded, "Nelson, recite The Creed." He sang the word "creed" just as he had done a few days before.

Jayson Nelson replied, "Yes, Baba." And he began to recite, "*The Vanguard Creed. We are Vanguardians, the tip of the spear…*"

As Jayson spoke, Baba Ojore walked among the ranks, inspecting each boy. There were no wandering eyes. This habit had been corrected during drill after many, many, many pushups. Once Jayson finished, Baba Ojore faced the entire group, "There is a beautiful quote by the great humanitarian, Mahatma Gandhi.

It says, 'I shall conquer untruth by truth. And in resisting untruth, I shall put up with all suffering.' Njama, tell me why this quote is so beautiful."

Kamau paused and took two deep breaths before responding. Then he said, "Baba Ojore, I do not regard the quote as beautiful. We have been taught that…"

Baba Ojore snapped, "I am not interested in what you have been taught!" He then continued in a calmer tone, "I am interested in what you have learned."

Kamau continued, unphased by the verbal chastisement, "There is no nobility, no beauty in suffering. We can live full lives without suffering."

Baba Ojore responded, "Hmmm. Well then Jekwa, perhaps the first part of the quote is beautiful. What of the idea that we can conquer untruth by truth?"

Bongani responded, "Baba Ojore, I do not regard that portion of the quote as beautiful. I believe it is confusing."

Baba Ojore furrowed his brow, "You insolent child. By what logic would you consider such a poetic statement to be confusing?"

Like Kamau, Bongani was unfazed by Baba Ojore's insult. "Baba Ojore, the term 'conquer' has military connotations; it suggests a physical enemy. When applied to a philosophical idea like 'truth,' it turns people away from a real physical enemy and puts their attention on a philosophical enemy. This is confusing, especially for people who are not clear on who their physical enemies are."

Baba Ojore smiled proudly, "You didn't learn that here, Jekwa. But you will."
Bongani replied, "Yes, sir."

Carl returned from the woods covered in dirt and debris and fell into formation. Baba Ojore's smile faded quickly, "Let us inspect Lofton's filter.

Baba Kojo gave several drill commands to move the Mkhosi into the woods. It also gave him a chance to show Baba Ojore how proficient the Mkhosi had become.

Carl's filter was built well. It was large, sturdy, and effective. Baba Ojore tested it with his own sample of contaminated water. Baba Ojore ordered the Mkhosi to the fire ring. Once there, he had each boy take off his Gink shirt and throw it near the ring. As the boys stood there grinning and bare-chested, he announced, "You are no longer Ginks. You are Vanguardians ready for training. Now I can train you!"

The Mwalimu distributed each man six Vanguard Steel shirts. Each shirt had a plain front, and on the back of each shirt was a different quote. Two shirts bore the words, "Self-respect is the foundation of justice." Two shirts read, "I have freed thousands of slaves and could have freed thousands more if only they had known they were slaves." The last two shirts read, "There is no progress without sacrifice."

SECRETS OF THE VANGUARD ORDER

Baba Ojore joined the Mkhosi during group reflection that evening. Wayne Scott asked Baba Abiola if his chest ever burned when running the Three-Mark. Baba Abiola replied flatly, "No. Not when running the Three-Mark. Yours shouldn't either in a few days. Our minds and bodies can adjust to a wide range of circumstances if we let them. And for the most part, they do this without being told. For most of you, your minds and bodies have already adjusted to the Three-Mark. For others of you, it will take a few more days. Pretty soon, the run will feel like a walk in the park."

Amari added, "I studied my pain when running."

Baba Ojore asked, "What did you learn?"

Amari explained, "I wasn't really in pain. My chest was heavy and tight. But it didn't hurt. I didn't feel any pain in my legs. I didn't feel any cramps after the second day. But in my mind, I just got tired of running. I felt like my mind wanted to do something else."

Baba Ojore asked, "How many others studied their pain during the run?" About half of the hands went up. He asked, "How many had the same experience as Danjuma?" Nearly every hand stayed up.

Baba Ojore explained, "Our brains are powerful, and they function in three parts. A portion of our brain, the lizard brain, is designed to ensure that we survive. It makes us run or fight when we are threatened. It makes us forget all reason and seek only food when we are hungry. Another portion of our brain, the limbic brain, is like a sophisticated lizard brain. This portion of our brain drives us to seek pleasure and avoid pain. This portion of the brain controls our memories, our habits, and our… passions." He elongated the word 'passions' and looked several of the VITs squarely in the eye. He continued, "These are the two parts of our brains that are at work when we feel that a task is too hard. It is these lizard and limbic brains that make us want to quit. But we are not lizards." He paused, "We are not lizards, are we?"

The Mkhosi erupted, "No, SIR!"

Baba Ojore smiled and continued, "We are not lizards. We are Vanguardians, and we also have a rational brain called the neo-cortex. The neo-cortex is responsible for reasoning, consciousness, abstract thinking, and kuumba, which means imagination and creativity. This is the portion of our brain that knows how valuable the Akhet is despite the hardship."

Wearing a puzzled look, James Dozier asked, "Baba Ojore, does this mean our lizard brain is bad for us?"

Baba Ojore responded emphatically, "No, sir! Every part of us is necessary and good. It works just the way God intended." He looked at each man as he continued, "What is bad is when we use our brains improperly. For example, it is bad when we let the lizard brain make rational decisions. That is one reason our first virtue is courage. Vanguardians don't make decisions based on fear. Fear is controlled by the lizard brain. Decision making is controlled by the neo-cortex. Uhh… Another example… We don't let our passions control our reasoning. Passions are controlled by the limbic brain. Reasoning is controlled by the neo-cortex."

Baba Chinua added, "In the dead world, you will find that people are mostly controlled by their lizard and limbic brains. They are governed by fear and by vice. They are constantly running from the slightest hint of discomfort or inconvenience, no matter how beneficial. And they are constantly running after any apparent pleasure or delight, no matter how destructive. This is one reason we train so hard. We are training our brains to function properly. This is also why we are going to win."

The Vanguardians in Training sat pensively as they took in what Baba Ojore and Baba Chinua shared. Over time, the reflections shifted to other events of the day, but most revolved around the theme of suffering. During a lull in the discussion, Baba Thulani said, "There is an African proverb, Tembo wanapopigana, ni nyasi zinazoteseka. In English it says, 'When two elephants fight, it is the grass that suffers.' What does this mean?"

Jayson responded first, "It could be talking about two parents as the elephants and their children are the grass. So, when two parents fight the children suffer."

Bongani added, "It could also be referring to two armies as the two elephants and the civilians are the ones that suffer."

To everyone's surprise, Chandler spoke up, "These interpretations are not mutually exclusive."

He sounded like an egghead. Kamau understood why he kept so quiet.

Egghead Chandler continued, "Two elephants represent large powerful forces, whether that be parents, armies, corporations, or governments. The grass represents forces that are weaker by comparison, whether that be children, civilians, employees, customers, or citizens."

A few other boys offered variations on the basic meaning that Chandler provided. Baba Chinua then asked, "For Vanguardians, what should we learn from this proverb?"

A number of suggestions were made about being careful with power and being protective of those that are weaker than us. One poor soul suggested that we shouldn't fight. He was roundly excoriated and nearly kicked out of Camp Furaha that night. Finally, during a quiet pause, Carl Lofton called out, "It seems to me, the moral of the story is, 'don't be the grass'!"

SECRETS OF THE VANGUARD ORDER

Everyone laughed uproariously. Laughing himself, Baba Ojore said, "That's right, Brother Lofton! Don't be the grass. God did not create us to suffer." The Mwalimu and the new Vanguardians in Training smiled and nodded as they contemplated that message. Baba Ojore then addressed the Mkhosi. "Fire is beautiful and life sustaining. It provides us with heat and safety. It allows us to manipulate and control the natural world. It is a companion." He paused and made eye contact with each Vanguardian. "Fire also purifies. Tonight, let it purify Mkhosi Kunye. There are no Ginks here!"

One at a time, and in complete silence, each Vanguardian took his Gink shirts and added them to the fire. Once all the Gink shirts were burned, the Mkohsi gathered for Mduara ya Heshima. They were grateful for many things: for their accomplishments of the day; for the encouragement they received from one another; for their transition from Ginks to Vanguardians in Training; for Baba Ojore, their new teacher; and for their brotherhood. In those moments of peaceful, reflective gratitude, no one would have guessed that in less than twenty-four hours their brotherhood and their strength would be put to the test.

CHAPTER THREE

The Losses of Kikuyu Squad

The First Cadence (Day Five)

Kamau didn't know it, but Friday of the first week would be a harrowing day. At Mti wa Umoja, the Vanguardians of Mkhosi Kunye were in high spirits. They had met the daunting challenge of running the Three-Mark in a respectable time. They passed Baba Ojore's inspection and earned the status of Vanguardians in Training. And they bonded with one another.

Later that day, the Mwalimu organized the Vanguardians into five squads of four. Each squad was assigned one responsible Mwalimu. The first was *Kikuyu Squad*. It was comprised of Kamau Njama, Raymond Hewitt, Chandler Gardner, and Alton Bailey. Baba Kahuthia took responsibility for Kikuyu Squad. The second was *Zulu Squad*. It was comprised of Bongani Jekwa, Wild-Eyed Deiondre Everly, Wayne Scott, and Keith Duhart. Baba Thulani took responsibility for Zulu Squad. The third was *Yoruba Squad*. It was comprised of Amari Danjuma, Carl Lofton, Kamal Ofori, and Basheeru Chiriga. Baba Kojo took responsibility for Yoruba Squad. The fourth was *Fulani Squad*. It was comprised of Charles "Little Bird" Hall, Albert Dorsey, James Dozier, and Jayson Nelson. Baba Abiola took responsibility for Fulani Squad. The fifth was *Mongo Squad*. It was comprised of Gerard Winford, Danny Echols, Michael Hedrick, and Omowale Ndukwe. Baba Chinua took responsibility for Mongo Squad.

Kamau became the leader of Kikuyu Squad. It was not that squads were assigned leaders. It was just that the others instinctively deferred to him. Their deference didn't mean much to Kamau. He was disappointed with this squad. *We would get trounced in a scuffle,* he thought. *In fact, we wouldn't fare well in a game of basketball or even ping pong.* As Kamau saw it, Alton and Chandler were incapable of doing anything physical. In fact, it was a miracle that Chandler's neck could support his head. And while Raymond was physically capable, his psychology was not suited to conflict and competition. He was too nice.

Well, whatever, he thought. *Just make sure that Kamau shines!* He had had the same dilemma on the basketball team last year. He was stuck with a big man, who was lucky if he could catch a pass, and a cast of mediocre players. Yet somehow, he made it work for himself.

Bausi Ojore led the morning run. He and the Mwalimu slowed the pace. This allowed the stragglers to no longer be stragglers. For the first time, the Mkhosi ran as one unit. What's more, they kept the line straight (no goose lines), and they kept the line tight. They looked good. During the run, Baba Ojore introduced the Mkhosi to cadences. He explained that the cadence had two purposes. First, it was intended to help the unit run uniformly. Second, it was intended to boost the morale of the unit. The person calling a cadence said a line and the rest of the Mkhosi responded by repeating that line.

After making his explanation, Baba Ojore called the cadence:

Mama, Mama can't you see
Mama, Mama can't you see
What the Vanguard done for me?
What the Vanguard done for me?
Mama, Mama can't you see
Mama, Mama can't you see
What the Vanguard done for me?
What the Vanguard done for me?

The Mkhosi finished the morning run in record time, and Kamau felt good. His foot was healing. He did not get cramps. His wind was good. Even the aches he felt earlier in his back and legs were gone. Most of all, however, he felt strong. He did not feel it in his body; he felt it in his mind. Kamau had been an athletic boy. He had always felt able to run as fast or jump as high as anyone, but this was different. Now he felt invincible. He felt like an invincible man led by six of the most invincible men he had ever known. And he was surrounded by nineteen other invincible men. Well, maybe eighteen others. He wasn't so confident in skinny Chandler. Well, on second thought maybe it was seventeen others. Wild-Eyed Deiondre was still a bit miffed by that beating he caught from Kamau. At any rate, those were details that didn't matter much. What did matter was that Kamau felt good.

Combatives Training

After breakfast, Baba Ojore took the Mkhosi to a large circular building. It was peculiar. It was shaped like a primitive hut, but it was much larger than a hut. It was made of stone, and it had a domed roof. There was an engraved stone just over the door with the words "Ukumbi wa Mapambano" etched in large type. In smaller type beneath these words was the word "Terrordome" enclosed in quotation marks.

As they stood outside of the hut, Baba Ojore began, "Men, this is the Ukumbi wa Mapambano of Mkhosi Kunye. We call it the Terrordome. Move inside and await my instruction."

As he moved inside, Kamau was struck by the enormity of the hut. It was a combination of an exercise gym, a dojo, and a boxing facility, and it was the largest he had ever seen. Although everything seemed to be under one roof in one big open-air room, it was organized by theme. There was a section that contained a large, elevated boxing ring. Positioned around that ring were speed bags, double ended bags, hanging heavy bags, and several other types of punching bags. There were also cleared sections of the floor that were marked off for individual training. There were mirrors and every imaginable type of boxing equipment. There were ropes, gloves, tape, handheld striking bags, striking mitts, helmets, and several other items that Kamau had never seen.

Another section looked like a karate dojo. This section had a large wooden floor partially surrounded by walls. The walls were decorated with motivational wall hangings and weapons. There were long staffs, short staffs, nunchacku, various types of swords, and many other weapons. There was one wall with mirrors, sitting just behind bins full of more striking pads. A third section was centered around a large pit. This pit was filled with sawdust. Around the pit was a wall lined with long padded sticks, padded vests, crotch pads, and helmets. These were just like the padded suits the VITs had worn in Combatives Training, over the past few days. At the far end of the hall was a section that contained weightlifting equipment. There were nautilus-style machines as well as various benches and racks. There were dumbbells, barbells, kettlebells, and more plates than the boys of the Mkhosi would ever be expected to lift. There were medicine balls, heavy ropes, and chains. It was endless.

Kamau continued to look around the room. He looked at Bausi Ojore and the Mwalimu. The faces of the Mwalimu were serious, almost reverent. These men weren't interested in good looks. These weren't puffed up gym rats out to score style points. These men were dedicated to honing themselves into weapons of war. This was their forge.

SECRETS OF THE VANGUARD ORDER

Baba Ojore's voice broke Kamau's reflection, "To the pit." He walked the Mkhosi to the area with the sawdust pit and the padded suits and sticks. Baba Ojore explained that the sticks were called pugil sticks, that the suits were for protection, and that the exercise was used in the military to imitate combat with a rifle and bayonet. He also explained that, for VITs, pugil training was designed to condition the men to exert and to withstand aggression while, at the same time, keeping their wits.

After that explanation, each VIT and each Mwalimu was given a padded suit and an unpadded stick. These sticks were weighted. They were much heavier than the padded sticks. The VITs were then organized into formation and spread out. They were instructed to place the stick behind their heads and over the tops of their shoulders. Baba Ojore then commanded, "Take a seat in the Vanguard Chair."

Confused, the VITs stood at attention until Baba Abiola demonstrated. With his feet shoulder width apart and the stick across his back, he squatted until his thighs were parallel with the floor. The VITs followed suit. Everyone sat in the Vanguard Chair except for Baba Ojore and Baba Kojo. As they sat, Baba Kojo spoke, "We are hard! Because we are hard, some do not like us. But we are not here to be liked. We are here to lead our people. Because we are hard, we will provide for our people. Because we are hard, we will protect our people."

Kamau's legs began to tremor just as Baba Ojore commanded, "VITs, stand up." He then looked at Baba Kojo, "Baba Kojo, was there anything more that you wanted to say?"

Baba Kojo responded, "Yes, Baba Ojore."

Baba Ojore commanded, "VITs, take a seat."

Again, the Mkhosi sat, and Baba Kojo continued, "We are men that other men fear in battle. We are men that other men respect." Baba Kojo continued speaking slowly and deliberately. "We are men that women love." There were a few giggles from the VITs. "We are men that women pursue. We are men to whom women run for security."

Kamau's legs burned, and he found it difficult to keep his back straight. He began to study his pain.

At just that moment, Baba Ojore commanded, "Mkhosi Kunye, rise up." He then looked at Baba Kojo, "Baba Kojo, are we ready to move on?"

Baba Kojo responded, "Not yet, Baba."

Baba Ojore shrugged, "Okay, Mkhosi Kunye, take a seat."

Kamau struggled to get into his squat position. He leaned forward, and his knees were bent only slightly. Baba Kojo began calling out the names of VITs whose form was sloppy. Kamau deepened his squat.

Baba Kojo continued, "We are men that children admire. We are men that children emulate." Kamau no longer heard Baba Kojo. It was all he could do to keep from collapsing. Baba Kojo continued, "We are men in whom children find security. Because we are hard, our people have life! We are Vanguardians." He then shouted, "Umoja!"

Baba Ojore commanded, "Mkhosi Kunye, say it together."

At that command, the entire Mkhosi shouted, "Umoja!"

Baba Ojore commanded, "Stand strong, Mkhosi Kunye."

Kamau wanted to collapse, but he knew better. He stood and allowed the burning in his legs to slowly subside.

Baba Ojore commanded, "Circle the pit! Quickly!"

Baba Chinua commanded, "Kikuyu Squad to the center." Alton, Chandler, Raymond, and Kamau all jumped into the sawdust pit. There were four pugil sticks there. Each man picked up a stick. Baba Chinua ordered, "On my command, you will fight. When a man falls, leave the pit and watch the remainder of the battle from the Vanguard Chair. You will continue until the last man is standing. Fight!"

When the command was given, Kamau found that Chandler was standing just to his right. *Last man standing?* he thought. *That should be easy with this group.* He struck Chandler forcefully in the head. Chandler flopped into the pit. In fact, he fell so quickly, it seemed that the blow was simply an excuse to quit.

Kamau watched Raymond and Alton wail at each other. He noticed that Alton used his pugil stick to push Raymond more than he struck him. This worked to Alton's advantage. His weight and strength forced Raymond to the edge of the pit. Kamau moved quickly towards the pair and began swinging away at Raymond. Between Kamau's head strikes and the shoving from Alton, Raymond couldn't keep his footing, and he fell.

Kamau turned carelessly away from Raymond and squared off with Alton. He began to strike forcefully. After being hit three times in rapid succession, Alton resorted to his pushing strategy and lunged towards Kamau. Kamau stepped back to give himself room for another barrage of strikes, but he did not realize that Raymond hadn't cleared the pit. He tripped over Raymond.

Seeing Kamau fall, Alton thrust his hands over his head in celebration, and the Mkhosi erupted in cheers. Suddenly, Alton's left leg gave way, and he was struck in the chest. The blow caused him to gasp. The next thing he knew, he was on the floor staring up at the ceiling of the Ukumbi wa Mapambano. Baba Kahuthia stood over him.

Baba Ojore commanded, "Bailey, what is your fourth general order?"

Alton looked around confused as to what had just happened.

SECRETS OF THE VANGUARD ORDER

Not receiving a quick response, Baba Ojore replied forcefully, "Chaki!" The VITs came to learn that "chaki" was a strong reproof. It was usually barked or growled and showed extreme disapproval. Baba Ojore continued, "Bailey, what are the four steps for disassembling a tent?" As he asked this question, Baba Kahuthia struck Alton with the pugil stick.

Alton gazed at Baba Kahuthia in disbelief. It was clear that he had no idea why he was being struck.

"Chaki!" Baba Ojore continued, "Bailey, recite The Vanguard Creed!"

Alton began clambering to his feet. But he was slow, and he did not recite The Creed. Predictably, Baba Ojore chastised him, "Chaki!" Baba Kahuthia struck him again, causing him to wobble awkwardly.

Baba Ojore turned to the Mkhosi, "Our greatest weapons are those that our enemy will never see. One of those weapons is our mind. To succeed in battle and in life, we must, at all times, keep our wits. Gardner lost because he was not prepared for attack. In fact, he was not prepared to fight. Hewitt lost because he panicked when he felt overwhelmed by the odds. Njama lost because he was not aware of his surroundings. And although it looked like Bailey won, Bailey also lost. His first defeat came when he was distracted by his apparent success. He was celebrating in the midst of combat. His successive defeats came when he was incredulous at the idea that someone was actually attacking him."

A number of the VITs nodded in understanding, Alton included. Baba Ojore continued, "Now, let's try again. Keep your mind in the fight."

For the remainder of VCT, the Mkhosi conducted intense exercises. They did the Warriors Edge, the Dying Cockroach, which Baba Kojo called "Dying Yurugu," whatever that meant, the Iron Cross, and Vanguard Bridges. During each exercise, the Mwalimu took turns telling them how great they were, how much they loved training, how invincible they were, and a host of other fictions that they really wanted to be true. Following the fiction-laden exercise, the newly formed squads took turns in the pit. After all squads had fought to the last man, the VITs were thoroughly exhausted.

Just before lunch, Baba Ojore assembled the Mkhosi outside of Ukumbi wa Kunye for an announcement. "Mkhosi Kunye, today is Friday, and we are near the end of the first week of the Akhet. We will have slightly modified schedules this weekend. Saturday and Sunday, we will have intersquad competitions. Saturday evening, we will enjoy a movie, and Sunday morning we will have chapel. We will continue with our Vanguard Games as normal.

When Baba Ojore dismissed them, Kamau asked Raymond, "What are Vanguard Games?" He imagined that he may have missed something when he was visiting with the nurse.

Raymond shrugged, "I have no idea. We didn't play any games at all this week."

Trouble at the Kambi

Later that day, just before dinner, Michael Hedrick and Jayson Nelson were sent back to the kambi to retrieve a notebook for Baba Kojo. He needed it for the evening instruction. When Hedrick and Nelson returned to Ukumbi wa Kunye, they were visibly shaken. Kamau saw Hedrick giving a report to Baba Ojore. As he listened to the report, Baba Ojore was composed.

Raymond, who also witnessed the report, was more alarmed. He leaned over to Kamau and whispered, "Something is wrong."

Kamau asked, "How do you know?"

Raymond explained, "I can tell from Baba Ojore's eyes."

Kamau looked at Baba Ojore. He could tell nothing. To Kamau, it seemed that Baba Ojore was processing what was being said. He asked Hedrick a few questions. When they were answered, he nodded and leaned over to whisper to Baba Kojo.

Raymond was right, however. Baba Kojo stood and abruptly announced that dinner had come to an end. Kamau was disappointed. He was just getting started on this meal. Although the food at Camp Furaha was mediocre, he was growing accustomed to it. And seeing that it was the only food he had, and he still had a tremendous appetite, Kamau found that he didn't hate it so much. In fact, for the past two days, he wasn't eating as much as he was devouring his food.

Baba Kojo ordered the Mkhosi out of Ukumbi wa Kunye. Once outside, Baba Ojore informed the Mkhosi that their kambi had been ransacked and pillaged.

In his shock, Kamau forgot about his lost meal. Baba Kojo commanded the Vanguardians in Training to form a column of two and double time it back to the kambi. When they arrived, the site was in total chaos. Tents were collapsed, some with poles and stakes missing. There was no order to the site. Provisions were missing from several of the carryalls. What wasn't missing was strewn about haphazardly. There was so much chaos that it was impossible to determine what belonged to who.

As he sifted through the wreckage, Kamau grew incensed, and he thought, *This couldn't have been wild, feral hogs. Hogs don't ransack.* His incense grew into rage, *This probably wasn't even thieves. Whoever did this wants to strike out at us. They want to hurt us.* Kamau heard grumblings from others at the site. He was not alone in his rage or in his speculation.

Baba Ojore called the Mkhosi together. "Mkhosi Kunye, it appears that there is an invader in Camp Furaha. Once upon a time... a long, long time ago... our people lived in a world where there was no theft. There were no locked doors, safes, and padlocks. There was no need for such measures because no one lurked about looking to steal the little trinkets and cheap trash that are so craved and coveted at sunrise only to be discarded by sunset. But alas, that time is gone, at least for now. We are Vanguardians. We do not steal. We do not steal because we know that life's greatest treasures cannot be stolen. They can only be earned by hard work, discipline, and commitment. We do not steal because we know that theft brings Isfet into our ranks. We do not steal because we know that Vanguardians will beat the brakes off a thief."

At this last suggestion, Bongani and members of Zulu squad responded with a strong affirmation of "Yebo!"

Baba Ojore continued without pause, "But although Vanguardians are not thieves, although Camp Furaha is an oasis of peace, love, and harmony, it exists in the muck and mire of mayhem." He paused. "Help me out, Baba Thulani."

Baba Thulani quickly added, "We are in the midst of macabre, malevolence, and malcontent, morbid, and malicious misanthropy. We are surrounded by miserable, murderous miscreants and their musty, mushy-minded, moronic minions."

Baba Ojore nodded to Baba Thulani, "Asante Sana, Baba." He continued, "It is our job to maintain the sanctity of our oasis. Beginning tonight, we will have Vanguardians stand post. We will have twelve rotations of forty minutes each. We will post two Vanguardians per rotation. Our sixth and seventh rotation will each have three men. Baba Abiola will take the first rotation. I will take the sixth rotation. Baba Kojo will take the seventh rotation. Baba Thulani will take the twelfth rotation. Baba Kahuthia, you and Baba Chinua work out the rest of the post schedule."

"Yes, sir!" Baba Kahuthia replied coolly.

Baba Ojore continued, "If any Vanguardian on post notices an invader, sound the alert of Guard Defend. Announce the alert twice. Give as many details as possible while interjecting the alert. Describe the size of the invading force, descriptions of the invaders, locations, genders, weapons, strengths, and weaknesses. Provide as much information as you can. Vanguardians, as you hear the alert, you join the Vanguardian on post immediately. Your charge is to defend yourself. Defend the kambi. You will defend Camp Furaha until the invaders can no longer do harm to anyone. You will not kill them! But you will beat them until they are close enough to death to smell their miserable graves." He snapped, "Do you understand me?!"

The Mkhosi responded with an enthusiastic chorus, "Yes, Baba!"

Daniel's Dilemma (O'Leary)

When Dan pulled his car up, Timothy could tell that something was wrong. "Are you alright, Dan? What's going on, buddy?"

Dan stared blankly. "No, I am not alright. But let's go to dinner. We've got to fix this."

Timothy had no idea what they had to fix, but he was concerned for Dan. As he pulled out of the parking lot, he nearly hit a pedestrian. Then, less than a minute later, he nearly ran through a red light into oncoming traffic. After the red light, Timothy got out of the car. "Dan, let me drive while you get yourself together."

Dan hollered out of the window, "No it's okay. I'm good now."

The light turned green, and Timothy stood there in traffic, looking at Dan defiantly. He yelled back over the traffic noise, "You either get in that passenger seat and hand me the keys or meet me at the restaurant. I like breathing." Horns blared at the two as Dan relented. He slid across the seat as Timothy got in behind the wheel.

Timothy buckled up and patted Dan's shoulder. "Don't worry, big guy. Whatever it is, we'll handle it."

Dan gazed off into nothingness throughout most of their time at the restaurant. He wasn't able to talk until after they had ordered their meals. When the waiter left, Dan looked at Timothy and said simply, "Someone stole my briefcase."

Timothy recoiled in horror, "That's terrible. Was your wallet in it? Your phone? Do you need to make some calls to cancel credit cards?"

Dan replied flatly, "No wallet. No phone."

Timothy was first confused, then worried, "So what was in it?"

"The plans for the big project I've been working on."

Timothy's eyes widened, "The complete project portfolio?! Oh, my goodness!" Timothy tried to calm himself down. He thought out loud, "What are we going to do?"

Dan continued, "This project has the potential to make TechInnoGen the biggest, wealthiest company in the world!" He continued, growing angrier as he spoke, "Forget executive vice president. I will *run the company.*"

Timothy listened quietly. Dan continued to fume "But all that, *all of it*, will be lost because of a homeless ni…" he caught himself, and tempered his tone. "It may all be lost."

Timothy took no offense at Dan's outburst. "Are you saying that your briefcase contained no phone and no money."

"Yes."

Timothy continued, "All you had in there was a complete project portfolio?"

"Yes."

Timothy's face was twisted, "And it was stolen by a homeless man?"

Timothy seemed dismissive, and Dan didn't understand why. He shrugged, "Yeah. That's what I am saying."

Timothy *was* dismissive, "Man, the homeless man can't use a project portfolio. He can't eat it, drink it, or smoke it. He probably can't even read it. The man was looking for money."

Dan showed a hint of surprised relief, "So do you think I should tell Erick?"

Erick was the CEO of TechInnoGen. Timothy responded quickly, "Sure, you tell Erick… if you want to lose your job." Dan grunted.

Timothy continued, "I wouldn't tell Erick anything. That briefcase and that portfolio are probably somewhere in a dumpster right now. And that homeless man is cursing you out for not having money in it."

Dan was still uneasy. "How am I going to move this project forward? What if the plans get out somehow?"

Timothy could see that Dan would not rest easy. So, he relented, "Dan, I can help to find your briefcase and, hopefully, the plans."

Dan brightened up. "You can? But how? You're not a…" He looked uneasy.

"I am not a what?" Timothy asked with a confused non-accusatory expression.

Timothy's innocent demeanor emboldened Dan, and he continued, "You're not a Black, Black. You know… you're not a thug. You don't have street cred."

Timothy paused before responding. Again, he did not take offense, "No, I am not. But I know people who could help. So, you move forward with the presentation and the project. I will work to get the briefcase back."

Dan grinned broadly, "Timmy, my boy, I knew we could figure it!"

Timothy then asked, "Dan, just to be sure, have there been any setbacks or strange happenings around this project?"

Dan replied coolly, "No. None at all."

Timothy was disappointed by Dan's response. Not long ago there was a fire at the R&D facility that housed an early version of the SEV Fitzroy. There were rumors that a number of key components were never recovered. Some believed these items were consumed in the fire. Others argue that the fire was a cover, and the parts were stolen. Timothy gathered these details from other sources. He was disappointed that Dan did not trust him enough to be forthcoming.

For the remainder of that meal, Timothy briefed Dan on key research developments in biocommunication. Dan still refused to give him any details on the project. So, Timothy asked pointed questions and provided relevant insight as best he could.

Chandler's Hack

Kamau's spirit was low. He did not have the energy and enthusiasm that he had had at the start of the day. Despite this, he went to work with the rest of the Mkhosi. They pitched their tents, secured provisions, folded clothes, organized their carryalls, and brushed debris from their sleeping bags. For the remainder of dinner, they worked to bring order to the chaos, and in a short time, they had succeeded.

Once order was restored, Baba Ojore reassembled the group. "We will not be deterred. Resume with the evening schedule."

That evening, as they read the *Autobiography of Malcolm X*. Baba Chinua and Baba Thulani asked the Mkhosi questions related to the book. The Mkhosi answered questions eagerly and even posed questions of their own. Kamau's participation was marginal.

During Group Reflection, Baba Ojore revisited the proverb presented earlier in the week, "Smooth seas do not make skillful sailors. Who knows what is meant by this proverb?" Several members of the Mkhosi talked about the importance of obstacles and difficult challenges in our growth. Others gave examples of the challenges faced during the Akhet. Some pointed to growth they had experienced in the past week. Baba Ojore concluded by discussing the implications for Vanguardians. He encouraged the Vanguardians to embrace hardship, to seek it out. He emphasized that hardship was not a source of failure but a source of growth.

Just before Group Reflection ended, Keith Duhart asked, "What are Vanguard Games? We haven't played any games."

Baba Kahuthia smiled, "Well of course you did, Duhart. We've played Vanguard games all week."

The Mkhosi protested. They had run. They had done PT. They had drilled. But they hadn't played any games.

Baba Thulani interjected, *"Put 'em Up, Take 'em Down* is a Vanguard Game. *Last Man Standing* is a Vanguard Game. We've played plenty of games!" The Mkhosi was visibly deflated. They were expecting something fun, and if those were games, they certainly were not fun.

Before the Mkhosi went to sleep that evening, Baba Kahuthia also gave each man his post assignment and instructions for keeping track of time and for notifying the next team on post. Kamau and Raymond would be on the ninth rotation together.

SECRETS OF THE VANGUARD ORDER

The following morning, Kamau could not keep his mind focused during Mti wa Umoja. He was still sleepy, in part from standing post for forty minutes and also from having his sleep disrupted after waking up at three o'clock in the morning. In the fog of his fatigue, Kamau failed to notice how perfect the Mkhosi ran that morning. No one struggled to complete the run. Not only did the stragglers finish with the group, but they finished strong. No one wanted to fall out at the end of the run. No one ran for water. It was just as Baba Abiola had promised. This run felt like a walk in the park.

The Mkhosi was permitted to speak during breakfast. This was the first meal since the start of the Akhet that they were permitted to speak. During breakfast, Kamau learned that no one saw or heard anything of interest during the night. The Mwalimu spent time teaching some of the VITs how to patrol the kambi. Chandler and Alton were on post with Baba Kojo, who taught them. They, in turn, shared what they had learned with Kamau and Raymond.

Raymond commented, "Wow! We were lucky that nothing happened on our watch. There was a lot we did wrong."

Kamau changed the subject, "Alton and Chandler, I have a question for you."

Raymond flashed a glance of agreement at Kamau, as though he knew what Kamau was thinking.

Kamau continued, "Are you two tired? Did you get enough sleep?"

Alton replied casually while gobbling up another serving of home fries, "No, we didn't get enough sleep. But we're not tired. Chandler has a hack for limited sleep."

Raymond and Kamau simultaneously looked over at Chandler. Seeing their gaze, he pushed his glasses up his nose and said curtly, "It's not a hack." He looked back down at his plate, and breaking off a small piece of his muffin, he murmured, "It's science."

What is the deal with this mealy-mouthed egghead, Kamau thought. Then he asked, "Chandler, what is the science? Can you explain it to us?"

Chandler focused even more intently on his muffin, "If you are not able to get a full night's sleep, you can feel well-rested by sleeping in ninety-minute increments."

Raymond began speaking, but Kamau interrupted him, "Why ninety-minute increments?"

Still avoiding eye contact, Chandler responded, "The natural sleep cycle, a complete sleep cycle, is ninety minutes. When we wake up in the middle of a sleep cycle, we feel less rested than if we wake up between cycles."

Kamau was processing what Chandler had shared. Raymond asked, "So is it better to have less sleep with complete sleep cycles than to have more sleep when the cycle is interrupted?"

As Chandler responded, Kamau noticed that now he was picking at his eggs. "It's not that simple. The sleep cycle adjustment works with small differences in sleep time, like thirty minutes or maybe an hour. But it doesn't work with large differences. Also, it doesn't work indefinitely. I've done experiments on myself, and I found that after a few weeks it doesn't work anymore. My guess is that there are limits on how well it works, because you can't eliminate the need for sleep."

Kamau watched Alton go back for another plate. He thought, *Maybe he's making up for that dinner that got cut short last night.* He asked Chandler, "So you've done experiments on this?"

Chandler replied flatly, "Yes."

A light bulb went off in Kamau's head, *That dude is smart!*

Vanguard Application Sets

After breakfast, the Mkhosi had their first Application Set. During Application Sets the VITs were given tasks that required them to apply the principles they had learned during the Instruction Sets. The first Application Set was called *Prepare for Battle.*

During this exercise, one VIT was given the task of moving the entire Mkhosi from the kambi to a second location where they were to line up in preparation for a mock battle. The VIT in charge had to move the Mkhosi, using only drill commands. Bausi Ojore complicated the task by locating the battle site on the other side of rough terrain such as woods, water, or tall meadow. The Mwalimu further challenged the VITs by creating distractions such as loud noises and "live grenades," which were actually water balloons lobbed into the ranks of the Mkhosi.

Each VIT had an opportunity to lead the Mkhosi. After each round, the Mkhosi and the Mwalimu debriefed. The debrief helped the leading VIT and others in the Mkhosi get an idea of how to improve drill practice. Each VIT was also scored on his performance in leading the Mkhosi. Kamau was one of four VITs to earn a perfect score. The other three were Bongani, Kamal Ofori, and Omowale Ndukwe. Omowale was surprisingly charismatic. The Mkhosi liked him and would follow him anywhere.

Alton scored poorly because he did not have mastery of the commands. He knew them well enough to follow them, but he had not thought about them much beyond following them. He also had trouble reversing direction.

While Raymond knew the commands much better than Alton, and certainly had no trouble with direction, he was too friendly and not commanding. His commands sounded like requests, and the Mkhosi was sluggish to respond.

SECRETS OF THE VANGUARD ORDER

Chandler, poor Chandler. Chandler's "command," if it could be called that, was a disaster. He made no eye contact, and he mumbled the entire time. The Mkhosi spent more time asking him to repeat commands than they spent actually executing his commands.

It was a sad, sad performance. VIT scores were tallied by squad, and Kikuyu Squad had the lowest score of all. They had even finished behind Fulani Squad, which was Charles Hall's squad. *How embarrassing*, Kamau thought.

A second Application Set was an obstacle. The obstacle was a relay in which each squad provided two, two-man teams. The first team would (a) complete a distance run that ended in a wooded area, (b) assemble a filter, filter tainted water, and drink the product (c) navigate an expansive creek, (d) defeat an enemy by striking him fifty times with the pugil stick (twenty-five hits for each man), and (e) take the defeated man's tent back to the starting point and assemble it. After the first team completed tent assembly, the second team would repeat the process.

When the exercise was completed, Raymond and Kamau had the second fastest time overall, beaten only by Bongani and Deiondre, the second fastest tent assembly time, beaten only by Alton and Chandler, and the fastest filter building time. This was offset by incredibly slow times from the rest of Kikuyu Squad. Alton and Chandler were slowest on the run, slowest in navigating the creek, and slowest in defeating the enemy. Kamau wanted to staple Chandler's glasses to his forehead. He had never seen anyone stop fighting to adjust his glasses. *That is such a stupid, stupid boy!* he thought. Again, Kikuyu Squad came in last.

Invaders

That day, Kikuyu Squad lost at everything. They were last among the five squads of Mkhosi Kunye, and it wasn't even close. Surprisingly, however, Kamau stood out as one of the strongest VITs. He had already garnered respect from the others when he beat up on Wild-Eyed Deiondre, and then again when he swallowed his pride to apologize to the Mkhosi. Now, the Mkhosi was beginning to see Kamau's quick wit, strength, and athleticism on full display. It was just too bad that it was wasted on Kikuyu Squad.

Later that evening, after reading the *Autobiography of Malcolm X*, the Mkhosi assembled in Ukumbi wa Kunye for movie night. They watched the first episode of *Roots*. Very few of the VITs had seen *Roots*. It was an old movie. It didn't have dazzling special effects or actors that they knew. Left to their own devices, none of them would have ever watched it. But after six days of standing, walking, running, constant physical exertion, and sleeping on the ground, they would have done anything for the chance to sit in chairs for two hours. After six days without computers, tablets, cell phones, or television, they would have watched G-rated Disney cartoons and enjoyed it. To sweeten the event, the Mwalimu provided popcorn, iced tea, and lemonade.

The idea of a film lifted Kamau's mood. He led the Mkhosi in a spirited celebration. Throughout the film, they cheered for the good guys. They boo'd and hissed at the bad guys. They laughed uproariously, and they gave warning and instructions to the actors. Ukumbi wa Kunye was full of energy.

At the end of the episode, Baba Ojore invited Baba Kojo to reflect on the film with the Mkhosi. Baba Kojo drew the boys' attention to the historical realities of slavery: how African people had whole intact families, customs, and institutions; how boys were taught to be men; and how white and Arab slave monsters destroyed these African societies. He also drew parallels between the historical incidents of slavery as seen in the film and the realities seen in Black communities today. Despite the heaviness of the film, Kamau felt good. The film helped him to forget about all the losses he had suffered that day and to feel the joys of brotherhood again.

Sunday morning, just before the Hwmanda Awakening, Kamau began to stir. His body knew it was time to get up. Saturday night, he had tried Chandler's hack for getting better rest, and it really worked. He felt normal, like he had gotten a normal night's sleep.

As he stirred, he was startled to full awareness by the alert, "Vanguard Defend! Vanguard Defend!" The cry woke up the entire Mkhosi. Raymond, too, popped up, and Kamau and Raymond both scrambled to get dressed. "Vanguard Defend! There's a sea of pink shirts, there're Ginks everywhere! Vanguard Defend!"

CHAPTER FOUR

Kikuyu Squad Takes a Stand

New Friends

The voice of the Vanguardian on post was trailing, "He must be following them," Kamau told Raymond. Kamau didn't want to miss the action. He scrambled out of the tent, leaving one boot behind. Looking around, Kamau saw the Vanguardian on post, and ran in his direction. As he approached, he saw the Ginks. They looked startled and afraid. Kamau didn't see what was behind him. He was leading the charge of a group of fire-breathing Vanguardians.

As he drew near, Kamau heard Baba Ojore's command pierce the morning air, "Guard, Attention!"

Kamau stopped instantly and stood at attention. The Ginks he was chasing also stood at attention. *Are they with us?* he wondered.

Baba Ojore appeared and stepped in front of Kamau, positioning himself between Mkhosi Kunye and their prey. He ordered Mkhosi Kunye into a column of five.

As he fell into formation, Kamau realized that the entire Mkhosi was with him.

Baba Ojore sized up Kamau, "Not even the lack of shoes will keep you from a fight. I love it Njama! Yebo!"

Kamau replied forcefully, "Yebo!"

Baba Ojore addressed the Mkhosi, "Mkhosi Kunye, this is Mkhosi Kubili. They are doing some early training exercises, and they need to move through our section of Camp Furaha. These are not our invaders. These are our brothers. Introduce yourselves."

Jomo W. Mutegi

So, there are more Mkhosi. I wonder how many, Kamau thought as he moved towards the Ginks to introduce himself. Kamau met several of the boys. They all had southern accents like Carl Lofton. Some were thicker and heavier than others. The boys must have been from different places in the South.

After a few minutes of introductions, Baba Ojore commanded, "Mkhosi Kunye, return to kambi for morning call. Double time!"

The Mkhosi ran back to the kambi and finished dressing for morning call. After morning call, Baba Chinua explained that, on Sundays, they rested from the daily run. Instead of the morning run, they had more intersquad competitions.

Baba Ojore then announced that, later in the day, they would conduct exercises with Mkhosi Kubili. Kamau was eager to train with the new Mkhosi, even though they were still Ginks. He was a personable boy and looked forward to making new friends. *Maybe we can beat someone from that group in a competition,* he thought sarcastically.

Following Mti wa Umoja, the VITs of Mkhosi Kunye and the Ginks of Mkhosi Kubili spent the remainder of day seven training together. Kamau's hope of Kikuyu Squad being better than these Ginks was not realized. Even the Ginks of Mkhosi Kubili beat Kikuyu Squad at most everything. But the novelty of a new group of boys was enough to distract Kamau from their losses.

During lunch, Kikuyu Squad sat at a table with Yoruba Squad and a group of four boys from Mkhosi Kubili who made up Xhosa Squad. Charles Lofton was in Yoruba Squad, and he asked one of the boys from Xhosa Squad, "So, what kind of thangs have ya'll been doing? Did you learn The Creed?"

A baby-faced boy with a bright smile named Ronnel responded, "Yep. We learned The Creed. We learned everythang we did today. We filtered water, learned drill, did combatives…"

Carl added, "Yeah! We worked with Hausa Squad this morning. They were good!" He inquired further, "Why are you still wearing Gink shirts?"

Ronnel rolled his eyes and said nothing. Another boy, Zach, answered, "We got scragglers. 'Dem boys try hard enough, but they just can't run."

Carl continued with his questioning, "How many stragglers you got?"

"Three."

Carl's eyes got big, as he wondered, *How could only three stragglers keep an entire Mkhosi in Gink shirts?* But he said nothing.

Zach took a big gulp of water before asking, "Ya'll didn't have no scragglers?"

Carl laughed, "We did." He looked at Alton and Chandler, "We had five stragglers for three days. Carl then gestured towards Kikuyu Squad, "Top of that, this whole squad was straggling last Thursday."

Zach perked up and looked squarely at Kamau, "How'd ya'll go from scragglin' to bein' VITs so fast?"

Kamau's mouth was full, and he couldn't respond. Carl answered for him, "Kamau was injured when he was stragglin'. When he got better, he ran with the stragglers and motivated 'em."

Zach looked at Kamau in disbelief, "What kinda motivatin' you do to make a boy run?"

Raymond answered, "We ran behind them and pushed them whenever they slowed down."

Chandler chimed in, "I was a straggler. After I ran the Three-Mark the first time, it got easier, and I didn't need to be pushed."

Carl smiled at Zach and Ronnel. "Yeah, make ya stragglers finish the next run. You'll be outta them pink shirts soon."

After lunch, Mkhosi Kunye and Mkhosi Kubili prepared for chapel. For the first chapel service, they listened to a lecture called the African Builders of Civilization. For the second chapel service, the VITs, Ginks, Mwalimu and the two Bausi discussed what they had learned from the speaker's message.

Baba Ojore emphasized the importance of applying the message. "Given what you learned from the message, identify one way that you could (or should) live differently."

Baba Ojore did not require anyone to share this publicly. In fact, he actually discouraged it saying, "Vanguardians do not stand behind a pulpit, proclaiming moral or spiritual superiority. We understand that our lives proclaim who and what we are. A person's religion is not what they say. A person's religion is what they do."

Kikuyu Squad and Baba Kahuthia worked with Oromo Squad and Baba Juma to discuss the lecture and the lessons learned. Kamau's mother and father had often talked about the accomplishments of Black people, so he had heard much of the lecture content before. However, today he was beginning to understand it in a much different way. He had never before considered how much time, work, energy, and sacrifice go into a small accomplishment, like learning to assemble a tent. He imagined that a big accomplishment, like developing a medical treatment or building a business, would require a lifetime commitment.

For the remainder of the day, the VITs of Mkhosi Kunye and the Ginks of Mkhosi Kubili spent time working, eating, and playing together, and they shared stories of their experiences at the Akhet. As the evening drew to an end, they parted and prepared for another day. But nothing could prepare Kamau and Kikuyu Squad for the challenge they would soon face.

Jomo W. Mutegi

Timothy walked briskly down to Coordination Center Two. He was planning to meet Anand Devi for lunch. Today CC2 was bustling with activity. "Anand are you ready for lunch?"

"Yes, Tim! Give me one minute."

Anand received cross looks from two of the research coordinators who were assisting him. Anand addressed them, "I will be back in thirty minutes. We are still permitted to eat, you know."

Timothy smiled. He was pleased to see Anand's assertiveness.

They ate lunch off site. Timothy spoke, "Anand, I know your time is tight, so I will get right to the point. The activity in CC2 makes no sense. You have a project set to launch in five months, but it looks like you are launching next week. I am trying to plan around this project, but it is very difficult."

"Yes. It is very difficult. The timing is not as planned. The preparation is not as it should be. And while we are scrambling to make it work, Daniel Silverstein is making impossible demands!" Anand was uncharacteristically angry, and he was growing angrier by the moment. "He is erratic. He knows nothing about the science. And he cares nothing about human life!"

Timothy nodded, "Yes, he can be difficult to work with. What is he requiring of you?"

Anand's tone was emphatic, but he lowered his voice to a whisper, "Timothy, this project involves sending a small expeditionary force to a new H-Zone planet."

Timothy recoiled in shock and surprise. His eyes grew large. He stammered, "This… this… this is unheard of." He smiled and clapped Anand on the back, "Anand, you are going to be a very rich and famous research scientist."

Anand shook his head, "Not working for Daniel Silverstein, I'm not. I'll be lucky to stay out of jail after this crew dies because of his negligence."

Timothy shook off his surprise and nodded his head in understanding. "OK. I get it. He is pressing you to do too much too soon."

"We cannot do six months of work in one month. The crew we are working with are mostly civilians. They are not experienced in space travel. They are not even very good scientists."

As Anand railed on, Timothy listened patiently. And in a moment of weakness, Anand begged, "Please save me from Daniel Silverstein. This project is going to be a disaster."

Timothy looked Anand squarely in the eyes, "Anand, my friend, I am out of the loop on this one. But if there is any way that I can keep you safe, both legally and within the company, I will do it."

Anand collected himself, "I know you will." After a pause, he grabbed Timothy's arm, "Timothy, the project has already launched. I shouldn't be telling you this, but the crew has been there for twenty-seven days. It is more than legal issues. There are many lives at stake."

Timothy nodded, "Understood my friend. Understood."

Unity, The Second Virtue

Kamau struggled mightily during Week Two of the Akhet. His struggle was unlike what he had experienced in the beginning. He had come to accept the bad food, the yelling, the bug bites, the heat, the constant pain. He had even come to accept the loss of his opportunity to play basketball for Coach Salters, and the certain poverty he would experience after not working all summer. What he could not accept, and what caused him to suffer more than anything, was being last in everything he did.

The worst of it was that he was powerless to effect any change. It wasn't Kamau that was losing. No, it was that fat, wheezing boy Alton. It was that happy, grinning, fool Raymond. But worst of all was that weak, egghead boy, Chandler. No matter what Kamau did, no matter how outstanding his performance on any task, these three found a way to mess it up. They were like a trio of two-ton anchors weighing Kamau down.

At Mti wa Umoja, on Monday, Baba Kahuthia's affirmation sealed Kamau's fate. "When one man succeeds, we all succeed. When one man fails, we all fail." This became the mantra of the Mwalimu throughout the week. Only it seemed a bit false to Kamau. His success never seemed to translate into success for Kikuyu Squad. But Kamau was certainly dealt the punishment and humiliation of all their failures.

This week, the Mkhosi learned a new poem and read a new book. The book talked about how horrible American food is. The VITs were astonished to learn that the diseases associated with Black people, like diabetes and high blood pressure, were actually diseases caused by white people and their processed food. Most of the VITs had always heard that these diseases were caused by eating soul food.

Throughout the week, they also reviewed all the material covered in Week One. While Kikuyu Squad didn't shine here (in fact, they didn't shine anywhere), memorizing poetry and reading didn't bring them great shame. But the Mwalimu also escalated their Combatives Training by providing formal instruction in boxing as a form of combat and taught them to make primitive shelters as part of their survivalism training. For Kikuyu Squad, both were a disaster.

Jomo W. Mutegi

Mkhosi Kunye began boxing instruction on Monday. The temperature had to be near 100 degrees. It did not matter to the Bausi or the Mwalimu. They trained outside in the sweltering heat, learning strikes and footwork. For the full period of the instruction, they were drilled for proper technique. As they blistered in the morning sun, Baba Abiola spent thirty minutes telling them how much Ra loved them and was giving them sunshine kisses; how much their families would love them; how much their enemies would hate them; how wonderful it was to sweat because their sweat made the grass grow; and how some people had a disease called hypohydrosis, where they could not sweat. It all sounded made up to Kamau. He wondered how much of what the Mwalimu said was true.

On Tuesday, it rained heavily. They trained outside in the rain, reviewing the strikes and footwork from the previous day and adding one defensive maneuver. They also practiced combinations. As they shivered in the cold, driving rain, Baba Chinua spent thirty minutes telling them how lucky they were to have a "pleasant drizzle" to keep them cool; how much Tefnut loved them and was giving them a refreshing drink; how much their families would love them; how much their enemies would hate them; how wonderful rain was because it made the grass grow; and how some people had a condition called "drought" where they had no rain. Near the end of Tuesday's training, Mkhosi Kunye could barely move their legs to step when striking, because the mud was so thick around their feet. By the end of training, their feet and trousers were filthy and caked in mud.

The weather on Wednesday was beautiful. Tuesday's storm had cooled the air. So, the temperature was in the upper seventies and the sky was clear. It was a perfect day for training. The VITs, who were excited to finally train outside in good weather, reported to the training field. Immediately upon his arrival to the training field, Baba Ojore ordered the Mkhosi to Ukumbi wa Mapambano. It appeared they would train indoors on this beautiful day.

Once at Ukumbi wa Mapambano, Baba Ojore walked the Mkhosi to the forest of hanging heavy bags. "Pair up with your quarter mate. Each pair should have two, ten-pound dumbbells."

Kikuyu Squad was grouped together. Raymond and Kamau were on one bag, while Alton and Chandler were on the adjacent bag. Baba Thulani wheeled a bin containing the dumbbells among the group. Each pair of Vanguardians in Training took out a pair of dumbbells.

Charles Hall grabbed his and blurted out, "These ain't so heavy."

This indiscretion was met with silence and blank stares. By this point, there were a few lessons that the Mkhosi had learned abundantly well. One of these lessons was to listen, to watch, and to keep quiet. Charles "Little Bird" Hall just would not learn. *Maybe he can't help himself,* Kamau thought. Kamau didn't know for sure why Little Bird couldn't keep quiet. But he did know that his moment of indiscretion would not be good.

Baba Ojore seemed to ignore Charles Hall's outburst. "Partner Kunye will strike the bag for one round while Partner Kubili will hold the bag and provide motivation." Baba Ojore continued, "All men will rest for one minute. Then Partner Kubili will strike for one round while Partner Kunye provides motivation. The striking partner will hold the dumbbells while striking." He paused, "Are there any questions?" There were none. "1-2 Combination. Begin!"

At Baba Ojore's command, nearby clocks flashed "3:00" and began counting down. Music began blaring. It was some old, high energy, rap song.

I got so much trouble on my mind
Refuse to lose
Here's your ticket
Hear the drummer get wicked

Kamau began while Raymond provided motivation. Fortunately, Kamau didn't need any motivation. Raymond didn't quite seem to know what to say. Kamau whaled away forcefully, violently. The high energy music fueled him. And his desire to outdo the rest of the Mkhosi drove him. However, after just thirty seconds of 1-2 combinations, he was getting tired. After one minute, he was spent. His arms began to drop.

Baba Kahuthia moved towards him, holding a stick with a gloved fist on the end. He thrust the stick into Kamau's chin. "Hold up your guard." He chastised Raymond, "Motivate this man. He is your brother. You will put your life and the lives of your loved ones in his hands. He needs to be strong."

Kamau was getting tired. Three minutes was a long time. It was a very long time. Ten-pound dumbbells were heavy. They were very heavy. Apparently, he was not the only one to think so. He heard Baba Ojore yelling over the music, "Keep fighting! Fight hard! Vanguardians never quit!"

With one minute to go, Kamau struggled to keep his hands up. But each time his hands dropped, Baba Kahuthia reminded his chin with the gloved stick. He struggled to punch. But each time his punch weakened, Baba Kahuthia intoned, "Fight, Njama! Finish strong!"

Baba Ojore continued motivating the fighters, "We are called Vanguardians for a reason. We are the tip of the spear! The tip of the spear must be sharp. Sharpen yourselves! We die with bloody knuckles. When necessary, one Vanguardian fights against the whole world."

Kamau watched time tick away on the clock. He summoned all he had to finish strong. He ignored the pain and ache in his shoulders. He tucked his elbows against his sides to help prop up his weary arms. But he held his guard. He threw weary, sloppy punches, but he kept punching. A bell chimed and the music faded.

Charles Hall flopped down underneath the bag he had been hitting, and Baba Abiola exploded. "Get up, Hall! You will not be flip flopping around this Terrordome like a fish! You will not bring dishonor to your squad, to your Mkhosi, to the Vanguard, or to yourself. Are we clear?"

Little Bird scrambled to his feet, "Yes, sir!"

Baba Ojore commanded, "Switch strikers." At the end of the one-minute rest, he commanded, "Begin!"

The clocks reset at "3:00" and the music resumed. Kamau watched Raymond intently and provided him calm counts, "1-2... 1-2... 1-2... good... 1-2... hold your guard... good... 1-2..."

While he was motivating Raymond, Kamau had an opportunity to watch Chandler. Predictably, Chandler had grown weary after the first or second combination. Alton never gave up on him. "Come on Chandler, you can do it. Hit harder. That's right. Knock him out!" It was inspirational... fruitless, but inspirational.

Baba Kahuthia continued to use the fisted stick to ensure that Kikuyu Squad kept their hands up. The Mwalimu continued to motivate the Mkhosi. And Bausi Ojore continued to drill them. After everyone had done a 1-2 combination, he commanded a 1-2-3 combination, then a 1-2-3-2 combination, then a 1-2-5-2 combination. They continued the training for an hour. Even the Mwalimu took breaks from motivating their squads to get time on the bags. Baba Kahuthia did his training with twenty-pound dumbbells.

When the VITs left the Terrordome, Kamau observed Bongani asking Charles Hall derisively, "How about those little dumbbells. Are they heavy yet?"

Charles Hall didn't respond; he just looked down sheepishly.

Kamau was impressed with Bongani. It was just the kind of sarcastic insult that he would have made.

Kamau's Lament

Each day of Week Two, the VITs learned to make a different type of primitive shelter, using only a tarp and materials found in the woods. On Monday, they made a debris shelter. On Tuesday, they made a wedge tarp shelter. And on Wednesday, they made a lean to. Each VIT made each type of shelter at least twice. But each VIT was also assigned a specialty shelter, which he made multiple times. Kamau's specialty shelter was the debris shelter. On Thursday, the Mkhosi assembled in a remote wooded area. It was an area they had not seen before. Baba

Ojore addressed the Mkhosi, "Over the past three days, you have learned to build three primitive shelters. Winford! What three shelters have you built?" Gerard Winford replied, "Baba Ojore, the three shelters we have built are the debris shelter, the wedge tarp shelter, and the lean-to shelter."

Baba Ojore continued, "The more you practice building these structures, the better you will become. Today, we will learn to build two more shelters. The first is designed for maximum concealment. It is the pit shelter. The other is for gathering. It is the round lodge. Baba Thulani, Baba Kahuthia, and Baba Abiola will demonstrate the construction of the pit shelter."

As the Mwalimu worked, Baba Ojore explained the process of construction. He shared diagrams with the Mkhosi of what the finished construction would look like. He described various conditions that would impact the effectiveness of this shelter. He led the Mkhosi in a discussion of the pros and cons of this shelter as compared to the other forms of shelter they had learned to build. Baba Ojore shared stories of Vanguardian success and failure with this shelter construction.

Baba Ojore pointed out, "While this shelter provides good concealment, it does not allow for quick access and egress. It also takes a lot of time to build."

Kamau asked, "Baba Ojore, can this shelter be used for storing provisions?"

Baba Ojore smiled, "That's good thinking, Njama. Vanguardians, what type of provisions might we store in a pit shelter?" The Mkhosi discussed the implications of storing provisions in a pit shelter. Would wetness cause metal to rust? Would it erode wood? Would insects or rodents eat food? Would the provisions mold?

Once the shelter construction was completed, the Mkhosi inspected it. Baba Ojore then commanded, "Mongo Squad, find a location approximately 200 yards north of this location and construct a pit shelter."

Mongo Squad huddled together with Baba Chinua. Baba Chinua did not appear to speak. Mongo squad could be seen trying to determine which direction was north and how to determine 200 yards. Eventually, they chose a direction, and they were off.

Baba Ojore continued, "Fulani Squad, find a location approximately 200 yards south of this location and construct a pit shelter." As Fulani Squad huddled together, Baba Ojore commanded, "Yoruba Squad, find a location approximately 200 yards east of this location and construct a pit shelter." He then commanded, "Zulu Squad find a location approximately 200 yards west of this location and construct a pit shelter."

Where do we go? Kamau thought. *All the directions are used up.*

Baba Ojore commanded, "Kikuyu Squad, find a location within a fifty-foot radius of our current location and construct a pit shelter."

Kamau led the squad in identifying a location. They positioned themselves a good distance from Baba Ojore and halfway between Fulani Squad, which was south, and Yoruba Squad, which was east.

Ever since they had been organized into squads, Alton, Raymond, and Chandler deferred to Kamau as the leader of Kikuyu Squad. Alton had had a deep-seated loyalty to Kamau that began when Kamau saved him from being beaten by a group of boys. Raymond recognized that Kamau was stronger, faster, and more knowledgeable than himself. What's more, Raymond's personality was too accepting of everything and everyone. He didn't possess the force needed to lead. Kamau had this in spades. Chandler didn't disagree with either Alton or Raymond. Even if he did, it would not have mattered. He was too weak to exert his will.

Ironically, Kamau did not care much for leadership. He would have been fine to have anyone lead besides himself. What Kamau cared about most was Kamau. After resigning himself to the rigors of the Akhet, he had embraced the idea of personal growth. He was interested in his own status as a Vanguardian. He cared precious little for Alton or Raymond, and he cared nothing at all for Chandler. As he saw it, these twits could do nothing for him. But he played along as best he could.

Chandler suggested working in teams. Kamau and Raymond would dig, initially. After fifteen minutes or so, Alton and Chandler would take over the digging duty. While Kamau and Raymond dug, Alton asked Kamau, "What can we do to help?"

Kamau thought for a moment. He couldn't think of anything that Alton and Chandler were able to do. "Just conserve your energy. You will need to dig pretty soon." So, Alton and Chandler sat and watched.

After fifteen minutes, they switched. While Alton and Chandler dug, Kamau and Raymond went looking for logs to cover the pit. They found about twelve logs. Two were thin and needed to be tested for sturdiness. They returned to the pit and noticed that the construction had gotten lopsided. Alton had dug twice the depth that Chandler had. Initially, Kamau said nothing. He just observed. Chandler stopped every two strokes to rub his shoulders and adjust his glasses. Kamau grabbed his shovel, "I got it." Without saying a word, Chandler clambered out of the pit and sat looking at the logs.

Raymond felt badly for him. "Come on Chandler, we need a few more logs." Together they ran off and gathered more logs. When they returned, Alton and Raymond switched. Kamau kept digging. Chandler sat and watched. Kikuyu Squad kept up with this inefficient rotation. Kamau never stopped, and Chandler never really started.

SECRETS OF THE VANGUARD ORDER

They heard Fulani squad walking back to Baba Ojore's location. About ten minutes later, they heard Yoruba squad making their return. They continued working but were making very little progress. Kamau was spent, and Chandler felt useless and shamed. Raymond and Alton were demoralized. They felt Chandler's hurt and wanted to help, but they didn't know how.

As the chatter of the Mkhosi grew, it became clear that everyone had returned except for Kikuyu Squad. Soon, Alton and Raymond stopped working. Kamau was digging alone. He seemed to be digging harder in denial of the fact that their shelter was not going to be built in a respectable time.

Baba Ojore and Baba Kahuthia approached the site. They were followed by the entire Mkhosi. Kamau kept digging. Baba Ojore asked, "Njama, why are you still digging?"

Exhausted, Kamau replied, "Baba Ojore, I am still digging because Vanguardians don't quit."

Baba Ojore nodded his head, "Njama, there's more than one way to quit. You quit before you started. Now get out of that pit."

Kamau dropped his shovel and stared up blankly. *What does he mean? I never quit,* he thought. *I've been doing the work of two men.*

Baba Ojore commanded, "Fulani Squad, show us your shelter."

As the Mkhosi headed towards the location of Fulani Squad's shelter, Baba Kahuthia held Kikuyu Squad back. He was direct and to the point, "We don't give participation trophies. You don't get credit for a good try. We either succeed or people die. Now, here today, you failed. And you failed because you did not work as a team. You did not function as a unit. You functioned like four individuals." He made eye contact with each member of Kikuyu Squad, and paused to let his words sink in. "Now look at my hand." He showed an open hand. "There is not one of my fingers, no matter how strong it is, there is not one strong enough to strike a blow. But together," he balled his hand into a fist, "together, they can strike a mighty blow. Either you learn to work together, or you will continue to fail. Are we clear?"

They responded affirmatively, "Yes, Baba."

Baba Kahuthia encouraged them on, "Let's join Mkhosi Kunye."

Although they understood Baba Kahuthia, none of the four members of Kikuyu Squad knew what he should do differently. Raymond continued to deferentially go along with whatever was happening. Alton continued to blindly follow Kamau. Kamau continued to dismiss the members of his squad as incapable, and Chandler continued to be dismissed. What was so ironic is that they did well individually. However, as the next few days unfolded, they continued to underperform as a unit.

They inspected the pit shelters of the other squads. Zulu Squad's shelter was especially well-built. Baba Ojore used it as an example and model for the entire Mkhosi.

The next day, Baba Ojore provided instruction in the construction of a round lodge, and each squad constructed one. Kikuyu Squad's shelter was the shabbiest of the bunch. In fact, that entire day, during Instruction Sets, during Combatives Training, even at meals, everything Kikuyu Squad touched seemed to turn to mold. No one in the Mkhosi said it aloud, but Kikuyu Squad was clearly the worst Squad in the Mkhosi.

That evening, after the VITs had written in their journals, the Baba's collected them. As Kamau lay on his bag, waiting for sleep, Raymond spoke to him, "Do you know why you are down?"

"No. I don't," Kamau replied.

Raymond began, "It's because you feel like a loser."

Kamau sat upright and glared in Raymond's direction. He was ready to pound the sass out of Raymond Hewitt and show him what a beating from a loser felt like.

"I am not saying you *are* a loser. I am saying you feel like one. Our squad is the worst squad out here. You are not used to being the worst at anything. That's why you're down. When our squad starts winning, you will feel much better."

Kamau lay down again. He didn't say anything, but he thought about Raymond's words. He was right. Kamau didn't realize it until Raymond told him, but Raymond was right. Kamau wasn't upset because Kikuyu Squad performed poorly. He was upset because he… Kamau… felt like a loser. And that feeling got stronger when he saw the unity and enthusiasm of the other squads, especially Zulu Squad. He spent his remaining waking moments thinking about what he could do to help Kikuyu Squad start winning.

The Cowing of Little Bird

The next day, the second Saturday of the Akhet, marked a turning point for Kikuyu Squad. All night, Kamau struggled with the idea that he was the leader of the worst squad at the Akhet. He slept very little. There was nothing to be done about the lack of sleep, but he had to figure out a way to help his squad improve. The problem was that he didn't know how. The best solution he could come up with was to work harder, to perform better himself to offset the poor performance of his squad members. He had tried this since the squads were formed, during the Application Sets of the first Saturday, during Combatives Training, during the construction of the pit shelter and the round lodge, and it did not work. But he had no better ideas.

SECRETS OF THE VANGUARD ORDER

After breakfast, the Mwalimu had the Mkhosi spend the morning and early afternoon playing a series of eight Vanguard Games. They were *Chaos, One Minute Please, Backstabbers, What Would You Do, Build It Again, Bear Burdens, Every Man,* and *Talk Straight.* Unlike many Akhet activities, the hardest part of *these* Vanguard Games was not physical. While the games required physical work and exertion, the greatest challenge was the mental, emotional, and social stress. After the fourth game, *What Would You Do,* a few members of the Mkhosi began to realize that each game reflected a different principle from the poem, *If.* While the VITs were proud of themselves for figuring it out, that knowledge did not make the games any easier. And it did nothing at all for Kikuyu Squad as they spent the morning and afternoon being trounced by the other four squads of Mkhosi Kunye.

As the day progressed, other VITs began to comment on Kikuyu Squad. After Kikuyu Squad's defeat at the *Battle of Bear Burdens,* Kamau received a snide remark from Deiondre that he tried to ignore. He had already given Deiondre the business once, and he didn't think he could do it again without catching heat from the Mwalimu. Then, after the defeat at the *Battle of Talk Straight,* Charles Hall made a derisive comment about Chandler, and the whole of Kikuyu Squad overheard it.

What made Charles Hall's comment so ironic is the fact that Fulani Squad was genuinely bad. They were just a tad less pathetic than Kikuyu Squad. Raymond was convinced that Charles innocently misspoke, but Kamau didn't care. In his mind, Charles Hall was not permitted to make innocent mistakes at his expense. And more importantly, while he couldn't stop the losing ways of Kikuyu Squad, he could stop the VITs from making Kikuyu Squad a laughingstock.

So Kamau approached Charles when he was with Fulani Squad. Without any warning or hesitation, Kamau walked right up to Charles, with Kikuyu Squad trailing him like baby ducklings, and asked flatly, "Charles Hall did you insult Kikuyu Squad?" His words were innocent enough, but everything else about Kamau was clearly a threat—his tone, his posture, his proximity to Charles.

Charles responded nervously, "N...n...no. I di..didn't..."

Kamau narrowed his eyes and interrupted him, "Charles Hall do you want to *fight* me?"

Maybe Charles remembered how Kamau had pounced on Wild-Eyed Deiondre. Maybe he just had a fearful respect for Kamau, as most of the boys did. Either way, he stammered, "No, no, not at all..."

"No. You just have a problem controlling your mouth." Here Kamau had won the support of all those present. Everyone knew that Charles could not control his mouth. They had all seen it on more than one occasion. His own squad suffered because of it. "You've got diarrhea of the mouth, don't you, Charles Hall?"

Charles Hall talked too much. But he did have pride. "Well, *no*, I don't..."

Kamau narrowed his eyes again, moved closer and cowed him, "DON'T YOU?!"

Charles' eyes grew wide, and he caved, "Yes?"

Kamau maintained his intense gaze, "Yes, you do! And it's caused by constipation of the brain, isn't it?"

Charles was silent.

Kamau barked fiercely, "ISN'T IT?!"

Shamelessly, Charles blurted out, "Yes!"

The other boys, Albert Dorsey, James Dozier, and Jayson Nelson were in stunned amazement. They stood there, mouths agape and dumbstruck, watching in disbelief that Kamau humiliated Charles Hall in front of their whole squad. They couldn't believe that Charles, or any boy for that matter, would allow themselves to be berated in that way. And for a brief moment, the losers of Kikuyu Squad felt proud.

Kamau's posture softened a bit. "Charles Hall, don't you insult Kikuyu Squad again. We are all brothers out here. I'd like for us to be friends, you and me." Without waiting for a reply, he turned and left. The rest of Kikuyu Squad scrambled after him.

Chandler Gardner thanked Kamau. He looked him in the eye, spoke in an audible tone on the first try, and thanked him.

Kamau accepted his thanks graciously, "Sure, Chandler, we are one squad, and you're a good Vanguardian. I won't tolerate any nonsense coming your way!" What Chandler did not know at that moment is that Kamau cared nothing for Chandler. He cared nothing for Chandler being insulted. The insult just gave Kamau an opportunity to vent his frustration on Charles Hall.

That afternoon, Mkhosi Kunye held intersquad competitions. Kikuyu Squad came in last in tug-of-war; last in the jump to safety drill, which was really a sack race; last in the grenade toss drill, which was really a balloon toss; last in the grenade catch drill; and last in the no man left behind drill.

The only competition where Kikuyu Squad did not finish last was the *Fallen Dane*, which was really 4 v 4 soccer. In an unexpected way, Kamau's verbal assault on Charles Hall and Fulani Squad helped a bit. Kikuyu Squad and Fulani Squad played each other last. And throughout their competition with the other squads, Fulani Squad played the game much better than Kikuyu Squad. Charles Hall was really quick, and Jayson Nelson was very good. Although Fulani Squad lost their first three matches, they barely lost. They lost to Mongo Squad in the very last seconds and played Yoruba Squad to a draw. They lost that one in overtime on penalty kicks.

Kikuyu Squad, on the other hand, was horrible. Raymond was capable, but deferential. He acted as though he didn't want to offend the other team by actually playing any defense. Alton was a good tryer. He worked hard, but that porky body was just not built for soccer. Chandler, poor Chandler, was afraid of getting hit, afraid of getting kicked, afraid of his glasses slipping too far down his nose. The only thing he didn't seem to be afraid of was losing. Kamau had no answers for this abysmal squad. So, he just ran around like a one-man show, humiliating opponents when he could, dazzling the Mkhosi with his own fancy footwork when he could, and smack talking when he could. Yet, his squad was losing badly.

So, when Fulani Squad and Kikuyu Squad finally met, it was assumed that Fulani Squad would wipe the field with Kikuyu Squad. But something strange happened. Raymond began playing defense. Alton and Chandler looked somewhat athletic. They looked capable. Kamau noticed the difference early on, and he stopped showboating. He started playing seriously. He barked out instructions, gave encouragement, took time to explain strategy, and of course, he played hard. He played harder than he had up to that point. At the same time, Fulani Squad was timid. They gave up on contested balls. They refused to body Kikuyu Squad off the ball, and all aggression was gone from their play. The match was still close, but Kikuyu Squad won by a slim margin. When the final whistle sounded, Alton, Chandler, and Raymond jumped about so wildly, you would have thought they had won the World Cup.

Kamau joined them to a lesser degree, but he thought the overexuberance was shameful. They were even celebrating like losers. Then he wondered, *Did we win or did Fulani Squad lose?* He wasn't sure. It seemed as though Kikuyu Squad played harder, and they played with more confidence. But it also seemed as though Fulani Squad played scared.

Kikuyu Squad Fights to Win

That evening, Kamau was able to sleep. Their victory over Fulani Squad gave Kamau hope that Kikuyu Squad could begin winning. At morning call, Baba Ojore announced that, later in the day, Mkhosi Kunye would spend time training with Mkhosi Kuthathu.

Because it was Sunday, Mkhosi Kunye did not do the morning run. Instead, they had more intersquad competitions. Today's competition would be combatives. The Mkhosi gathered at the Ukumbi wa Mapambano, and each squad was to compete in boxing matches against the other four squads.

For each boxing match, contestants were chosen at random. There was no effort to match contestants by size. According to Baba Ojore, "In this life, Vanguardians don't pick our enemies. We beat every imbecile that God sends our way. And we thank him for the opportunity."

The combatants wore sixteen-ounce boxing gloves, protective head gear, and a mouthpiece. Squad members gathered in the corner of the combatant from their squad, along with the squad Mwalimu. Baba Ojore officiated the matches. Everyone else stood around the outside of the ring.

For their first match, Kikuyu Squad fought Mongo Squad and, to everyone's surprise, even Baba Ojore's, they won. Raymond fought Danny Echols, Mongo Squad's smallest man. Danny didn't put up much of a fight, and Raymond beat him handily. The one sour note was that Raymond shamed himself and the squad by trying to apologize to Danny after the fight. Kamau gave him an earful for that pathetic display. "Did Danny apologize to Kikuyu Squad when we got beat from sunup to sundown yesterday? I think not."

Alton fought Omowale Ndukwe. Omowale was one of the very large stragglers. He was growing fitter every day, but he was still a fat boy. It wasn't his size that cost him the fight. It was his attitude. He just didn't try very hard, and Alton was just the opposite. Alton would never quit. He would punch one hundred times, one thousand times, ten thousand times if he had to. He would just never quit. He beat Omowale on sheer determination.

Kamau fought Michael Hedrick. Michael was the other straggler from Mongo Squad. He was big, but that meant nothing to Kamau. Kamau was quick, mean-spirited, and tired of losing. He hit poor Michael fifty times if he hit him once and never got touched. Then he danced around the ring in a display almost as shameful as Raymond's apology.

Chandler fought Gerard Winford, if it could even be called a fight. It was more like a flop at the idea of fighting. Gerard was the toughest VIT in Mongo Squad, but that didn't matter. Chandler would have flopped to a flag with Mongo Squad written on it. Kamau didn't care much, in part because he thought there was no hope for Chandler, but mostly because they won.

Kikuyu Squad's second match was against Yoruba Squad. Again, Raymond, Alton, and Kamau each won their match. And again, Chandler lost. This time Chandler lost to Carl Lofton, who had very good hands. Chandler was also improving. He didn't just flop at the sound of the bell. He threw a few haymakers before Carl knocked him into the ropes. Kamau made sure to encourage him to try to bolster his confidence.

By the time they faced their third opponent, Kamau was on cloud nine.

SECRETS OF THE VANGUARD ORDER

Kikuyu Squad had won two matches, and now they faced Fulani Squad. When the combatants were selected and announced, Raymond whispered to Kamau, "We'll win this easily, and Chandler can win his match too."

Puzzled, Kamau asked, "What makes you say that?"

Raymond explained, "Look at them. They're still afraid. All Chandler has to do is stand and fight."

Just as Raymond had predicted, Alton beat the stew out of Charles Hall, who barely lifted a glove to defend himself. Raymond politely defeated Albert Dorsey. Not wanting to shame him, Raymond didn't come close to giving one hundred percent. Chandler was matched up against James Dozier, Fulani Squad's smallest man. Before the match, Kamau gave Chandler some pointers. "When you fight him, look at his chest. Pretend that he is the bag we punched during the combatives drill. Hit him with the 1-2 combination, nothing else. If he raises a hand to hit you, step towards him and let loose with the combination. You're going to win this."

When the bell rang, Chandler looked like a real fighter. He kept his guard up, and by looking at James' chest, he kept his chin tucked low. James was also a bit timid. For a while, neither boy threw a punch. They just danced around. Raymond shouted from the corner, "Strike now! 1-2!"

Hearing this, Chandler exploded. The haymakers he had thrown in the previous match were now transformed into a series of jabs and crosses. After being hit once, James moved back and tried to cover up to keep from getting hit. His backward movement must have emboldened Chandler who followed him back into the ropes and continued throwing a barrage of punches. The rest of the fight followed the same pattern, Chandler attacking with a simple combination and James looking for a way to escape. Chandler won his first match handily, and Kikuyu Squad celebrated. Even Baba Kahuthia nodded and flashed a proud grin as he congratulated Chandler.

Kamau won his fight against Jayson Nelson. Jayson was a decent-sized boy, but not much of a fighter. Kamau beat him quickly and without any fanfare. Everyone knew Kamau would win. He had already established himself as one of the strongest fighters in the Mkhosi. Besides that, after Chandler won, it was clear that Kikuyu Squad would win the match. So, Kamau didn't want to pile on. *How beautiful!* Kamau thought, *We beat Fulani Squad twice in two days. And they had the nerve to insult our squad.*

After winning three matches and seeing Chandler win his fight, Kamau believed that Kikuyu Squad had turned a corner. One more victory, and they would be on top of the first intersquad competition of the day. Their last match was against Zulu Squad, which had also won three matches. This would be a tie breaker.

Chandler fought first against Keith Duhart. Keith wasn't a good fighter, but he was better than Chandler. For his part, Chandler looked like a new person. He was confident and aggressive. Even with these changes, Kamau didn't think Chandler would win, but he did. He got lucky and caught Keith stepping carelessly into a right cross. Keith should have seen it coming. Chandler only used two punches.

Kamau could taste the sweetness of their victory. With Chandler winning, they couldn't possibly loose. The worst they could do was tie. Alton was up next. He would fight Wayne Scott. Wayne was a thickly built boy. He was one of the stragglers, but he wasn't porky. He was just very big. He was easily the biggest boy in the Mkhosi.

Just as Alton stepped in the ring, Deiondre walked by Kamau and commented, "It's about time you losers return to your losing ways."

Kamau kept his cool. Raymond and Chandler looked at him. "Don't worry about him. I'm not going to beat him. I'm going to humiliate him."

Alton fought hard, but in the end he lost. His punches didn't seem to have any effect on Wayne Scott whatsoever. Wayne's punches, on the other hand, knocked Alton down twice. That was enough for Alton to lose the bout on points.

Kamau was up next against Wild-Eyed, Deiondre Everly. As they entered the ring, Deiondre commented, "Ain't gone be no sucka punches like last time."

Kamau responded coolly, "Naw. It's just be a sucka getting punched." The Mkhosi hooted and howled. It seemed that Kamau had amassed a following.

Seeing the support Kamau had, Deiondre tried to save face, "Put something on it."

Still in good humor, Kamau remarked, "I'm gon' put these hands on it as soon as you stop talking." Again, the Mkhosi roared.

Trying to regain the Mkhosi's attention, Deiondre blurted out, "An extra run."

Instantly Kamau responded, "Fine."

Seeing he wasn't fazed, Deiondre wanted more, "To the Six-Mark."

"Fine."

He increased the stakes, "To the Twelve-Mark."

"Fine."

Fuming, Deiondre blurted out, "To the Never-Mark."

Kamau was unperturbed, "Everly, you can wager a run to the Ohio state line and around the perimeter. It don't matter to me because I won't be running it. You will. And just for good measure, you're going to run it with one eye, because as soon as you shut your mouth, I'm gon' shut that left eye." The Mkhosi lost it. Even Baba Chinua and a few of the Mwalimu joined in the howling.

Deiondre tried to shout over the din, "To the Never-Mark."

Baba Ojore loved the spiritedness of the VITs. He had not expected a bet like this, but he saw no harm in it. It would toughen the boys and teach them. He confirmed the bet, "The loser will run to the Never-Mark!" The Mkhosi hooted and howled and cheered wildly.

When the bell rang, Kamau went right to work. He knew that he was a better fighter than Deiondre, but Deiondre was good. He wasn't a slouch. Besides that, Deiondre was wild and unpredictable, and Kamau didn't want to take chances and risk losing the match. So, he hit Deiondre with his jab to keep him off balance and waited for an opening. Kamau went to work on that left eye just as promised. He would throw the left jab to the body, and as Deiondre dropped his hand to defend it, Kamau would counter with the right cross. The headgear protected the eye, but after the first two clean hits, it became irritated, and so did Deiondre. He lunged at Kamau wildly, and Kamau stepped back and hit him with a left hook.

Baba Ojore was impressed. It was obvious that someone had been teaching Kamau to fight long before he arrived at the Akhet.

Kamau continued working on Deiondre, who was now protecting his left eye. His hands were high, so Kamau moved in close and began hitting him with uppercuts to his body. When they were close, Deiondre caught Kamau in the side of the head with a right hook. It was the first time Kamau had been hit today. He stepped back to get his bearings.

Deiondre was still protecting his eye, but the punch he landed gave him confidence, and Kamau knew it. With Deiondre's hands high, Kamau went back to work on his body. This time, he let his right guard hang low. Deiondre wound up to hit him with a left hook. Seeing it, Kamau bobbed and stood up into a right cross to Deiondre's eye.

Ahh. Got 'em, Kamau thought. It was a solid hit, and Kamau fulfilled his promise of shutting Deiondre's eye and, hopefully, his mouth.

Deiondre stepped back and clutched at his eye. While he tended to his injury, Kamau stepped back and turned towards Kikuyu Squad. As he walked towards his corner, Kikuyu Squad began yelling and pointing. Just then, Kamau felt a blow to the left side of his midsection, followed by a blow to the side of his head. His right hand touched the canvas as he tried to keep himself from falling. He looked to his left, and the next thing he remembered was looking up at Baba Kahuthia who was kneeling over him and calling for the nurse.

Kamau heard boos and hisses from the Mkhosi. He heard Alton yelling over the din, "He cheated! He cheated!"

Groggy, Kamau asked Baba Kahuthia, "What happened?"

Baba Kahuthia held up three fingers, "How many fingers do you see?"

Kamau reported, "Three. What happened?"

"You got knocked out, Kamau."

He was incredulous, "Knocked out?! I can't get knocked out!"

"Hmph. Not now cause you're on the ground. But you got knocked out when you were standing up. Now, let's get up. The nurse will be here shortly." Baba Kahuthia spoke plainly, but he had a touch of sadness in his voice. He stood Kamau up, and everyone cheered.

As he walked back to the corner, Kamau's head cleared. He asked Baba Kahuthia, "Is the round over? Do I still have time?"

Baba Kahuthia replied, "No. You're done, Son."

Alton protested to Baba Kahuthia and anyone else who would listen, "But it's not fair. He cheated. Baba Ojore should let Kamau finish."

Baba Kahuthia looked at Alton and the rest of Kikuyu Squad, "What does 'fair' mean? Life ain't fair. It fell within the rules. There was never a whistle blown. There was never a bell rung. There was never a stop to the fight, and Deiondre attacked when Kamau let his guard down. Use this as a lesson and get better."

Kamau glared across the ring at Deiondre. He was grinning from ear to ear and leering at Kamau and the rest of Kikuyu Squad.

"Where's the lesson in this?" Raymond asked bitterly.

To everyone's surprise, it was Chandler who answered, "Don't let your guard down."

Baba Kahuthia looked at Chandler, "That's right. Don't let your guard down. Now Raymond, get your head together, you still got a fight."

By this time, Mama Zuri had arrived to check on Kamau. She drew long awkward stares from the Mkhosi, even Raymond and Bongani Jekwa who were supposed to be fighting. Seeing this, Baba Ojore instructed Baba Kojo to find a private place for Kamau to be examined. Once Nurse Zuri was out of view, Baba Ojore called for the start of the final match.

Raymond was a decent fighter. His technique was excellent. But fighting is much more than technique. It is also attitude. And Raymond's nature was too noncombative. As a result, he didn't realize his full fighting potential. Bongani Jekwa was quite different. He was stern, serious-minded, and mean. He was a controlled version of Wild-Eyed Deiondre. Under the best circumstances, this fight was a mismatch. But these weren't the best circumstances. Raymond's head was not in the fight. He was still distracted with thoughts of Kamau's defeat. Raymond Hewitt didn't stand a chance. He lost to Bongani handily. Fortunately,

Bongani did not try to pile on. He made no effort to humiliate Raymond. He beat him on points and secured a victory for Zulu Squad.

After his fight, Bongani never cheered or celebrated. He congratulated Raymond and Kikuyu Squad. The other members of Zulu Squad followed his lead, all except Wild -eyed Deiondre. Deiondre was running around with one eye swollen shut, pumping his fist yelling, "We won! We won!" And "Go run, Njama! To the Never-Mark, Njama!" Deiondre was making himself into a very unlikable character.

Once he saw Deiondre's antics, Bongani approached him and spoke quietly in his ear. Deiondre grew silent and congratulated Kikuyu Squad.

Baba Ojore looked across the Ukumbi at Baba Kahuthia. They flashed glances of regret at one another. Baba Ojore announced, "This was our first Intersquad Combatives competition. We will have many more. Brothers, keep in mind that we are not here to destroy one another. We are here to strengthen one another. When we fight, we fight hard so that we can become better fighters and so that our brothers can become better fighters. In this way, we become a better, stronger Vanguard. We learn from every victory, and we learn from every defeat."

Mama Zuri came from behind the screen with Kamau. Kamau rejoined Kikuyu Squad, and the Mkhosi clapped and cheered loudly like they were welcoming home a returning hero.

The Never-Mark

Baba Ojore nodded and addressed the Mkhosi, "Now, Brother Njama fought valiantly." There were more cheers. Baba Ojore continued, "But he lost."

There was grumbling and a low murmur from the Mkhosi. And one boy said audibly, "He was cheated." No one knew who said it, but no one tried too hard to find out.

Baba Ojore ignored the outburst and continued, "Brother Njama lost his fight, and he also lost his bet. He will run the Never-Mark. We will accompany him to the edge of the path and see him off." The Mkhosi formed a column of two and marched to the edge of the path. Once they were there, Baba Ojore gave Kamau advice. He spoke so that the entire Mkhosi could hear him. "Njama, this is another trial. It is a very, very difficult trial. But you can do it. Your body will want to quit, but you will press on. Your mind will tell you that you must quit, but you will press on. You will find within you a strength and resolve that you never knew you had. And this trial will help you to find it."

Baba Chinua moved to the front of the column. He took his stopwatch in hand. "I will keep time. We should record this." Baba Ojore nodded in agreement. Baba Chinua began to count, "Ready…"

Before he could start, Alton broke formation and ran to stand by Kamau. Baba Ojore looked at him inquisitively and spoke sternly, "Bailey, what are you doing?"

Alton looked at him with a tear in his eye, "When one man fails, we all fail. When one man succeeds, we all succeed."

As he spoke, Raymond and Chandler also broke formation and joined Kamau and Alton. Baba Ojore chastised them, "Kikuyu Squad, this was Njama's bet. He did not bet on behalf of the whole squad."

Kamau looked at Kikuyu Squad, "I'll be back. I can do this. Stay here."

Chandler looked Kamau in the eye, "No. We are one unit… one squad."

Seeing this, Baba Kahuthia whispered to Baba Ojore, "Baba Ojore, let them go. They need this. I will give them some provisions."

With a very subtle smile, Baba Ojore nodded his approval.

Baba Kahuthia ran off and quickly returned with a small daypack and a hand radio. He gave the daypack to Kamau. "These are provisions for all of you. There is water and food. Eat and drink before you are hungry or thirsty. Your bodies will need it. You don't have to finish fast, just finish. Keep your bodies moving. You can walk, but do not stop to rest. Do not sit down. Your body will lock up on you if you do. There is also a radio if anyone should get hurt, or if anyone wants to quit," he didn't say any names, but both he and Kamau were thinking about Chandler, "use this radio to contact me. I can have someone come to assist you. When you run, you will see a marker that says, 'Thirteen-Mark.' You keep going. Shortly after that, you will see a marker that is slightly bigger than the others. It will say nothing. It will be blank. Everything will be downhill from there. It will be hard. It will be very hard. But it will be downhill."

Kamau nodded, "Yes, Baba."

Baba Chinua began the count again, "Ready…"

Baba Kahuthia said hurriedly, "We are with you. Even when we are not there, we are *all* backing you up!"

Baba Chinua continued, "Begin!"

The Mkhosi erupted in motivations and cheers. They heard Charles Hall hollering above the din, "Kikuyu Squad, we are with you! Vanguardians never quit!"

As they began the run, no one spoke. Kamau was focused on finding his pace. The pace of the morning run was a bit slower than his natural pace, but this was his run, and Kikuyu Squad would support him. Once he found a good rhythm, Kamau reflected on the morning's events. He thought of how Kikuyu Squad was winning in the intersquad competition. He thought of Alton's never-quit spirit, Raymond's insight, and Chandler's transformation into a halfway decent fighter. He even got to see Nurse Zuri. It was a perfect morning. At no moment this morning did he imagine he would be running the Never-Mark on the one day he was given to rest from running. *It was my own fault*, he thought. *I was arrogant. And I did let my guard down. I know better and should have done better.* Kamau saw the run as his punishment for not being more disciplined.

As these thoughts raced through his mind, Kamau looked at Kikuyu Squad. Raymond was running faithfully at his side. Alton and Chandler were already exasperated trying to keep up, but they ran behind him dutifully. *What am I doing?* he thought. *This is my punishment. Not theirs.* Then he stopped.

Confused, Raymond asked, "What you doing, man?"

Alton added, "Baba said we can't stop. We'll get lock joint."

"It's lockjaw," Chandler panted.

"Huh?" Alton asked, confused. "He said we can get lockjaw?"

"There's no such thing as lock joint. There is such a thing as lockjaw," Chandler tried to explain while gasping for air. "Baba Kahuthia did not say we would get either. He said our bodies would lock up if we stopped."

Raymond interrupted, "Kamau, why are you stopping?"

"I'm sorry. I need to apologize to you."

Alton interrupted angrily, "Naw! You don't need to apologize to nobody! Deiondre cheated! And we 'gon get that boy when we get back."

"Okay. Slow down. I do need to apologize." Kamau began walking and remained silent for a long time to recollect his thoughts. The rest of Kikuyu Squad followed, saying nothing. For the first time all summer, Kamau was honest with himself. He had been incorrigible. He was not a terrible person, but he was far from being his best self. He could have been a much better brother to Rafiyah, a more respectful son to Mr. and Mrs. Njama, a friendlier quarter mate to Raymond, a more committed squad captain, a less brash and abusive VIT to his Mkhosi. He didn't have to threaten Charles Hall. He didn't have to embarrass Deiondre Everly. It was certainly fun doing so, but was it necessary? Well, a guy's got to have some fun.

At any rate, the version of Kamau he had given the world this summer was unacceptable by his own standards. He was running an ungodly distance (he still didn't know how far it was), and three of the boys he disregarded the most, voluntarily committed to running it with him. What better friends could a person have? He didn't deserve these friends.

Kamau stopped again, "I need to apologize because I have not been as good of a squad captain as I can be. If you accept my apology, I promise to be a better captain and a better friend."

Alton got teary-eyed and hugged Kamau. Raymond smiled broadly and shook his right hand, giving him a hug with his left. Chandler beamed and clapped his back.

Kamau started walking again and spoke while he walked, "First of all, my pace was too fast. This is not my run. This is Kikuyu Squad's run. We will run the pace of our slowest man. So, let's start slow, and when the run gets hard for anyone, speak up, and we'll slow down."

Chandler yelled out, "Yebo!" This caught everyone off guard, and Chandler smiled at the looks of surprise.

Kamau continued, "Second of all, Alton Bailey, were you crying?"

"Hmm?" Embarrassed, Alton Bailey quickly wiped his face.

"Alton Bailey, the Vanguardians of Kikuyu Squad do not cry." Kamau's tone turned playful. "Now, we might dot yo' eye."

Chandler added parenthetically, "Deiondre Everly." Everyone snickered.

Kamau continued, "We'll definitely make you comply."

Raymond added, "Charles Hall." The squad giggled again.

Kamau continued, "But we do not cry!" Pleased with their collective wit, they hooted and cackled in a moment of self-congratulatory bonding.

Soon, the squad found a comfortable running pace. The pace was slow enough that everyone could talk comfortably. Kamau announced, "Consider this to be the first official training session of Kikuyu Squad. I wish I knew how far we are running."

Chandler replied, "We're running 26.2 miles."

Everyone looked at Chandler in amazement. Raymond asked, "How do you know?"

Chandler explained, "I counted my steps."

"Counted your steps?" Alton asked.

Kamau encouraged Chandler, "Explain the whole process, Chandler. We've got time."

Chandler explained, "Okay. So, my average stride length when running is three-and-one-half feet. There are 5,280 feet in one mile. That would be 1,508½ steps for each mile. It took 4,627 steps when we ran the Three-Mark. That is about three miles."

"Are you doing this math in your head?" Kamau interrupted with a hint of amazement.

Chandler replied flatly, "Yes."

Kamau was in disbelief. "Okay, go ahead."

Chandler continued, "The measurements are not perfect. Stride length varies with road conditions, fatigue, and even cadences cause us to adjust our stride a bit. But it is a close approximation."

Alton, too, was in disbelief, "You counted all those steps during the entire run?"

Chandler asked rhetorically, "What else was there to do?"

Raymond asked, "So, if the Three-Mark is three miles, how do you conclude the Never-Mark is 26.2 miles? Would it be the Twenty-six-Mark?"

Chandler explained, "Remember Baba Kahuthia said that after the Thirteen-Mark the run would be downhill. So, I took that to mean that the Thirteen-Mark was the halfway point. If the Thirteen-Mark is thirteen miles and it is half of the Never-Mark, then the Never-Mark is twenty-six miles. I said twenty-six point two because that is the official distance of a marathon. The Bausi and Mwalimu are too precise to be careless about two-tenths of a mile."

Kamau asked, "So Chandler, have you figured out how long this run will take us?"

Chandler smiled. Finally, his talents were being recognized. "Sure. If we run an average of ten minutes per mile, we will finish in just over four hours and twenty minutes. If we run an average of twelve minutes per mile, we will finish in just about five hours and fifteen minutes."

Kamau realized that Kikuyu Squad had a talking, breathing computer on the team, and they had failed to use him all this time. *He, Kamau, failed to use him all this time.* Up to this point, Kamau was frustrated that his human computer wasn't a bouncer. How foolish! He wouldn't make that mistake again. He asked, "What pace do you think we will run?"

Chandler continued, "The pace for our daily morning run is eight minutes per mile. That's what we are running now."

Raymond interjected, "Are you counting steps now?"

Chandler smiled. He was brainy, but he couldn't count, do math, run, and have a conversation all at the same time. "No. It just feels like our normal pace." He continued answering Kamau's question, "So, we are running eight-minute miles now, but I don't think we can keep it up for twenty-six point two miles. We have never trained for this type of run, and our bodies will start to give out after a while. I think it is reasonable to plan on averaging twelve minutes per mile. That would give us plenty of time to walk for rest."

Kamau was processing what had been said. "Okay, we'll slow down to walk at the Six-Mark. We will also eat at that time, then we'll pick up our run after we're done."

CHAPTER FIVE

Kamau's New Squad

Kamau Meets His New Squad

Kamau wondered what else Chandler knew. *What else could he do with that mind of his? What about Raymond or Alton, did they have any hidden secrets or abilities?* He grew excited at the thought, *I bet this squad is a goldmine of talent. We could crush Zulu Squad and dominate the entire Mkhosi if we maximize our talents.* He determined then that he needed to learn more about the members of Kikuyu Squad. He needed to know more than just their talents. He needed to know their hopes, fears, tendencies, and desires. He needed to know them as well as he knew himself. No. He needed to know them better than he knew himself; and he needed to know himself better. He didn't tell the squad his purpose. He just started getting to know them. "Raymond, tell us about yourself." Throughout the next hour, the boys poured their souls out to one another, even Kamau.

> Raymond's Story: Raymond's father is an entrepreneur. He owns real estate throughout the city, and he runs a carpentry business. His mother teaches chemistry at the local community college. Raymond is the fourth of nine children—five girls and four boys. Raymond's three oldest siblings (two sisters and one brother) all work for his father's business. Raymond has worked for his father every summer since he was eight. Each summer, he learns a different aspect of the business. This summer, his father told him that the Akhet was more important than working on the business. He said, "Building strong buildings was easy compared to building strong men." He sent Raymond to Camp Furaha so that he could take on hard challenges

and grow from it.

Being away this summer is hard for Raymond. His father is getting older and is not able to keep up with the workload the way he did when he was younger. Raymond and his older siblings are trying to learn the business so that if something happens to their father, they can keep it going to support the family. Mr. Hewitt provides substantial support to three other households in their extended family, in addition to supporting his own family.

Chandler's Story: Chandler lives with his mother's parents. He has younger twin sisters who live with one of his aunts. Neither his mother nor his father has a stable life. Chandler's father had been an accountant for a well-respected accounting firm. When Chandler was three and the twins were six months old, Chandler's father was accused of embezzlement by a partner in the firm. The charges were false, and there was no physical or documentary evidence to support the accusation, but that did not stop the wheels of justice from grinding Mr. Gardner into pulp. On the basis of testimonial evidence alone, he was convicted of a felony and served three years in the state penal institution. He was eventually released when an appeals court overturned the conviction. The district attorney had no stomach for a new trial; besides that, the accusing partner was serving time for misappropriating more than $750,000 dollars from several non-profit and religious clients. By this time, however, the damage was done. Mr. Gardner was no longer able to ply his trade as an accountant. In fact, he was not able to get meaningful work anywhere. He turned to odd jobs and petty crime, and he's spent the past eight years in and out of jail.

Chandler's mother did not handle the stress well. Raising three children alone, being a legal expert for her incarcerated husband, and being a bread winner was more than she could bear. She began to self-medicate. Now, she struggles to stay clean and sober. Chandler spends a great deal of time with his grandfather, working around the house. He learned to fix cars, do carpentry, plumbing, and mason work. He also learned quite a bit about electrical work. Chandler has his own workshop set up in the basement right next to his grandfather's work area. When he is not working with his grandfather, Chandler is reading or doing various science experiments. Books help him escape from the pain of not having his parents and sisters nearby.

Alton's Story: Alton is the youngest of two children. He has a sister who is three years older than him. His parents are divorced, and he lives with his mother. His father is a good man who earns a very good salary as a regional manager for a national retail store. He also does landscape work on the side. Although he earns good money landscaping, Mr. Bailey doesn't landscape for the extra money. He doesn't need it. But landscaping gives him two things that he enjoys: demanding physical labor and a chance to be outside. Physically, Alton's father is a larger version of Alton. He is not muscular, but he is very strong. He is also very generous and has few expenses. He lives in a small three-bedroom house within walking distance of Alton's mother. He keeps two extra bedrooms one for Alton and one for his sister. He drives a simple car. He has no debt. He does not use credit cards. It is rumored that he has a net worth of $1.5 million, but Alton does not know for sure. He is also the sole financial supporter of a local football league. The league was started by mothers in the community who could not afford AAU but wanted something for their sons. Alton played in the league when he was younger. Mr. Bailey is very fond of Mrs. Bailey. Alton once asked his father why they divorced. Mr. Bailey said, "Your mother is a good woman. She just wasn't good for me. I had to learn to love her from a distance."

Alton's mother has been dating a new man for the past twelve months. They are planning to get married within the year. The man that she will be marrying lives in Kamau's community. Alton believes they will be moving to that community once his mother gets remarried.

Kamau also shared details about his own life. He told Kikuyu Squad about his sister, about his father and mother, about Imani, about the hot, moist, delectable, intoxications that are served at their dining table three times a day. He told them about the community in which he lives, about the rules that the Njamas live by, and about his initial resistance to the Akhet.

Raymond asked, "How is it that you didn't know about the Akhet? Back in November, we had to sign a form agreeing to attend."

Kamau looked surprised, "Really? I don't remember signing any form." Chandler and Alton both agreed with Raymond that they, too, had signed forms. Kamau wondered if he had indeed signed a form and simply didn't remember. He felt foolish.

The other boys also could not understand why Kamau held so much bitterness towards his father. Chandler saw Mr. Njama as a man who provided a good home and who was there with his son. Raymond saw him as a man who was still vigorous. He had taught Kamau how to fight. He made it such that Kamau did not have to work. Alton saw Mr. Njama as a man who kept his family intact. He still lived with and loved Kamau's mother. After hearing the stories of the squad, Kamau began to rethink his animosity towards his father. *These boys have much greater challenges in their home lives than I do, and they're still full of love for their parents. I have a lot to be grateful for.*

In their getting to know one another, they found out that all of them would be going to the same high school next year. Raymond and Chandler both went to Hickory Middle School. Alton and Kamau both went to Washington Middle School. Both Hickory Middle School and Washington Middle School were feeders for DuBois High School.

They also learned that everyone, except Chandler, had some connection to the small community in which Kamau lived. Kamau lived there; Alton's mother was dating a man who lived there; and Raymond's father was instrumental in helping to renovate the houses in the community.

They approached the Six-Mark sooner than expected. The slower pace and the conversation made the time pass quickly. They felt good and wanted to keep running, but Kamau remembered Baba Kahuthia's advice to eat and drink before they were hungry and thirsty. So, they slowed down to a walk, and they ate and drank. As they passed the Six-Mark, Kamau took the radio that Baba Kahuthia had given him and placed it at the base of the mark.

Chandler asked nervously, "Why are you leaving the radio?"

Kamau looked at him reassuringly and said flatly, "There are no quitters in Kikuyu Squad."

Raymond interjected, "Yeah, Kamau, but what if someone gets hurt?"

Kamau replied, "If any one of us gets hurt, the others will help that man to finish the run." He then paused, looking each VIT squarely in the eye. Everyone nodded in understanding. They continued talking and joking with one another. After they had eaten, Kamau said they would take another break at the Thirteen-Mark.

Over the next six miles, they shared what they had learned or observed about the Mwalimu and about the other boys in the Mkhosi. Here Raymond shined. He was intuitive and incredibly observant of people. With the subtlest of cues, he was able to form accurate conclusions about people's true thoughts and feelings.

Alton asked, "Raymond, you seem to know people pretty well. Why is crazy Deiondre so crazy?"

Raymond responded matter-of-factly, "Deiondre's not crazy. He's angry."

Shocked, Kamau asked, "Angry? Why is he angry with us?"

Raymond shook his head, "He's not angry with us. He's angry at the world. Something bad may have happened to him. Sometimes when people suffer, they lash out at anyone they can, anyone that comes close."

Alton asked, "Well, why does he keep beefing with Kamau?"

Just as Raymond flashed a look of disbelief at Alton, Chandler snapped, "Kamau started it."

Raymond answered in a calm, friendly tone, "When Kamau challenged Deiondre, he became a convenient target. But if Kamau was not here, Deiondre would have beef with someone else."

Alton snarled, "Yeah, well, I don't care what his problem is. When I get a chance, I'm gon' fix it for him."

Kamau was about to temper Alton's hostility, but before he said anything, he thought better of it. Instead, he asked Raymond, "How do you know so much about people?"

Raymond shrugged, "I don't know. I have eight brothers and sisters. I guess I learn a lot from them. And in my dad's business, we have to work with different types of people, so I guess I learn a lot there as well." The truth is Raymond Hewitt had no idea *how* he knew. In fact, until the Akhet, he never realized *that* he knew so much about people.

After a lull in the conversation, Alton blurted out, "Have you noticed that Baba Ojore seems to appear and disappear every morning like magic?!"

Raymond exclaimed, "I thought it was just me! I thought I was having trouble seeing. He does seem to appear out of nowhere!"

"I've seen it too. It's got to be some sort of optical illusion. Do you think it's magic?" Kamau asked sarcastically.

Alton asked emphatically, "What kind of optical illusion could make a *whole* person, big as Baba Ojore disappear?!"

Kamau turned to Chandler, "Chandler, could it be an optical illusion?"

Chandler thought for a moment. "It could be. It could be both."

"It could be both… what?" Raymond asked, confused.

"It could be both an optical illusion and magic," Chandler replied. He went on, "Have you ever noticed in the summertime, when you are driving, if you look at the pavement at an angle, you can see the reflection of cars, trees, and the sky above the pavement. It looks like the reflection you would see when looking at water."

Kamau laughed in surprise, "Yeah, I've seen that."

"It's an optical illusion. It's a mirage. But really it is just science. The light is being reflected off the pavement. It is similar to the way light reflects off a mirror, a body of water, or sand. It's simply the reflection of light."

"Well, it's not magic," Alton snorted.

Chandler replied, "Magic is just science that we do not understand."

As Kikuyu Squad approached the Twelve-Mark, Kamau noticed that Chandler was laboring to keep pace. He asked, "How's everyone doing?" Everyone responded enthusiastically about how good they felt and how motivated they were. Although this is not what Kamau wanted to hear, this type of response was a typical part of Akhet culture. All the VITs adapted to it very quickly. They found that a good show of enthusiasm and joy in the face of hardship made the work easier to bear. It also kept the Mwalimu from giving them more hardship. Kamau wanted to be sure that no one was injured, but he didn't want to mess up the warrior spirit of Kikuyu Squad, so he said nothing more. Instead, he made sure to maintain the slow pace.

At the Thirteen-Mark, Chandler began to walk. Kamau kept running, "We will break soon. Keep pushing." Chandler nodded and began running again. Kamau observed Chandler closely. The squad could have stopped. It was only a tenth of a mile more. But Kamau wanted to see how Chandler would respond.

The squad soon reached the halfway point, and they all slowed to a brisk walk. As he reached into his bag to share the food that Baba Kahuthia had given them, Kamau commanded, "Injury report?!"

The rest of Kikuyu Squad snapped attentively. Kamau's tone was different. For the first time, he commanded attention. He sounded more like one of the Mwalimu than a VIT.

Raymond responded first, "No injuries. I am one hundred percent."

Alton added, "I have a tightness in my right calf. But I can push through."

Chandler added, "I'm okay too… one hundred percent."

Kamau looked squarely at Chandler. "Chandler, there is no shame in being injured or sore. I noticed that you ran the last mile slow, and now you're limping. We can't function as one unit if we are not honest with each other."

Chandler looked down sheepishly. "It's my left shin. I have a shooting pain running through it, off and on."

Kamau nodded, "That's good to know, soldier!"

After their Thirteen-Mark break, Kamau had the squad alternate between running one mark and then walking the next. They did this through the Nineteen-Mark. Alton's calf got tighter. It was to the point that he could not flex his foot when running. So, with each step, he swung his right leg around in an arc. Chandler's shin was much worse. He found some relief by running on the grassy area that ran adjacent to the paved path. But his real relief came when they walked. During this stretch, Raymond began to feel soreness in his lower back. For his part, Kamau also had soreness in his lower back and in his feet. He suspected that he might be developing blisters again.

By the time they reached the Nineteen-Mark, Kikuyu Squad had eaten all their snacks. Given their injuries, Kamau thought it best that they walk the remaining seven miles. He asked, "Chandler, how long will it take to walk the last seven miles?" "My guess is that we are walking somewhere between three to four miles per hour, so we should be able to walk the rest in about two hours."

Kamau was concerned about Kikuyu Squad's ability to finish. He asked, "When we started, you said that, eventually, our bodies would give out. Do you think we can go for two more hours without food?"

Before Chandler could respond, Alton barked a favorite line of Baba Kojo, "If it's difficult, we do it right away. If it's impossible... we may take a tad bit longer."

Kikuyu Squad walked to the Twenty-one-Mark, from there they ran to the Twenty-two-Mark. By this point, the entire squad was a wreck. While walking slowed the progression of their various injuries, it did not heal them. Chandler could barely shuffle, let alone run. With every step, he seemed to be in excruciating pain. Alton's sidewinder limp had also lost its vigor. He seemed to be dragging his right leg. Kamau and Raymond struggled to run upright. Seeing this, Kamau announced that they would walk three miles to the Twenty-Five Mark, and they would run to the finish.

Kamau spoke energetically, "We'll finish strong. Mkhosi Kunye may be waiting for us. They may not be. But if they are, we will show no weakness. We will run confident, strong, and energized to the kambi. Are you with me?"

In unison, Kikuyu Squad responded, "Umoja!!"

Over the next three miles, Kikuyu Squad made up their own cadence. There were lots of bad rhymes, nonsense statements, and, of course, boyish humor. Once these were taken out, the squad had a nice cadence. They called it a few times to help them remember it. They each took a turn calling one verse, except Kamau. He called the chorus.

<u>Kikuyu Squad's Cadence</u>
Had a good home but they made me leave,
Had a good home but they made me leave,
So, Baba could teach me to achieve.
So, Baba could teach me to achieve.
They sat me in a barber's chair,
They sat me in a barber's chair,
And zip, zip, zip, I had no hair.
And zip, zip, zip, I had no hair.
They yelled and screamed all day and night,
They yelled and screamed all day and night,
Until I finally got it right.
Until I finally got it right.
Sound off
One, Two
Sound off
Three, Four
Break it on down now

SECRETS OF THE VANGUARD ORDER

One, Two, Three, Four, One, Two… Three, Four

Get off the sidewalk, get off the grass,
Get off the sidewalk, get off the grass,
Kikuyu Squad is coming past.
Kikuyu Squad is coming past.
We don't mind that morning run,
We don't mind that morning run,
Kikuyu Squad can't be outdone.
Kikuyu Squad can't be outdone.
We don't mind the flies and fleas,
We don't mind the flies and fleas,
We just want some more PT.
We just want some more PT.
Sound off
One, Two
Sound off
Three, Four
Break it on down now
One, Two, Three, Four, One, Two… Three, Four

We will run with a broken leg,
We will run with a broken leg,
Anything to get ahead.
Anything to get ahead.
Eenie, Meenie, Miney, Moe,
Eenie, Meenie, Miney, Moe,
Let's go back and run some mo'!
Let's go back and run some mo'!
No slackers ever won no war,
No slackers ever won no war,
That's why we are so hardcore.
That's why we are so hardcore.
Sound off
One, Two
Sound off
Three, Four
Break it on down now
One, Two, Three, Four, One, Two… Three, Four

As they limped and lurched to the Twenty-Five-Mark, Kamau looked at the squad. "Are we ready?"

They shouted enthusiastically, "Ready! Let's go!"

Kamau began running. He intoned, "Finish strong!" The enthusiasm of the moment caused him to run a bit too fast. Once he settled down to a comfortable pace, they ran quietly for three minutes or so.

At that point, Raymond began calling the cadence. For the remainder of mile twenty-six, they ignored their pain. They forced themselves to stand erect. They refused to limp. They held their heads high and in unison. They called the cadence they had created together. As they approached what they believed was the Never-Mark, they could see two figures about a quarter mile in the distance. As soon as they saw them, one of them disappeared.

Who is that? Kamau wondered. They continued chanting and running.

As they neared the Twenty-Six Mark and turned a corner, they saw a sea of people. Raymond murmured in surprise, "It's the whole Mkhosi."

Chandler corrected him, "No. That looks like two Mkhosi."

It was Mkhosi Kunye and Mkhosi Kuthathu. Thirty-six VITs, ten Mwalimu, and two Bausi ran towards them, cheering and shouting motivations. This outpouring, this show of support energized Kikuyu Squad. As they met the Mkhosi, all the VITs, Mwalimu, and Bausi turned to run with them, laughing and cheering.

Kikuyu Squad forgot about their nagging aches. They stood taller. They ran stronger. Kamau felt invincible. With his heart pumping fire, he began the cadence again, shouting over the din, "SOUND OFF!"

To this, Raymond, Alton, and Chandler shouted, "*ONE, TWO!*"

The second time Kamau intoned even louder, "SOUND OFF!"

Kikuyu Squad responded, "*THREE, FOUR!*"

"BREAK IT ON DOWN NOW!"

"*One, Two, Three, Four, One, Two… Three, Four!*"

With this, Chandler called his portion of the cadence, "Had a good home, but they made me leave." To his surprise, everyone there, all fifty-two VITs, Mwalimu, and Bausi gave the response. He had never heard so many men speaking in one voice. And he was leading them.

This unity continued to the finish. Kikuyu Squad called their cadence with enthusiasm, and the Vanguard running with them responded with joy and admiration for what they had accomplished. As they crossed the edge of the path, Baba Chinua looked at his stopwatch and shouted, "Four hours and fifty-five minutes!" The Vanguard erupted in cheers and applause.

The Seeds of Friendship

Kikuyu Squad had finished their run during the middle of lunch. Immediately after their triumphant return, Mkhosi Kunye and Mkhosi Kuthathu rushed back to Ukumbi wa Kuthathu to finish their meal before the lunch hour ended. Hearing they had an opportunity for food, Kikuyu Squad wasted no time in joining them. The Squad learned that while they were running the Never-Mark,

Mkhosi Kunye had spent the morning training with Mkhosi Kuthathu.

As lunch ended and everyone prepared for chapel, Baba Ojore approached Kamau. He snapped, "Njama!"

Kamau snapped to attention and replied, "Yes, Baba Ojore."

"Get your squad to the infirmary. Mama Zuri will check you over for injuries and clear you for action. Baba Kahuthia and I will meet you there."

Kamau tried to suppress his excitement, "Yes, Baba."

As they headed to the infirmary, Alton was disappointed. "Aww man! We're going to miss the whole day. We won't get to spend time with the new Mkhosi."

Kamau looked at Alton and shook his head. "Raise your hand if you would rather spend the afternoon with thirty-six crusty boys instead of looking at Mama Zuri."

Both Chandler and Raymond gave Alton the side-eye. Alton smiled, "Oh! I forgot about Mama Zuri."

Seeing that no one raised their hand, Kamau smiled. "Good! There are no fools in Kikuyu Squad." The boys laughed and limped their way to the infirmary.

Mama Zuri had each of the boys complete a body scan. Then she gave each a personal check up.

Kikuyu Squad was a bit banged up after the run to the Never-Mark. Chandler had shin splints that mostly affected his left leg. Alton had Achilles tendonitis that affected his right heel. Kamau's blisters had never fully healed, and because he had not planned to run this Sunday morning, he had not applied the moleskin that Mama Zuri had given him. So, the blisters became reaggravated. Raymond was fine. He was sore from the run, but he was not injured in any way.

Seeing Kamau's injury, Baba Ojore grew stern, "Njama, are you trying me?"

Confused, Kamau responded, "No, Baba Ojo…"

Baba Ojore cut him off, "Do you think we have little elves knitting behind the kambi?"

Still confused, Kamau tried to respond, "No, sir. I…"

He was cut short again, "Do you think we run a sock factory?"

Now Kamau understood, "No, sir."

Baba Ojore clasped his hands behind his back and slowly walked up to Kamau. He got very close, and their noses were almost touching. He spoke slowly and deliberately. "Njama, you bloodied a second sock. And as I see it. You owe me for one… 'nother… sock." Then he erupted, "Now get down and give me twenty!"

His eyes wide, Kamau quickly fell to the floor in the pushup position. Before he could begin, Raymond dropped down next to him. Alton and Chandler followed Raymond's lead.

As he began the pushups, Kamau was uncertain as to who should count. Baba Ojore never said, "On my count." Kamau didn't want to count himself, because there was no way he was going to voluntarily do twenty pushups counted "The Vanguard Way." And if he counted wrong, he would be scolded and given more hardship. So, he sang a simple cadence. "Kikuyu Squad, Ready. Down. *Up, Down, Up... Up, Down, Up...*"

This squad unity and Kamau's quick thinking surprised Baba Ojore. He looked at Baba Kahuthia, smiled, and gave an affirming nod. Baba Kahuthia smiled and nodded in agreement. When they had done twenty pushups, Baba Ojore said, "Asante Sana, Kikuyu Squad. Njama, your sock debt is paid."

Together, Baba Ojore, Baba Kahuthia, and Mama Zuri decided that Kikuyu Squad should have three days of rest from the morning run. Mama Zuri wanted a week, but Baba Ojore was concerned about the boys getting soft and spending too much time away from the Mkhosi. Baba Kahuthia suggested that Kikuyu Squad ride bikes to the Six-Mark in place of the morning run. This would help them to maintain their conditioning. Baba Ojore agreed. Alton and Chandler were also required to ice and elevate their injuries three times each day. They would do this at mealtimes.

When Kikuyu Squad finished, they hobbled back to the Mkhosi. On the way back, all they talked about was Mama Zuri, how beautiful and kind she was, and how they hoped to have wives like her one day. During this conversation, Raymond mentioned offhandedly how lucky Baba Kahuthia was.

"What makes him so lucky?" Alton challenged.

Wrinkling his forehead and looking sideways at Alton, Raymond answered matter-of-factly, "Because she is his fiancé." Raymond thought that should be obvious.

Alton, Kamau, and Chandler stopped and asked in shocked surprise, "Fiancé?!"

"Yes," Raymond responded. "Didn't you see her ring? Didn't you see how they looked at each other?"

Kamau was crushed. He didn't see any of that. All he saw was Mama Zuri in all her perfection.

Up to this point, Kikuyu Squad liked and respected Baba Kahuthia. But after realizing that he had won the attention and affection of Mama Zuri, they admired him. They practically worshiped him.

Kikuyu Squad returned in time to catch the latter half of the first chapel service. They were listening to a lecture called the European Origins of Violence and Criminality. As they had done the week prior, second chapel service was used to discuss what they had learned from the speaker's message.

Throughout the remainder of the day, the story of Kamau's fight with Deiondre was told and retold dozens of times. And the story of Kikuyu Squad's run to the Never-Mark was told even more than that. The VITs of Mkhosi Kunye and Mkhosi Kuthathu learned about each other's hometowns, families, and upbringing. They had opportunities to see each other's strengths and weaknesses. The VITs didn't know it, but the seeds of lifelong friendships were being planted.

That evening, Kamau went to bed with great satisfaction. When the day began, he was surrounded by a bunch of boys he cared nothing about. And he was saddled to three boys who were destined to lose every competition they touched. However, as the day ended, he was surrounded by boys who respected and admired him and who he was learning to respect. Most importantly, he found friendship in those three boys who were destined to lose. And even if it meant losing, Kamau would rather lose with them than win alone.

The Gift Exchange (O'Leary)

Dan walked into his office to find a package on his chair. It was wrapped in brown kraft paper and topped with a red bow. The attached card read, "Another problem solved."

"What is this?" he murmured.

At just that moment, Marlene stuck her head in his office and said, "It's a package from Tim. He wanted to give it to you in person, but he has to leave town for a few days. He said it's a family emergency."

Puzzled, Dan muttered, "Thanks, Marlene." He closed the door so that he could open the package in private. It was the stolen briefcase. In the weeks that had passed since it had been stolen, Dan had focused so intently on moving the project forward, that he had forgotten about the briefcase. He also forgot about Timothy's promise to find it.

Even though he had forgotten about the briefcase, a wave of relief flooded his chest. He breathed deeply as stress and worry dissipated. Dan noticed that the case had been treated roughly. The leather was torn in some places. The latches had been pried open. The pockets inside were pulled loose of their fittings. But despite the damage, there it was. The full project report remained in the briefcase. It had clearly been rifled through by someone with filthy hands. There were human paw prints all through the report. The pages were dog-eared and out of order, but everything was there. Dan buzzed Marlene. She replied, "Yes, sir?"

Dan spoke solemnly, "Marlene, send Timothy and Daphne a nice gift. Send them a very *expensive,* nice gift. He is probably the best and most loyal friend I have in this world."

She smiled and replied, "Yes, sir!"

Acceptance, The Third Virtue

Despite their injuries, Week Three of the Akhet proved to be a turning point for Kikuyu Squad. While Kikuyu Squad was still the last squad to complete many challenges, no one had the sense that they were losing. One reason for this was that they had earned the respect of the entire Mkhosi. They had done the impossible. They had run the Never-Mark. They had done it voluntarily and with no preparation. And they never complained. Another reason is that they were no longer trying to compete against other squads. They seemed to focus so intently on developing themselves that they were oblivious to what was happening with anyone else.

For example, on the first day of Week Three the Mkhosi was learning to make fire. After demonstrating, "the Four Steps to Building a Vanguard Fire," Baba Kojo commanded, "Light 'Em Up!"

After all squads had a fire going, Baba Chinua announced the time, and Baba Kojo commanded, "Put 'Em Out!" And the fires were doused with water. Once the squads extinguished their fires, Baba Kojo commanded, "Light 'Em Up!" and the process would begin again.

All squads got faster with each new fire, except Kikuyu Squad. While most squads worked together by having each VIT do one task, Kamau made each member of Kikuyu Squad go through the entire process alone. The other members watched and made suggestions. Throughout the process, they frequently stopped to discuss strategies for completing the task more efficiently. Chandler was especially useful. He suggested two modifications that each member of Kikuyu Squad was able to practice. Eventually, each member of Kikuyu Squad became very proficient at fire craft.

Also, during Combatives Training, Kamau no longer seemed interested in whooping other members of the Mkhosi, not even Wild-Eyed Deiondre. Instead, he used Combatives Training as an opportunity to study his various opponents and to practice new techniques. He also worked intently on helping the other members of Kikuyu Squad to become better fighters.

On Monday of Week Three, the Mkhosi learned and practiced throws. Kamau made sure that, Kikuyu Squad watched one another and made suggestions for improvement. These were always stolen moments, as there was not as much time during Combatives Training. So, Kikuyu Squad began meeting during personal time to practice combatives.

SECRETS OF THE VANGUARD ORDER

Meditations on Death

There were several disturbing activities during Week Three. One of them was the Mkhosi's meditation on death. During Monday's group reflection, Baba Ojore talked to the Mkhosi about death. "Most people have an irrational fear of death. Vanguardians do not fear death. But to not fear death takes training. We must reject the mental programming of the dead world and reprogram our minds."

Few of the VITs understood what Baba Ojore was saying. Seeking clarity, Keith Duhart asked, "Baba Ojore, why do we not fear death? I don't *want* to die."

Baba Ojore responded, "Thank you for your question and your honesty, Duhart. Many times, our *wants* are irrational and irrelevant. How many remember last week when it stormed all day and we trained in the rain?"

Hands and groans went up all around the campfire.

Baba Ojore continued, "How many of you *want* it to storm tomorrow?"

No one responded.

"How many of you don't *want* it to storm tomorrow?"

A few hands went up. Baba Ojore looked at Omowale, "Ndukwe, you did not raise your hand. Do you *want* it to storm tomorrow?"

Omowale responded, "Baba Ojore, I don't think it matters. If it rains, we will train. If it doesn't rain, we will train."

Baba Ojore smiled, "That's right, soldier! We are not children groaning and whining about what we want and what we don't want. We live in the world that is, not the world that we want to be." He paused to look at the VITs, then continued, "If we *want* the moon to stay out and delay the rising of the sun so that we can get more sleep, will it?"

A few of the VITs laughed, "No, sir!"

Baba Ojore smiled, "No. It will not. If we *want* the earth to slow its revolution around the sun and give us four more weeks of summer, will it?"

Again, the VITs laughed as they responded in chorus, "No, sir!"

Baba Ojore nodded and smiled, "No. It will not." His smile faded, "And if we want to live past our allotted time, will we?"

The spirit of the Mkhosi grew solemn. There were faint murmurs from the group.

Baba Ojore responded, "No. We will not. Vanguardians… Brothers… Death is inevitable. It is the proper conclusion to life." Baba Ojore watched as the VITs pondered those words.

After a long silence, he continued, "But don't worry. We are not here to die. We are here to live. In the dead world, many people …most people… fear death. Their fear is debilitating, and because of it, they never really live. Some spend the greater portion of their lives trying to avoid death. Others spend most of their time engaged in umm… uhhh…" He searched for words. "…uhhh,"

Baba Thulani chimed in, "Self-gratification…"

Baba Ojore continued, "Yes, self-gratification." Baba Ojore smiled and nodded, "So, to live this life to the fullest, to be of the greatest service to each other and to ourselves, we must rid ourselves of irrational fear. And fear of death is one of those irrational fears."

This discussion was Mkhosi Kunye's introduction to Vanguard Meditations on Death. Throughout the remainder of the week, they engaged in exercises where each VIT, Mwalimu, and Bausi imagined his own death. They wrote newspaper articles describing fictional scenarios of their death. They wrote eulogies to be read upon the commemoration of their deaths. They engaged in mental exercises where they imagined everything they owned and everyone they loved, even themselves, being taken away.

One day, during an exercise, Charles Hall found a dead squirrel at the edge of the woods. The Mwalimu had the entire Mkhosi sit in a semicircle around the squirrel's corpse and imagine the squirrel's birth, its life, and its experience at the time of death.

Kamau had heard his father use the word "macabre" to criticize white America's fascination with death. Halloween was his preferred time of year to make this observation. Initially, he thought the Vanguard Meditations on Death were macabre. However, after a time, Kamau realized that the exercises and activities made death "normal." He began to see many aspects of death that he had never before considered. For example, he began to consider the death of non-human creatures such as animals, plants, even microorganisms. He thought about the attitude other creatures might have towards death. They clearly had an aversion to it. Everything living makes efforts to stay alive. He considered how death affected those who are left living. He began to take notice of the benefits of death. Almost everything he ate was once living. Death was necessary for his survival, for the survival of every living thing. He thought about the purifying function of death, and how death removes weakness from a group, making the group stronger.

In all, the Vanguard Meditations on Death made the concept of death less of a boogie man and more of a real aspect of life. As the concept of death became more real for Kamau, he realized that he was also developing a greater respect for both life and death.

Hunger in Mkhosi Kunye

On Tuesday of Week Three, the Mwalimu extended the morning training exercises through lunch, so the Mkhosi missed lunch. That evening, they extended evening training exercises through dinner, so they also missed evening personal time and dinner. Just before Group Reflection, the VITs decided that they should ask the Mwalimu and the Bausi why they were being denied meals. However, they were cautious. They knew that approaching the Mwalimu or Bausi in the wrong way could incur additional work, greater denial of meals, or some other hardship. This would all be couched as a "lesson" of some sort, but it was hardship, nonetheless.

They all decided that Kamau would speak on their behalf. The VITs had come to accept that, in many ways, Kamau was the best of them. He was the best fighter and the most athletic. He was one of the smartest VITs with a quick wit. And as time went on, he was demonstrating that he could be a good friend. Surprisingly, Kamau did not accept this responsibility. He said simply, "No. I am not the best VIT to represent the Mkhosi to the Mwalimu. They will listen to Bongani far better than me."

Kamau did not need to say any more. Once he pointed their attention to Bongani, everyone knew he was right. Since their very first day at Camp Furaha, Bongani was more serious and more manly than any of the VITs. Although he was the same age as the others, he was not marked by any of the boyish foolishness that exuded from the others. He was probably the only VIT that could command the respect and attention of Wild-Eyed Deiondre. And the Mwalimu would take Bongani's concern seriously.

That evening, near the end of group reflection, Bongani spoke plainly, "Baba Ojore, today we have not eaten lunch or dinner. Is there a lesson that we should be striving to learn?"

Kamau was impressed. Bongani's words were succinct and to the point. There was no hesitation, no accusation, no demand, no wry sarcasm. It was far better than he himself would have done.

It was Baba Kojo who responded, "You have not eaten because you have not provided food for yourselves. An infant whines and cries, begging for an opportunity to suckle at his mother's nipple. A man provides food and sustenance for himself, his family, and his community."

For a long time, an awkwardly long period of time, Baba Kojo stared blankly at Bongani. Bongani said nothing, for there was nothing to be said. He stared blankly off in the distance as they were taught to do during drill. Many of the VITs followed suit.

Baba Abiola broke the silence, "Are you infants?"

The response was a weak and dejected response as few VITs murmured, "No, Baba."

Baba Abiola repeated his question with force, "Are you infants?!"

The Mkhosi responded more enthusiastically, "No, Baba!"

Baba Kojo concluded the evening group reflection, "Well then, you are dismissed."

That evening Kamau's stomach gurgled until he fell asleep.

The next morning, during personal time, the VITs conspired to discover ways to feed themselves. Their idea was to seek permission to hunt for food in the woods. Bongani would make the request, but he did not like it. He thought it was ill-conceived. They didn't know how to hunt. They could not be specific as to what they were hunting for. They did not have any tools for hunting. They would not have known what to do with an animal if they were lucky enough to catch one. Then there was also the problem of scale. If they caught a bird or a rabbit, it would not be enough to feed twenty hungry VITs. Bongani, Kamau, Amari Danjuma, and Albert Dorsey raised these objections. These were leaders of four squads. The leader of Mongo squad and his squad members argued vehemently against these objections. Ultimately, the leaders of the four squads relented, primarily because as bad as the plan was, they had no alternative suggestions, and everyone knew they had to do something.

As suspected, breakfast was being replaced by an additional Instruction Set. Just before the Instruction Set began, Bongani addressed Baba Kojo who was leading the exercise, "Baba Kojo, the VITs of Mkhosi Kunye request permission to use this time to provide food and sustenance."

Baba Kojo responded with a look of shock. He murmured, "Provide food and sustenance?" His words were barely audible.

Baba Kahuthia shook his head and shrugged.

Baba Chinua mumbled, "What in the world?!"

As he observed the theatrics of their responses, Kamau pursed his lips to stifle his laughter. Few of the other VITs found this funny. They were hungry and growing aggravated.

Baba Ojore shook a look of disbelief off his face and asked, "Jekwa, how are *you* and the *VITs* going to provide food... and sustenance?"

Keeping his composure, Bongani responded flatly, "We will attempt to capture a small animal."

A look of pity overcame Baba Ojore, and he shook his head as he responded to Bongani. In his response, Baba Ojore raised every objection that Bongani, Kamau, Amari, and Albert raised to the rest of the Mkhosi. Then he concluded, "But... young men must learn to be men at some point. Yes, Jekwa, the VITs of Mkhosi Kunye can use this time to provide food and sustenance."

Without being commanded, the VITs immediately clustered into a circle, where they loosely organized themselves into their respective squads. The leaders of each squad were at the center of the circle where they could confer.

As the VITs coordinated their efforts, Baba Kahuthia spoke up over the din, "Mkhosi Kunye, you are hungry, but hunger is not starvation. And hunger will not kill you. Poison on the other hand... poison *will* kill you. As you search for food, be careful not to consume any plant, animal, insect, or fungus that is poisonous, diseased, or infected in any way. If you are uncertain, do not eat it. You bring it back here first."

With these words, Baba Kahuthia raised another concern that the VITs had not considered. How would they know if an animal they captured was safe to eat? For the twenty hungry teenagers, the question was academic. They were ravenous. They had not eaten in almost twenty-four hours. If their only hope of eating was to catch something, then that's what they would do.

The squad leaders agreed that each squad would canvas a different area of the woods to look for food. They also agreed to make no attempts at catching birds. It was seen as too difficult, and birds would not yield much meat. They decided to focus on squirrels and rabbits. They agreed to a central meeting location, meeting time, and a call that could be used to alert the other squads should they catch something.

After an hour of chasing rabbits and squirrels through the woods, the VITs learned that eating was not an easy endeavor. The VITs were too loud and too slow. And the squirrels and rabbits were not enthusiastic about being food. Many times, they did not wait to be chased. They simply ran off upon being seen.

At the end of the allotted time for breakfast, no one had captured an animal, and no one had eaten. The Mwalimu had the Mkhosi assemble in Ukumbi wa Kunye. Each VIT was given a cold, sweet, peppery drink and vitamin supplements. Baba Thulani led the Mkhosi in a discussion of what they had learned while trying to capture food.

He then talked about eating as one of the natural challenges of human beings. "Most Westerners spend their entire lives having someone else catch food for them... having someone else plant, grow, water, weed, and harvest food for them. Most Westerners never do the hard work that comes with eating."

As Baba Thulani spoke, Kamau thought about the delectable meals his mother served, and how much he loved eating at the Njama table. He reflected shamefully on how he often complained about having to go to a neighbor's house to pick up the food. He now saw that it was an easy price to pay for good food.

Baba Thulani continued, "Most Westerners spend their entire lives having someone else kill their food for them... having someone else skin, defeather, scale, disembowel, and fillet food for them. Most Westerners never do the dirty work of eating."

Baba Thulani then provided an explanation of what they should do when they catch their first animal. He described "the Four Steps to Field Dressing Game the Vanguard Way." Following that, Baba Chinua took the Mkhosi outside. He introduced the Mkhosi to traps and snares. He explained the difference between the two and provided instruction in building a fixed snare and a deadfall trap.

After the VITs had practiced making the trap and snare, Baba Ojore dispatched them a second time to "provide food and sustenance."

Although they went off with much more confidence than they had the last time, they returned with the same amount of food. That afternoon, there was no lunch provided. Instead, the VITs sat in Ukumbi wa Kunye, drinking the sweet pepper juice and eating vitamin supplements. Just before dinner, they were given personal time, during which most of them slept. Again, there was no dinner.

The next morning, the morale and energy of Mkhosi Kunye was low. The morning run was slow and labored. The VITs spoke very little. They looked lost, dejected, and a few were visibly angry. Following the morning run, the VITs checked their traps and snares. All were empty. The Mwalimu gave them pointers on positioning, on bait, and on general set-up. They made these changes during the time they would have normally eaten breakfast. Each squad was given permission to set one additional trap or snare. There were now a total of fifteen traps and snares distributed throughout the woods.

Just before lunch time, the Mkhosi checked the traps. All were empty. But two traps, one set by Yoruba Squad, and the other set by Mongo Squad, had bait missing and animal dung where the bait had been. In both cases, the triggering mechanism was not sensitive enough. Both traps were adjusted and re-baited.

Since there was no food captured, there was no lunch. Following lunch, Baba Ojore appeared with a wild rabbit in his left hand. Many in the Mkhosi were absurd in their excitement. They had forgotten all discipline: singing, dancing, falling out of formation. Kamau could not believe his eyes. They seemed to have forgotten all their training of the past three weeks. He looked at Kikuyu Squad to be sure they were steadfast in their discipline. And they were. He also noticed that Zulu Squad had not succumbed to foolishness. Bongani's expression was impassive, but Wild-Eyed Deiondre had such a look of disgust, Kamau would not have been surprised if he had begun spanking the VITs who got out of line.

Baba Abiola's voice rang out, "Mkhosi Kunye! Give me twenty."

Kikuyu Squad, Zulu Squad and the others joined the rabble of Mkhosi Kunye as they regained their discipline. After eighty pushups, interspersed with three lectures on discipline, Mkhosi Kunye was permitted to stand in formation.

SECRETS OF THE VANGUARD ORDER

Baba Ojore was amused. He smiled as he spoke, "You think this rabbit is one that you caught, don't you?" A few VITs could not control their faces as they smiled through pursed lips. Michael Hedrick and James Dozier were not even trying to control their faces. They were outright grinning.

Baba Ojore continued, "You think the fact that I am holding this rabbit means that you are going to eat, don't you?" No one responded. So, he urged them, "Tell the truth."

Still wearing that stupid grin, James Dozier nodded as he responded, "Yes, Baba!"

Baba Ojore continued smiling for a moment. Then suddenly, his face was straight, and he snapped, "Well it doesn't! Now give me ten, Dozier. And get that foolish grin off your face!"

Mkhosi Kunye joined James Dozier in his punishment. They were hungry and weak, and the push-ups took a very long time. After forty pushups and two lectures on acceptance, Mkhosi Kunye was back in formation.

Baba Ojore walked among the ranks. "Soon, your traps will reward you with prey. It will be your job to convert that prey into food." As he walked, Kamau noticed the strange way that he held the rabbit. He grabbed the rabbit by its neck with his right hand. He held the rabbit's hind feet with his left hand. As he walked, he kept the rabbit's head pointed towards the ground. "When you capture an animal in a trap or snare, the first step to converting that prey into food is killing it."

As Baba Ojore said the word, "killing," he quickly pulled the hind legs upwards. There was an audible cracking sound, and the rabbit went limp. The VITs gasped in shock. Baba Ojore handed the rabbit to Baba Thulani who produced a large knife from somewhere in his BDUs, severed the rabbit's head, tied the rabbit's hind legs, and hung it upside down on a nearby tree. He performed these actions very quickly.

As Baba Thulani prepared the rabbit for food, Baba Ojore narrated, "Vanguardians field dress an animal in four steps. Step one is to convert. Here we convert the animal to meat. We catch it, kill it, remove the head and feet, and drain the blood." While describing the four steps, Baba Ojore pointed out things to consider when field dressing such as the method of death, the outside temperature, and the amount of time between the animal's death and the butchering. He explained how these various factors impacted whether the animal would be good for food.

Baba Thulani worked as quickly as Baba Ojore spoke. "Step two is to skin. Here we remove the feathers and fur." Baba Ojore explained other uses for feathers, fur, and skin and explained why they might need to be saved, depending on the circumstances.

Baba Thulani was removing and inspecting the internal organs as Baba Ojore announced, "Step three is to disembowel. Here, we remove the internal organs." Once the internal organs were removed, the Mwalimu encouraged the VITs to inspect the carcass and the organs. Baba Kahuthia and Baba Abiola pointed out the heart, lungs, liver, and stomach and showed the VITs how to identify each.

After the Mkhosi examined the organs, Baba Ojore explained that inspection of organs was important as it was one way to determine if an animal had a disease or infection.

By the time Baba Ojore concluded, "Step four is to butcher and prep for cooking." The rabbit no longer resembled a rabbit. It looked like meat that was ready for the grill. Kamau stared blankly, uncertain of what he should feel about this transformation.

His spell was broken by Baba Kahuthia, "Gentlemen, we take no undue pleasure in killing. Now, we will kill. In fact, we do kill. And we do it because it is necessary for our survival. This simple process of converting prey to food is one that our ancestors did almost every time they ate. Any apprehension or discomfort you feel is because Yurugu has built a wall between us and the natural world. No, Vanguardians do not take any undue pleasure in killing. But it is important to us. It is important because it reminds us of our place in the natural order of things. It reminds us that we are capable of taking care of ourselves. We are not living like domesticated dogs relying on a disinterested master to feed us kibble when it suits him. It reminds us that the food we eat comes from other living, breathing beings. And it reminds us that we need to live humbly and to respect life."

Raymond's Dinner

Between lunch and dinner, the Mwalimu allowed the VITs to check their traps. They also provided guidance as the VITs made modifications to the traps. This time, the modifications were minor. Baba Chinua mentioned to Mongo Squad that traps are rarely active during the heat of the day. Dawn and dusk are the best times for catching rabbits. That is when they are most active. He also mentioned that it is best not to check traps too frequently as they had been doing. Too much human activity would often scare away prey.

When others expressed frustration at not catching anything, Mongo Squad shared what Baba Chinua had told them. This gave the VITs hope that they might still eat soon.

Friday morning, the VITs missed their third breakfast. This missed meal was partly their own fault. The Mwalimu gave them permission to check their traps during their morning personal time. The VITs believed that if they had been able to trap any food, they would be permitted to field dress it and eat it. However, drawing on the information provided by Mongo Squad, the squad leaders decided that they should check their traps less and only after dawn or after dusk. Checking the traps before breakfast would likely mean they were scaring away potential prey.

This decision was made the night before, and it was far from unanimous. Kamau and Bongani led the effort. The opposition was fierce because this plan guaranteed that they would miss another breakfast. Kamau argued that missing one breakfast was far better than missing three meals, which they were likely to do if they scared away food that morning.

But it was not his reasoning that won over the Mkhosi. He had the support of Kikuyu Squad because he was their leader. He had the support of Zulu Squad because he was aligned with Bongani. He was still enjoying the unmitigated support of Fulani Squad, which he had earned ever since he cowed Little Bird. As for Yoruba Squad, they were split. Carl Lofton and Amari Danjuma were supportive, but Kamal Ofori and Basheeru Chiriga were not. They eventually went along because Kamau extended them enough flattery to make them feel good about themselves.

Ironically, it was Mongo Squad that was staunchest in their opposition. The very VITs who provided the critical information did not trust it. *What gives with them?* Kamau thought. After he had tried sound reason, emotional appeals, flattery, chumming it up, and all other methods of influence that he knew, Kamau threatened them into submission. He said simply, "If I have to go one more day without eating because someone in this Mkhosi is either too weak or too stupid to see good reason, I am going to beat someone until my belly is full." With these last words, he stared intently at the members of Mongo Squad. They each fidgeted nervously, and not one of them returned his gaze.

Bongani allowed Kamau's words to sink in, then he asked, "So, are we agreed?" And they agreed.

The Mwalimu allowed the adjustment. The Mkhosi's patience was rewarded. Of the fifteen traps, three had rabbits. The VITs were ecstatic. In part because they would be able to eat soon, but mostly because they had succeeded in trapping food for themselves.

Baba Ojore led the Mkhosi through a dense section of woods that opened into a large clearing. At the edge of the clearing was a structure, a wooden rabbitry. Kamau's eyes grew large. He had never seen so many rabbits in one place before. There was an array of wooden cages. The cages were stacked three cages high and ten cages long. Each cage held two white rabbits. Not far from the rabbitry were four worktables, next to each was a wooden post. There were knives, gloves, water, and buckets at each table.

Baba Ojore announced, "Kikuyu Squad, step forward. Each of you should grab one rabbit from a hole and proceed to a dressing station."

Kamau and Alton were excited. They ran to the rabbitry. Kamau did not notice how reluctant Raymond and Chandler were. He was too eager to eat. At his dressing station, Baba Abiola worked with Kamau. Even though he was overcome with hunger, the process was more difficult than he thought it would be. First, the rabbit scratched at him ferociously. Baba Abiola showed Kamau how to hold the rabbit such that his legs were away from Kamau's arm. After a time, Kamau got the hang of it. And once the rabbit was in his hands, he could not see it as food. He hesitated, and Baba Abiola saw it.

Looking at him empathetically, Baba Abiola said, "Kamau, if you do not want to kill this rabbit, you do not have to. We'll make other provisions for your lunch and dinner this evening."

"Yes, Baba."

Baba Abiola continued, "But before you decide not to kill this rabbit, remember that…" Baba Abiola heard a sharp crack.

Kamau looked at him squarely, "I understand Baba." He then placed the dead rabbit on the worktable, took a knife and continued dressing it.

Baba Abiola nodded, "Okay." He then talked Kamau through the dressing process.

Alton, who was being guided by Baba Chinua, was making good progress. Chandler was being guided by Baba Thulani, and although he was making progress, it was slow progress. On two occasions, he turned his head and tried to vomit. He might have succeeded if his stomach wasn't empty from three days of fasting. As it were, he simply filled his mouth with the wretched taste of bile. But he did not complain. He kept working.

Raymond was guided by Baba Kojo, but he never found it within himself to kill his rabbit. Initially, he tried to summon the courage. He tried to override his care and compassion for the animal. But it was to no avail. After a few minutes of internal struggle, he realized that he would rather be hungry than to kill. So, Raymond sat holding his rabbit while the rest of Kikuyu Squad dressed their meat.

After Kikuyu Squad processed their rabbits, the remaining squads did the same. Working one squad at a time, the Mwalimu guided the VITs through the process. Baba Ojore continued to give pointers, identify ways of expediting the process, and make notes about safety and the unique features of the rabbits being processed. The rest of the Mkhosi watched and listened. Aside from Raymond, three other VITs did not process their rabbits. These were Danny Echols from Mongo Squad, James Dozier from Fulani Squad, and Basheeru Chirigia from Yoruba Squad. Everyone from Zulu Squad processed their rabbits.

That afternoon, lunch was served. In fact, it was more than lunch. It was a feast. It was the largest meal that had been served at the Akhet. The portions were not large. In fact, they were smaller than normal portions, but there was a great diversity of food. There was even pound cake and peach cobbler served for dessert. Akhet meals never included dessert. To ensure they had enough time to enjoy the feast, the VITs were given an extra thirty minutes for lunch.

Everyone was permitted to eat except Raymond, Danny, James, and Basheeru. These were the four VITs that did not process their rabbits. They sat at a separate table, and were given the sweet, peppery juice and vitamin supplements. Baba Ojore joined them, "Young men, you are not being punished because you did not dress your rabbits. We want you to understand and experience what it means to provide for yourselves and for others. Do you understand?"

After they reluctantly acknowledged their understanding, Baba Ojore replied, "OK. I know you don't like it, but it is important that you understand it. I will sit with you and forego lunch as well."

A few tables away, Kamau, Alton, and Chandler were just sitting down to their dinner. It was the first time that Raymond was not at Kamau's side for a meal. Kamau looked and saw Raymond sitting with the other VITs. He also noticed that Baba Ojore and the other Mwalimu were not eating. He stared blankly and murmured, "No." At just that time, Alton was raising a dinner roll to his mouth. Still staring blankly, Kamau smacked the roll from Alton's hand and repeated more firmly, "No."

Alton protested, "Kamau, what's wrong with you, man?!"

Kamau seemed to be broken from his trance. "I'm sorry, Alton." He then looked at Alton and Chandler, "Are we one squad?"

They replied emphatically, "Yes, sir!"

He pressed them, "Are we one squad when it is convenient, or are we also one squad when it is hard?"

They were beginning to get his meaning. Alton looked over at Raymond, who was oblivious to this conversation. He then spoke forcefully, "He should have killed that rabbit, Kamau! I need to eat!"

Kamau replied coolly, "Yes, Alton. We all need to eat. But Raymond needs our brotherhood." Kamau led them as they sought permission to return the food. Normally, this was anathema as food was never wasted at the Akhet. However, the Mwalimu allowed an exception in this case.

The three then joined Raymond, Danny, James, Basheeru, and Baba Ojore. Although members from the other squads saw Kikuyu Squad join Raymond, none of them were moved to join their respective squad member. Kamau made a mental note of this, but he said nothing. At one point during the meal, Baba Ojore commented in an offhanded way, "Passion is slavery. We must continue to learn restraint."

Following lunch and between Instruction Sets, Raymond, Danny, James, and Basheeru were given another opportunity to field dress a rabbit. Everyone did so except for Raymond. For the remainder of the Instruction Sets, Alton was livid with Raymond. He knew that Raymond's failure would mean yet another missed meal. During their personal time, Kikuyu Squad discussed Raymond's dilemma. As Raymond tried to explain his opposition to killing "an innocent rabbit," Chandler demonstrated the illogic of Raymond's position.

Chandler asked, "You eat chicken, beef, fish, turkey, duck... Do you eat duck?"

"Yes. I have eaten duck before."

"Those are all animals. I don't know what moral code makes them innocent, but I imagine they are as innocent as the rabbits." Chandler's words suggested that Raymond was a hypocrite. However, his tone was so impassive, so logical, and he himself was so nonjudgmental, that Raymond never took offense.

Alton said nothing at all, which is probably a good thing. Instead, he bit his tongue and scowled at Raymond the entire time. Kamau said relatively little. He focused on positioning himself between Alton and Raymond to make sure that they did not come to blows.

Chandler continued, "So your issue is not that you are opposed to animals being killed. You are opposed to doing the killing. Is that correct?"

Raymond hesitated, "I am not sure."

"Some people are opposed to animals being killed for food. In response they often adopt vegan diets. As I understand it, they don't want to be responsible for causing an animal pain." At this point, Chandler sounded like a university professor, which is probably for the best, as it prevented him from being accusatory as he spoke to Raymond. "Now I am not here to judge the morality or ethics of the vegan, but the irony is that there is scientific evidence that plants also feel pain."

At this, Kamau, Raymond, and even Alton jerked their heads towards Chandler and stared in disbelief.

Kamau added reflectively, "Wow. Well, if that's true, then causing pain is completely unavoidable. Either we cause pain to other creatures in order to survive, or we cause ourselves pain in the process of dying."

Raymond added, "I suppose that is another way to understand acceptance. Many of the 'bad' things that we run from—death, pain, discomfort, work—are all normal parts of living. Rather than running from them, we should just accept them for what they are."

Alton responded sarcastically, "How about hunger. How much longer do I have to accept that?"

Kamau grabbed him and wrestled him to the ground. "You sound like me, Big Man!" The four tussled and bit. With the tension gone, they talked and played for the remainder of their personal time.

That evening at dinner, everyone ate except for Kikuyu Squad, the Mwalimu, and Baba Ojore. Tonight, the VITs were served the rabbit that they had processed. There were four rabbit dishes: rabbit cacciatore, southern fried rabbit, rabbit confit, and slow cooked rabbit stew. Raymond watched everyone sit down to eat. Then he looked at Kikuyu Squad. No one complained. Even Alton's hostility seemed to have subsided. Yet, he realized that he could not hold out forever. At some point, they would need to eat. He would need to eat. Was that rabbit's life more valuable than his own? He spoke to Kamau, "I'm ready."

Kamau asked no questions. He knew immediately what Raymond meant. He stood and commanded, "Squad." The others stood with him. Kamau approached Baba Kahuthia, "Baba Kahuthia, Kikuyu Squad requests permission to provide food and sustenance."

Baba Kahuthia nodded. There was a trace of pride on his face. He turned to Baba Ojore, "Baba Ojore, Kikuyu Squad requests permission to provide food and sustenance."

Baba Ojore replied curtly, "It's about time. Permission granted. Let's go."

Baba Kahuthia, Baba Ojore, and Kikuyu Squad left Ukumbi wa Kunye in a column of two. As they left, the entire Mkhosi erupted in cheers and shouts of "Yebo!"

An Unwelcome Messenger (O'Leary)

Timothy O'Leary stepped reverently into the garden courtyard. A dark complexioned, old man, with short-cropped, grey hair walked by and smiled at him brightly, "Good day, young fella!" He waived his wrinkled hand at Timothy as he passed.

Timothy returned the smile and bowed slightly, "Good day, sir." As he took a seat on a nearby bench, he felt out of place. He was younger than anyone present. He was still wearing his business suit, which was very different from the clothing worn by the men and women in the courtyard. Worst of all, he was not invited to be there. He had come of his own accord.

As he sat waiting, an abnormally tall, abnormally lean, bald man walked towards him briskly. The man, who appeared to be Timothy's age, was at least six feet eleven inches tall and could not have weighed more than 200 pounds. He was a very thin man. His face was cold and angry, and he spoke curtly, "You should not be here. This is a violation of protocol that compromises you and many others."

Timothy kept calm, ignoring the chastisement. "Yes, I understand. My message is short. I will be brief. There was no other way to deliver it."

Thin man's eyes narrowed as he leaned forward. He looked as though he wanted to physically attack Timothy. O'Leary sensed this threat but kept his composure while watching the man intently.

Thin man continued to examine Timothy but said nothing. After a time, he nodded, apparently satisfied that he had learned something from this strange staring contest. "InDuna will see you. But make it quick. You should not be here!"

Timothy nodded. As thin man gangled off, a normal-sized man approached. He was stern and powerfully built. Clean cut with a receding hairline that was greying on the temples, this man was about fifty years of age. As he approached Timothy, he narrowed his eyes and greeted him, "Nnamdi Edozie! My brother! How are you?!"

Timothy greeted him in return, "Baba Taharka, thanks for agreeing to see me. I know this visit is a violation of protocol. I will be brie…"

Taharka interrupted, "It is good to see you, Warrior. You look strong and you are in good health! Come, break bread with me."

As they walked, Taharka engaged in all the pleasantries of civilized discourse. He asked about Daphne, Timothy's job, his health, and his emotional satisfaction. He also shared with Timothy how his own life and work were progressing. By the time they sat down to eat, he cut straight to the point, "Brother, why are you here?"

Timothy explained, "The expeditionary project that TechInnoGen is planning has been moved up from the initial commence date. This is a very recent change."

Taharka showed no surprise or emotional response. "So, when is the project set to launch?"

Timothy responded, "One month ago, tomorrow."

Now, Taharka showed a bit of surprise, "They've been on the ground for a month?

"Yes, sir!"

Taharka paused, gathered himself, and began thinking aloud, "So, they accelerated this project by over six and one-half months?" Considering this, Taharka turned to Timothy and inquired further, "*A person who is in too much of a hurry stubs his toe.* Do you think this project is likely to succeed?"

"*If the rabbit is your enemy, admit that he can sprint fast.* Even when they fail in their evil machinations, they fall forward." Timothy paused to gauge Taharka's response. He continued, "Columbus was lost, but he still ushered in the demise of the 500 Nations. Rochambeau was defeated at Vertières, but the French still robbed Haiti of its..."

Taharka interrupted, "I get it. I understand. Asante Sana, Warrior. You should hurry back. Do not reach out to us again before this is over. We will obtain everything we need through surveillance."

"Asante Sana, Baba."

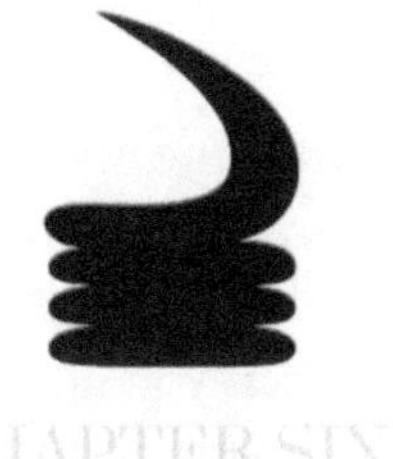

CHAPTER SIX

New Challenges, New Strengths, New Men

Service and Sacrifice, The Fourth Virtue

Among the VITs of Mkhosi Kunye, Week Three came to be known as "The Week of Starvation." Ironically, they each looked at the week with fondness. As if they were not already brimming with confidence, the experience of going multiple days without food and the newfound ability to catch and prepare food if needed, made them feel invincible.

By the fourth week of the Akhet, it was difficult, at times, to distinguish the VITs from the Mwalimu. The VITs had grown serious. They were much more solemn faced. They wore a steely-eyed determination, and they embraced hardship. When the Mwalimu increased the morning run to the Four-Mark, they beat their chests and gave shouts of "Yebo!" They embraced Combatives Training. It was almost impossible to get them to stop training. Following the lead set by Kamau and Kikuyu Squad, other squads began training during personal time.

The instruction for Week Four centered around service and sacrifice. Throughout the week, the Mwalimu emphasized the role of Vanguardians as leaders. Vanguardians were expected to be leaders in their homes and communities, and for their race. Baba Ojore stressed the way that Vanguardian leadership differed from leadership in the dead world. "As Vanguardians, we are leaders. And as leaders, we serve the people. We sacrifice for the people. In the dead world, the people are used as footstools and servants for the so-called leaders."

Kamau had his own challenge throughout Week Four. It seemed as though Baba Kahuthia and the other Mwalimu were harder on him than normal. Bongani was also being targeted.

During PT on the first day, while the Mkhosi sat in the Vanguard Chair, Bausi Ojore said, "Lofton, you're a funny man. Come out front and tell us a joke."

Smiling and speaking from his "seated" position, Carl spoke cheerfully, "Bausi Ojore, if you're African when you go in the bathroom and African when you come out, what are you in the bathroom?"

Bausi Ojore answered, "I'm an African, Son."

Carl smiled, "No, sir. European." He laughed as he repeated himself, "You're a-peein'. Get it?"

The Mwalimu smiled and a few of the VITs snickered.

Baba Ojore smiled and looked over the Mkhosi. "Njama, you thought that was funny. Do you know how I know?"

Kamau replied, "How do you know, sir?"

Bausi Ojore's smile faded, and his tone grew stern, "Because you are smiling. Now, as we continue and for the remainder of this day, the following VITs will practice controlling their expressions: Njama, Jekwa, Danjuma, Hall, and Winford." Bausi Ojore named the captains of the five squads.

He continued, "When your face betrays your heart, you are defeated. When your face betrays your mind, you are defeated. A defeated leader cannot lead a successful squad." He spoke a Kiswahili phrase to the entire Mkhosi, "Mnyama anayeongoza anapokuwa kilema, kundi hushindwa kufika malishoni." For the next five minutes, while sitting in the Vanguard Chair, Baba Ojore had the Mkhosi memorize that phrase. Later that evening, at Group Reflection, they would learn the translation of that Kenyan proverb, "When the leading animal is lame, the herd fails to get to the pasture."

After Mkhosi Kunye had memorized the phrase, Baba Ojore announced, "Mkhosi Kunye will do twenty pushups on my count, each time a squad leader's face betrays his heart. These twenty pushups belong to Njama." Following the pushups, Mkhosi Kunye again sat in the Vanguard Chair and Baba Ojore turned to Carl, "Lofton, that last joke was good. Tell us another one."

Carl again spoke cheerfully, "Bausi Ojore, why does Snoop Dog use an umbrella?"

Baba Ojore smiled, "I'm not sure about that one Brother Lofton. Why does Snoop Dog use an umbrella?"

Carl replied, "For drizzle."

This time the Mwalimu laughed openly and heartily. Again, some of the squad leaders snickered. And again, the Mkhosi did pushups. This Vanguard Game went on throughout the remainder of PT.

Baba Ojore enjoyed this Vanguard Game. He had them play it every day that week. On Day Two, the VITs laid prone in the Warriors Edge as they were peppered with personal and hurtful insults. Yet, they worked to remain impassive. On Day Three, they held the plank position as they were showered with news stories and historical accounts of horrific suffering, death, disease, and destruction. Yet, they worked to remain impassive. On Day Four, they meditated as they were subjected to loud crashes, the sound of falling trees, blood curdling screams, and other startling, random noises. Yet, they worked to remain impassive.

After a week of these drills, the VITs of Mkhosi Kunye were becoming very good at controlling their facial expressions. They were adopting the habit of controlling their expressions automatically and without being told. Kamau was beginning to understand how and why his father was so skilled at appearing indifferent and impervious to anything happening around him.

During Week Four, Mkhosi Kunye extended their Combatives Training to include defensive maneuvers in hand-to-hand combat. They learned counters, blocks, and avoiding maneuvers. They boxed on Saturday and Sunday to hone each other and the VITs of the other Mkhosis. All the VITs were becoming proficient fighters. They no longer feared being hit. They did not lose their composure when attacked unexpectedly. They were less wild and less emotional when fighting. Even Wild-Eyed Deiondre, had learned to control his wild impulses and to channel his rage. As fighters, they were very formidable. Kamau was still the best fighter in the Mkhosi. However, the distance between him and the others was not quite as great as when they first began.

He was still more athletic and a bit more courageous. But this is not what set Kamau apart from the others. What most distinguished Kamau from the other VITs was the attitude with which he fought. He fought with joy. He seemed to genuinely enjoy the act of engaging in physical combat. Raymond noticed, and mentioned to Alton and Chandler, that Kamau's eyes lit up when it was his turn to fight. He sometimes smiled after being struck by an opponent. And he was almost giddy after winning a bout. When Kamau fought, there was no stress, no angst, no doubt, there was just joy.

During Week Four, the Mkhosi also added to their knowledge of trapping by learning to forage for food. They were taught to identify edible plants and mushrooms. They learned which seeds, leaves, roots, and flowers were safe for consumption. They also learned the more common plants and mushrooms to avoid. One evening, their dinner was comprised solely of plants gathered by foraging. A few of the VITs gave that food back to nature in an inglorious fashion.

That week, Mkhosi Kunye read a book about the horrors of television. The book described how television viewing led to a decreased attention span, insensitivity to real crisis issues, excessive attention to unimportant phenomenon, and a host of other social and psychological maladies. Kamau had heard many of these arguments from his father, and it was one reason that the Njamas watched very little television. What was interesting was that Kamau had always thought that TV was a conspiracy against the Black Man. At least that is what he heard from Jabari Njama. So, it was surprising to see that these arguments were being made by a white professor. The author of the book argued that TV was a conspiracy against *everybody*. Kamau asked Baba Ojore about this. "Baba Ojore, is television bad for Black people or is it bad for everyone?"

Baba Ojore looked at him thoughtfully. He had a sense of where this question was coming from, as he had heard it before. "Njama, if you swim in sewage, will you get dirty?"

It was a repulsive metaphor, but Kamau did not recoil. He replied simply, "Yes, Baba. Anyone in that sewage would get dirty."

"Well, Son, that is what we live in now. Western society is analogous to sewage. The more we immerse ourselves in it, the more corrupted we become." A few of the VITs gave nods of understanding. Baba Ojore continued, "We talk about the negative impact television, industrial food, or other Western practices have on us as African people, but that does not mean they *only* impact us as African people. We work to avoid these corrupting influences because we desire a better life for ourselves."

Near the end of that week, the Mkhosi memorized the poem, "Phenomenal Woman." A few of the VITs took issue with the poem, protesting that they were training to be men and didn't need to know anything about being phenomenal women. Baba Kahuthia asked the VITs, "What type of women do you want in your life?"

Charles Hall replied enthusiastically, "One like Mama Zuri!" To this, there were cheers, hoots, amens, and attaboys.

Baba Kahuthia smiled and nodded, "Yes, she is a desirable woman. In fact, she's phenomenal." He turned serious, "And if we are going to be men who select good African women, who guide our women in fruitful directions, who raise our little girls to be strong members of our race, then we need to study women."

Jomo W. Mutegi

The Last Straw (O'Leary)

Timothy arrived at work early and hung his blazer on the back of his office door. He expected that this day would be a busy one. The first thing he did was call his wife, Daphne. "Hey, Sweetheart. How are you?"

He laughed, "I know it's only been twenty minutes. But I forgot to tell you that I will meet Anand today for lunch. We will probably meet off site at the Farmacy Café. I am sure he wants some privacy. I haven't spoken with him in a while, and we have a lot of catching up to do. I expect he has a lot to tell me about how his work is coming along." He paused to listen, "Yes, Love, I will be back at the usual time. Bye bye."

That afternoon, Timothy and Anand walked to the Farmacy Café together. As they walked in, Timothy noticed two strongly built men sitting at a table near the door. This is where he normally sat. Seeing the seat was occupied, Timothy smiled uneasily and began scanning the café for another seat. With this, the two men arose and one of them said to Timothy, "Please, sir, take this seat. We were just leaving." Timothy shook the man's hand, thanking him as the two left the café.

They sat down to lunch, and Timothy noticed that Anand looked more ragged than when they had met a week ago. "Anand, my guess is that things are not improving on the project. Why don't you tell me where you are, and I will tell you what I see."

Anand began, "Thank you, Timothy, for meeting with me. As I mentioned, the first problem is the crew. We have one former astronaut who was an Air Force Colonel and one former Marine fighter pilot who trained as an astronaut, but he never had a mission. That is it! Two men who are marginal scientists at best! Yes, they were accomplished military men, but as scientists, they are no good!" Anand calmed himself, "They are not best suited for this job."

Timothy nodded to show he understood, "Yes, I'm with you. Go on."

Anand continued, "The remaining eight are women with no space training. And of those eight women, only four are scientists. There is a biological engineer, a biologist with expertise in biocommunication, a medical doctor, and an ecologist. The other four, I have no idea what they do. They look like hot, body building women. But they do not know science. They do not understand how the spaceship works. They cannot fix systems if they go down. They have never lived in zero gravity. They have no skills that are useful to this project."

Timothy listened intently. "How has the crew's poor qualifications impacted the project so far."

Anand hesitated and began to speak, but he stopped himself.

177

SECRETS OF THE VANGUARD ORDER

Timothy allowed himself to sound exasperated, "Look, Anand, I get that you are in a horrible situation. But I cannot help you if I am in the dark. So, you need to decide that either you are going to deal with the bad consequences of telling me what is going on and receive help, or you're going to deal with the bad consequences of *not* telling me what's going on and receiving no help!"

Anand shook his head in approval, "Yes, I understand." He took a deep breath. "Okay. There are many insights that we can get from this planet. One is biocommunication. We have many examples of biocommunication here on earth, of course, but this planet seems to have a much more highly integrated interspecies communication system. This is the first thing that we should explore."

Timothy stared intently at Anand and nodded, encouraging him to continue. Anand continued, "The crew is supposed to be gathering samples of flora and fauna from the planet. They are supposed to conduct a set of basic experiments to determine which specimens to bring back for further analysis. They are supposed to map the topography of the geographic region from which the specimens were collected. They are supposed to collect environmental data from that region. You know, winds, precipitation, sunlight, temperature, etc. We need this data on the climate to help study the specimens when they return.

Timothy nodded that he understood. "So, what is actually happening?"

Anand responded curtly, "Nothing! Nothing is happening. Nothing that is supposed to happen is happening. At first, I thought they were just inept. Their journals were sloppy. Their data collection was haphazard. They were not methodical in how they canvassed the region. Now, I wonder, maybe they are just sloppy. Maybe they do not care enough to do good work. Whatever the cause, they are wasting lot of money. They are putting their own lives at risk."

Timothy looked puzzled, "Anand, sloppy data collection and management is a bad practice, but it's not life threatening."

Anand responded sharply, "You go wander all over a strange planet, you are risking your life." He lowered his voice to a whisper, "And this planet has sentient beings. Our scout team saw evidence. We placed EVC Fitzroy in an unoccupied area. But these yahoos, they wander aimlessly each day, getting closer and closer to native populations."

Timothy stared at him piercingly. "Anand, stop giving me information piecemeal. Either tell me everything, or let it go."

Anand's shoulders slumped. "I don't want to make accusations…" Timothy rolled his eyes and prepared to leave. Anand blurted out, "I think they are trying to colonize the native population!" Now, he had Timothy's attention. Anand continued, "I said they wander close to the native population. That is not true.

They have interacted with the native population a lot. There are growing native encampments just outside our landing zone. Two different times, crew members accompanied new encampment natives when they attacked other natives."

Timothy flopped back in his seat, dumbfounded. "Wow! This is a catastrophe. How did you learn this?"

Anand's eyes grew wide, "Timothy, you cannot tell anyone. I will lose my job. A lot of data is collected, but much of it requires high clearance. I…"

Timothy cut him off, "Say no more."

Anand pleaded, "I know! But even without that, poor research practice and poor project management should be enough. I have been trying to tell anyone who will listen."

Timothy inquired further, "Has Dan been any help?"

"Timothy, I know he is your friend, but Dan is very bad man… a very bad man. He is a part of the problem. First, he hired these incompetents against the advice of the project team. Then, he rushed the project beyond anything that is reasonable. Then, he is nowhere to be seen. How do you run a project, but you never come to the Command Center? Now, we raise issue, he send new people, add confusion."

The longer Anand spoke, the angrier he got. And as he lost his cool, he also lost his ability to moderate his Hindi accent. By this point in the conversation, Timothy had to focus intently to make out what Anand was saying. Timothy asked a question to slow him down, "So that must be the cause of the chaos in CC2?"

"Yes. Very much. Each new addition comes with different personality, expertise, security clearance, and with no background knowledge. The busyness you see is not managing the mission, it is managing the people Dan keeps sending to cover for a poorly run project."

Again, Timothy nodded, "I see." He paused, then asked in a slow deliberate way, "You mentioned that the crew had a military background. Did they have any weapons?"

Anand's eyes widened, and he raised his hands in exclamation, "Oh my goodness! I almost forgot. In the beginning, there was a big push for weapons. In fact, Dan wanted so many weapons that he began removing research equipment from the cargo manifest. We laughed. It was so foolish. So, we refused all firearms, explosives, and incendiaries. So, if they need weapons (which they should not), they will have to use sticks and stones."

Timothy looked at his watch, "Look Anand, it's getting late. But we need to get moving on a solution. What is one change we could make, that you believe would help?"

Anand responded immediately, "Get Dan into the Command Center. If you can do that, it will solve many problems. In his absence, I should be the lead. But they do not listen to me."

"Don't worry, Anand. I am on it. It may take two or three days, but I will make it happen."

Loyalty, The Fifth Virtue

As the Akhet progressed into Week Five, the VITs continued to receive new challenges. Kikuyu Squad rose to meet some of these challenges, like the new morning run that was now increased to the Five-Mark. Other challenges, however, set them back. On the first day of Week Five, Baba Ojore assembled the Mkhosi at the kambi for the start of Combatives Training. This was strange, as no formal training had ever taken place at the kambi.

Once the VITs were in formation, Baba Abiola went into a tent and threw many of the provisions out into the open courtyard. The provisions just happened to belong to Jayson Nelson. Jayson stared blankly as though he was unfazed by his provisions being violated in such a disrespectful manner.

Baba Ojore and Baba Kojo walked in and around Jayson's provisions, periodically stepping on them. They both seemed not to notice but, by this time, Kamau knew better. Jayson's discipline was extremely impressive. Amidst all the offense to his provisions, his face remained impassive. Baba Ojore spoke, "Winford, show me the weapons in these provisions."

Gerard Winford stepped forward and surveyed the provisions. He moved things about, lifting the sleeping bag and rummaging through the duffle. After a few moments, he stood and faced the Bausi. "Baba Ojore, there is no weapon in these provisions." Gerard Winford's words were strong and clearly spoken. He stood straight as an arrow with a quiet confidence. Gerard was the toughest member of Mongo Squad and was well-respected by the VITs. He was clear-headed and strong. He never seemed out of sorts. It is for this reason that what happened next was so startling.

Just as Gerard announced to Baba Ojore that there was no weapon among the provisions, Baba Kojo picked up a makeshift pillow. Most of the VITs converted their small stuff sacks into makeshift pillows. They took the stuff sack that would normally hold their sleeping bags and stuffed it with clothes. This gave them something to prop up their heads while sleeping. As Baba Kojo held the sack in his right hand, he grabbed the back of Gerard's head with his left hand. Baba Kojo then yanked Gerard's head forward in a violent sweeping motion, forcing his face into the pillow. Baba Ojore's head snapped in the direction of Baba Kojo, and for a brief moment, he looked surprised.

Gerard began to struggle. The VITs heard muffled grunts and screams coming from the pillow. Gerard's arms flailed about wildly and without purpose.

Baba Kojo snarled as he barked, "If there are no weapons among these provisions, Winford, then why are you struggling to breathe?" As Gerard continued to struggle, Baba Kojo addressed the VITs, "Your failure to recognize a weapon or any type of threat could mean the difference between life and death for you and your loved ones. Now, let's see what becomes of Winford's failure."

At those last words, Kamau's eyes widened. He tried to control his response, but he could not. Neither could the other VITs. They grew uneasy. Baba Kojo held fast as Gerard continued to struggle. Kamau expected, in fact he hoped, that Baba Ojore would intervene, but he did not. Baba Kojo continued holding Gerard. Raymond nudged Kamau and whispered desperately, "Shouldn't we help him?"

Dumbfounded, Kamau simply responded, "I don't know."

Again, Baba Kojo spoke to the Mkhosi, "Your next breath is your most important. Don't let a cavalier attitude cause you to miss it."

The VITs were clearly concerned. Many had dropped their looks of impassivity. A few stared, slack-jawed, and others seemed to be gathering the nerve to rescue Gerard. At the same time, Gerard's muffled screams and uncontrolled flailing stopped.

Thinking Gerard had passed out, Kamau stepped out of formation and moved towards him. Kikuyu Squad began to follow. Kamau had taken no more than two steps, when Gerard struck Baba Kojo's chest with a left hook. Still snarling, Baba Kojo dropped the pillow and released Gerard.

Baba Ojore shook his head and exhaled heavily, "It took you long enough, Winford." He then commanded Mkhosi Kunye, "Back in formation!" As Kamau returned to formation, he noticed that Bongani and Zulu Squad had also moved towards Gerard.

Baba Ojore spoke privately with Baba Kojo who was not seen any more that day. In Baba Ojore's absence, Baba Kahuthia addressed the Mkhosi, "The first lesson is incidental, but no less important. If your life is under attack, you fight. You fight, and you make no apologies for it. Our enemy is tricky. He uses relationships, status, rituals, ceremonies, and a host of other social and psychological strategies to trick us into accepting our own death. Do not fall victim to those tricks. It does not matter who is attacking you. And the reason given for the attack does not matter. Vanguardians do not walk peacefully to our deaths. We are hard to kill! Are we clear?!"

Shocked by the demonstration, the Mkhosi murmured haphazardly and with little enthusiasm, "Yes, Baba."

To that weak response, Baba Abiola roared, "Are we clear?!"

The thunder bellowing from Baba Abiola's chest snapped the VITs into consciousness, and Mkhosi Kunye erupted in unison, "Yes, Baba!"

Having returned to the group, Baba Ojore continued, "The second lesson is the reason we are here this morning. Anything at your disposal can be a weapon for you. And anything at your enemy's disposal can be a weapon against you. Today, we will focus on primitive physical weapons."

Beginning that day and for the remainder of Week Five, Mkhosi Kunye learned to identify and use natural physical weapons. On Monday, they learned to find and fight with sticks. They focused specifically on two types of sticks: the long stick and the short stick. They learned basic offensive and defensive maneuvers with each one. On Tuesday, they learned to find and fight with stones. They learned the properties of different types of stones. They discussed the advantages and disadvantages of fighting with these different stones as well as the ways to use stones of different sizes. They practiced throwing stones by hand and striking with a stone in hand.

On Wednesday, they learned to find and fight with shivs. These were pieces of wood, stone, or bone that could be used for slashing or stabbing. It would be used much like a knife. Throughout the week, the Mwalimu drew the VIT's attention to the advantages and disadvantages of the weapons they were learning to use. Prior to this experience, Kamau always had the idea that a knife was a good fighting weapon. However, Kamau soon learned what a poor weapon a shiv or a knife would be in a fight. Baba Abiola and Baba Kojo demonstrated several shiv attacks and fights with shivs against other weapons. Although a well-crafted knife would be an improvement over a primitive shiv, the wielder of the shiv or knife always had the disadvantage of range. He had to get within arm's reach of his opponent. Kamau thought to himself, *If I can give you the business from two to three feet away, why would I get close enough to get hit, kicked, or stuck?* So, while a shiv or knife was better than no weapon at all, it would not be his top choice.

By Thursday, they began modifying their "natural" weapons into "primitive" weapons. On Thursday, they learned to craft and fight with a bow and arrows. This was Kikuyu Squad's greatest challenge. For some reason, the entire week on weapons proved to be a challenge for Kikuyu Squad. They had difficulty finding good weapons, modifying those weapons, and fighting with the weapons. But they were especially bad with the bow. They struggled crafting the bow. They struggled making good arrows, and they were horrible marksmen. They hit nothing.

On Friday, they learned to make and fight with two types of spears. The first was the long spear, which was modeled after the assegai used by the Maasai. The second was the short spear, which was modeled after the iklwa used by the Zulu. For some odd reason, Zulu Squad was quite pleased with this acknowledgment. As the Mwalimu led instruction, they puffed out their chests and nodded smugly at the mere mention of the word, "Zulu."

The peacocking of Zulu Squad was a minor irritant to most of the Mkhosi, but it must have struck a nerve with Chandler. At one point, he stared daggers through big Wayne Scott and asked derisively, "Why are *you* so proud? Did you invent it?"

Chandler's response caught everyone off guard. Mostly, because it was so out of character for Chandler. But also because Wayne Scott was easily the biggest boy in the Mkhosi. Chandler, on the other hand, was clearly the frailest, if not the smallest. Wayne, who was as shocked as anyone, said nothing. So, after a long awkward silence, the Mwalimu returned to instructing, the Mkhosi returned to learning, and Zulu Squad returned to peacocking, though they were a bit more subdued about it.

Raymond had noticed something different in Chandler all week. And that evening, he mentioned it to Kamau after the group reflection. "Have you noticed that Chandler has been acting a bit different?"

Kamau was oblivious, and his response proved as much. "Of course, he acts different. He's an egghead. He reads books, does experiments, and he knows a lot of stuff. He's the brains of this operation. We need him to act different."

"That's not what I mean. Did you notice, today, how he tried to start a fight with Wayne Scott?"

Kamau laughed indifferently, "Yeah, I almost forgot about that! That was great. I thought Chandler was gonna pop him." Still laughing, he added absent-mindedly, "Lucky he didn't. Wayne would pull his insides out."

Raymond persisted, "But what would have been Chandler's reason for fighting him?"

This question stumped Kamau. He himself never needed much of a reason to want to fight anyone. In fact, the idea that someone would need a reason to fight was an idea that he had never considered. Kamau was barely audible when he repeated the question, "What would have been his reason?" He stared blankly as he pondered that simple question.

Seeing that Kamau had no ideas, Raymond continued, "It's not just the fight. Chandler has not been adjusting well this past week. He's losing touch with who he is."

"Yeah? And who is he?" Kamau's tone turned sarcastic. "If Chandler is tired of being an egghead, good for him. Nobody wants to go through life getting pushed around. Save the concerns for real problems."

SECRETS OF THE VANGUARD ORDER

Raymond thought Kamau was too dismissive. He also thought Kamau was wrong. But he let it go. If Chandler had been out of sorts for the past week, so had Kamau. In fact, ever since Week Four, Kamau had been getting a lot of criticism and punishment from the Mwalimu. Added to that, Kikuyu Squad had performed poorly the previous week during Combatives Training. And Kamau never accepted losing very well. So, Raymond kept quiet and hoped things would get better.

Although learning to identify and fight with primitive weapons occupied the hearts and minds of Mkhosi Kunye during Week Five, this was not the overarching lesson. The emphasis for Week Five was on loyalty. Throughout every meal, Instruction Set, run, Vanguard Game, and even the lectures they received during PT, Bausi Ojore and the Mwalimu emphasized to the VITs that, "Our purpose is to provide and protect." They emphasized that protection and provision applied to the VITs themselves and extended to the VITs families, communities, and ultimately to the race.

During one evening reflection, Baba Ojore pointed out that providing and protecting is every man's purpose. He went so far as to say, "Providing for and protecting our families and communities is the reason Amon put us on this earth." But several of the VITs, led by Wild-Eyed Deiondre, pointed to dozens of men that they knew personally who did not provide for or protect anyone.

Baba Ojore explained, "Yes, Everly, there are many among us who are living outside of their purpose. These people are a threat to everyone's well-being, even their own." Baba Ojore went on to provide examples of how entire communities suffer when members of the community live outside of their purpose or fail to meet their responsibility in some way.

During Week Five, Mkhosi Kunye read a book about Christopher Columbus and how his actions laid the foundation for racism, racial stereotypes, and religious justifications for abuse of Black people that still pervade society. Although Kamau's father had often talked about the history of Black people and modern society, this book drew clear connections between slavery, capitalism, and the modern-day conditions of Black people. For some reason, this book helped Kamau to see himself as part of a long, historical chain of people and events that were far bigger than himself.

The end of Week Five was especially exciting. Up to this point, Mkhosi Kunye spent a portion of the weekend with each of four different Mkhosi's. At the end of Week One, they spent time with Mkhosi Kubili, with Mkhosi Kuthathu at the end of Week Two, with Mkhosi Kune at the end of Week Three, and with Mkhosi Kuhlanu at the end of Week Four. During these times, the Mkhosis trained, ate, studied, had chapel, and played Vanguard Games together.

Through their interactions, they learned that each Mkhosi was comprised of young men from different parts of the country. For example, the VITs from Mkhosi Kubili were all from the South. Kamau knew this right away from their southern accents. And the VITs from Mkhosi Kune were from the Northeast. They never got enough of talking about how tough and hard it was to live in their cities. *Well, why don't you move?* Kamau thought. *There's bound to be more livable cities.* So, over the course of four weeks, the VITs of Mkhosi Kunye had an opportunity to meet VITs from all over the country.

At the end of Week Five, however, all five Mkhosi's gathered for the entire weekend at Ukumbi wa Kunye. It was a joyous surprise. There was more food than was normally served. The Vanguard Games were intense as the VITs were eager to compare their knowledge and skill. The Ukumbi roared throughout the weekly movie as the VITs cheered, jeered, and held running dialogue with the actors on screen. The weekend had the usual rigor and hardship that is typical of the Akhet. However, it was peppered with an extra measure of enthusiasm, humor, and cheer. Even the Mwalimu seemed to relish the extended brotherhood.

The weekend was a godsend for Kamau, Bongani, and the other squad leaders of Mkhosi Kunye. The presence of the other Mkhosis took the Mwalimu's attention from them, if only for two days. Raymond noticed that Kamau's spirit was lighter. He was joyful again. And for the first time in five weeks, he saw Bongani laughing. The act of laughing made Bongani Jekwa look like a different person. In all, it was a tremendous time of learning and brotherhood.

A New Plan (O'Leary)

Taharka felt anxious as the pouring of libations and other formal introductory ceremonies were concluded. He breathed deeply and worked to soothe his spirit and still his mind. Taharka viewed the ceremonial activities as a distraction from the work that needed to be done.

As inDuna, Taharka was commander of the Vanguard Order, the Abantu's warrior faction. And while Vanguard Warriors were known to wear their authority lightly, they were also known to act. They were not pontificating, talking-about-what-should-be-done, type of men. They would consider all known factors, make reasonable decisions, and act. Taharka, like most Vanguardians, enjoyed ceremony and ritual, but he rarely let either stand in the way of action.

However, inDuna was something of a political position. In addition to serving as leader of the Vanguard Order, Taharka was responsible for coordinating Vanguard activities in service to the life of the larger community. This meant that he held a seat on the Elder Council and, as such, he learned to sit patiently through many ceremonies and much talking-about-what-should-be-done.

As the libations were concluded and the eldest elder granted permission for the ceremony to begin, an attractive older woman smiled and spoke, "Baba Taharka, what brings us here today?"

Makeda Genet was not as old as the elders in the room. In fact, she was only a few years older than Taharka. The Iya Iyaba was typically old enough to command the respect of elders, but young enough to engage in the daily rigors of the job. There had never been an Iya Iyaba who was younger than fifty, and none ever served beyond the age of sixty-two. Despite her relative youth, Makeda made everyone feel as though she was their grandmother. She was genuinely warm and inviting. Her hair, worn in locks that extended to the top of her back, was tinged in grey and framed a beautiful face. Every part of her face smiled and said welcome: her cheeks, her eyes, her mouth. She was a stout woman, wearing the portliness one would expect from a well-fed grandmother. And she had some unknown magic, something in her demeanor, in her being, that compelled one to serve her, defend her, and obey her.

Even the battle-hardened Taharka was not immune to her spell. "Yes, Mama Makeda. I am here seeking approval to alter the plans for Prince Henry's Demise." Prince Henry's Demise was the name of a military operation being organized by the Vanguard Order. It was named for the Fifteenth Century, Prince Henry of Portugal, who is credited as the first European to circumnavigate and systematically explore the southern coasts of Africa.

Members of the Elder Council sat patiently, waiting for Taharka to continue. Taharka, however, said nothing more.

Mama Makeda smiled warmly and interrupted the awkward silence. "Baba Taharka, in what ways would the Vanguard Order like to alter the operation?"

With this question, the tension in the room mounted. The relationship between the Vanguard Order, the Elder Council, and Iya Iyaba was a strained one. It was strained, not by the good will of the people involved, but by their respective roles and responsibilities. The Vanguard Order was a warrior cult. They were charged with protecting the Abantu and securing ever increasing space of self-determination for the Abantu. Long ago, it was determined that these charges could not be fulfilled with strongly worded letters. No. Fulfilling these charges required that many men would get their hands dirty as they did ugly things that needed to be done.

Two measures were taken to protect the Abantu. The first is that the

Vanguard Order was required to act in secret, never divulging any details to the Elder Council or any other non-Vanguard Abantu members. The second is that the Abantu, through the Elder Council, had to approve major Vanguard operations. The arrangement was a messy one. How could the Elder Council approve an operation of which they had no knowledge? The tension being felt by Taharka, Mama Makeda, and the Elder Council on this day was not new. It was a tension that often pervaded these gatherings.

Taharka responded, "Esteemed Council, when Operation PHD was last presented to the Council, it was to be a preemptive, non-confrontational intervention. We would like to accelerate our timeline and prepare for the possibility of a small-scale confrontation." Here, Taharka began speaking in the vaguest of terms. Yet, no one was offended. Everyone understood the balancing act he was required to perform. Taharka continued, "We have good reason to believe that the timeline has shifted. If we continue as planned, our intervention cannot be preemptive. In fact, there will be no intervention at all. We will be too late."

One of the elders, a frail, petite, dignified woman spoke, "Brother Taharka, you have been a strong voice for our people. I have watched your work for the past twenty years, and I am impressed by the way you sacrifice for others. We need more men like you."

As the Elder droned on, Taharka was careful to remain respectful and attentive. It was hard. Here he was, on the cusp of a crisis, in need of a quick decision, and the elder was singing his praises. His mind drifted to the Vanguard motivation, *Acclaim, accolades, applause, we don't need 'em. Just give us an enemy and a chance, we'll defeat 'em!* Then came the thundering chorus of *Yebo!*

Although Taharka's best fighting days were behind him, his war spirit was as strong as ever. Deep within him, that war spirit was begging the Elder Council to stop talking and to get out of the way. *Just step aside. Let us fight!* The elder continued, "If this were anyone else, I would question the reliability of this information. But you are a man of integrity, and you would not bring us an unfounded request."

Taharka saw the psychological maneuver. She praised him, presented herself as an advocate, then tied his integrity to the veracity of his message. This move would apply psychological pressure to a person, making it difficult for that person to be deceitful. The average person would want to live up to the fine reputation that the elder laid out and justify the advocacy of the elder. But Taharka was not the average person. He was a Vanguardian. He was the leader of the Vanguardians. And while he appreciated the elder's kind words, he could not be moved by them. He was driven by his ideals and mission; and the elders were wasting time.

The elder concluded, "Given the changed circumstances, is the Vanguard Order *able* to be successful even with a modified timeline?"

Taharka should have been offended. The Vanguard Order was solely responsible for the Abantu. The Vanguard Order alone secured the various communities, ensured the financial well-being of those communities, and obtained the financing for the very facilities in which the Elder Council met. To question the ability of the Vanguard Order was unconscionable. Yet, Taharka appeared unperturbed. He replied, "We should put out the fire while it is still small. Neither I nor any Vanguardian could guarantee a successful outcome. But history shows us that if we do not take a stand now, we will be unable to take a stand years and maybe even months from now."

This time, a stately, older gentleman with a full head of closely cropped grey hair spoke. And he spoke slowly, "The chameleon looks in all directions before moving. Forgive us for being so slow to conclude this business. Old age is constantly trying to take our hearing, eyesight, strength, and sadly, it tries to take our nerve. We fight father time with the same intensity that you fight Yurugu. Baba Taharka, what will this modified operation cost?"

Taharka knew very well that the elder was not asking about money. Money was never a concern of the Elder Council. Instead, the Council was concerned with the human cost of the Vanguard Order. Would Vanguardians be lost? Would members of Abantu be lost? They were even concerned about the loss of enemy lives. Taharka responded, "You cannot climb to the mountain top without crushing some weeds with your feet." He paused and examined each of the council members. From anyone else, this might have been poorly received. It was almost a chastisement. In a rather direct way, Taharka was reminding the Elder Council that sacrifice was necessary, even inevitable. However, Taharka was well respected by the members of the council. He held a seat on the Council. In many ways he was one of them.

After an awkwardly long pause, Taharka continued, "If a small-scale confrontation is inadequate in getting the job done, we will return to the Council before extending the operation."

Mama Makeda turned to the Council to determine if there were any additional questions. Seeing that there were none, she asked, "Baba Taharka, would you please allow the Council time to deliberate?"

"Yes, Mama Makeda." Taharka took his leave.

Restraint, The Sixth Virtue

The trials of the Akhet continued unabated into Week Six. The VITs began the week by running the Six-Mark. They learned two new cadences and a new poem called, "Good Timber." Although the daily routine was firmly set, the Mwalimu continued to push and challenge the Mkhosi. The VITs were given unique Application Sets. They were sometimes required to draw from things learned early in the Akhet to successfully complete a challenge. These unexpected variations to the routine kept the VITs from getting complacent.

At this point, the Mwalimu almost never yelled at the VITs. Not to say that there was not plenty of yelling. There certainly was. But it was not directed at the VITs. Everyone yelled, and they yelled at everything. They yelled cheers for one another. They yelled warnings and instructions during drills, Instruction Sets, and Application Sets. They lifted their heads towards the sky and yelled cries of triumph at every success. In fact, after completion on the run to the Six-Mark they looked like a pack of wolves hooting and howling at the moon, except there was no moon.

Mkhosi Kunye continued learning to use weapons in Combatives Training. That week, they focused more on crafting primitive weapons from natural materials. They, once again, crafted the bow and arrow and the two spears. That week, they learned to craft the sling, and they used it to throw stones.

Baba Kahuthia demonstrated this by throwing several stones with near perfect accuracy at short distances. He was also able to consistently throw stones hard enough to penetrate large pieces of fruit and planks of wood. The VITs were amazed that a simple sling could be deadly. Most thought of it as a child's toy. But that week, they learned that in the right hands, a sling could project a stone with great force and accuracy. In addition to making primitive weapons, the VITs focused heavily on learning defensive maneuvers against these same weapons.

They also read a new book during Week Six. The book was written by an economist. In it, the author described how he worked for an American consulting firm to convince developing countries to take out large loans for construction projects. The countries would only hire American companies to do the construction, and the debt from the loans would leave the countries beholden to the US.

The book was a challenging read for many of the VITs. However, they were stunned that such a thing could take place. With each day that passed at Camp Furaha, Kamau began to see his father less as an extreme conspiracy theorist and more as a brilliant tactician. All he could think about while reading this book was how knowledgeable and insightful his father was.

In many ways, Mkhosi Kunye continued to grow during Week Six. The VITs were no longer the frail, scared, whiney boys that had arrived at the Akhet in early

June. They were still boys, but they had the look of men. Their mentality, determination, and resolve had changed. It would be impossible to get any one of them to put on a pink, Gink shirt, and it would be foolish to try.

Baba Ojore was pleased with this transformation. He expected it, for he had seen it many times before. However, the transformation from boyhood to manhood was a process of growth that came at a cost. And like any growth process, it entailed a degree of pain. But Baba Ojore and the Mwalimu were ready.

The number of fights between the VITs increased quite a bit during Week Six. There were a few reasons for this. First, the VITs were increasingly familiar with one another. And while they had begun to see the bad traits in each other, they had yet to accept those traits. Second, they were less afraid than they had been. They were no longer afraid of the wilderness, the distance from their families, the hardship, or the Mwalimu. Third, the organization of the Mkhosi into squads promoted in-group bias.

During Week Six, there were three fights. This was quite a bit. For the first five weeks, there had been only one fight. But in a strange way, each fight was understandable. On Monday, Jayson Nelson and Danny Echols had a brief scuffle. During Combatives Training, the VITs were shooting arrows on a primitive archery range. Baba Thulani called for a break so the arrows could be retrieved. After some time had passed, Danny Echols picked up his bow and began shooting again. However, Jayson Nelson was still downrange, retrieving arrows. Seeing that Danny was shooting in his direction, Jayson sprinted towards Danny, from downrange, and tackled him, screaming threats as Gerard Winford and Omowale Ndukwe pulled them apart. Danny apologized profusely, claiming not to know that Jayson was downrange.

The Mwalimu and, in fact, the entire Mkhosi expressed their disappointment in Danny. Although a lot of time had passed for arrow retrieval, he did not wait for the "all clear" signal, and his carelessness put a man's life at risk. Jayson was also chastised by the Mwalimu. However, he was chastised for losing his composure. The VITs were expected to keep their wits regardless of the circumstances, and Jayson failed to do so.

Surprisingly, Charles Hall (the leader of Fulani Squad) and Gerard Winford (the leader of Mongo Squad) received the worst chastisement of all. As Squad leaders, they were responsible for the conduct of the members of their squads. According to the Mwalimu, specifically Baba Kojo, Gerard failed to ensure that his squad members took safety seriously.

Baba Kojo grilled him horrendously. It wasn't the theatrical, borderline playful, grilling they had become accustomed to. Baba Kojo's tone was a berating one. He accused Gerard of being stupid—"having a profound loss for knowledge and reason" were his exact words. He also threatened him with Vanguard Study. No one knew what Vanguard Study was, but if it was anything like Vanguard Games, it probably wasn't good.

As Baba Kojo railed at Gerard, the other Mwalimu looked uncomfortable. Kamau had the feeling that Baba Kojo was coming unhinged. Then he turned his venom to Charles, "Hall!"

Stunned, Charles Hall stammered, "Yes, Baba."

"Hall, what kind of squad are you running? Do you want to pack up your things and transfer to band camp? Cooking camp?" He was yelling uncontrollably, "Hall, you have four men in your charge. You are responsible for them. We all rely on you to do your job. If *that* man loses his head, we all suffer!" Baba Kojo stabbed a finger in Jayson's direction when he said, "that man." The point was made.

Kamau's stomach dropped at this display. As leader of Kikuyu Squad, how was he expected to be responsible for three other people. He liked his squad members. They were his friends. In fact, they were his best friends. But how was he to account for their every action?

On Tuesday, Carl Lofton and Michael Hedrick came to fisticuffs, in a manner of speaking. Following the morning run, Michael was in a cross mood. Seeing that Michael was down, Carl, in his normal, jovial way, began joking with him, trying to cheer him up.

Michael was not interested. He snapped, "Leave me alone, Carl. I ain't wit' it today."

Omowale Ndukwe and Amari Danjuma were both nearby. So, Carl had an audience, and he continued to perform. Michael continued ignoring him so, at one point, Carl tapped Michael on the shoulder to get his attention. At that tap, Michael spun round and cracked Carl in the side of the face.

Dazed, Carl staggered, and his head wobbled. As he got his bearings, he began to smile, "Michael! You got hands." With that, Carl put his hands up in a fighting stance and began to dance around. He then began taunting Michael, "Face all frowned up, fists balled up too? Let's us all see what big Mikey gon' do."

Michael charged towards Carl. Although he was much bigger than Carl, Carl was fast, and he had very quick hands. Almost instantly, the Mkhosi circled around and watched.

Michael, who was clearly frustrated, began swinging. Carl was having a good time. He ducked, bobbed, and weaved, and was never touched. In fact, he began coaching Michael as he danced about. "Watch your left shoulder, Big Mike. You're telegraphing your cross. Keep your feet underneath you. You're off balance."

Even the Mwalimu watched. It was odd that no one tried to break it up, but there really was nothing to break up. Aside from the first blow, Michael never landed a punch, and Carl never threw one.

After a minute or so, Michael stopped swinging. He very likely felt silly swinging and never landing a punch. What's more, he was pooped. When Michael dropped his hands, Carl ran to Michael, gave him a hug and lifted his hand in the air announcing, "Big Mikey! They can't handle the two of us, Big Mike!" With that, Michael Hedrick smiled.

The third fight took place on Thursday, and it didn't end as happily as the second. There had been ongoing tension between Kikuyu Squad and Zulu Squad even before the squads were formed. Kamau's goading Deiondre into a fight and Deiondre beating Kamau in a boxing match were the beginning of the tension. Since that time, however, Bongani and Kamau had worked to ease tension between the two squads. Bongani was firm in his expectations of Zulu Squad and Kamau, while not as heavy handed as Bongani, made it clear to Kikuyu Squad that there should be no conflict.

Despite the efforts of the squad leaders, members of each squad remained at odds with one another. The biggest sources of tension were Wild-Eyed Deiondre Everly, who still harbored deep-seated animosity towards Kamau, and Alton Bailey, who was fiercely loyal to Kamau. Keith Duhart and, recently, Chandler Gardner also contributed to the tension, though to a lesser degree.

For the day's second round of Vanguard Games, the Mkhosi played the Fallen Dane. In their second match, Kikuyu Squad was playing against Zulu Squad. The first time Kikuyu Squad played the Fallen Dane, they had lost to every other squad except Fulani Squad. And they almost lost that one. But now, Kikuyu Squad was very good. In fact, they typically dominated all other squads in this game.

From the beginning, their game with Zulu Squad was chippy. It began with a lot of trash talking. Deiondre talked incessantly to Kamau. Deiondre talked about how slow Kamau was, how he had beaten Kamau in a fair fight, how weak Kikuyu Squad was, how bad they were at fighting with weapons, and how his "pansy squad" was going to lose yet another game. Kamau was proud of himself. To all this, he said nothing in response. He simply played.

Kamau's silence could have been taken as a sign that he chose to take the high road. But in reality, he noticed that Deiondre was aggravated more by being ignored. In fact, Kamau was a much better athlete than Deiondre. He was faster, more agile, and stronger. So, with each criticism, Kamau worked harder and looked for opportunities to make Deiondre look hapless. He would change pace suddenly to blow by Deiondre. He would let Deiondre get close to the ball, then shield it with his body and move away. He would feint in one direction and, rather than playing immediately, he would pause, drawing attention to Deiondre's missteps.

But Deiondre wasn't the only trash talker. Chandler, for some odd reason, talked a lot of trash to Big Wayne Scott. Wayne was gracious in not pummeling skinny Chandler, and he never spoke back. But he did take every opportunity to bump him. Chandler's frail bones rattled every time Wayne's massive torso made contact. Yet, Chandler kept talking.

Although Wayne and Kamau did not respond to Chandler and Deiondre verbally, tensions in the game still rose. Keith Duhart and Alton joined Deiondre and Chandler in playing more aggressively than was necessary.

Then it happened. Kamau went a step too far. He was moving up the right sideline with the ball, and Deiondre was challenging him. Kamau took a jab step to the left and Deiondre lunged. It was a feint and Kamau, who still had the ball, passed it between his legs to Raymond. As Deiondre lost his balance and fell, Raymond scored Kikuyu Squad's fifth point.

Baba Chinua announced, "5-0 Kikuyu Squad!"

Kamau then proclaimed loudly, "Keep it coming, baby! We gotta lotta mo'!"

Deiondre jumped to his feet in protest, "He pushed me!" He then walked up to Kamau, yelling about being pushed.

Out of nowhere, Alton charged chest-first into Deiondre, knocking him to the ground. He growled, "Back down, boy!"

Deiondre jumped up and lunged for Alton, who charged him again, and again knocked him to the ground, "Stay down, boy!"

Kamau stared at Alton wide eyed, "What are you doing?"

Alton pleaded his case, "He out of pocket, Kamau!"

Chandler began skipping around wildly, beating his chest, and yelling, "That's right, boy! Stay down, boy!"

Kamau looked at him bewildered. Chandler looked like he had gone crazy. Kamau wondered, *What is wrong with him?*

By this point, Baba Chinua and Baba Thulani had stepped between the two squads. And Baba Kojo was giving Kamau and Bongani an earful. According to Baba Kojo, as leaders, it was their responsibility to ease the tension between their squads. Instead, they let it fester. According to Baba Kojo, they needed Vanguard Responsibility practice. So, they were responsible for gathering firewood and stacking it neatly at the kambi. They would do this during the remainder of the Vanguard Games, during their free time, and through dinner.

SECRETS OF THE VANGUARD ORDER

Kamau is Out of Reach

During Group Reflection that evening, Baba Ojore led a discussion on passions and restraint. It was a topic the Mkhosi had studied all week. Baba Ojore and the Mwalimu worked to help the VITs understand how men are often made slaves to their passions. Baba Ojore reminded the Mkhosi of the lizard brain. He reminded them that passions are base human desires that the lizard brain uses to drive us to action. "Passions drive many people to excess, so they indulge in things like food, sex, drugs, alcohol, and even comfort. Evildoers dangle these things in front of people as enticements, and that is how people are made slaves to their passions."

Baba Ojore addressed the group, "Men, today we saw first-hand how our passions, when unrestrained, can lead to destruction. What destruction did we see?"

Charles Hall was the first to respond, "We saw lack of responsibility."

Kamau looked at Charles and kept his face impassive as he thought, *Keep it up, Little Bird.*

Baba Ojore responded, "No, Hall. There was the need for a better exercise of responsibility, but that was not where we saw destruction. What destruction did we see?"

A few other VITs offered up responses, but all were rebuffed. When finally, Bongani responded, "Baba Ojore, we began to see destruction in our brotherhood."

Kamau looked at Bongani and smiled proudly. Prior to today, he and Bongani respected each other. In fact, they liked each other. However, after suffering punishment together, they grew closer. Without saying it, both boys knew that they were the leaders of Mkhosi Kunye. They knew that the other VITs would follow the lead that they set.

Upon hearing Bongani's response, Baba Ojore responded enthusiastically, "Yes, Jekwa! We saw cracks in the foundation of our brotherhood." He spoke slowly and deliberately with these last few words. After a brief pause, he continued, "And we must fix it. So, what unrestrained passions caused this destruction?"

After a very long pause, Kamau spoke, "Misplaced loyalty." As he responded, Kamau looked at Alton. When their eyes met, Alton looked down in shame.

Baba Ojore responded, "Mkhosi Kunye, can misplaced loyalty be a passion?" A few doubted whether misplaced loyalty could be considered a passion. It was nothing like food or alcohol.

Basheeru said, "My Dad told me about a pastor who molested boys in his church. When the congregation found out, they did not punish the pastor. They rallied around him, and they protected him. They were loyal to him when they should have been loyal to their beliefs."

Baba Abiola chimed in, "That's an excellent analogy, Chiriga. How would restraint help in a situation like that?"

Basheeru remained quiet as he had no response. But his quarter mate, Kamal, offered a response, "We need restraint whenever the lizard brain causes us to act against our best interest. The problem is not the thing we desire (like food, sex, or people to whom we might be loyal), the problem is our *overindulgence* in the things we desire. If eating leads us away from good health, then we need to restrain our eating. Food is not the problem. If our loyalty leads us away from our intended goal, then we need to restrain our loyalty. The object of the loyalty, like this pastor, is not the problem."

Kamau noticed how the Mwalimu beamed with pride upon hearing Kamal's response. Kamau thought, *He might be almost as smart as Chandler.*

Baba Ojore smiled broadly, "That's very good, Ofori. I really appreciate the way you unpacked that idea. That's excellent." Baba Ojore then chuckled, "Uh. Now, just to be clear…a child molesting pastor is *always* a problem. In fact, uh… any child molester is a problem. And sure as we live and breathe, Vanguardians are problem solvers."

The Mkhosi shouted enthusiastically, "Yebo!"

"But Ofori, your point is well taken. The secondary problem, in your scenario, was the failure of those parishioners to deal with their wayward pastor." Baba Ojore continued, "Mkhosi Kunye, were there any other unrestrained passions that caused destruction in our brotherhood?"

There was a brief pause during which Bongani stared daggers through Deiondre. In response, Deiondre stared back, his eyes growing wilder with each moment. Then finally, he pinched his lips into a snarl, rolled his wild eyes, and responded, "Pride, Baba Ojore. My pride is a passion that I did not restrain, and it contributed to the destruction of our brotherhood."

In that moment, Kamau was proud of Deiondre too. For all his shortcomings, Deiondre had a lot of redeeming qualities. He was courageous and confident. He followed the chain of command. And, here, he showed that he was humble enough for self-criticism.

Baba Ojore was proud as well. He did not say it, but everyone heard it in his voice, "That's right, Everly. Pride can be a passion that we all may need to restrain."

That evening, before lights out, Kamau called Kikuyu Squad together. He spoke first to Alton, "Alton is your first loyalty to me or to Kikuyu Squad?"

Alton looked surprised. "Kamau you're like a big brother to me." He hesitated.

Kamau pressed, "Talk straight!"

Alton continued, "My first loyalty is to Vanguard." He paused to weigh Kamau's reaction, "…then Mkhosi Kunye." He paused again, this time looking at Chandler and Raymond, "…then Kikuyu Squad… then you."

Alton's response reflected the command structure that the VITs had been taught. Kamau suspected that Alton was giving the correct answer rather than the truthful answer. His initial inclination was to push him. But he decided to let it go. Alton's admission of the truth would not make any difference.

Instead, Kamau reassured him of their friendship. "Alton, I want you to know that I am not upset with you. I appreciate you and everything you bring. Keep giving us your best!"

Alton responded with a surprised smile. He nodded, "I got it!" He expected to be chewed out for getting Kamau in trouble. But he understood that Kamau was now protecting him.

Kamau then turned to Chandler, "Chandler, what's gotten into you?"

Chandler replied innocently, "What do you mean?"

Kamau's expression was sincere, "Why were you running around beating your chest? Why were you antagonizing Wayne Scott?"

Chandler straightened up, and his face took on a thinking expression. He seemed to be at a loss. After a moment, he responded simply, "I don't know."

He had never seen Chandler "not know" something. Now Kamau was at a loss. He shrugged and furrowed his brows, "Well don't do it again. How can you help the squad if Wayne beats you senseless?"

With that, they said their goodnights and retired to their tents. As Raymond and Kamau walked off, Raymond commented, "Kamau, Chandler is trying to prove himself. He wants to be tough. He wants to be strong physically not just mentally."

Kamau turned dismissive, "Yeah, well, we all want something. I want to be home eating my mother's cooking, playing basketball, and making money. But instead, I'm here… carrying bug-infested firewood and missing dinner because my squad can't keep it together." With that he walked off, leaving Raymond behind.

Raymond said nothing. For the second time in two weeks, Kamau ignored Chandler's issue. Even in the face of clear evidence that the issue was getting worse and could cause problems for the squad, Kamau refused to do anything about it. But now Raymond was at a loss because he did not know how to reach Kamau.

Jomo W. Mutegi

Honor, The Seventh Virtue

The weekend brought a welcome relief from the tensions of Week Six. The entire weekend was spent at Ukumbi wa Kubili and, again, all five Mkhosis gathered. That weekend they learned that, as a collective, the five Mkhosis were referred to as an Ibutho. On the first day of the gathering, Baba Ojore announced that the weekend would begin the Ibutho Intersquad Competition. All twenty-five squads would compete against one another and earn points. At the end of the Akhet, the three squads with the highest point totals would earn a special recognition. This announcement excited everyone, even the Mwalimu.

Kamau and a few others from Mkhosi Kunye noticed that Baba Ojore seemed to be in charge. Even though each Mkhosi had its own Bausi, they all deferred to Baba Ojore. Kamau had noticed that he took leadership last week as well, but he assumed it was because Mkhosi Kunye was serving as host. That weekend, it became clear that Baba Ojore oversaw everyone. This gave the VITs of Mkhosi Kunye a sense of pride. But it also gave them added pressure. Now, they would be expected to perform better than the other Mkhosis.

Among the intersquad competitions that took place that weekend was a boxing tournament, Fallen Dane tournament, chess tournament, and Combatives tournament. For the Combatives tournament, the VITs wore full pads and used pugil sticks.

The Mwalimu also had the Mkhosis take part in two non-scoring competitions. On Saturday, they held the Vanguard Contest of Merriment. The task for each squad was to earn as high of a score as possible by singing "Asafo the Wide-Eyed Warrior." Squads were rated on singing quality, singing coordination, and enthusiasm. The score in each category was determined by the volume of the Ibutho's cheers. Baba Kofi, a Mwalimu from Mkhosi Kuthathu placed a flat black stone on a table. When Baba Ojore asked the Ibutho, "How do you rate this squad's singing quality?" the Ibutho cheered, and a holographic number was projected in the air above the stone. This process was repeated for the singing coordination and enthusiasm.

As a means of encouraging the merriment of the VITs (or humiliating them, Kamau wasn't sure which) the Mwalimu required that each VIT dress for the occasion by wearing an artifact of "the Merry Mess." Some wore green or red elf hats. Others wore reindeer antlers. Others wore Santa bibs. These paper artifacts were made by the VITs.

Kikuyu Squad was the fourth squad to sing, and the first squad from Mkhosi Kunye. Unenthusiastically, they took to the stage of the Ukumbi. They were almost sheepish. And they began singing.

SECRETS OF THE VANGUARD ORDER

Asafo the wide-eyed warrior
had a very tight-strung bow,
and if you ever saw it,
you wouldn't be around for long.

The song was supposed to be sung to the tune of "Rudolph the Red-Nosed Reindeer," so Kikuyu Squad knew the song. But from them, it sounded more like a funeral dirge. They sang horribly. Not one of them could carry a note. And they were obviously embarrassed. Aside from the fact that they should have been embarrassed singing so badly, they were embarrassed to be on stage singing in front of the entire Ibutho. They dragged themselves through the second verse.

All of the other Warriors,
they were jealous and ashamed,
they wondered how Asafo
invented all the Vanguard Games.

Bongani had seen enough of this travesty of music and shaming of Mkhosi Kunye. He marched Zulu Squad to the front of the stage, furrowed his brows, and commanded Kikuyu Squad, "Sing Vanguardians! Sing with enthusiasm!"

At this show of support, Kamau was reminded that he did not lose. He knew that he could not sing well, but he could certainly sing all out. And that is what he did. He sang louder, and Kikuyu Squad followed his lead.

Then one rainy Akhet Eve,
Bausi came to say,
"Asafo with your bow so tight,
Go and lead my troops tonight."

After each line, Bongani and Zulu Squad shouted motivations at them like, "Sing strong!" and "That's right!" and "Bring it home!" By the time Kikuyu Squad began the fourth stanza, all of Mkhosi Kunye was gathered at the foot of the stage, cheering the most horribly sung song they had ever heard.

Then all the Warriors loved him,
and they shouted out with glee,
Asafo the wide-eyed warrior,
He destroyed the enemy.

By the end of the song, Kikuyu Squad was moving like the Four Tops, only without practice. They were swinging their arms, doing little two steps, kneeling for the crowd. Alton even had the audacity to repeat the last line a second time, changing the pitch of the last few words and throwing his hands to the ceiling while holding the note.

When Baba Ojore asked the Ibutho to rate Kikuyu Squad on singing quality, you could have heard a pin drop. No one dared move for fear that a chair might squeak and give points for Kikuyu Squad's screeching and squawking. They scored a three. It was probably due to some deaf cricket who didn't know what was going on.

When Baba Ojore asked the Ibutho to rate Kikuyu Squad on singing coordination, they received better scores, but they still weren't very high. However, when Baba Ojore asked the Ibutho to rate Kikuyu Squad on enthusiasm, Ukumbi wa Kubili erupted. They earned the highest points of any of the twenty-five squads for enthusiasm.

And when they left the stage, there was a good deal of glad-handing and back-slapping going on among the squads of Mkhosi Kunye. The way they had fought with each other throughout that week, one would never have imagined the camaraderie they now showed.

The winner of the Vanguard Contest of Merriment was Mossi Squad from Mkhosi Kune. While most squads had one or two VITs who could sing well or at least hold a tune, Mossi Squad had three of the best singers that Kamau had ever heard. And their fourth man was an average singer with a very deep man voice, in a little boy's body. They easily won the singing quality portion of the contest. Then to cement their victory, they changed the arrangement to match the version of the song sung by the Temptations. They coordinated beautifully. Sekou Konate was the lead singer. Tatenda Murangi and Jerome Hill sang backup. And George Wilson used his baritone to wow the Ibutho with speaking parts. The Ibutho erupted in cheers of appreciation for the talent of Mossi Squad.

Dishonor in Mkhosi Kunye

By any standard, Kamau's experience at the Akhet was life changing. He met new friends, learned to survive in the wilderness, became a better fighter, read books that most people would never read, and was exposed to ideas that most people would never even consider. He found within himself abilities that he never knew he had. At the start of Week Seven, Kamau would have told you that he was a new person.

But as life changing as his experience at the Akhet was prior to Week Seven, nothing would compare to what happened to him at the end of Week Seven. The week began like all the others: the Hwamanda awakening, Mti wa Umoja, the morning run, and the Instructional Sets after breakfast.

Throughout Week Seven, the squads learned land navigation. They learned to determine direction by the sun and by the stars. They learned to use a manufactured compass and to make a primitive compass. They learned to keep track of the distance they traveled, to read topographical maps, and to take a bearing.

They extended their Combatives Training by learning to move, attack, and defend in units. First, they learned strategies for squad movements, then they learned strategies for Mkhosi movements. The next logical step was to move with an entire Ibutho. Maybe they would learn those strategies on the coming weekend. Many of the VITs also expected that there would be some new Vanguard Game in which the Mkhosis competed by attacking each other.

As part of these war game simulations, Mkhosi Kunye learned the importance of "holding the line." This was a phrase that Baba Ojore and the Mwalimu used frequently throughout Week Seven. Under different attack scenarios, the VITs learned quickly how an uneven line could lead to the destruction of an entire attacking force. So, while "hold the line" came to refer to the line of attack during combat, it was also a reminder that VITs should live in a way that is aligned with Vanguard ideals and with other Vanguardians.

The predominant theme throughout Week Seven was honor. Baba Ojore led discussions each night during group reflection. At every opportunity, he pushed the VITs to understand what honor is and to see the importance of honor in the lives of Vanguardians. Baba Ojore's definition of honor was simple, "...to be consistent in thought, speech, and action." The VITs soon learned that doing so, being consistent in thought, speech, and action, was not easy for many people.

With so much focus on honor, it was ironic that it was an act of profound dishonor that led to Kamau's life changing experience. It began on Wednesday evening during the Reading Set. This week Mkhosi Kunye was reading *Miseducation of the Negro*. As always, the Mwalimu stopped frequently to explain portions of the text and asked questions aimed at getting the VITs to think more deeply about the text.

Since the first reading weeks ago, Chandler had always been one of the most eager VITs to engage in these discussions around the text. And here, seven weeks later, he still got excited about the readings and the discussions. For some reason, during Wednesday's reading, Wayne murmured, "Neeeerrrd," when Chandler spoke.

Chandler was highly irritated. Raymond noticed that Chandler looked as though he was ready to pounce on Wayne. Alton was ready too. When Raymond mentioned it to Kamau, Kamau looked around cluelessly and shrugged as though he had not even heard it.

At a later point in the discussion, Wayne repeated his nerd comment. This time, Deiondre joined him in snickering. Chandler pursed his lips into a sneer, and his eyes grew large. Alton's fists balled up into knots, and he looked at Kamau, begging for permission. This time Kamau did hear it. He motioned for Chandler and Alton to remain calm, then he looked at Bongani who nodded.

Through all this, the Mwalimu never responded. They clearly saw what was happening. They looked squarely at Wayne, at Chandler, at Deiondre, and Alton. But they said nothing. They simply continued with the reading.

When it happened a third time, Chandler looked to be on the verge of tears. He was trying with everything he had to subdue his pride and to remain seated. Kamau dropped his book on the floor, turned towards Bongani and threw both of his hands up while raising his eyebrows. Bongani was visibly agitated and, without even looking at Kamau, he walked over to Wayne, whispered in his ear, and Wayne stopped. But the damage was done. No one from Kikuyu Squad spoke for the remainder of the Reading Set.

Over the next two days, things had returned to normal. Chandler and Alton seemed to have forgotten about Wayne and Deiondre, and Bongani seemed to have gotten Zulu Squad back under control. Kamau was pleased that this situation did not escalate. He wasn't interested in missing any more meals or suffering any other type of punishment. He was focused instead on preparing for the Ibutho Intersquad competition. He had Kikuyu Squad use their free time to practice the land navigation and the Combatives strategies they had been learning that week. Kamau was pleased with their progress.

That Friday evening, just as the Mkhosi sat down to Group Reflection, everything changed. Kikuyu Squad was sitting together, all except for Chandler, who had gone back to his tent to leave something. About a quarter of the way around the fire, sat Zulu Squad. Just before Baba Ojore began, Kamau noticed that Chandler was walking towards the seat occupied by Zulu Squad. *What in the world?!* Kamau thought. *Has he forgotten where to sit?*

Just as he thought those words, Chandler swung at Wayne from behind. His first arced around Wayne's head and struck him in the nose. An audible "pop" was heard around the campfire, followed by a hushed, "Oooh." Everyone was shocked. Even the Mwalimu looked stunned and confused.

Wayne, who was completely defenseless, toppled over sideways, and blood gushed from his face. The scene was horrific. To make matters worse, Chandler began taunting Wayne, "Yeah, boy. Who's the nerd now? Who's the nerd now?" Chandler skipped around doing the same ape dance that he had done in Week Six. Kamau wanted to choke him. But it looked as though Zulu Squad might get to him first. Seeing this, Kamau jumped up, followed by Raymond and Alton.

Kamau stood face to face with Chandler and grabbed him, pinning his arms down and walking him away from the fire and away from Zulu Squad. He spoke in a low, calm tone, "Calm down and shut your mouth." Feeling the strength of Kamau's grip and hearing the determination in his voice, Chandler did just that. He stopped struggling and stopped talking.

Behind Kamau, Alton and Raymond positioned themselves between Zulu Squad and Chandler. Raymond noticed that even Bongani wanted to get at Chandler. Seeing this, he put both hands up and said, "Bongani, Kamau will get him straight. He'll take care of it."

This seemed to settle Bongani a bit. Bongani and the rest of Zulu Squad turned to take care of Wayne. Keith Duhart and Baba Thulani took Wayne to see Nurse Zuri. While they were gone, the Mkhosi continued with Group Reflection as planned. But to Kamau and the rest of Kikuyu Squad, it felt less like Group Reflection and more like a sermon aimed at Kikuyu Squad, courtesy of Chandler.

How foolish that Chandler would sucker punch a fellow VIT... at the start of Group Reflection... during the week that focuses on honor! Kamau was livid. The thought of Chandler made him sick on the stomach. *That boy is a fool!* he thought. *Why'd they put that dummy in my squad?*

For thirty-five minutes, Kamau suffered through the agony of having to listen to what he already knew—that Chandler's conduct was dishonorable. That it brought shame to Kikuyu Squad, to Mkhosi Kunye, and to the Ibutho. And that, as a leader of Kikuyu Squad, he was responsible for the conduct of his squad members.

The greatest agony of all was that, following that Group Reflection sermon, Mkhosi Kunye closed the day with Mduara ya Heshima, the circle of honor. What in the world was Kamau going to say to Mkhosi Kunye?

That evening, before lights out, Baba Kahuthia came to speak with Kikuyu Squad. "Before I begin, I should ask you, do you want to be of service to Black people?"

Kamau had no idea what this question had to do with the punishment they were sure to receive. He was overwhelmed by the shame and embarrassment he felt after Chandler's conduct, and he didn't have the energy to decipher Baba Kahuthia's riddle. He and the others responded with a very lackluster, "Yes, sir."

Baba Kahuthia continued, "Okay. Well, you already know that there will be a consequence to Chandler's misbehavior. Rather than taking part in the Ibutho Intersquad Competition this weekend, you will serve as gophers for the Ibutho. Now, you know there is no punishment at Camp Furaha. Every misstep is an opportunity for growth. You should look at this as an opportunity for growth. You said that you want to be of service to Black people. Now, this is an opportunity for you to practice aligning your thoughts and actions with your words. This weekend will require you to work. It will be hard work. Your first task is to remind yourself of how you are being of service to Black people through this work. Your second task is to find joy in it."

Kikuyu Squad responded, "Yes, Baba."

Baba Kahuthia began to walk away but paused and turned to Chandler. "Chandler, I am curious to know, do you feel any remorse for hitting Wayne?"

Chandler's response was emotionless, "No. He deserved to be popped in the nose. But I shouldn't have done it when I did, and I shouldn't have hit him from behind."

Baba Kahuthia replied, "Thanks for your honesty. Just so you know, his nose is broken. But it will heal just fine."

This was the start of Kikuyu Squad's life altering adventure.

Author's Note

Dear Reader,

At the outset, I said that Kamau's story was difficult to believe. Yes, it was a great story to tell around a campfire. But was I really to believe that the things told to me were true? That these things really happened? Was I really expected to go out into the world and pass off these fictions as a retelling of actual events?

Well, up to this point in the story, I would say that the events were fantastic. Not fantastic in the sense of being extraordinarily good, but fantastic in the sense of being imaginative or fanciful.

Could Kamau and his friends have been abducted and taken to a remote location? It's not likely, but I suppose it's possible. Could he have been subjected to an underground boot camp of sorts? It's hard to imagine, but it doesn't violate the known laws of physics.

Up to this point in the story, I was an entertained, yet skeptical, listener. But it was here that my skepticism ended. What follows is flatly unbelievable. Initially, I did not believe the remainder of Kamau's tale. Here, we began to violate known laws of physics, at least as I initially understood them. But as I have mentioned, time and study have changed that for me.

Kamau and his friends are fully aware that their tale is unbelievable, yet they insist that it is true. What's more, I have tried to disprove the facts that they present, yet I cannot.

Sincerely,
Jomo W. Mutegi, Ph.D.
"The Professor"

BOOK 3

An Unexpected Journey

A New Day

The next morning when he was awakened by the Hwamanda Horn, Kamau found that he was still angry with Chandler. While getting dressed, Raymond commented, "Today, we will miss the Ibutho Intersquad Competition."

Kamau stared straight ahead and spoke slowly and deliberately, "Hewitt, I don't want to hear the name Chandler Gardner, and I don't want to see that fool... all day." With that response, Raymond also knew that Kamau was still angry.

That morning, the entire Ibutho joined together for the morning run. The cadences were beautiful. One hundred and thirty voices, thundering away, filled the air with unity, strength, and harmony. Although Kikuyu Squad ate breakfast with the Ibutho, Kamau seemed unable to enjoy it. He was so cross, he barely spoke. Chandler, too, was quite withdrawn. He felt Kamau's anger. How could he not? Kamau refused to even acknowledge his presence. Alton and Raymond, on the other hand, enjoyed their time with the other VITs, knowing that it would be limited.

Following breakfast, Baba Kahuthia assembled Kikuyu Squad outside of Ukumbi wa Kuthathu. Baba Ojore was with him, and he addressed each member of the squad directly and deliberately. "Njama, Gardner, Bailey, Hewitt, we are human. We make mistakes. There will never be a time in this life that you, or any of us, will be beyond making mistakes. The important thing is to learn from those mistakes. Now, work to forgive yourselves... and each other."

After he spoke, the mood lightened a bit. He eyed each of the VITs and added, "That's an order." Relieved to have Baba Ojore's support, Raymond and Alton smiled a bit. And while neither Kamau nor Chandler smiled, the scowls were wiped from their faces.

As Baba Ojore left to command the Ibutho, Baba Kahuthia took Kikuyu Squad to begin their gopher duties. Using formal drill commands, he organized them into a column of two and ran them to a location they had not seen before.

They stood outside of a large, very modern building. In fact, the building was more than modern. It was futuristic. The base of the building looked to be about four stories high. It was made of a black stone, like the granite countertops in Kamau's home. On top of the base, the rest of the building was shaped like a pyramid. It was made of black glass, except for the very top, which was made of clear glass with a green tint.

Kikuyu Squad stood there, mouths agape, as they stared breathlessly at the massive structure. "How in the world did this get here?" Raymond wondered aloud. "I thought Camp Furaha was in the wilderness."

Alton looked questioningly at Baba Kahuthia, "Baba, did Vanguardians build this?"

"Yes, Bailey. Vanguardians did build this… in a manner of speaking."

After giving Kikuyu Squad a few more moments to ooh and aah at the magnificent edifice, Baba Kahuthia reclaimed their attention. "Gentlemen, this is not a fieldtrip. You have a responsibility to serve as gophers for the Ibutho."

Losing the opportunity to commune with, train with, and compete against the rest of the Ibutho was bad enough. But being referred to as gophers was more than Kamau could stand. Each time he heard it, he cringed, and his aggravation with Chandler grew.

At the base of the building was a ramp that led to the side of the building. As they approached, Alton asked, "Why does this path lead into the wall?"

At just that moment, Baba Kahuthia placed his hand on a black glass panel just to the right of the path, and the wall parted, revealing a double door. Kikuyu Squad again stared in awe. From the exterior, there were no visible signs of a door.

Once inside, Baba Kahuthia had Kamau press his hand against a panel that was very much like the one he had just used to get inside. Another portion of the granite lit up to reveal an alphanumeric pad. Baba Kahuthia began pecking away on the pad as he spoke, "Njama, you will be able to open this door until 1900 hours. Kikuyu Squad will be running back and forth all day. Whenever one of you needs to gain access to this building, you will need Njama to be with you."

Baba Kahuthia then led Kikuyu Squad down the hall and to a stairwell. They took the stairwell down four flights and exited the stairwell at B-4. Here, they stood, peering down a dimly lit hallway. As they walked, however, lights on the ceiling and walls flashed on and brightened their path. About halfway down the hall, on the left, there was a doorway. Atop the doorway was a sign that read, "Warfare in the Dark Ages." Baba Kahuthia led them into that room.

Once inside, they stood in awe. Chandler broke his silence, "Baba Kahuthia, is this a museum?"

Baba Kahuthia chuckled slightly, "No, Gardner. A museum would have real artifacts. These are all replicas. We have no money to waste on showpieces. Maybe one day we will. What you see here is a collection of warfare instruments used by Europeans in the Dark Ages. We use these to help us better understand warfare tactics. We want our simulations to be realistic."

Baba Kahuthia gave Kikuyu Squad a list of items they were to transport to the War Zone, which was the Ukumbi wa Mapambano of Mkhosi Kuthathu. Baba Kahuthia's list included offensive weaponry (swords, mace, axes, long bows, crossbows, spears, and a variety of polearms) and defensive weaponry (helmets, gorgets, pauldrons, guntlets, couters, vambraces, and mail). The offensive weapons were made mostly of wood. This would ensure that no one would accidentally lose an appendage during the simulation. The defensive weaponry was made mostly of metal. All of it was very large, bulky, and heavy. This guaranteed that Kikuyu Squad would have a long, arduous day.

They began with offensive weaponry. Each man carried four weapons. The route they took to the War Zone was a ten-minute walk. To shorten the time, they tried running. But this turned out to be a bad idea. First, because it was difficult to run carrying the awkward wooden weapons. Second, because they were not running together. Kamau was still sour and barely spoke to anyone, and Chadler remained withdrawn. It took nine trips and three hours to deliver the offensive weapons.

When they had finished, Baba Kahuthia allowed them to have personal time and then lunch with the rest of the Ibutho. Throughout both personal time and lunch, Kamau and Chandler remained quiet and withdrawn. Raymond was growing agitated by the tension, and he wondered how long they could go on without speaking.

After lunch, they returned to their gopher duties. Now they would need to deliver the defensive weaponry. As they descended the stairwell to B-6, Alton turned right down the hall instead of left. Just as he realized his mistake, he noticed a room with some wheelbarrows just across from an elevator. "Yo, Kamau look! There's wheelbarrows and an elevator. Man! we can get this done so much quicker than walking up six flights of stairs and carrying everything by hand!"

Chandler repeated in a low murmur, "Six flights of sta…? We are on the wrong floor. This is B-6. We are supposed to be on B-4."

Alton stepped into the elevator, "Let's take this up to B-4."

Raymond looked at Kamau, wondering if it was okay. Chandler followed Alton, ignoring Kamau completely. Raymond then took a risk. He stepped into the elevator, leaving Kamau in the hallway.

They all looked back at Kamau. Alton said cheerily, "Let's go, Chief! We still one squad, even though you mad at us."

As Kamau smiled and joined Kikuyu Squad, Chandler moved to select B-4 from the wall panel.

Kamau responded to Alton, "I am not mad with you all. I am disappointed in the behavior. It keeps getting me, actually us, in trouble."

Chandler, who seemed to be in his own world, murmured again, "There's no buttons."

Alton turned to Chandler, "Put your hand on that black stone. It's like the one outside. It'll probably light up."

As Chandler reached for the stone, Raymond grew tense and barked at Kamau, "Kamau, the trouble is you own fa…"

Then suddenly, they vanished.

Where's Dan Silverstein? (O'Leary)

Timothy slowly poked his head into the executive suite. He then stepped into the suite, looked around, shrugged, and began speaking to himself. Suddenly, his thoughts were interrupted. "Timothy? Is everything alright?" It was Erick Sabbatini, the CEO of TechInnoGen.

Timothy jumped as he turned and saw Erick, "Oh! Mr. Sabbatini, you startled me." He laughed slightly as his heart rate came down and he regained his composure. "Is everything fine? No, everything is not fine. I am looking for Dan and I thought… I was actually hoping that he might be here."

"No, he's not here," Erick responded firmly. Then with genuine concern in his voice, he asked, "Why? Is something wrong?"

Mr. Sabbatini's concern was warranted. He knew Timothy well, as he was one of the rising stars at TechInnoGen. And while some employees frittered company time away traversing the halls like they were at a picnic, Timothy O'Leary did not. He was out of place, and this was very uncharacteristic. To Erick's mind, if Timothy O'Leary was futzing about, then something was definitely wrong.

Timothy gave a deep sigh, as he said reluctantly, "Yeah. I hate to bother you with this, but I'm concerned. I have been trying to find him for two days. There is a project in CC2 that seems to be on the edge of collapse, and Dan is the project lead. Normally, I would not interfere with a project, with which I am not involved, but this project is large and growing, and a few people that I have tapped for a project that I am leading have been pulled in. So, I can't plan without a clearer sense of what's going on in CC2."

Timothy caught himself and stopped abruptly, "I am sorry Mr. Sabbatini. I am thinking out loud and I shouldn't do that. I'll find a way to handle this. Forgive me for interrupting." With that, he turned and quickly walked away.

Not Our Grass

Hearing Raymond, Kamau's eyes narrowed, and he scowled. *Who does he think he is, raising his voice at me? I'm gonna shake that foul tone out of his mouth.* No sooner had he thought these words, than the elevator dropped suddenly and forcefully. And it continued dropping for about thirty seconds, which is a long time for an elevator to drop.

As it dropped, Kamau noticed that everything around him was blurred. He could not clearly see the faces of Raymond, Chandler, or Alton. He only saw their blurred outline. He could not see the walls of the elevator. He also noticed that he couldn't speak, hear, or move. After a while, the elevator stopped. It didn't slow down. It just stopped. And once it stopped, there was no elevator at all. Kamau's legs felt weak, and he wobbled.

Alton looked around bewildered. "Why are we outside?"

After a moment, Kamau got his bearings. The first thing that came to his mind was that disrespectful Raymond Hewitt. Then he turned to Raymond, "Were you saying that it is my fault that we are gophers... running back and forth all day, carrying wooden weapons... missing the competition?!"

Raymond ignored Kamau as he looked around in awe.

Alton continued, "Where is the elevator? Where is the building?"

Kamau, still burning mad at Raymond, snapped at Alton, "What building?!"

Alton shrugged at Kamau. "The big glass pyramid building that we have been going in and out of all day! It's gone! The building is gone!"

Kamau was finally broken from his self-indulgent stupor. He then noticed that the building was, indeed, gone. "What is this?" he asked.

Raymond suggested, "Maybe it's a test. Maybe the Mwalimu want to see how we conduct ourselves alone in the woods."

Alton was livid, "That's ridiculous. What kind of test is that? We had those tests." He walked towards Raymond, speaking more deliberately, more forcefully, "And even if this was a test..." he paused and began yelling again, "...how did we get in the woods? We was just in a elevator!"

Kamau stepped between Raymond and Alton. "Calm down. We'll figure this out. But to do so, we need each other."

Raymond stepped back and looked at Kamau disapprovingly. "Really? We need each other now? Kamau, you have been ignoring Chandler for the past two weeks."

Kamau looked confused. "I have not been ignoring Chandler for two weeks." He then took on a defiant tone, "I have been ignoring him today! After he got..."

Chandler jumped in and scowled at Raymond. "I'm not an infant. I don't need Kamau to look after me. I can..."

Alton began yelling at the squad, "Would you stop it? Look around! These are not our trees! This is not our grass! The smell is wrong. This ain't our smell!"

Everyone stopped bickering. Alton finally had their attention, and everyone began to focus on the situation.

Kamau spoke up, "Alton's right. This is all wrong. Chandler, you haven't said anything. What do you think?"

Chandler was reluctant and slow to respond, "Well, what I think is pretty outrageous. That's why I haven't said anything."

Alton pressed him, "Don't hold back. We need you. What is it?"

Chandler nodded and continued, "I think we are on another planet."

Raymond cried out, "Another planet?! How in the world could we be on another planet?"

Kamau motioned to Raymond to stop protesting. His eyes narrowed, "Raymond, let him speak."

Chandler continued, "Alton is right. These are not our woods. In fact, we have never seen these trees before. Look around. Point to a maple tree. A beech tree. A dogwood. An oak."

As Chandler named trees that should be familiar to them, Kikuyu Squad looked around, surveying the surrounding trees. They had learned to identify major tree species when learning fire craft. And Chandler was right. They did not see one tree that they recognized.

As they turned back towards Chandler, he explained, "I know that there could be other places on earth that have trees that we do not recognize. But we should recognize the sun anywhere on earth. Look at this sun. What do you notice?"

Raymond must have noticed something as he exclaimed, "Wow!" but he never said what it was.

Alton looked at him, "What is it?"

Kamau interjected, "It's dim. The sun is not bright."

"Right," Chandler added. "And we just had lunch. So, it should be about 1300 hours. But does this sky look like the end of lunch?"

Alton responded, speaking very slowly, "Naw. This is at least 1900 hours. That's what the sun looks like at Group Reflection.

Kikuyu Squad was in awe, and they stood quiet for an extremely long time, observing their surroundings, but not moving too far or saying too much.

A Lead on Kikuyu Squad

Mkhosi Kubili and Mkhosi Kune stood on opposite sides of a huge field. Baba Ojore and Mwalimu from each Mkhosi stood in the middle of the field, while the Bausi of each Mkhosi gave them battle instructions.

Baba Ojore stopped and looked to the edge of the field for the Mwalimu from Mkhosi Kunye. He spoke playfully to Baba Kahuthia, "Baba Kahuthia, we need defensive weaponry for the next set of drills, and it looks like we've lost our gophers. Is there any chance that there was too much tryptophan in the lunch? Do you think they are somewhere in the woods napping?"

Despite Baba Ojore's lightheartedness, Baba Kahuthia began to worry. The culture and structure of the Akhet would not allow any of the VITs to shirk their responsibilities, especially not this late into the experience. Baba Kahuthia responded in earnest, "No, sir. Something must be wrong. Kikuyu Squad would not miss an assignment."

Baba Ojore replied sternly, "Agreed! Kikuyu Squad is your charge. Take Baba Munjuku and Herero Squad to assist. If there is trouble, you have a Vanguard Ibutho backing you up."

Baba Kahuthia smiled slightly, "Yes, sir!"

Baba Kahuthia gathered Herero Squad and briefed them on the situation. They would first check the Ebe Nyocha. If Kikuyu Squad was not there, they would spread out and methodically canvas the area.

Upon arriving at Ebe Nyocha and seeing the massive futuristic structure, Herero Squad responded with the same shock and awe as Kikuyu Squad. Baba Kahuthia and Baba Munjuku went inside, while the VITs stood post. The Babas went to B-4 and the room marked "Warfare in the Dark Ages." They searched the room thoroughly and found nothing strange or out of place. As they stepped into the hall, however, Baba Munjuku sniffed the air. "Do you smell that?"

Baba Kahuthi tilted his head back and inhaled deeply through his nose. He caught the faint scent of scorched metal. He nodded, and they followed the smell to B-6 where they found an open elevator and four technicians working.

Baba Munjuku recognized one of the men. "Brother Bakari! How have you been, Warrior?! Have you seen a squad of VITs in the past hour or so?"

Brother Bakari's eyes grew large, "No, but we have noticed some irregularities that we are trying to figure out."

Baba Kahuthia asked, "Brother, what is this that you are working on?"

Bakari grew uncomfortable, "InDuna has ordered that this project be treated as classified. But it looks like your VITs have been poking around in here. There is also a missing item. They may have run off with it. Maybe they are on the grounds playing games."

Baba Kahuthia smiled uncomfortably, "No, sir. They would not be on the grounds playing. I could guarantee that."

Bakari responded, "The only other explanation is that they have engaged Chumba cha Usafiri. But that's not possible. Its not operational."

Munjuku said, "I'll report back to Baba Ojore. We probably need to search the grounds."

Kahuthia nodded in agreement, then asked, "Brother Bakari, is there any way to verify that Chumba cha Usafiri is not operational?"

Bakari nodded, "Let's check with Brother Adio. He's the Communications Technician on duty." Munjuku left to report to Baba Ojore as Kahuthia and Bakari went in search of Adio. Bakari spoke to the Engineering Team, "This is probably nothing to worry about, but just in case, don't adjust any settings. Take a break until this is done."

Kikuyu Squad is Found

Kikuyu Squad stood in a circle as they tried to make sense of their situation. They had considered Chandler's suggestion that they were on a different planet, but they weren't all convinced.

"Chandler, I understand what you're saying. But I think there is another explanation, a simpler explanation." Raymond had calmed down. In fact, they had all calmed down. The stress of the Akhet, the humiliation of their punishment, and the shock of being thrust into an unknown situation would have been a lot for anyone to bear, but these young men found it within themselves to push past those challenges and to deal with circumstances as they were. And in that moment, they felt like brothers again.

Raymond continued, "There is still a chance that this could be a test. I believe the Mwalimu could change, or at least make it look like they have changed the trees, grass, the smell... and yes, even the sun."

Alton posed a question, and his tone was sincere, "But how could they do that?"

Raymond shrugged and tilted his head, "I don't know *how* they could do it. If I knew *how*, we'd be rich." Kamau laughed, as Raymond continued, "But I can tell you why I think they could do it."

SECRETS OF THE VANGUARD ORDER

No one spoke as they waited for Raymond's revelation. "Remember after we ran the Never-Mark , how we went to Nurse Zuri and she put us in this machine that scanned us?" They nodded in agreement. "That scanning machine told her everything about us. It told her our height, weight, age, blood type, cholesterol level, cortisol levels, percentage of body fat, and key incidents in our medical history…" Raymond had not completed his list, but he felt that he had made his point. Have you ever seen anything like that at a doctor's office before?"

The rest of Kikuyu Squad sat quietly as he continued, "This is a camp nurse. But her equipment is better than I have ever seen in a hospital."

Alton began to speak slowly, interrupting Raymond's explanation, "Yeah…. But…"

Kamau cut Alton short, "Let him finish, Alton. We'll all have a say."

Raymond continued, "Remember when we first arrived here, how Baba Ojore did not camp with us?" Again, they nodded in agreement. "He would come in, tell us how horrible we were, and then leave… every morning." The others laughed at this memory. "We never really saw Baba Ojore walk up or walk away. He just appeared at the edge of the kambi when he was coming, and he disappeared at the edge of the kambi when he was leaving."

"Yeah!" Alton exclaimed excitedly. "He would be walking and just disappear like it was a movie."

"And the building we were in… Look, we have been living in nylon tents, sleeping on the ground, eating in a log cabin. It makes it look like everything here is primitive. But that's all a trick. The Mwalimu and Baba Ojore have very advanced technology. I think they have the technology needed to create an illusion. I think they can make us think that we are in a strange place, like a new planet, when really, we are right where we have always been."

Kamau asked, "But if they have advanced technology, couldn't they also use it for space travel?"

Raymond responded, "But why would they? Everything they have done is to give us challenges, to make us stronger. Giving us a challenge by creating an illusion does that. But sending us to another planet? What does that do?"

Chandler spoke up, "Well, first, if we are on another planet, they didn't send us here. We did. We were never told to use the elevator, or whatever it was. We were not even told to go on B-6. Second, just because they have advanced technology, does not mean they have space travel technology. Space travel, teleportation, travel through wormholes, whatever it would take to get us to another planet, would require so much more than the other technology we have seen."

Chandler's points were well taken, but Alton was now confused. "So,

Chandler, which side are you on? Do you think this is another planet or is it an illusion?"

Chandler responded flatly, "There are no sides. I'm looking at all the evidence, trying to figure out what's going on."

Kamau had been quiet throughout the discussion. He was taking it all in and considering all sides when Alton asked, "What do you think, Kamau."

Kamau looked at each man before responding. Then he asked, "Is there anything we haven't thought about?" The squad was quiet. "Alright then. We'll gather more information. But we'll do it with two thoughts in mind. First, we will assume that we are still at Camp Furaha and that this is an illusion. Second, we will move and act with the same caution we would have if we knew that this was actually a strange planet. That means we stay together, don't eat or drink, and limit our contact with plants and animals."

They agreed to assume they were still at Camp Furaha and to try to determine their location. Drawing heavily on the land navigation skills they had learned in Week Seven, they constructed a makeshift compass, marked their current location, then set out in one direction for about a mile. Upon seeing nothing familiar, they returned to the original location. Again, they tried to determine their location, traveling in a different direction the second time. Doing this process twice, they were exhausted and could not figure out why.

Kamau spoke, "This should have been a four-mile walk. I feel like we just ran the Six Mark twice." The others agreed.

As they sat to rest, Chandler commented, "If this is another planet, it is probably larger than earth... maybe three times larger."

Curious, Raymond asked, "What makes you say that?"

Chandler explained, "A larger planet would have a stronger gravitational pull. A planet that's twice as large as earth, would have twice the gravitational pull, which would make us work twice as hard. What we did feels like it was about three times as hard as it should be, so I'm guessing that, if this is a new planet, it is three times as large."

Kamau listened with great surprise. *Man, this guy is brilliant.*

Seeing the shocked surprise on the faces of Kikuyu Squad, Chandler added, "We all learned this in school. Remember, the reason astronauts bounce so easily on the moon is because the gravity is one sixth that of the earth's gravity?"

Alton laughed, "Yeah! That's right."

Chandler added, "My estimates are rough guesses."

Kamau then asked, "So, if this is *not* another planet, if this is an illusion, how could we explain our walk being three times harder than it should be?"

They looked around, and no one responded. It seemed that no one had an answer for that. In Kamau's thinking, that translated into one point for the new planet theory.

After a moment Alton asked, "But if this weren't earth, the compass wouldn't work right?"

They all seemed to agree that the working compass suggested that this was earth, when Chandler clarified, "Not necessarily. Some planets have magnetic fields, and some do not. We can't assume that it's earth because of the magnetic field."

After resting a bit longer, Kikuyu Squad took a bearing in a third direction and began walking. They were exhausted, so they did not speak. Fewer than two minutes into their walk, they heard the faint sound of Baba Kahuthia's Cajun accent calling, "Kamau? Kamau Njama!"

Cleaning Up His Mess (O'Leary)

Dan could no longer avoid Command Center 2. A representative from the CEO's office called Dan and read him the riot act for the hot mess he had made of the SEV Fitzroy project. Dan was chastised for running a project that fell so far out of company protocol. Dan had violated company policy regarding timing, project planning, recruiting, and project transparency. He was putting lives and company money at risk. As Dan listened politely while being excoriated, he wondered how the CEO's office had found out what he had done.

Dan started with a small team to keep the operation under the radar. He stayed away from CC2 for the same reason. It was not his fault that Apu, or whatever his name was, could not keep his team on track. At any rate, the jig was up. Dan had better go fix Apu's mess.

As Dan left his office, he called to Marlene, "Marlene, we've got a project in CC2. We will be here for a few weeks. Bring a mobile office down as soon as you can."

Marlene was aghast as she thought, *What?! A project in CC2? Just like that?* Apparently, she had been out of the loop as well. But being a dutiful assistant, she quickly prepared to provide administrative support to Dan Silverstein, who was, by now, halfway there.

Dan thrust open the glass door of CC2, like a cowboy walking into the saloon of a new town. The response in CC2 was what you might expect if it were a saloon. A hush came over the room. As he entered, Dan confidently announced that he needed a debrief, and as he walked to the glass office reserved for the project leader, Anand moved to join him.

Udhibiti wa Dhamira

Kahuthia and Bakari went up one flight to B-5. Turning right out of the stairwell, they walked down a short hall and towards a large, open room enclosed in glass. The room was empty except for one person who seemed to be working at a very leisurely pace. Outside the entrance door stood a tall, muscular, young man, with close-cut hair and a neat goatee. This man stood guard at the entrance to Udhibiti wa Dhamira, which was the command center of the Vanguard Order. All operations that required monitoring and real-time coordination, and there were very few, were managed from this location.

Bakari addressed the guard. "Good day, Brother Leboo. We need to speak with the communications technician."

Leboo Naengop stood fast, and when he responded, his deep voice rumbled, "Good day, Baba Bakari. You know that Udhibiti wa Dhamira is off limits without clearance. I'm sorry, I cannot let you in." Despite his size, everything about Leboo screamed, *I'm a gentle giant and I'm not that bright.* Perhaps this is why he was assigned the easy responsibility of "guarding" an area that was never in any danger.

Bakari remained calm but firm. "Brother Leboo, I understand that you do not want to violate protocol. So, I will ask you, 'Would it be a violation of protocol to block a Mwalimu from carrying out his training duty?'" He gestured to Baba Kahuthia as he asked this question.

A gust of dopiness swept across Leboo's face, and with a somewhat confused look, he responded, "Uhhh? Yes, sir."

Baba Bakari continued, "Would it be a violation of protocol to sit idly by while VITs were hurtled through space-time?"

Now, Leboo's posture softened, and his body seemed to crumple a bit. His once stern expression morphed into a look of sheepish concern. "Yes, sir?"

Kahuthia was taken aback at the mention of VITs hurtling through space-time. Bakari continued, "Brother Leboo, would it be a violation of protocol for you to…"

Pressed by an increasing sense of urgency, Kahuthia cut him short, narrowed his eyes, and growled, "Brother Leboo, I suggest you shut your mouth and get out of my way before I violate your protocols."

Leboo's reply was snappy, yet deferential, "Yes, sir," and he quickly moved aside.

Kahuthia and Bakari entered the Udhibiti wa Dhamira and approached the communications technician on duty. Bakari spoke, "Brother Adio, I need your assistance. Four VITs have gone missing, and we want to confirm that they have not disappeared from the transmission chamber. Do you have a record of any transmissions?"

Adio's eyes grew large, "Brother Bakari, my understanding is that Chumba cha Usafiri is not operational. So, there should be no transmission."

Bakari responded, "Yes, Brother Adio, this is what we expect, and we want to confirm it to be so."

Adio swallowed and moved towards a computer terminal. "Baba Bakari, your team has been working on the chamber for the past few weeks. The log will show dozens of transmission signals. Each time a system is tested, it creates a ghost signal. The problem is that these ghost signals are indistinguishable from signals generated with actual transmissions." He began pecking away at his terminal.

Baba Bakari inquired further, "Do these signals indicate the transmission destination?"

Adio paused from his pecking, "Well, they do. But we have been testing dozens of destinations."

Baba Kahuthia continued, "Okay. Do we have any information that would allow us to narrow the possibilities?"

Adio's response was delayed. He first completed what he had been typing. Then he spun in his chair to face Baba Kahuthia, "I've initiated a scan to look for variations in the transmission signals. If any are detected, it may help me to distinguish a real transmission from the ghost transmissions. As for narrowing the possibilities…" Adio shrugged apologetically, "I don't know. This technology is new to us. We have never used it in a real scenario before."

Baba Kahuthia worked to remain composed, but he was in disbelief that a squad in his charge could be hurled through space *accidentally*!

Adio returned to the panel, squinted, and began speaking slowly, "Hmmm… Okay… It looks like that… Argh! That was a dead end. The signals are indistinguishable from one another."

Baba Kahuthia did not respond to this bad news. Hearing it, his facial expression never changed. In fact, he was calm. Adio watched his face and noticed his lack of expression, wondering if he understood what was happening.

After a lengthy pause, Bakari asked, "If we can't locate them, maybe we could at least communicate with them. Brother Adio, can you communicate with them?"

Adio smiled excitedly, "Brethren, I think we have a solution!" He then began feverishly pecking away on his keyboard. He spoke as he typed. "There are a few things that have to be in place for them to receive the communication."

Baba Kahuthia stood quietly as Adio seemed to be rambling on to himself. "The first and most important thing is that they must have Akofena with them.

Would they have known to keep Akofena? I don't know. Why would they? Then… the transceiver on Akofena has to be on. Do they know how to work Akofena? I doubt it. How would they?" Adio continued typing and talking. It seemed he had forgotten that Kahuthia and Bakari were even there. "And the volume has to be high enough to be heard. It's not a transistor radio. Adjusting the volume is not easy. Of course, it's most likely that the audio level set by the technicians hasn't been changed."

Adio punched one last key defiantly and turned to Baba Kahuthia as he sat back away from the terminal, "There."

Baba Kahuthia looked at Adio questioningly, and he spoke softly, "Is that a live line of communication?"

Adio nodded but said nothing.

Baba Kahuthia stepped forward and spoke directly into a microphone suspended over Adio's terminal. "Kamau? Kamau Njama! Chandler Gardner! Raymond Hewitt! Alton Bailey! Kikuyu Squad, if you can hear me, then you are safe. Steady your mind and listen. We are working to determine your location. Once we have your location, we will come to get you."

Adio tapped a button, which muted the microphone. "Tell them to speak. We need to see if they can communicate with us." He unmuted the microphone.

Baba Kahuthia continued, "Now, can you hear me?"

Hope for Anand (O'Leary)

It was only an hour after Anand briefed Dan on the status of Project SEV Fitzroy when the Research Team opened communication. Typically, Anand led the communication. And just as typically, he asked for a report on the status of data collection. Today was no different than in times past.

Anand began, "SEV Fitzroy, Health Status. Report."

A gruff, gravelly voice came, "Health status, good. All team members report top physical condition. Daily measurements reveal that vitals are within ideal range. We are ready to rock and roll, Project Leader!"

Anand continued, "SEV Fitzroy, Provisions Status. Report."

Again, the gravelly voice responded, "Provision Status, good. All supplies are holding steady at planned rates. We have identified four native species that may be edible in a pinch."

Anand shook his head. The Research Team was not there to find new food for themselves to eat. "Why were they wasting time in this way?" Anand continued with the check-in. "Habitat Status, Report."

The response, "CC2, we have experienced some minor damage to our antigravity generator. We've looked at it, but we can't understand what's wrong with it. I have commanded that it be taken offline for four to six hours a day. I expect less frequent use will reduce strain on the unit and prolong its useful life. Additionally, this will allow our crew to adjust to the planet's gravitational force."

The antigravity generator counteracted the effect of the planet's increased gravitational force. The more time the Research Team spent with the aid of the antigravity generator, the more energy they would conserve for their data collecting forays.

Anand replied, "Crew Commander, the decision to take the generator offline for one-third of the waking day ensures that your crew will experience greater fatigue. You are already behind schedule with your data collection. Now you will have an even greater challenge completing data collection."

The response, "Yes, CC2. In the short term, our data collection efforts will be limited. However, as our bodies adapt to the increased gravitation pull, we will be better able to return to our usual pace."

Your usual pace is crappy too, Anand thought. He looked at Dan to gauge his response to the SEV Fitzroy. Dan seemed unbothered by the decision. *This is a sad, sad state of affairs,* Anand thought.

Anand continued, "Data Collection Status. Report."

The response, "CC2, we are making progress with data collection. We have completed sample collection for two sectors."

Anand pursed his lips in frustration. His reply was firm, "SEV Fitzroy, how do you call that progress? That is half of what it should be. You are everyday further and further behind. You must stop wasting time with other activities. You are there to collect data, first and foremost!"

The tension in CC2 was thick as no one responded. Dan approached Anand and placed his hands on Anand's shoulders in a show of support. Dan broke the awkward silence, "SEV Fitzroy, this is Dan Silverstein, Project Leader. None of us in this room is in your situation. Tonight, we will sit in the comfort of our own homes, eating freshly prepared food and enjoying the company of our loved ones. So, we respect your sacrifice and your need to make command decisions in real time. However, Project Coordinator Devi is correct. We need that research data. It is the sole purpose of this mission. On next check-in, please provide a plan of how you will compensate for the time lost and complete data collection in time for you to return home safely."

The Research Team Leader responded, "COPY THAT, Project Leader."

Dan ended the transmission, and Anand felt a wave of hope that the project might be saved.

Jomo W. Mutegi

A Familiar Voice

Upon hearing Baba Kahuthia's voice, Kikuyu Squad froze and shouted, "Baba Kahuthia!" In their excitement, they didn't hear what he said after calling Kamau's name. They also noticed that his voice was faint, so he must have been far away.

Chandler squinted and peered through a stand of trees murmuring, "Where is he?"

By this time, they had heard Baba Kahuthia call Alton's name. And Alton quieted the group, "Shhh! He's in Chandler's leg." Alton moved nearer to Chandler listening carefully to Baba Kahuthia. The others followed Alton.

When Baba Kahuthia asked Kikuyu Squad if they could hear him, everyone stopped and looked to Kamau, who responded, "Yes, sir. We can hear you!"

Baba Kahuthia commanded, "Njama, tell me what you see." Kamau reported everything the squad had seen and everything they suspected. He reported that they were in a wooded area similar to that of Camp Furaha. He reported that none of the trees were familiar to them, that the sun was small in the sky and dim, that it seemed to be near evening. He reported that the work seemed to be three times as strenuous as they would expect. He also reported that they had not eaten or taken water.

When he concluded, Kamau added a detail that the squad had not discussed. "Baba Kahuthia, it feels like we have been lost for about two hours or so, but the sky has not changed. The sun hasn't dropped. It's at the same place it was in when we first noticed it."

Baba Kahuthia spoke, "Kikuyu Squad, you are doing an excellent job. Keep your wits about you and continue working together. The information you have provided is very useful."

Kamau hurriedly interrupted him, "Baba, where are we?!"

There was a pause and a solemn response, "Kamau, at this time, we do not know where you are. But Baba Ojore and our scientists are going to figure that out. Now, you do your job. Stay strong, and we will have you home soon."

Before Kamau could respond, another voice, an unfamiliar voice spoke, "There is only enough energy for a three-minute conversation. Following that, Akofena has to recharge."

Again, Kamau asked hurriedly, "What is Akofena?"

The voice became garbled, "Ako... fe... is... th..." suddenly, communication stopped.

When the transmission broke, Kikuyu Squad sat stunned for a while. They had not made sense of what was happening, and they were uncertain as to what they should do.

After a very long period of silence, Kamau spoke, "So, we *are* on another planet."

Raymond protested, "He didn't say that. You asked him where we are, and he said he didn't know. So why would you think we're on another planet?"

Kamau looked at Raymond and wondered why he was afraid of the idea of being on another planet. To Kamau's mind, no matter where they were, they were just as lost. But realizing that Raymond was struggling with the idea, Kamau let it go. He wasn't trying to win any arguments about their location. He wanted to find a way home. And he needed the entire squad to be at their best.

Kamau looked over the squad and said, "OK. Let's finish our exploration." He really wasn't sure what to do, but he knew that he didn't want everyone sitting around. He wanted to keep everyone focused on something other than their bad circumstances.

As they began to walk, Alton spoke up, "Are we gon' act like Baba Kahuthia didn't just talk to us from Chandler's leg?"

Baba Ojore Goes to Ebe Nyocha (Taharka)

As Baba Ojore approached Ebe Nyocha, he slowed his pace. He saw InDuna Taharka and another man approaching the complex to his right. As they got closer, Baba Taharka smiled broadly and called, "Montsho! Do we ever grow weary?!"

To this, Baba Ojore responded back, "No, Baba! No!" Taharka had been Ojore's Mwalimu when he himself was a VIT, and this call and response was one of Taharka's favorites.

Taharka's broad smile returned as he greeted Ojore with the handshake and embrace that is characteristic of Vanguardians. "How goes it brother?"

They stood together just feet away from the entrance. Ojore's expression turned solemn. "Not too good, I'm afraid. We have a squad of VITs who went missing just hours ago. We may need to assemble a search team to canvass the grounds.

Taharka nodded, "Young men keep us vigilant, don't they?" He then turned to his companion, "Chiumbo, this is Baba Ojore Montsho. He is lead Bausi of this year's Akhet."

Baba Ojore smiled warmly and greeted Chiumbo, "Yes, Brother! How are you? It's good to see you again."

Chiumbo returned Baba Ojore's greeting, though with much less warmth and enthusiasm. Chiumbo was a slight-built man who was given to dourness. His face always suggested that something was wrong, like he had just eaten a bit of spoiled food or smelled the scent of a decaying animal. He served as Chief Adjutant to Baba Taharka. In this role, he was responsible for assisting Baba Taharka in his professional and personal daily tasks. So Chiumbo answered phone calls, handled correspondence, scheduled appointments, arranged travel, and was the first and primary representative of the InDuna. Typically, if an order was given by Baba Taharka, the recipient of the order heard directly from Chiumbo.

So, most Vanguardians knew Chiumbo, and those who did not know him personally, knew *of* him. He was often referred to as Chief Agitator. His personality was abrasive. He was smug and condescending, which was contradicted by his frail physique. But he was completely confident in his authority, which of course wasn't really his. However, after years of serving as Chief Adjutant, he had grown comfortable and secure under the cloak of Taharka's authority.

Baba Ojore ignored Chiumbo's aloofness.

Together, the three men entered the building and walked to the Command Center. As they approached the glass room, seeing Baba Kahuthia inside with a technician, Ojore grew concerned. He quickened his pace.

The guard on duty was visibly nervous on Ojore's approach, "Uhhh. Good day, Baba Ojore?" He barely got that first awkward greeting out of his mouth when he saw Baba Taharka. "Baba Tahar..."

Sensing Ojore's urgency, Baba Taharka commanded, "Step aside, Son." Leboo could not clear a path quickly enough, and Taharka and Ojore took command off the room.

Friends and Foes

Kikuyu Squad Makes Camp

In the excitement of hearing from Baba Kahuthia, after the shock of knowing for certain that they were lost, possibly in the far reaches of space, given the stress of trying to determine what to do to save themselves, they had forgotten the absurdity of Baba Kahuthia communicating to them through Chandler's leg, as it were.

With Alton's reminder, Kamau and Raymond both looked up quickly, as though they had just remembered something. Raymond spoke first, "Yeah. What was that about?"

Chandler responded absentmindedly, "Oh, I almost forgot. It wasn't my leg." He then dug his hand into the cargo pocket on his BDU pants. "It was this," he said as he pulled out the black panel from the elevator. When we were in the elevator, or whatever it was, I went to select B-4. There were no numbers so I put my whole hand on the panel, thinking that it would light up... like the outside panel did for Kamau. Well anyway, I must have hit the wrong lights because the next thing I knew, we were falling and everything got blurry. I must have grabbed this panel trying to hold on to something. The next thing I knew, we were here."

"Well why didn't you say you had it?" Kamau asked. He tried to ask in a curious tone. He didn't want Chandler to get defensive or to feel like he was being accused.

Kamau's tone must have worked because Chandler answered like he was back to his old self. "I forgot. When we got here, we were arguing. I must have stuck it in my pocket without thinking."

Kamau smiled, "Okay, Chandler! You are the keeper of the panel. If anyone tries to take it, you give 'em the business. You beat 'em till you get tired, and then… you beat 'em some mo'.'"

Chandler beamed and nodded, "'Dats right!'"

For the next two hours, they explored the last two cardinal directions. So, for one mile in each of the four cardinal directions, they saw nothing of consequence. They saw no structures, landforms, trees, and no plants that they recognized. They saw few animals. But that was not unusual. Even at Camp Furaha, animals scurried off at the smell and sight of the VITs. They often heard the scurrying, but they rarely saw the animals. This day, they saw a good number of birds, but that meant little to them. There were very few birds that they were able to identify.

On their return from exploring the final direction, they stopped to discuss their situation. Kamau spoke first, "It's been about four to five hours since we have been here, which means it's somewhere between 1700 and 1800 hours. I don't understand why it's not getting dark."

Chandler spoke up, "Day and night are caused by a planet rotating on its axis. During the daytime, a person is on the part of the planet that is facing the sun."

Raymond interrupted, "I'm not following you. Can you repeat that."

Chandler continued, "Sure, and I'll demonstrate." He stood up and repeated his explanation, while also demonstrating a planet's rotation and revolution. "So, a planet rotates on its axis. It's like a top spinning." He spun around a few times to illustrate. Whatever part of the planet is facing the sun is experiencing daytime." He paused and motioned to Kikuyu Squad as though they were the sun. Whatever part of the planet is facing away from the sun is experiencing nighttime."

Kamau interrupted rudely, "Well, I hope we all knew that much."

Alton jumped in, "I didn't."

Kamau nodded, "Okay. Thanks, Chandler. Please continue."

"Well, because a planet rotates on its axis, we get night and day. But a planet also revolves around a sun." He then began walking around Kikuyu Squad in a big circle. "Each time it revolves around the sun, we get one year."

Alton smiled, "Chandler, you're a good teacher! I get it."

Chandler continued. This time he spun circles and walked around Kikuyu Squad at the same time. "So, earth spins on its axis and revolves around the sun at the same time. It spins on its axis 365 times for every one time it goes around the sun."

"Got it." Kamau responded.

Chandler paused, "Raymond, are you following."

Raymond, who had grown quiet, nodded, "I got it."

"Okay. So, every planet is different. Some are faster and some are slower.

They rotate at different speeds, and they revolve around their suns at different speeds." He paused to see if everyone was understanding him. Seeing they were, he continued. "Some planets rotate on their axis at the same rate that they revolve around the sun."

Chandler began rotating and revolving again, "When that happens, one side of the planet is always facing the sun, meaning that it is always daytime. The other part of the planet is always away from the sun, meaning it is always nighttime." He walked around Kikuyu Squad facing them the entire time. "This is called tidal locking."

Kamau was bewildered by Chandler. "Man, how do you know all this stuff?!" he thought out loud.

Alton then asked Chandler directly, "So, is it possible that it will always be daylight here?"

Chandler responded, "Yes, that's possible. In fact, from what we have seen, it is likely."

Raymond yawned and spoke in a deep growling voice, "Well, maybe we should walk to the Dark Side, Luke, and get some rest." Laughing, they each tried their own Darth Vader impersonation.

When Kamau broke up the comedy, he said, "Okay, let's make kambi. The best shelter would be the pit shelter. But we don't have anything to dig with. We could use primitive tools, but I don't think we have the time or energy for that. So, I recommend we build the lean to. What are your thoughts?"

Together, they discussed the pros and cons of those options. They ultimately agreed with Kamau's suggestion and began building two lean-to shelters.

Conflict Resolution (Taharka)

"Where's the Engineering Team?!" Chiumbo's voice screeched at the technician.

Adio was completely taken aback. He was a tall and, at one time, physically imposing man. In terms of size, he would have dwarfed Taharka. But alas, time and the chair from which he plied his trade had eroded that once-great physique. Now, he was still tall, but as for the rest of him, he was a bit... puffy. Despite his physical puff, he was, in every other way, a man. And he was not accustomed to being yelled at, nor did he like it.

On hearing Chiumbo's screech, Adio paused at his terminal, bit his lip, and gave Chiumbo the side eye. He calmly responded, "Brother Chiumbo, the Engineering Team is not aware of the situation. They went on break. Brother Bakari is looking for them now."

In addition to being frail and overly confident, Chiumbo was a very poor judge of people. He often missed the subtle cues that marked social interactions. So, it was no surprise that he was oblivious to the fact that Adio was on the verge of stomping him senseless. And being unaware, he continued his foolish screeching, "Brother Technician, we need that Engineering Team here this instant!"

Adio paused again. At the first instance of Chiumbo's rudeness, no one noticed. The air was tense, and the setting was new. Baba Ojore and Baba Taharka were strategizing with Baba Kahuthia on ways to support Kikuyu Squad.

This time, however, everyone did notice. Adio paused again. He bit his lip again. He was very clearly trying to restrain himself. He stood, faced Chiumbo, and spoke directly without any of the formality characteristic of the Vanguard Order, "Yo, my man. You gon' stop all that loud screeching. We all facing a tense situation. But if you can't find it within yourself to speak with some respect, you gon' be facing a hospital situation." With that, Adio stared daggers through Chiumbo. He wanted to be sure the message was received.

Apparently, Chiumbo understood. His chest rose and fell heavily, and he said nothing. He simply looked down like a scolded puppy. Kahuthia, Ojore, and Taharka watched as Chiumbo and Adio resolved their differences.

Seeing that the two had come to a resolution, Baba Taharka smiled at both men, "Very well then… That's one problem solved. Now let's fix this last problem and we can all go home."

He patted Adio on the back, and the computer tech returned to his station. He then faced his adjutant, "Brother Chiumbo, I think it might be more effective if you took to the grounds of Camp Furaha to help find the Engineering Team. When you find them, let them know it is urgent that they report to the Udhibiti wa Dhamira."

Chiumbo nodded and headed out. Taharka turned to Kahuthia and Adio, "What updates can you provide?"

Adio provided the debrief. Uncertain of what Baba Taharka knew, he started at the beginning. He told Baba Taharka about the likely breach of Chumba cha Usafiri, the estimated time of transmission, their inability to determine the location, and their brief communication with Kikuyu Squad.

At this last bit of information, there was joy as a surge of hope bolted through the room. Baba Ojore was especially excited. He had grown fond of these VITs, and though he did not mention it, he saw great potential in what they could bring to the Vanguard Order, the Abantu, and the entire Pan Afrikan community.

Baba Kahuthia shared what he had learned from Kikuyu Squad. It was clear to him that all this information was new to Baba Ojore. As for Baba Taharka, he was not so sure.

Over the next twenty minutes, the group discussed the challenges they faced in communicating with Kikuyu Squad and in bringing them back. They also explored possible solutions. Taharka spoke very little. He listened, asked pointed questions, and took notes. They were interrupted when Chiumbo returned followed by four men. The discipline of these men was evident in their crisp movements and posture. Before they spoke, Baba Taharka commanded, "Chiumbo!"

Chiumbo stepped away from the men and approached Taharka. Baba Taharka handed him a sheet of paper, whispered some instructions, and off Chiumbo went. Taharka then stepped towards the four men. He was flanked by Ojore and Kahuthia. He smiled warmly at them and spoke, "Greetings, Warriors."

They returned his greeting. He then spoke directly to the leader, "Brother Bakari, your report?"

One man stood forward as the leader of the team. He glanced at Ojore and Kahuthia, then looked squarely at Taharka and said solemnly, "Brother Chiumbo has briefed us on the situation. Sir, we have bad news."

An Anonymous Tip (O'Leary)

Tim strolled into his office early. He whistled and had an extra bounce in his step. The previous night had ended in spectacular fashion, and the morning was off to a great start. He began his workday as usual, with a call to Daphne, a review of his daily calendar, and a bit of stage setting. He turned off all email and phone notifications; and he pulled a scientific article he had earmarked for reading. Years ago, Tim had developed the practice of spending one to two hours each day reading current research. He found that it helped him to stay light-years ahead of his peers, many of whom stopped reading current research shortly after they had written their dissertations.

Once his workday was ready to begin, Dan made a slight deviation from his routine. He closed his office door. He took a cellular phone from his briefcase. It was a cheap phone; one of those flip phones that can be purchased from a department store without a contract. He then placed a call.

Timothy spoke from the back of his throat and dropped his R's. He sounded as though he was from Boston. "Yes, I'd like to repawt a theft, and uhhh, I'd like to remain anonymous."

He waited for a reply. "Okay, uhhh, look I'm an employee ovah heeuh at uuuhhh, TechInnoGen. As you know, we have a lot of highly sensitive scientific products. Yeah, well, faw one of those products, the cawmpany plans... the official documents weeuh stol'n. And they weeuh stol'n from the briefcase of one of ah top executives."

He paused to listen, "No, sih. You ah not undahstanding me. This has got to be anonymous. I got kids to feed. Anyway, these plans describe a project that could threat'n national security if it gets in the wrawng hands." He then added for good measure, "Sahgeant, if you find these plans quickly, you might be saving hundreds of thousands of lives. And I'm pretty sure the top brass at TechInnoGen would want to show theih gratitude to the police department. Thanks."

The Prep Team Reports (Taharka)

Bakari Njeri, Okello Ogutu, Mungai Wachira, and Macharia Kabui stood tall and strong in the presence of Baba Taharka.

As team leader, Bakari addressed the InDuna. "Baba Taharka, to begin, we have been running tests on Chumba cha Usafiri for several weeks now. We are still learning the technology. We did not expect that it would be operational. At the time of the transmission, Chumba cha Usafiri was set for transport to an H-zone planet orbiting a star in the constellation Libra. This is the location for Yurugu's pending exploration." He turned to Macharia, "Brother Macharia, please provide Brother Adio with the interstellar coordinates so that he can locate the planet. Once he is satisfied, provide him the planetary coordinates so that we can locate the VITs."

"Yes, sir!" Macharia snapped, as he headed over to Adio.

Bakari knew they would need to account for how and why they left Chumba cha Usafiri unsecured. But for now, the lost VITs was a more immediate concern. He continued, "Baba Taharka, the planet is slightly over twenty light-years from earth. It is about three and one-half times larger than earth, so it has an intense gravitational pull. This will make labor difficult for the VITs."

No one spoke. They all listened intently to Bakari's report. "There are several species on the planet that make for edible food. This includes both plants and animals. There are also many sources of potable water." At this last bit of information, Baba Kahuthia began taking notes. He then asked, "Brother Bakari, what are the two or three most easily accessible and healthful foods available on the planet?"

Bakari turned to Okello Ogutu, who gave Baba Kahuthia a detailed description of a few of the available foods on the planet. Once Okello had finished his description of food sources, Bakari resumed his report. "There is water within a mile and a half of their arrival location. We can provide them directions."

Kahuthia replied, "Thank you, Brother Bakari!"

Bakari continued, "There are a number of small groups, tribes, and other factions of humanoids throughout the region. Our intelligence report shows that two of these groups are hostile for no good reason." Baba Kahuthia recoiled slightly at the reference to humanoids. But he quickly composed himself.

Baba Ojore inquired, "Are they likely to encounter any humanoid species at their current location?

Bakari responded, "If they stay within a two-mile radius of their current location, there is a very slim chance that they will encounter any humanoids."

Hearing this report, Taharka looked at Bakari and asked flatly, "What's the bad news?"

Bakari responded, "Yes, sir. First, the energy coupling on Chumba cha Usafiri needs to be replaced. We have an acquisition team working on it, but we expect it will take three days to have the replacement."

Taharka snapped, "Three days?"

Bakari remained quiet. Ojore nodded his head in quiet acceptance. Then simultaneously, he, Taharka, and Kahuthia stared back at Bakari.

After an awkward pause, Taharka asked, "Brother Bakari?"

"Yes, sir?"

"What other bad news do you have? You said, 'First, the energy coupling needs to be replaced.' What is second?"

Bakari responded absentmindedly, "Yes, sir. The Akofena device taken by the VITs is glitchy. The global positioning module is providing inaccurate readings. And the communication module comes in and out."

Taharka, Ojore, and Kahuthia received this news without any apparent concern. Once Bakari finished his report, Baba Taharka said, "Thank you, Warrior. Keep your squad around.

He then turned to Ojore and Kahuthia, "So we've got to figure a way to support four VITs on a planet 20 light-years away for *three days*?!" He continued, "And when we provide them instruction on how to return, we will communicate through a device with unreliable communication?"

Ojore chimed in, "And they will travel using a transport device that is malfunctioning?" They paused in contemplation. Ojore shook his head, "I don't like this situation."

Kahuthia spoke, "When a monkey doesn't get a banana, he eats chilies."

Ojore and Taharka looked at Kahuthia and at one another. Taharka smiled, "Yes, Brother Kahuthia. If the situation doesn't work for us, we change the situation."

Kahuthia offered, "We send a team with a functioning Akofena, and we bring them out." Ojore and Taharka nodded their approval.

Ojore offered, "Excellent, Brother Kahuthia. How about Mursi Squad. They are quite…"

Taharka cut him off, "Chaki!" Ojore and Kahuthia were taken aback by Taharka's response. Taharka continued in a more pleasant tone, "I have another squad in mind that would be perfect. I'll have Chiumbo get them here tomorrow."

Kikuyu Squad Receives Instructions

Alton heard Baba Kahuthia's voice and startled awake. Chandler was also stirring. They crawled from behind the lean-to and woke Kamau and Raymond. Chandler responded, "Yes, Baba, Kikuyu Squad is here. We're getting Kamau and Raymond."

Kamau was groggy, but the circumstances alerted him enough. "Squad reporting, sir."

Baba Kahuthia chuckled slightly at the formality, "Okay, listen. We have only three minutes to communicate. After that you will need to wait another twelve hours to hear from us. I have a lot to tell you. Are you ready?"

Kamau looked at the squad. They were listening. "Yes, Baba," he replied.

"We now have your location. You are on a planet in the Libra constellation, about twenty light-years from earth. That planet is in a captured rotation around its star. What that means for you is there will be no daytime or nighttime."

Kamau interrupted the explanation, "Yes, Baba, we understand. Chandler explained tidal locking to us. And it has remained dusk since we arrived."

Baba Kahuthia was taken aback, and he responded, "Oh. Well, that's outstanding."

Baba Taharka and Baba Ojore both looked at each other with expressions of surprised satisfaction.

Baba Kahuthia continued, "As long as you find a clean water source, the water is safe to drink. In terms of its molecular composition, it is the same as our water."

Although they were listening intently, Kamau thought it was important to let Baba Kahuthia know that they were still there. So, he periodically responded with a simple, "Yes, sir."

"There is food that is safe for you to eat. I will describe to you three types. The first is a nut about the size of a balled-up fist. These nuts range in color from orange to brown. The shells are easy to crack, and the meat inside can be eaten raw; it can be roasted in an open fire; or it can be ground into a powder and boiled in a bit of water to make a paste. The nuts are tasty, filling, provide good nutrition, and they are found everywhere. Do not eat the nuts when they are still green. They are poisonous when they are green. Make sure they have turned brown or orange.

"The second is a very large leaf. These leaves grow in clumps from the ground, much like collard greens. They are the huge leaves. One leaf will be more than you can eat in a meal. They can be eaten raw or boiled. These are safe to eat. There are no known similar species, so identifying them is relatively easy.

"The third is a small animal similar to a rabbit. It has soft rabbit-like fur, and it produces in large numbers like rabbits. It walks upright like a raccoon, but it is docile, slow, and safe to capture. The meat is not the best, but you can live off of it."

The transmission had grown quiet, and Baba Kahuthia asked, "Njama, are you still with me?"

Kamau responded, "Yes, Baba. We are listening."

Baba Kahuthia continued, "Very well. Now about …ing, follow… yo… n…al in…tions." The transmission had begun to go out. Kikuyu Squad looked at each other in confused frustration, but they remained quiet and strained to listen. The transmission continued, "The …ues have …at hel… … mon…tor earth …for …now." There was a loud crackle and hiss and the transmission ended.

In his frustration, Alton snapped, "What we 'sposed to do with that, Kamau?!"

The rest of Kikuyu Squad was quiet. Chandler and Kamau seemed to be thinking. Raymond was growing despondent.

Alton continued, "All this fancy technology… but the radio don't work!"

Kamau looked at Alton and spoke sternly, "That's enough, Alton. Keep your head. Otherwise, you'll get us all in trouble." He then spoke to everyone, "That goes for all of us. If one of us loses his composure, or makes a bad decision, or acts carelessly in some way, that one person puts the whole squad at risk."

Kamau looked around to see that his message had gotten through. When he was confident that it had, he continued, "Now, forget about what we didn't hear. What we did hear is that we can eat. And I, my friends, am hungry!"

They smiled and got a bit giddy at the idea of eating. Even Raymond's spirits seemed to be lifted. Alton clapped his hands and rubbed them together, "Oh yeeeesss." He then pretended to be a smug aristocrat, "Uhh, Garcon, I will have a serving of the slow moving racoo-rabbit, roasted please." They cackled with excitement.

Adopting a very poor British accent, Raymond added, "And for myself, I would like the balled-fist alien peanuts." He then turned to Kamau, "And you, sir?"

Kamau noticed that everyone was laughing except for Chandler. He responded to Raymond, with the same bad accent, "My associate…" he said gesturing to Chandler, "…will have the lettuce that's big as your head."

Chandler was humored, but he did not join in. Kamau knew what this meant. Chandler had thought of something that they had not. The realization gave him pause, and he asked, "Chandler, are we missing something?"

Chandler looked at him squarely, "Yes, we are missing a lot. We are missing rope or string that we need to trap the racoo-rabbit. We're missing knives that we need to skin and butcher it. We are missing matches or tinder that we need to build a fire to roast the racoo-rabbit, and we are missing water. Remember, we walked four miles yesterday; I guess it was yesterday… We walked four miles… one mile in each of four directions and we saw no water. There was no river, creek, pond, not even a puddle."

The Squad sobered a bit. Chandler's realism put things in perspective. While they now knew what they could eat, they were many steps away from being able to actually eat it. After the limitations of their situation set in, Kamau nodded and redirected the energy of Kikuyu Squad, "Thanks, Chandler. He's right. We can eat, but we have a lot of work to do."

The experience they had had at the Akhet of going days without eating, until they were able to catch their own food, gave each of them an appreciation for how hard it is to eat. Even when foraging for food, they learned that searching for, gathering, transporting, preparing, and cooking seeds, plants, and mushrooms is still quite a bit of work.

So, with Chandler's admonition and Kamau's words, they mentally prepared themselves for a long day… or whatever this period of time should be called.

Kamau made a suggestion, "Let's try to cover new ground. We can travel further, we can travel a new direction, or we can do both. What are your thoughts?"

It was agreed that they should cover new ground in hopes of finding water. It was also agreed that traveling too far would make the task of returning with food difficult. So, they agreed to travel a new direction, and they would travel until they had all the nuts and leaves they could comfortably carry.

The Squad Feasts

The search for food and water was not as successful as the squad had hoped. They found the balled-fist peanuts, which they ate raw. They also found the lettuce that was as big as your head, which they ate raw. As for the racoo-rabbit, they found none. Neither did they find water.

SECRETS OF THE VANGUARD ORDER

After they had finished eating, Alton spoke in a dejected tone, "Well, it sure wasn't a feast, but at least my stomach's not growling anymore."

They all concurred, when Kamau added cheerily, "Yeah? Well, who needs racoo-rabbit anyway. I'll tell you what, when we make it back to Camp Furaha, when we *win* the Intersquad Competition, *when* we finish the Akhet as the greatest squad ever, then, in celebration, Kikuyu Squad will feast at my home—at the Njama table."

Kikuyu Squad watched Kamau and began smiling. He spoke with joy, and his playfulness took their minds off their troubles.

He continued, "And let me tell you something, sirs—let me tell you sirs something, I promise you—you have never had a culinary delight anything like you will experience at the Njama table. You will enjoy succulence unlike any you have had anywhere on earth."

The smiles grew large, and Chandler added quickly, "Or any other planet for that matter." With that, their smiles transformed into outright laughter, and they each began naming the various dishes they wanted to eat at the Njama table.

After some time, Kamau added, "Well the food helped a bit, but we won't make it very long without water. I say we go looking for some. We've got time. That's for sure."

Everyone nodded in agreement. As they set out in search of water, they decided to follow the path they took on their very first exploration. They traveled in a direction they believed to be north. They also resolved to go farther than before. Their *confidence* was high as they had contacted Baba Kahuthia. Their *energy* was high after having rested and eaten. And now, it seemed their *spirits* were high. After walking about a mile, Kamau commented, "We are too loud."

"What do you mean?" Raymond asked. "We haven't spoken for the past ten minutes."

"I'm not talking about our voices. I'm talking about our heavy feet that keep cracking twigs and crushing leaves. Our shoulders keep rustling leaves. Our loud breathing…"

"What difference does it make, Kamau?" Alton asked.

Before Kamau could answer, Chandler spoke up, "It doesn't make any difference if we're moving through our own woods with sixteen other VITs and six Mwalimu, and when our food is always waiting for us at Ukumbi wa Kunye. But if we need to sneak up on dinner, it makes a big difference."

Kamau nodded, "That's right!" He said nothing more about it.

At that point, there was little they could do to learn to be quieter when moving through the woods. However, the realization of how loud they were helped Kamau to put their new skills in perspective. On one hand, they felt invincible. Physically, they were each stronger than they had ever been. They could run any distance and could carry or move any load. And they could do both all day. Many days, they actually did. Mentally, they were stronger and more disciplined. They could endure pain. They could accept hardship without reservation. They could focus amidst distraction, and they could dismiss passion and emotion to think clearly. They had learned to fight with and without weapons. They had learned to function as a unit. They had an impressive set of new skills. But in all this, they couldn't walk quietly through the woods. They couldn't see, let alone catch, a slow, defenseless rabbit-like animal. And if they didn't get lucky soon, they might die of thirst, all because they couldn't even find water to drink.

Kamau kept these wicked thoughts to himself. He didn't want to demoralize the squad. But having considered their limitations, he now noticed the sounds of the woods. Leaves rustled as small unseen animals scurried on their approach. There seemed to be a sphere of quiet that surrounded them. As they traveled, the woods grew silent to watch them pass, as though they knew that Kikuyu Squad did not belong.

After walking the second mile, Alton asked, "Kamau, what are we going to use to carry this water back?"

Kamau said nothing, as he had no answer. The question was yet another reminder of their ineptitude. After some time, and seeing that Kamau would not respond, Chandler offered, "We're going to use our bodies to carry it back."

Raymond smiled, and Alton responded, "Well, I guess I'll get the most water, seeing as I got the biggest container!" That was their last exchange before the unthinkable happened.

The Brief (Taharka)

The last members of the Support Team had arrived, and they were all assembled in the briefing room at Ebe Nyocha. A Support Team was assembled for any operation that required monitoring and real time support. Although it was rare, it was frequent enough that the Vanguard Order had established protocols for assembling and managing the Support Team.

A typical Support Team consisted of eight persons: four Abantu members and four members of the Vanguard Order. The four Abantu members for this particular team were Nicole Richardson (physician), David Knight (psychologist), Anthony Howard (historian), and Beatrice Turner (a female elder and playwright). To the Vanguardians, the female elder represented the grandmother of the community. Vanguardians were quick to strike. They were eager to settle conflicts and to settle them definitively. The female elder was a counterbalance to their extreme and decisive aggression. It was believed that if a situation was so dire that the community grandmother gave permission for the Order's unique form of justice, then they should not hesitate to enact it.

The four members of the Vanguard Order were Adio Bankola (the Communication Technician), Oko Addo (military advisor), Osei Yeboah (weapons expert), and Fenuku Akoto (physical scientist). It was not expected that these eight Support Team members had answers to all questions in their area of specialty. Instead, they had expertise, so they knew a lot. But most importantly, they knew the limits of their knowledge. Each had ready access to a team of other experts that they could draw on during an operation.

This mission was unique in three ways. First, a typical mission consisted of a single squad of four people, whereas this one consisted of eight. Second, the VITs were not trained Vanguardians. Their seven-week Akhet experience was little more than a cursory peek into the type of life that Vanguardians lived. Their training counted for nothing, and they could not be relied upon to function independently in any way. Third, this mission was rushed. Because of intelligence received by InDuna Taharka from an incognegro Vanguardian, the mission was moved up several months from the original planned mission. Most importantly, while there had been missions conducted in strange lands and distant locations, the Vanguard Order had never executed a mission on another planet.

Joining the Support Team in the Command Center were the four members of the Engineering Team, Kahuthia, Ojore, Dembe Akello (a pediatrician), and Natukunda Nngobi (a child psychologist).

As he began the brief, InDuna Taharka was flanked by Chiumbo, who positioned himself to Taharka's left, and Ojore, who stood to Taharka's right. Baba Taharka asked Baba Kahuthia to stand post, just inside the door, as a failsafe. Leboo stood post on the other side of the briefing room, and Taharka was not confident in his ability.

Taharka began, "Welcome, family! I'll not waste time with pleasantries as time is of the essence. I will begin with historical context. Recently, a tech company began using newly developed teleportation technology to explore planets that could be mined for their resources. Their first mission was launched a little over a year ago. It was a scouting mission that was successful. They confirmed the trustworthiness of their technology by transporting a scout team to a planet, gathering pertinent data, and safely returned to Earth.

"The Vanguard Order first became aware of this mission through an intelligence operative. We have been monitoring their activity, looking for opportunities to disrupt their efforts."

A few members of the Support Team nodded at Taharka and took notes as he spoke. Others sat patiently and listened.

He continued, "Based on our intelligence, we believe the threat posed by this company to be credible and imminent. If not addressed, we believe that harm to the Abantu and the larger community will be far-reaching and irreparable."

Taharka paused to give those assembled an opportunity to interject with any questions they might have. However, there were no questions, and there was no discussion. Perhaps a different group may have had uncertainty, but the men and women assembled here were students of history. They knew of the scramble to colonize Africa, of the East India Trading Company, and of the colonization of the Americas. The idea of Europeans traveling the globe to destabilize cultures for the purpose of exploitation was not foreign to them. They also knew, better than most, that the harm caused by this European recklessness was both far-reaching and irreparable. Those assembled were victims of it.

Seeing that there were no questions, Taharka continued, "We have had a series of unexpected developments related to this mission. First, our enemy has accelerated their planned launch by more than six months. They have had a group of invaders on the ground for over a month now. So, we have lost our opportunity to prevent them from returning to this planet." Taharka paused to survey the room before continuing, "Our second unexpected development is that a squad of VITs inadvertently transported to the planet." There were audible gasps from some of the members as heads shot up in shocked surprise. "We have established communication with them, and our last contact was at 0700."

Mama Turner asked in stark amazement, "How were our young men able to transport to another planet? How do we have this technology?"

Taharka answered her plainly, "Mama Turner, we liberated a prototype version of this technology from the enemy. And for some months, we've had our scientists and engineers studying it. Our Engineering Team," Taharka motioned to Bakari, "has been working to backwards engineer the technology. They were not aware that it was operational."

Ojore began to look uncomfortable. For a moment, his eyes moved about the room in an agitated way, and he fidgeted with his hands. However, after a minute or so, he regained his discipline.

Taharka's tone remained strong and unaffected. "This is the context in which we are now operating. Our job is to support the Extraction Team as they return our VITs home safely. Now, I'd like to brief you on the relevant details of the destination. One of the most impactful distinguishing features is that the planet in question is in a tidal locked orbit around its sun. What that means for us is that there are no regular periods of day and night. Our VITs have been on the ground for just over twenty-five hours."

SECRETS OF THE VANGUARD ORDER

Oko Addo asked, "Of all the challenges we face, how is that a concern? Young men can go a day or so without sleep."

Dembe Akello explained, "The twenty-four-hour cycle to which African people have grown accustomed over tens of thousands of generations is deeply ingrained not only in our biological and psychological makeup, but it's encoded in our ancestral memory. The effect of circadian rhythms has been seen in everything from animals and plants to fungi and microorganisms. On Earth, most things have evolved to rely on cyclic periods of activity and rest."

Oko interjected, "I understand the importance of circadian rhythms to normal human functioning. But these are not normal circumstances. Humans can survive brief periods of abnormal circumstances."

Natukunda added, "In humans, the cycle not only regulates sleep and rest, but it also controls temperature fluctuations and the release of hormones. Studies have shown that disruption of the circadian rhythm results in a wide range of physical and psychological problems."

Oko shrugged. He still didn't see an answer to his question. He was familiar with the concept of circadian rhythms. He also knew that modern life was already disrupting the natural rhythm right here on Earth. For the past several hundred years, Europeans had been in the process of turning the normal day and evening cycle on its head. Now, in the past one hundred years, with the advent of electric lighting, they have turned urban centers into twenty-four-hour day-zones, and there is no true nighttime anymore. Both diurnal and nocturnal animals that rely on periods of darkness are struggling to adapt to this new development. *I'd better not raise this issue*, he thought. *It would just muddy the waters.*

At that thought, Baba Kahuthia spoke up, "Brother Oko, the circadian disruption is not life threatening in and of itself. But we should consider it among the many factors that are affecting Kikuyu Squad. They are working against the confusion brought on by constant daylight. They are working to overcome the fatigue of heavier gravity. They are operating on limited rest. And they are working in the face of a traumatic shift in their understanding of the world. Two days ago, they likely had no idea that interstellar space travel was even possible. Now today, they are themselves on a planet that is light-years away.

Oko nodded at Kahuthia, "Understood. Thank you."

Osei Yeboah interjected, "What weapons will the team have?"

Taharka responded curtly, "No weapons." Osei's head jerked up in surprise.

Bakari explained, "Weapons add a substantial amount of weight. We are already pushing the limits of our technology by transporting eight people.

Taharka continued, "Brother Osei, there are other considerations. We should impact the native population as little as possible. The presence of advanced weaponry could greatly upset their development."

Osei nodded, "Very well."

Taharka smiled, "Besides all that, on this mission our team should be picking our VITs up and coming home."

After a short pause, Fenuku Akoto asked, "What do we know about the chemical composition of the planet?"

Taharka nodded towards the Engineering Team, "Brother Bakari?"

Bakari stood to address the group, "Yes, sir. In terms of its molecular and chemical composition, the planet is Earth-like in every way. Water is water. The air is similar to our air. It contains carbon dioxide, nitrogen, and oxygen. There is a good deal more carbon dioxide (about 20%) and more water vapor than we are accustomed to. The amount of oxygen is about the same. The flora and fauna are different enough to let us know that we are not on Earth, but it is all very Earth-like. Based on the reports we have seen, everything can be categorized using our own binomial nomenclature."

Mama Nicole looked puzzled, "What does it mean when you say, 'water is water'?"

Bakari smiled, "Yes, Mama. Not all water is created equal. Many of you have likely heard of heavy water from your college chemistry classes. Normally, hydrogen has one proton, one electron, and no neutrons. However, there is an isotope of hydrogen, called deuterium, that has one proton, one electron and one neutron. This extra neutron makes the hydrogen 'heavy'. When these deuterium atoms (or heavy hydrogens) bond with oxygen to form water, the result is heavy water. In small amounts, deuterium is no problem. In fact, we all have small amounts in our bodies at any given time. However, when consumed in large amounts over prolonged periods of time, deuterium can cause dizziness and lowered blood pressure."

Mama Nicole nodded in understanding. David Knight asked, "So, is heavy water the only variation of water?"

Fenuku interjected, "No, Brother David. Tritium is another isotope of hydrogen that can bond with oxygen to form water. Tritium is rare here on Earth, but it has two neutrons and it's radioactive. There are also multiple forms of water with normal hydrogen isotopes, ortho-water and para-water. These two forms of water have slightly different shapes based on the direction that the hydrogen atoms in the water spin."

David nodded in understanding. "I see."

Fenuku continued, "The issue here is not so much the variations of the water, air, or soil that we know. Our real concern is the possibility of molecular structures that we don't know. What the scout team is providing is a measure of confidence that, chemically, the planet reflects what we would see on Earth."

The briefing continued for another forty minutes with InDuna Taharka leading the discussion and members of the Support Team alternately asking questions of one another and answering questions for one another. Following the briefing, they took time to read materials provided to them.

When the team seemed to have completed their work, Taharka announced, "The Extraction Team will arrive first thing in the morning." At this mention, Ojore again appeared agitated. He looked as though he wanted to speak, but he restrained himself. InDuna Taharka observed Ojore's agitation, but he said nothing. Instead, he continued addressing the Support Team, "The Extraction Team will also need to brief, prepare for transport, and make final arrangements."

Mama Nicole looked at InDuna Taharka with shocked concern, "Final arrangements?! Do you mean…"

She was unable to complete her sentence. Baba Taharka helped. "Yes, Mama Nicole, Vanguardians always make final arrangements prior to an engagement. We take nothing for granted."

As he observed the manner with which Baba Taharka engaged the Support Team, Baba Kahuthia was impressed at his brilliance. He never lied or misrepresented the truth. But he also never let the Support Team see fully the warrior aspects of Vanguard life. Making final arrangements was an ongoing aspect of Vanguard existence. It went hand in hand with Vanguard Meditations on Death. Vanguardians were prepared to fight, kill, and die on a moment's notice. And this constant state of preparation took work. This was an aspect of Vanguardian life that most in the Abantu could never understand, but it was necessary to ensure the survival of the collective.

As the Support Team broke, Bausi Ojore turned to InDuna Taharka. "InDuna, permission requested to join the extraction team on this mission." Although Ojore was requesting permission, he spoke to Taharka as a peer.

Taharka looked at him squarely, sized him up. He then turned away as he responded, "Permission denied."

Ojore stood firm, "InDuna, these are my VITs. I am charged with securing their well-being. Why would you deny me this?"

Taharka responded flatly, "Because you are old."

Ojore's eyes grew large, and his voice rumbled, "Old?! I'll show you old!"

Unfazed, Taharka responded wryly, "You'll show us all old when you get to that planet, fumbling and stumbling about." He looked Ojore directly in the eyes and smiled.

Ojore's anger subsided, if ever it really was anger. But he was still very serious about his request. He said nothing but waited for a real answer to his inquiry.

Jomo W. Mutegi

Taharka indulged him, "Look, Bausi, you are in line to be the next InDuna, and there is no other. I am an old man. I cannot do this job much longer. What would it do to the Order if we lost you in a mission that you did not need to join?" He then answered his own question, "It would set us back. There is a team of men in place. This squad is trained. This squad has prepared. You should know that better than anyone. You trained them. Now, let these men do the job that they have been prepared to do." He paused and looked Ojore in the eyes, trying to gauge his receptiveness. What he learned was that Ojore accepted his decision as InDuna, but he did not like it.

Seeing as much, Taharka smiled and added, "Besides that, my friend, you too old."

That afternoon the Support Team ate lunch together as they rekindled old friendships and began forging new ones.

Captives

Raymond looked up in a start. "Do you hear that?!"

Chandler returned his whisper, "No what is it?"

"I think I hear water running. It sounds like a river."

They stopped walking and strained to listen.

Alton smiled and nodded, "Yeah! I hear it."

The sound was coming from their left. They could not see the river from where they stood. Eager to get water, Alton moved in the direction of the sound. But Kamau called for him to wait. "Alton!" As Alton turned back, Kamau began to explain, "We are walking a straight line from our kambi to that bearing we took. If we deviate from this line, we might not find our way back." The others nodded in agreement. They began looking around for some natural marker in the landscape, some abnormally large or distinctive plant that they could use for reference, but they could find none.

Then Raymond suggested, "Let's take turns. Two of us can go to drink, while the other two remain on the line. After the first two have their fill, then the other two will go. If the two going for water get turned around, the two on the line can holler, and we can follow the sound of our voices."

The squad paused for a moment to think this idea through. Alton added, "Maybe we should talk while the two water drinkers walk away. That way, we won't accidentally walk outside the sound of our voices."

The whole squad looked at each other. And for a moment, they stood there nodding with dopey grins, impressed with their cleverness. Alton looked at Kamau, "Okay. So should me and Chandler go first?"

Kamau responded, "No, you and Raymond should go first." So, Alton and

Raymond went for water.

For about two minutes after they had left, Kamau and Chandler called the cadence that Kikuyu Squad had created when they ran the Never-Mark. Raymond and Alton gave the response. After two minutes, Kamau and Chandler could still hear the response, but they could no longer understand it. After four minutes, they no longer heard a response.

It was atypical for Alton to work with Raymond. Typically, if the squad broke up into pairs, they paired with their quarter mate. On this occasion, however, Kamau wanted to speak privately with Chandler. He wanted Chandler to know that he was no longer sore about what had happened at Camp Furaha. So, during this brief time alone, the two made amends.

Kamau had begun to worry. It had been about four minutes, and they heard nothing from Alton and Raymond. They should have returned by now. Or, at least, they should have called out for direction. Just as he thought this, he heard a wretched screech coming from the direction that Alton and Raymond had traveled. As he looked in that direction, he saw a large, hideous creature. It looked like a horse that stood almost upright, but it had none of the grace and elegance of a horse. It foamed at the mouth, had jagged teeth, and a rat-like snout. Its front legs were raised off the ground, and they beat against the air. The legs looked deformed. They were small with no musculature and were shorter than a horse's legs should be. The creature looked like a cross between a horse, a rat, and a *T-Rex*.

Both Kamau and Chandler were frozen by shock and fear. They stood there, mouths agape, just staring at the beast. And suddenly, the creature bolted directly towards them. Neither of the boys knew what to do. Should they run? Where would they run to? Should they fight? How on earth would they fight? What about Alton and Raymond?

If shock and fear froze Kamau, this whirlwind of questions racing through his head completely cemented him in place. He didn't move. He had no idea what to do. The next thing he knew, something fell from the creature. Whatever it was, it fell right on top of Kamau and pinned him to the ground. As Kamau worked to free himself, he realized that it was a person.

The creature was so grotesque, so repulsive, that he had not even noticed that someone was riding on top of it. The rider must have jumped from the creature and tackled Kamau. The person wrestling with Kamau on the ground seemed to be a boy about his same age. He was much thinner than Kamau, but very strong, much stronger than Kamau.

Kamau managed to roll to his stomach. He pulled his left knee up towards his chest, then his right knee. Now Kamau was on his hands and knees, on all fours like a child pretending to be a dog. The boy grabbed at him from behind. Just like his father taught him, Kamau pulled his left leg forward, planting his foot firmly on the ground. He then mustered his strength to step forward and away in one quick motion. He then turned quickly to face his attacker. As he did so, he heard a cackling that sounded like laughter, and he noticed that he was surrounded by other boys, some standing and some sitting on these hideous beasts. He didn't take time to count those around him. He was focused on his attacker.

He did, however, hear one voice that stood out from the rest. Although he had no clue what this voice was saying, he sensed from the tone that it was the voice of the boy in charge. The boy in charge barked out commands to Kamau's attacker and to the others present. The boy facing Kamau rocked back and forth as though he was doing some sort of dance. Suddenly, he lunged at Kamau and swung at his head. Kamau ducked to avoid being struck. But he did not counterattack, which he should have done. He was confused by the attacker. He was trying to make sense of what the attacker had done. The attacker's arm did not attack in a way that Kamau recognized. It was not a jab, a hook, or a cross… or even a haymaker. The arm swung as though the elbow weren't a hinge. It was like the attacker's entire forearm could spin in a complete circle. The strike was as though the attacker threw his arm at Kamau.

While Kamau stood there, trying to understand the anatomy of his attacker, the attack continued. This time, he connected. Kamau doubled over with a strike to his midsection. Then after a strike to the back of his head, he crumpled to the ground. Kamau groaned in pain. He had never been hit that hard. Not even Wayne Scott could hit that hard.

As he lay there, he heard what sounded like cheers coming from the other boys. Kamau's attacker then began pulling him from the ground by his neck. As he pulled Kamau up, the boy jabbed his midsection, kneed his kidneys, and kicked his lower extremities. The grip exerted on Kamau's neck was choking him.

Kamau saw Chandler out of the corner of his eye. He was standing there being restrained by one of the attackers. Kamau also tried to count the attackers. It appeared that there were about ten boys and three of the creatures. As Kamau began to get his bearings, there was a great commotion among the attackers. The leader barked commands. Kamau's attacker dropped him. The attacker who restrained Chandler lost interest, and the other attackers began scrambling away as another group approached.

This second group was larger in number than the first. This group also consisted of boys who appeared to be about the same age as Kamau. But there were also older men. Strangely, one younger boy seemed to be in charge, and even the older men followed his direction. He did not bark commands. He spoke in more subdued tones, but he was clearly in charge. The way he carried himself, the way he spoke, reminded Kamau of Bongani Jekwa. This boy wore a short fur cape that extended from his shoulders to his lower back. The cape was attached to his shoulders by what appeared to be two paws. Each paw grasped one of his shoulders.

Some of the attackers helped Kamau to his feet. Others removed the ropes that had bound Chandler's hands. Two of the boys used pointed spears to prod both Kamau and Chandler to walk. As the entire group moved, Kamau's head began to clear. He began observing and thinking again. He noticed some of the differences in the attackers' anatomy and physiology. Their joints were not as stiff. They were leaner, yet stronger, and their movements were more fluid. By their dress, they looked like they came out of the pages of National Geographic. They were fully clothed, wearing mostly animal skins, and they adorned themselves with bones, feathers, stones, and paint. As for their language, Kamau was unable to make any sense of it.

After some time, Kamau spoke to Chandler. "Are you Okay?"

"Yeah. I'll be fine." Chandler sounded like his old self.

Kamau asked, "What happened to you back there? I didn't see it. There was so much confusion going on."

Chandler answered, "Same as you. They jumped off that horse creature, knocked me down, and tied me up."

Kamau nodded, "Okay." He then tried to reassure Chandler, "We're going to get out of this. We will be fine."

Chandler then asked a question that Kamau was not prepared to answer, "What about Alton and Raymond? How will we find them?"

Kioko's Misfortune (Taharka)

Kioko King'ori glanced at his watch again. He wanted to finish his errands so that he could be well rested for his early morning flight. He had finished his banking and eaten lunch with his girlfriend. One more stop for groceries, and he would be home.

Looking in his rear-view mirror, he noticed a dark brown sedan speeding up on him. Shaking his head, he thought, *This fool.* He had seen this same car just two minutes earlier when getting on the highway. The driver was trying to cross three lanes of traffic to get into the turning lane. He had almost hit a pedestrian trying to do so. Now it was clear that the driver was not only inconsiderate, but also reckless. Kioko could barely see the driver's head as he sat with the seat laid back. And he was driving very fast. Kioko wanted to get over and make way, but there was traffic in the next lane and nowhere for Kioko to go.

The brown sedan pulled up dangerously close to Kioko's bumper, trying to intimidate him out of the way. Kioko remained calm as he thought, *Look genius, I'll be out of your way as soon as I am able.* Not long after, an opening cleared and Kioko changed lanes to clear a way for the sedan. Now, with all the freedom Kioko could offer, instead of simply passing, the driver slowed down just enough to sneer at Kioko and make a rude gesture. Seeing this, Kioko shook his head and thought, *Unbelievable!* He then turned away and continued driving. The sedan sped away with music blaring.

About three miles later, Kioko saw the sedan pulled over on the side of the road. It appeared that the driver was receiving a citation. Kioko took note of the irony and kept driving. It was quite a surprise when, five minutes later, the sedan was back on the road... still speeding and still bouncing recklessly in and out of traffic.

Again, Kioko saw the car in his rear-view mirror. This time the sedan was speeding in the adjacent lane. As the car passed, with music still blaring, the driver looked over and saw Kioko. The driver's initial expression was surprise. That expression quickly gave way to anger. *What's his deal?* Kioko thought. Then he wondered, *Do I know this guy? Have I done something to him?* Kioko was genuinely confused. He was no angel, and he had had a few run-ins. Well, actually more than a few. In his youthful exuberance, Kioko had run roughshod over enough people that, periodically, a fellow who still harbored ill-feelings would resurface. Kioko didn't even know all these people. In these instances, Kioko would simply apologize and make amends where possible. Where apologies were not possible, he would stomp them anew, removing all hope of a future reckoning. *What could he do here?*

At the sight of Kioko, the sedan sped forward slightly and jerked suddenly into Kiko's lane. Instinctively, trying to avoid contact with the sedan, Kioko jerked his car right, leaving his tires nearly perpendicular to the path of his forward momentum. In doing so, Kioko's car continued forward, but now in a tumble. The car flipped over twice and came to rest on the side of the highway.

Kioko woke up to the sound of sirens whirring and EMTs yelling at one another. His left arm and lap were covered in glass. He felt a sharp pain in the left side of his torso. He had a broken rib. The feeling was one that he recognized, as it wasn't the first time. The passenger side of the car was crushed. It was pushed in so far that it was nearly as close to him as the driver's side door.

Just outside of his window, a fireman yelled to Kioko, "Sir, do not move. We will help you exit the vehicle." Hearing this, Kioko thrust his large shoulder into the door, forcing it open.

Again, the fireman called to him, "Sir, please remain seated."

Kioko was a very large man. He was naturally tall and thickly built. He took this natural, massive frame and honed it with regular weight training. He practiced parkour, which conditioned his body and mind to be flexible and creative. He practiced Krav Maga, which conditioned him to inflict and to endure pain. In addition to his physical prowess, he was a young, handsome man. He had an infectious smile. His white teeth gleamed against the backdrop of his deep brown complexion. He looked like he belonged in a men's fashion magazine. Women could not get enough of him, and men either clambered to hang out with him or looked at him with jealous disdain.

All of this combined to form a young man that was not one to follow instructions. So, Kioko ignored the fireman's commands and turned to step out of his car. As he stood, he dwarfed the fireman who looked up at him, "Sir, are you okay?"

Kioko felt a shooting pain run though his left knee and up through his torso. The pain was intense. It was so intense that it made him feel nauseous. He did not answer the fireman's question but, instead, began walking towards a nearby ambulance. With his first step, he collapsed.

The Potakwe

The attackers marched Kamau and Chandler into what appeared to be a village. There were many people waiting there. The group that held them captive was comprised only of men and boys. Now at the village, there were also women, girls, very young children, and very old people. As they entered the village, the attackers dispersed, walking off to greet the women, children, and others of the village.

It was strange to Kamau that even the two attackers that prodded him and Chandler left. They, too, went to greet their women. Kamau wasn't sure how to feel in that moment. Confused, he asked Chandler, "Are we still being held captive?"

Chandler huffed, "Humph. I don't think so."

Kamau grew indignant, "Then why'd they attack us in the woods? Why'd they tie us up?" With each question, his volume rose, and his tone grew more indignant. "Why'd they march us here to who-knows-where?"

Chandler took no offense to Kamau's temper or his tone. But he had no answers.

At the last of Kamau's questions, the leader of the attacking group, the man with the short cape, walked to Kamau and Chandler. He said something that neither of them understood, then gestured for them to follow. As they moved through the village and past the people, Kamau realized that this world that was very strange and new to him was actually quite familiar. While, in one sense, he knew nothing of these people or their customs, in another sense, he knew them very well. He saw warmth and joy. He heard passion and laughter. Here were the same familial bonds, friendships, and camaraderie that marked his experience in the Akhet, in his neighborhood, and in his home. He had traveled twenty light years from the only life he knew, only to find other people just like him.

The leader approached another young boy, slightly leaner and slightly taller, who wore a similar cloak, except this boy's cloak was longer. It was made of fur, and it looked to be the skin of a large animal, and rather than having two paws grasping the shoulder, it showed two paws crossing each other and forming an "X" just below the wearer's neck. The boy with the large fur cloak was flanked by two hard-faced, young men holding spears. These young men also wore red sashes around their waist. And in a protective crescent around this boy with the fur cloak, stood several other young men. These young men also wore red sashes and carried some sort of weapon that looked like a curved scoop on the end of a long stick. Now, it was clear to Kamau who the real leader was. The boy they had encountered must have been the leader of that smaller group, but the boy in the fur cloak was the leader of this village.

He gestured to himself and spoke, "Guh-Dal." He paused, watching Kamau and Chandler. He repeated himself, nodding towards the VITs, "Guh-Dal."

The second time the boy spoke, Chandler looked at Kamau, and Kamau repeated, "Goo…DOLL."

The leader laughed. Then everyone around them laughed as well. He gestured toward himself, repeated his name, then motioned to Kamau and waited.

Kamau spoke, "Kamau."

He repeated as best he could, "Ka…MOW." As he spoke Kamau's name, he over enunciated the K, so that it almost sounded like a click followed by "mau."

Kamau smiled, nodded, and repeated his name. And again, everyone laughed.

They continued in this way. Kamau introduced Chandler who they called "Kahn…dler." They seemed unable to reproduce the "ch" blend used in Chandler's name. And the "d" that appeared in the middle of his name was lost. It was barely audible when they spoke it.

Kamau and Chandler also met Jah-Bil, who was the boy that led the group that attacked them; and Das-Bel, who was an older man, and an advisor to Guh-Dal. It was during these introductions that Kamau and Chandler also learned that, as leader, Guh-Dal's title was Tado. So, it was proper to address him as Tado

Guh-Dal.

Kamau and Chandler were introduced to more people than they could possibly remember. The people seemed intrigued with them. They inspected their hair, facial features, and clothes. A few of the younger children touched or poked Kamau and Chandler inquisitively. But the adults gently pulled the children away.

That was another oddity that Kamau noticed. The age sequence seemed off. The leader looked to be the same age as the VITs, about fourteen years old. Boys and girls just a few years older, maybe sixteen or seventeen, had children. Adults who were the age of the Mwalimu, in the twenty-two to around twenty-six-year-old range were present, but they did not exert the same adult authority that Kamau was accustomed to. The oldest members of the village were slightly older than Baba Ojore. There was no one as old as Grandma Charline.

Over time, interest in Kamau and Chandler seemed to wane, and the villagers began moving about as though they were getting ready for something. With the inattention, Kamau and Chandler began to look around the village. The village had four sections, each separated by a two-foot-high wall of small stones. Within each of these sections was a tree surrounded by a ring of tree stumps and stones.

As Kamau made note of what was there, he speculated as to what the trees and the rings of stumps and stones might be used for. When he asked Chandler for his thoughts, Kamau was, again, amazed at the brilliance of his friend.

"What I've noticed is what's not here," said Chandler. "There are no homes or any other type of sleeping quarters. There are no signs of cooking or food. There are no signs that people *live* in this village."

Kamau nodded in understanding. Chandler offered a perspective that he had not considered. Chandler added, "All they do here is sit around those trees. They also spend a lot of time socializing. But they don't live here."

As they spoke, Tado Guh-Dal approached them flanked by two of his guards with a contingent of ten men in the red sashes following closely behind. He smiled broadly and motioned to his mouth, "Poh? Poh?" He then rubbed the right side of his torso with his left hand and again motioned to his mouth, "Poh?"

Kamau nodded and motioned to his own mouth, "Poh!"

He nodded and motioned for them to follow. As Tado Guh-Dal turned to walk, his guards positioned themselves between him and Kamau and Chandler. So, they followed the entourage. As they walked, it seemed that they were leaving the village. And they were not alone. The entire village moved in a massive train. Within minutes, it appeared that no one remained in the village.

Tado Guh-Dal and his entourage were in the middle of the caravan. There were two men who rode the hideous horse-rat. Suspended between these two beasts was an ornate litter. Given where it was in the caravan, Kamau assumed it was meant for Guh-Dal. But he did not ride in it. Instead, he walked. As he walked, he bounced and smiled. He seemed to be full of joy. He talked enthusiastically with members of his entourage. Das-Bel walked nearby, listening but saying very little. And Jah-Bil walked behind Kamau and Chandler, accompanied by two men with spears. Kamau was beginning to feel like a captive again.

They walked about two miles. In that time, Kamau and Chandler discussed whether they should escape. Earlier in the day, it seemed obvious that they should escape. But now, Kamau wondered if they needed to. Tado Guh-Dal seemed to welcome them. They were not being restrained. Kamau imagined that if he knew their language, he could simply ask for help. He decided to wait and observe a bit more. But they would certainly make a firm decision before they grew too weary.

During this two-mile walk, they also noticed that the path they traveled was like a trampled highway running through the woods. So many people moving in such a wide formation destroyed vegetation and created a path that was at least ten feet wide. Instinctively, Chandler whispered to Kamau, "They must travel this every day."

Kamau answered curtly, "You don't have to whisper. They don't understand a thing you are saying. If you whisper, it will look suspicious. Speak normally."

Chandler nodded and repeated himself, "I think they travel this path every day."

"Why do you say that?"

Chandler answered, "This vegetation has been trampled, not cut. Vegetation grows back quickly if it is not trampled on continuously."

Kamau didn't disagree with Chandler, but he didn't know what to make of Chandler's suggestion. "I guess it makes sense. But why would they march the whole village for such a long distance every day?"

At the end of the two-mile walk, they entered another village. And again, they were met by more villagers. This time, it was a very small group. As they approached, Chandler gazed intently at the villagers as though he saw something. Kamau, however, watched Chandler as he waited for Chandler's reply. Chandler's eyes grew large, his mouth fell open, and whatever he saw made him stutter incomprehensibly, "K… K… K… Kamau!"

A Military Solution (O'Leary)

When CC2 opened communication with SEV Fitzroy, Anand began with the status check routine. The results were the same as they always were. Anand was not the only employee bothered by these events. Other employees in CC2, mostly members of the original project team, were becoming visibly agitated. Anand muted the transmission and spoke in frustration, "I am coming very close to aborting this mission."

With those words, Dan's normally cheerful disposition turned to controlled rage. He snapped, "You will do no such thing! Step down, Anand!" The change in Dan was striking. He was always cheerful and good spirited and never confrontational. This was a side of Dan that no one present had ever seen.

Anand was especially taken aback. He turned to Dan and spoke in a stunned slow cadence, "Yes, sir. You have the com."

Dan paused, gathered himself, and smiled. He then addressed Anand before the entire project staff, "Anand, forgive me for being gruff. This situation is a challenging one. It is hard on all of us, myself included. But that is no excuse for poor behavior. Forgive me." Then turning to the project staff, he said, "We have a responsibility to support the Research Team. Now, we have asked them to develop a plan to complete data collection. Let's see what they have come up with."

Dan unmuted the transmission, "SEV Fitzroy, this is Dan Silverstein, Project Lead. You are currently behind in your data collection schedule. When we last spoke, you promised to develop a plan for getting back on schedule. Are you prepared to share that plan?"

The Team Leader responded, "Yes, sir. We have been challenged these past few weeks by the presence of a hostile band of natives. The presence of these natives has impeded our ability to effectively complete our mission."

Anand's eyes grew large, and he whispered to Dan, "That is not true."

Dan hushed Anand as the Team Leader continued, "We have engaged a second group of friendly natives. They, too, have had difficult encounters with the hostiles. According to our intelligence…"

Anand interrupted the Team Leader and spoke loudly and desperately to Dan, "These are lies! There has been, for a whole month, no mention of hostile natives in any report. This Team Leader is…"

Dan interrupted Anand. This time he kept his composure and his usual smile, "Anand, please, let the Team Leader finish." He turned towards the primary monitor and spoke directly to the Team Leader, "Forgive me, Team Leader. Please continue."

The Team Leader continued, "According to our intelligence, the friendly natives are preparing for a peacekeeping incursion into the hostile native territory. If we can support the friendlies, and if they can impress upon the hostiles the importance of peace, then we will be able to resume our data collection, and we can do so at an accelerated pace."

Anand's anger was visible. He looked as though he wanted to have a peacekeeping incursion on the Team Leader's face. But alas, he could not. So, he stood in the corner and fumed.

Dan, on the other hand, seemed to like the idea. "Team Leader, when do you expect this incursion to take place?"

"It is imminent. Our best guess is that it will take place within twenty-four Earth hours."

Dan replied, "How can we support you?"

The Team Leader responded, "Simply monitor the situation, sir. We have already taken measures to provide support here on the ground."

Anand was incredulous. Again, he burst out, "They were to make a plan yesterday. Now, in just twenty-four hours, they have engineered a war between two peaceful people?"

Dan tried to calm and quiet Anand, but he grew louder and more indignant. "They have been planning this all along. This is why they collect no data. They are playing war…"

Dan finally yelled, "ENOUGH!" His eyes were turned down into a scowl, and he peered directly at Anand. Anand breathed heavily and peered back, saying nothing.

Dan's face softened a bit as the scowl morphed into a look of stern resolution. He then turned away from Anand and commanded, "End the transmission." Turning back to Anand he said, "Anand, you are dismissed."

What Raymond Learned

Chandler ran ahead, grabbed Alton in a bear hug, and lifted him from the ground. This show of strength would have surprised all of Kikuyu Squad if they were not so overcome with joy and relief at being united once again. For about five minutes, they shook hands, hugged one another, high-fived, slapped one another on the back, laughed, and exchanged stories about all the horrors they had imagined during their separation.

The villagers observed them casually but made no effort to interfere with their reunion. After a time, everyone began to take seats. They sat on the ground in loosely configured circles. Each circle included four to six adults and many children. It seemed that each group had two or three families. Kikuyu Squad sat alone.

Young boys, just a bit younger than Kamau, had the responsibility of bringing clay pots to each grouping. When the pots arrived, food was ladled into each person's bowl. It was a thick, pasty stew, and everyone either drank the contents of the bowl or scooped it out with their hands. As the food was being served, Kamau and the others shared their experiences of the past few hours and what they had learned.

Kamau pointed out, "Well one thing we know for sure is that they hike a good distance every day."

Raymond asked inquisitively, "How do you know that?"

Kamau went on to point out Chandler's observation and explanation of what they had not seen. "This is actually the second village that we've been to. The first village had no place to eat. It had no place to sleep. This village looks like it is just for eating. There are no sleeping quarters."

Chandler added, "I think I know what's happening here. These are a migratory people."

Alton interrupted, "What does that mean?"

Chandler elaborated, "When a species migrates, it moves from one location to another at regular time intervals. The most obvious example is when birds fly south for the winter. Each winter they fly south, and each spring they return. Usually, species migrate with changing seasons. They are moving about for different weather conditions or different food sources." Everyone nodded their understanding and listened intently.

As Chandler spoke, food was brought to Kikuyu Squad. They looked at it, but no one ate any of it. Chandler continued, "I think the villagers here migrate at different times and for a different reason."

Kamau, Alton, and Raymond looked at Chandler intently. But Chandler sat there as though he had nothing more to say. After a moment, Kamau pressed him, "And?"

Chandler continued absentmindedly, "Oh. Yes. The people here migrate the same basic route every day. I think they do this to create a sense of day and night."

Kamau was disappointed in Chandler's big conclusion. He was also uncertain of it. "Why do they need to hike for day and night?"

Chandler jumped at the chance to answer this question. "Remember, this planet is in a tidally locked orbit around their sun. If they stay in one place, it will be daylight all the time. Since the planet's movement on its axis doesn't give them day and night, they create day and night by moving across the line that separates the light side of the planet from the dark side of the planet." The squad sat there in stunned silence.

Chandler asked Kamau, "Have you noticed that the sun seems to be a little closer to the horizon than it was at the village we came from?

Kamau was nodding his understanding when a young boy came and asked if they wanted to eat. "Poh?" he said as he gestured to his mouth.

Kamau did not know how to ask for the foods they knew were safe. So, he tried to ask by speaking slowly, and by using hand gestures. It was then that Raymond interrupted and spoke as he motioned to his own mouth, "Tahtiki? Poh Tahtiki."

The boy laughed and jumped in delight. He then ran off laughing and repeating, "Poh Tahtiki."

Kamau and Chandler stared in disbelief. "How do you *know* that?" Chandler asked indignantly.

Alton replied casually, "Raymond knows some of the words. He can understand them a little bit."

Kamau's eyes grew large, "You can?!"

Raymond smiled, "Yeah, the words in their language follow patterns. Once you know the patterns, it's easier to figure out what the words mean. So, all the words used to describe plants end in 'tiki.' The plant that produces the balled-fist alien peanuts is called 'TAH-tiki.' The plant that makes lettuce as big as your head is called 'POOH-tiki.' So, any time you hear a word that ends in 'tiki' you know they are talking about some sort of plant."

Kamau asked, "How did you figure that out?"

Raymond shrugged, "I just listened to them." He thought about it. Then he explained, "Well, at first, I just listened. Then I tried to speak to the doPotakwe. That's …"

Kamau cut him off to ask excitedly, "Who's that?"

"Who's who?"

Growing frustrated, Kamau began to raise his voice, "Who's the dotakwe?!"

Raymond laughed, "The *doPotakwe*. Okay, let me back up." Raymond realized that, in their excitement to see each other, he and Alton never explained to Kamau and Chandler what had happened once they were separated. So, he began by recounting their experience of the past few hours. As Raymond explained it, "Alton and I began walking towards the river. After a few minutes, we couldn't understand the words of the cadence that you and Chandler were calling. It didn't matter much because we knew the words. So, we gave the response to what we thought we knew the call should be. We also weren't concerned because we knew that as long as we could hear your voices, we could find our way back to the line."

Kamau and Chandler listened intently.

Raymond continued, "But soon after we couldn't understand you, we were attacked by a rogue band of doPotakwe." Raymond digressed to explain that "The land we are on is called Potakwe. It's pronounced Po-TOCK-Way, and the people were called DOH-Potakwe. Anyway, when the rogue band attacked us, we started yelling for help. But you never came. Afterwards, we figured that you didn't know we were yelling for help. If we couldn't understand your words, you probably couldn't understand ours."

Chandler added, "Yeah, we never heard any calls for help."

Raymond continued, "Right. So, when the rogue band attacked us, we didn't put up much of a fight. We were outnumbered, and they were so much faster and stronger than us that we didn't have much of a chance. So, they whooped up on us, tied us up, and then walked us through the woods."

Kamau's mind drifted momentarily as he thought about Raymond's words, "…we didn't put up much of a fight…" and "…they were so much faster and stronger than us…" With so much going on, he had forgotten that he had been beaten by the doPotakwe. In that moment, Kamau felt a surge of fear and doubt. It was an unfamiliar feeling. He had never before felt that he couldn't win a fight. Now, he began to be overcome with a sense of his own weakness.

Unaware of Kamau's mental anguish, Raymond continued explaining their adventure. "So, they had us walking behind those horrendously awful-smelling beasts." He pointed to one at the edge of the village. "They call them, wahtaka. When we were first attacked, it was the sight of the wahtaka that did it for us. The beast was so hideous, it stunned and shocked us. We weren't ready to fight after seeing it."

"Yes! We had the same experience when we got captured!" Chandler added excitedly.

"So, we walked for a very short time, being tied up and pulled by this rogue band. Then, suddenly, out of nowhere, came another group of doPotakwe. I know they knew each other. They had to have known each other. There were no war shouts and drums. They didn't even really fight. The leader of the second group of doPotakwe spoke like he was chastising the leader of the rogue group. The rogue group leader argued verbally. He looked around at the second group, then he commanded his group, and they left. The new doPotakwe group untied us and let us walk with them to this village."

"Did they hold you at spearpoint?" Kamau asked excitedly.

"No," said Raymond. "It was actually kind of strange. Initially, it seemed like they didn't really expect us to stay with them. But we had already lost our way. We couldn't have found our way back to the line. They seemed friendly, and I figured that if we got to know them, they would help us to find our way back to you. They also gave us some protection against the rogue group."

Kamau smiled and nodded, "That's good thinking, Raymond!"

Chandler then asked, "So, how did you learn the language?"

"Okay. So, when we were walking, I picked up a balled-fist alien peanut, and

I asked one of the doPotakwe what it was. I just held it up and said, 'Nut?' He took it from me, pointed to a tree and said, 'Tahtiki.' Sure enough! That tree was full of the nuts. So, I pointed to the tree and repeated, 'Tahtiki.'"

Alton interjected, "That was Gan-Jof. For the rest of our walk here, Gan-Jof and Raymond talked."

Raymond continued, "Yes, he taught me the names of trees, animals, and people. So, look. The land is called Potakwe. The people are called doPotakwe, but doPotakwe-*am* refers to all the elder women and doPotakwe-*awa* refers to all the elder men. Their culture is embedded in their language."

Kamau asked curiously, "What do you mean?"

Raymond continued, "Okay. All the boys' names are one syllable when they are young. So, Gan-Jof was called Gan until manhood. At that time, a second syllable was added to his name, Jof."

Chandler asked, "Would Gan-Jof be considered a man? He seems to be our age."

Alton interrupted, "Yeah. They look like boys, but they are men. We would be men up in here."

Raymond explained, "When they reach puberty, it's called 'The Seeding' and they have a 'Seeding Ceremony.' Then when they reach elderhood status, 'awa' is added to their name. So, one day, when he is old enough, Gan-Jof will be called Gan-Jof-awa. When girls reach puberty, it is called 'The Receiving,' and they, too, have a ceremony. It is 'The Receiving Ceremony.' When females reach elder status, "am" is added to their name."

Kamau expressed awe at the way their names conferred so much meaning, "Wow. That is cool."

Alton laughed and turned to Raymond, "Yeah. And your name don't mean nothing. You just plain old Raymond." He then mocked in a grandmotherly tone, "Come o'er her' Ray Ray."

One of the young boys brought three dishes of Tahtiki to Kikuyu Squad. Each dish was prepared differently. They ate their fill and drank water for the first time since arriving.

Shortly after everyone had finished eating, the children played, and the young girls watched them, the young boys collected the clay pots from each group, the women cleaned the dishes and the eating area, and the men prepared the belongings to be moved. Everyone had a role, and the village functioned smoothly. Kikuyu Squad helped the men prepare to move.

When traveling to the next village, Kikuyu Squad did not stay together. When they first set out, Raymond was engaged with Gan-Jof in conversation. Kamau, however, kept asking questions about hunting, weapons, and the red-sashed guard. Seeing this, Gan-Jof "introduced" Kamau to Jah-Bil, the stern-faced lieutenant that Kamau already knew. However, this time, seeing that Kamau had an interest, Jah-Bil engaged with Kamau cheerfully.

Kamau applied what he had learned from Raymond, as he spoke with Jah-Bil. He listened for patterns in the language. He asked specific questions, initially about names for items, but he soon found that he was learning much more.

Similarly, Gan-Jof encouraged Chandler to speak with Das-Bel. He did so after Chandler continued asking about the planet, its geography, the climate, and the path of the migrations. Das-Bel, too, was very eager to engage with this new stranger, and they learned much from each other.

Alton and Raymond spoke with Gan-Jof, learning more of the doPotakwe language and customs. After an hour or so of walking, the doPotakwe entered another village. This village was clearly a place for sleeping. There was a very large gathering space in the center of the village. There was a huge stone fire ring at the center of that gathering space. And, throughout the village, there were several smaller structures that looked like huts. As they arrived, the doPotakwe dispersed into these many huts. Jah-Bil showed Kamau and Kikuyu Squad to two huts near the center of the village. After inspecting the huts, Kamau, Chandler, Alton, and Raymond sat out in front of the huts, sharing what they had learned on their walk.

After a time, Jah-Bil returned with Gan-Jof and five other red-sashed men. Kamau recognized one of these men as the leader of Guh-Dal's private guard. Jah-Bil was in good spirits, smiling and joking with the other men. Upon their approach, Kikuyu Squad stood to greet them. Just as Jah-Bil began to speak, a voice came from Chandler's leg. "Kikuyu Squad, this is Baba Kahuthia. How are you making it?"

At the sound of the voice, Jah-Bil's smile contorted into a scowl, and the red-sashed guard drew spears and pointed them at Chandler.

Seeing the commotion, a hush came over the villagers who were nearby. All that could be heard was Baba Kahuthia's entreaty, "Kikuyu Squad? Come in. Kikuyu Squad, can you hear me?"

CHAPTER THREE

Yurugu Falls

Kamau Explains

Thinking quickly, Kamau stepped in front of Chandler and spoke loudly enough for Baba Kahuthia to hear him, "Jah-Bil, this is Baba Kahuthia. He is from our home world. We mean you no harm. Put down your spear."

Jah-Bil looked at Kamau in confusion. He barked commands at Kikuyu Squad that none of them understood. Kamau then barked a command of his own, "Raymond, translate!"

Raymond tried to translate Kamau's message, but he did not know enough words.

Kamau continued speaking, "We thank you for feeding us, for allowing us to migrate with you from village to village, and now to the dark side of this planet. We hope you will allow us to rest with you at this new location."

Raymond grew frustrated as he struggled to keep pace with the translation. Gan-Jof focused on Raymond and began helping him to make sense of Kamau's words.

Seeing that Gan-Jof was distracted and some of the Tado Guard was confused, Chandler understood Kamau's idea and began to help. He began speaking directly to Jah-Bil using the few words he had learned and trying to get Jah-Bil to help him translate others.

Meanwhile, Alton, who had positioned himself between Kamau and the many spears, frowned and said nothing.

Kamau continued to speak, "Jah-Bil, ever since you rescued us from the rogue doPotakwe, you have been friendly. Let's return to friendly relations. We have no way to return to our kambi. We have walked with you for many miles today, and we are not sure of our current location."

SECRETS OF THE VANGUARD ORDER

Frustrated and confused, Jah-Bil struck Alton so that he crumpled to the ground. As he did so, Kamau felt a spear pressed against the right side of his torso, just below his armpit. The spear made no attempt to break flesh. But it certainly could have. This was simply a warning, and it was accompanied by a loud, staccato command that could only mean "Quiet!" With that harsh, definitive command, all talking ceased immediately.

Jah-Bil and his men marched Kikuyu Squad to Tado-Guh-Dal's quarters in the center of the village. There, they waited, surrounded by the Tado Guard. After a time, Tado-Guh-Dal appeared. He was joined by his two primary guards, Das-Bel (his advisor) and Goh-Del (his uncle). This was Kamau's first time seeing Goh-Del. He stood out from the rest because he wore a distinctive headdress. It was fashioned from the skin of an animal that had the look of a weasel. The animal's head sat at the front of the headdress. Then behind the head was a typical, circular fur hat. Behind the circular fur hat was a tail that draped down the back of the wearer. It looked like a version of Daniel Boone's coon skin cap. Nowhere in the village was there another hat like it.

For the next thirty minutes, Kikuyu Squad was maligned, accused, and threatened. Their maligners, accusers, and threateners sneered, scowled, and barked at them. Kamau stood strong and bravely argued in defense of Kikuyu Squad, while Raymond tried to interpret. The gist of the dispute was why Kikuyu Squad came to the doPotakwe. Some, led by Goh-Del, believed that Kikuyu Squad had been sent to kill Tado-Guh-Dal to gain access to Potakwe. Goh-Del was chief among the advocates for killing Kikuyu Squad.

Kamau had no idea where Goh-Del got the idea that Kikuyu Squad was some sort of assassination team. It was pure fantasy, a foolish fiction. Kamau tried to impress the truth of their arrival on Goh-Del. He explained that they were accidentally transported from their home planet twenty light-years away. But reason seemed to be lost on him.

What made the communication more difficult for Kamau is that Raymond struggled to represent abstract ideas. Learning the terminology for concrete ideas was rather simple. He could point to a rock and one of the doPotakwe would say the word associated with rock. But what could he point to that would represent a light-year or space travel?

After struggling with this language barrier for a time, Raymond had an epiphany. He noticed that, periodically, Goh-Del, who was Tado Guh-Dal's uncle and their chief adversary, would huff, turn away, and mutter, "Fahtahu!" or "Gahtahu!" in exasperation. Initially, Raymond thought it was a curse, and he ignored it. But he remembered that the language was patterned, and he was desperate, so he stopped translating and interrupted Kamau with one word,

"Tahu."

At that, the buzz of the inquiry slowed to a low murmur, and he repeated himself, "Tahu." Raymond was beginning to feel foolish as Tado Guh-Dal stared at him blankly. The other doPotakwe simply stared as well. No one said anything. Raymond persisted, "What is Tahu?"

At this point, Gan-Jof came to his aid. Gan-Jof was not officially a part of this interrogation, but he was sitting with many doPotakwe who formed a ring surrounding Kikuyu Squad to watch. On hearing Raymond's question, Gan-Jof stood and broke the silence. "Onka ne tahu."

Tado Guh-Dal and others looked at him inquisitively. Gan-Jof spoke again. This time he gestured to Raymond, "Ise te aba, Onka ne tahu."

Tado Guh-Dal's eyes brightened as he looked again at Raymond, "Aaaah!" he exclaimed. He nodded his understanding and repeated, "Onka ne tahu." He then gestured and made a command to one of his assistants. Within moments, a very old, but very capable man walked towards the center of the gathering. The man took out a satchel, knelt and smoothed a section of dirt with his hands. He then shook the satchel and began chanting. The doPotakwe were silent, and all that could be heard was the sound of stones rattling inside the satchel and the rhythmic chanting that accompanied it. Without warning, the elderly man opened the satchel, casting the stones onto the cleared ground. He then stared intently at Kamau for what seemed like an eternity. Unfazed, Kamau returned the gaze. The elderly man then nodded to Tado Guh-Dal.

Tado Guh-Dal motioned for Gan-Jof to join him. For the next hour or so, Raymond translated Kamau's English into the little bit of doPotakwe that he knew. Gan-Jof translated Tado Guh-Dal's doPotakwe into the little English that he knew. The elder listened intently, moved stones about, and made incomprehensible incantations. And with hand gestures, drawings, enactments, and other theatrical tools, the interrogation proceeded.

Kamau would later learn that the elder with the stones was a man named Geh-Dol-Awa. Geh-Dol-Awa was a spiritual leader and healer of the doPotakwe. Tado Guh-Dal called for him to divine the truth of Kamau's words. He also learned that "tahu" is a word used to characterize ideas that the doPotakwe believe to be unreal or mythical.

Goh-Del's reference to "Fahtahu!" and "Gahtahu!" was a dismissal. It was the equivalent of Kamau dismissing an idea as a fairytale. Goh-Del was essentially saying that Kikuyu Squad's explanation deserved no further consideration. Fortunately for Kamau, he was not the decision maker in this matter. Tado Guh-Dal was.

Kamau used his facility of reason to argue for the lives of Kikuyu Squad. He pointed out that they were too young and inexperienced to be an effective team of assassins; that they very likely would have died of thirst had they not been saved by the doPotakwe; and that they had no weapons with which to fight. Then, to his shame, he pointed out that, at every encounter, the doPotakwe outfought Kikuyu Squad with ease. Kamau concluded with what he thought to be the quietus of the matter. He reminded Tado Guh-Dal that it was the doPotakwe who found Kikuyu Squad, not the reverse.

Although Tado Guh-Dal heard these arguments, he did not seem moved. As it turns out, it was Kamau's innocence, his openness, more than anything that won over Tado Guh-Dal. Kamau had bared his soul and explained everything: that they arrived accidentally after mistakenly tampering with an unauthorized elevator; that they struggled to keep pace given the stronger gravitation of the planet; that they were expecting a team of people to return and take them back home. Kamau even had Chandler show Tado Guh-Dal the black panel. Several doPotakwe ooohed and aaahed at the sight of it, but no one dared touch it. Perhaps they were afraid of being transported some great distance to an unknown place.

With his stones and incantations, Geh-Dol-Awa attested to the purity of Kamau's heart. So Tado Guh-Dal declared his story to be true. At this declaration, Gan-Jof (Raymond's translator) nodded his agreement. Jah-Bil (Tado Guh-Dal's lieutenant) softened his hardened posture and nodded his agreement. The Tado Guard stood in formation, snapped to attention, and, together, nodded their agreement. The tension throughout the village was eased as doPotakwe nodded their agreement, then dispersed into smaller groups and returned to their respective activities. It was only Goh-Del who seemed not to accept Tado Guh-Dal's declaration. Upon hearing it, he sneered and huffed as he turned to walk away.

That evening as the doPotakwe communed around the fire, Kikuyu Squad sat on the outer edges of the group. They watched the communing, but they did not take part. They spoke very little. Their hearts were heavy with the realization that they were nearly killed by alien people in an alien world. The reality and stress of their situation was beginning to take a toll. That night, they slept without speaking much to one another.

Oversight in CC2 (O'Leary)

As Anand scrambled out of bed and looked back at Kuyili sleeping peacefully, his chest felt heavy with the weight of his decision, but he knew it was his best course of action. He had spent the night before deep in meditative contemplation. It was in those quiet reflective moments that he began to see the situation for what it was. He saw that Dan was not a gifted scientist. Dan's gift was being able to strategically position himself for advancement. He saw that behind Dan's friendly, aw-shucks façade was a man who was desperate for control of this new planet and its resources. If this desperate man was willing to sacrifice his own people by sending them twenty light-years away to destabilize and possibly destroy another race of people, he would not hesitate to crush Apu, or whatever his name was.

No. There was too much money and too much power at stake. Anand could not expect good conduct from this juvenile and desperate man. And so, Anand packed a bag for Kuyili and the kids, placed it by the door, and went to the kitchen to draft a letter.

> Dear Mr. Sabbatini,
>
> I write this letter with a heavy heart, but also with a hopeful spirit. In the past four years, TechInnoGen has been a fabulous home for me. Here I have learned to become a better worker, a better scientist, and a better person. Here I have made many friends and become part of a special TechInnoGen family. I have come to believe in the company and the good that we do in the world.
>
> Recently, I have witnessed decisions that do not represent the company I have come to know and love. I currently serve as Research Coordinator for Project SEV Fitzroy, v2. There are several problems with the execution of this project. First, the data collection team hired for this project have neither the expertise nor the will needed to complete this mission. Second, the time frame for this mission was pushed up by six months, two weeks. Given that rush, we launched before we were adequately prepared. Third, the Coordination Center Staff was brought together in a way that strains the group's ability to work together as a unit. Finally, the Research Team is currently on the ground, and they are tasked with collecting data in a way that does not interfere with native populations. However, they have collected very little data and have committed to a path of military intervention in the affairs of the native population.
>
> To say that this project is being poorly executed is an understatement. With this way of operation, there is a very high probability that we will lose the lives of the eight-person crew as well as hundreds of millions of dollars that we have invested in this project. Worst of all, the PR damage could be insurmountable. The potential harm that this action could have for the company is incalculable.

SECRETS OF THE VANGUARD ORDER

I have exhausted all means that I know to remedy this situation. Having found no success thus far, this is my final attempt. In addition to providing this letter to you, I am filing a formal grievance with the Internal Review Board that oversees TechInnoGen research. I have also prepared a formal grievance to be filed with the World Commission on the Ethics of Scientific Knowledge and Technology (COMEST) at UNESCO. The grievance to UNESCO is scheduled to be sent in two weeks. If we can address this situation before then, this grievance can be abandoned.

I am not blameless in this matter. If I had been a better leader, or had a stronger voice, I believe I could have helped us to avoid the present circumstance. As such, I am also submitting my resignation.

Sincerely,
Anand Devi
Research Coordinator

Later that day, Anand moved his family into an extended stay hotel that was two hundred miles southwest of their home. He moved himself into an inexpensive hotel that was just ten miles from the office. He submitted his letter to Erick Sabbatini; filed an internal grievance with TechInnoGen; provided his attorney with a secondary grievance for UNESCO with instructions that it should be sent in two weeks should anything happen to him; and sent copies of everything to his close friend, Timothy O'Leary.

That evening, in Command Center Two, Dan was keeping everyone's spirits high. He was telling jokes and offering words of encouragement. He reviewed protocols to be sure that everyone knew their roles. Dan, whose back was to the door, noticed that the excited buzz of CC2 died quickly when the door was opened. His smile faded as he turned to see Erick Sabbatini walk in. Without saying a word, Mr. Sabbatini walked to Anand's station and sat in Anand's chair.

Kikuyu Squad Prepares for War

Kamau did not wake up as he normally did. Since his first week at the Akhet, his body had grown accustomed to the routine of the Hwamanda horn. He typically woke up just moments before it sounded. Today, however, even with no clock or sunrise to confirm it, he was certain that he had slept longer than normal.

What woke him was the bustle of doPotakwe moving about the village. He leaned over and shook Raymond. As Raymond stirred, Kamau was struck by the sour stench of breath and the foul smell of sweat and body odor that wafted from his clothes. Then another worry was added to his ever-growing list. *Oh, my goodness!* he thought. *We stink!* Together, Kamau and Raymond woke up Alton and Chandler.

As Kamau watched the group come alive, he realized that they had begun to abandon the many routines of the Akhet. The Hwamanda Awakening, Mti wa Umoja, the morning run, regular meals, the Vanguard Shower, Mduara ya Heshima, and Group Reflection, among many others. He also noticed that not having those routines was beginning to take a toll on their psyche. He wondered if it was also taking a toll on their unity and performance. They could not replicate all the routines, given their present circumstances, but they needn't abandon them all. Once everyone was ready, Kamau announced that they would begin the day with Mti wa Umoja.

As they formed a circle, Chandler protested, "Kamau, we don't have any water… and we don't have a unity tree."

Kamau responded confidently, "We'll sacrifice water from our bodies." He then led the Squad to the edge of the path that marked the boundary of the village. On the other side of the village were a few small, low-lying trees. The trees around this village were smaller and sparser than the trees at the other villages. This was, perhaps, due to the low light in that portion of the planet.

As Kamau led Kikuyu Squad to one scrawny tree, Alton protested, "Kamau that little tree can't be no unity tree!"

Again, Kamau responded confidently, "Alton, the tree does not strengthen our unity. Our unity strengthens the tree." With that, they circled the tree and grasped hands in the customary way.

Kamau began, "We who are gathered here, affirm the unity that we share with one another, that we share with our forebearers, that we share with our ancestors, and that we share with the unborn. The tree of African unity must be watered by the blood, sweat, and tears of our enemies and of Vanguardians."

As they continued through the morning ritual, Kamau felt a surge of strength course through him. He stood taller and felt his chest fill with air and expand. It was strange how this simple act made him feel connected to Baba Kahuthia, Baba Ojore, and all the Mwalimu of the Akhet. He felt connected to the sixteen VITs of Mkhosi Kunye and the ninety-six VITs of the Ibutho. They were no longer a lone group of boys on a distant planet. They were part of a vast fighting force that was conditioned and trained to withstand hardships, overcome odds, and succeed.

They completed the ritual with the recitation of the Vanguard Creed. During that recitation, Kamau realized that he was not alone in this feeling of connection and resurgence of strength.

Soon after that, the doPotakwe began their daily migration. Unlike previous migrations, the group did not all move together. The young men gathered and journeyed separate from the women, children, and elders. As the groups split, Jah-Bil motioned for Kamau to join him. So, Kikuyu Squad joined Tado Guh-Dal, Jah-Bil, Gan-Jof, Goh-Del, and the other young men of the village.

After an hour or so, they stopped walking and approached a village. The village was unlike the others. It was in disrepair. It was overrun with flora, and the stone walls were crumbling. There was an excessive amount of dirt everywhere. It seemed the village was rarely, if ever, used. The men went to work quickly, cleaning the village.

Jah-Bil took Alton and Chandler away to assist with the cleanup of the village. Gan-Jof motioned for Kamau and Raymond to follow him. Gan-Jof took them to speak with Tado Guh-Dal. This was the first time that Kamau had been in the presence of Tado Guh-Dal without the Tado Guard being present. Now, he spoke directly and privately with Tado Guh-Dal. Raymond and Gan-Jof were present to serve as interpreters.

Guh-Dal began by informing Kamau that Kikuyu Squad would fight with them. This came as a surprise to Kamau. He was not aware that Guh-Dal was going to fight. So, he asked Tado Guh-Dal to tell him more about this fight. Tado Guh-Dal smiled, nodded, and explained that when he was very young, his father had died unexpectedly. He was to become Tado-Potakwe. But he could not become Tado prior to the seeding. So, his mother ruled in his stead until he was ready. This upset some people because women are not permitted to serve as Tado.

Kamau interrupted to ask why women were not permitted to serve as Tado.

Tado Guh-Dal explained. "Tado is too dangerous, and women are too valuable. They produce children. One man can produce thousands of children at one time. If we lost one man, we would be sad, but the doPotakwe would continue because another man could produce many children. If we lost all the men, except for one, the doPotakwe would continue. But one woman can produce only one child at a time. If we lost all the women except for one, the doPotakwe would be lost. Every time we lose one woman, the doPotakwe suffer. Women do not do dangerous jobs, because we want to keep them safe. We want to protect them."

Kamau nodded his understanding, and Tado Guh-Dal continued. "So, when my mother took the role of Tado, some doPotakwe left. Each year that she served, more doPotakwe left. These are now dewa do-Potakwe."

Raymond stopped to explain that dewa referred to something that was lost. So, the literal translation would be "the lost people of Potakwe."

Tado Guh-Dal continued, "Some of those who left wanted my uncle, Goh-Del, to serve as Tado when my father died. But during the proving trials, Geh-Dol-Awa would not approve him. His heart was not deemed to be pure."

Tado Guh-Dal paused to see that Kamau understood the story. Raymond and Kamau assured him and Gan-Jof that they understood. Tado Guh-Dal then explained that it was dewa doPotakwe that abducted them when they were looking for water.

Kamau then asked if it was the dewa doPotakwe that they were going to fight. Tado Guh-Dal sighed heavily and said something that Raymond translated as, "Yes. In part..." Tado Guh-Dal then continued his explanation, "Strangers have come to Potakwe. They have come to the doNiOutokwe. They have seduced and confused the dewa doPotakwe and turned them into nne-ato doPotakwe."

Again, Raymond stopped to explain that doNiOutokwe meant "people of the dark rocks." Both Raymond and Kamau concluded that these were yet a different group of people. He also explained that "nne-ato" referred to something that was adversarial or opposed to something else. So, the literal translation would be "the opposers of the people of Potakwe."

Kamau's heart sank when he understood this distinction. Lost people could be found. They could be reclaimed. But opposers were true enemies. Here Kamau saw clearly how a small fissure in a people's unity could be made into something much greater. *Who were these strangers?* he wondered.

When Tado Guh-Dal gave his description of the strangers, Kamau understood why he and Kikuyu Squad came under such harsh scrutiny. By the description provided, the strangers were incredibly similar to humans. But then again, so were the doPotakwe. The strangers also used communication devices that the doPotakwe described as "talking rocks."

Tado Guh-Dal explained that, in one migration, the doPotakwe would battle with the dewa doPotakwe and the NiOutokwe. They would battle their own people to rid Potakwe of the trouble-making strangers. And Kikuyu Squad would bring them good luck and favor by fighting with the doPotakwe.

Kamau's eyes grew large as he protested, insisting that Kikuyu Squad could not fight. All he could envision was Kikuyu Squad getting slapped around by thousands of strong, disjointed doPotakwe and trounced by stinky, rat-faced wahtaka. Raymond informed Kamau that Tado Guh-Dal was not giving Kikuyu Squad an option. Dejected, they joined Alton and Chandler.

Having heard the story from Tado Guh-Dal, it was plain to Kamau that they were preparing for war. At one station, they were crafting bows and arrows. Spear shafts were being inspected at another. At a third station, arrow tips and spear tips were being molded and hardened in a fire. Most interesting of all the weapons was the stick with the curved spoon-like end. As they watched these sticks being crafted, Kamau asked one of the men to explain how they were used. Rather than try to explain, he grunted and demonstrated. He reached into a satchel and pulled out a tahtiki nut, loaded it into the curved spoon structure of his staff, and hurled it. It traveled a great distance and at a great speed.

As the time of crafting weapons came to an end, the men sat to eat. Following that, they began their journey to the next village.

The Extraction Team Arrives (Taharka)

"Good morning, gentlemen!" Chiumbo was back to his abrasive, screeching ways as he greeted the Extraction Team. On their arrival, three of the four men reported directly to the briefing room at Ebe Nyocha. The first was Funani Lungisi. Funani was a serious-minded man who smiled very little and spoke even less. He was always visibly alert. He had a habit of attending to everything said with the utmost care. He was also diligent in taking notice of his surroundings. One might not know it from looking at him, but Funani was a fierce fighter. Although he was shorter than most Vanguardians, with a lean, very slight build, he was the most formidable fighter present. He was especially skilled in close quarters weapons combat. He was an expert at using his smaller size to his advantage. Being very quick, he learned to present himself as a target that was impossible to strike. And at the same time, he wore down his opponents with well-timed blows that seemed to never stop coming. He had made a study of human anatomy and physiology. He learned to identify sensitive areas and pressure points. He was known to identify specific weaknesses in an opponent that he would later exploit to his advantage.

The second man was Mandla Masuka. In stark contrast to Funani, Mandla was a physically imposing man. He had a naturally lean build, that he honed over time into a very muscular, fear-inducing physique. But those who knew him did not fear him. He was one of the most good-natured Vanguardians one could ever meet. He had a joyous spirit and was easy to get along with. While he was a capable fighter, he was nowhere near as good as Funani or any other members of the Extraction Team. His strength was as a tactician. He had a natural instinct and feel for tactical maneuvers. He applied his skill as a tactician, not only to battlefields, but also to guerrilla encounters, street fights, barroom brawls, public relations, and political campaigns. He was a true student of his craft. He studied warfare, violent encounters, espionage, politics, corporate histories, and seduction. He didn't expect to be able to conduct these missions all his life, so he was preparing now for his life as an older man.

The third man was Manqoba Zama. Like Mandla, Manqoba was a physically imposing man. He was more thickly built than both Mandla and Funani, but he was also quicker and more lithe. Although he was a very skilled fighter, it was not his size, nor his fighting ability that distinguished him from the others. What distinguished him from the others was his sheer ruthlessness. The other members of the squad affectionately called him "Man Cobra." His ferocity was unnerving, and it was not employed as much as it was unleashed. In mixed company, he was quiet. And as long as he remained quiet, he could pass for a normal person. But the other members of his squad had seen him in other contexts. And they saw him for what he was, a powder keg waiting for an opportunity to explode. It was his good fortune to be surrounded by such capable men—men whose personalities counterbalanced his own so well. With his watchfulness, on multiple occasions, Funani was able to steer Manqoba away from explosive encounters. Mandla was able to do the same by reading danger before it manifested and exerting his joyful spirit to help Manqoba redirect his murderous impulse. And with these great friends, Manqoba could not have asked for a better leader than Kioko. Kioko was one of the few leaders that Manqoba could follow without question.

Seeing the three members of Bassari Squad, Chiumbo screeched again, "Where's Kioko?!"

Funani stirred uneasily. He watched as Manqoba's eyes grew large and he sat up straight and leaned in the direction of Chiumbo. Mandla smiled and spoke up quickly, "Brother Chiumbo, he's on his way. He had a little mishap yesterday, which delayed his trip. But he promised he would be here. You know he has never missed an assignment?"

Chiumbo stared at Mandla, saying nothing. His nose was scrunched up as though he smelled flatulence in the air.

Mandla spoke again, "Brother Chiumbo, I know it's typical to do the briefing first, but since we are waiting on Kioko, why don't we prepare the transport? That way we won't mess up your schedule." The suggestion of keeping Chiumbo on schedule resonated with him, and he relented.

So, for the next two hours Bassari Squad worked with the Engineering Team at Chumba cha Usafiri. It was a reunion of sorts. The eight men had been part of the same Ibutho many years ago. And while individual members maintained contact with one another over the years, this was the first time, in a very long while, that they were able to work and commune together. So, they calibrated the energy requirements for the outgoing journey. They used Mama Zuri's medical data on Kikuyu Squad to estimate the energy requirements for the return trip. They calibrated the newly installed Akofena. And Bassari Squad reviewed the operation of Chumba cha Usafiri. Having done all this, they then worked with Brother Adio to ensure that all communication systems were operational.

By 1100 hours, Bassari Squad and the Engineering Team had completed transport preparation. Having completed this work, all seven men then reported to the Command Center at Ebe Nyocha. InDuna Taharka, Bausi Ojore, and Baba Kahuthia were all awaiting their arrival. The men greeted each other with the customary Vanguardian greeting. They also took time to reconnect with one another.

Chiumbo, who stood apart from the group throughout this period of reconnection, handed a note to InDuna Taharka. The note indicated that Kioko had a "personal mishap" yesterday and would be joining them today, but there was no indication of the time.

Reading this note, InDuna Taharka commented jokingly to Bausi Ojore, "If Kioko doesn't show up soon, you might find yourself on this mission after all."

And after about twenty minutes, Chiumbo cleared his throat loudly, in an awkward attempt to get everyone's attention.

InDuna Taharka remarked playfully, "Brother Chiumbo, we still speak English. You can get our attention with words."

Bausi Ojore added, "Pia tunazungumza Kiswahili," which is to say, "We also speak Swahili."

Bakari added, "…kanye nesiZulu," which is to say, "…and Zulu."

InDuna Taharka adjusted his voice to match Chiumbo's voice and his curt snappy tone, "Hey guys, enough camaraderie. Let's get down to business!" He laughed as he patted Chiumbo on the back.

For a moment, Chiumbo's dourness seemed to melt away, and he enjoyed the humor of the moment with the others. He then said in the warmest, yet most masculine voice he could muster, "Vanguardians, there will be more time for camaraderie as the day progresses. But for the moment, we have business to attend to." At this display, everyone present erupted in cheers and applause.

As they were applauding, Kioko limped into the room, wearing a cast on his left leg. Kioko smiled as though the applause was for him. However, when those gathered saw him and his debilitated state, all applause, all cheer, all mirth ceased. Even Chiumbo stared at him uncomprehendingly.

InDuna spoke slowly, "What happened to you?" Then as Kioko began to respond, Taharka interrupted him, his tone a bit more indignant, "You do know that you have a mission?" As Kioko began to reply, Taharka continued, and his tone was very stern this time, almost irate, "Didn't you think to notify your squad so that alternative arrangements could be made?!"

Bausi Ojore placed a hand on Taharka's shoulder and addressed Kioko, "What happened, Son?"

Kioko addressed InDuna Taharka and Bausi Ojore, "Babas…" He then turned to Bassari Squad, "Brothers, please forgive me. Yesterday, shortly after 1300 hours, I was in a car accident. My car flipped multiple times, and I passed out during the collision, then again when I was trying to step out of my car. I had surgery last night and checked myself out this morning. I'm mission ready. I'm good to go."

Taharka squinted and looked at Kioko with skepticism, "Kioko were you discharged or did you just leave the hospital?"

Kioko stood straight as an arrow, "Sir, I'm good to go!"

Taharka shook his head in exasperation.

Kioko protested, "Baba, its just one knee. I have started and finished missions in much worse shape."

To an outsider, Kioko's insistence that he was mission ready might seem an act of false bravado. But in fairness to Kioko, his outlook reflected a cultural ethos that was instilled in Vanguardians even before they became Vanguardians. From their very first days as Ginks, they were conditioned to never complain, to ignore discomfort, to learn to manage pain, and to complete the job in front of them. For most everyday pursuits, this ethos worked well. It instilled in men a commitment to work hard towards accomplishing their goals. But in other pursuits, like traveling through space on a rescue mission, it came across as foolhardy.

Baba Ojore sought to bring balance to the conversation, "Induna, Kioko is committed to his mission. He is trying to do what we taught him to do."

Taharka nodded and said, "Chiumbo, please bring Mama Nicole, Baba Adio, and Baba Fenuku. We need their expertise." He then addressed the men present, "Okay. Let's figure this out."

Over the next hour, InDuna Taharka, Bassari Squad, the Engineering Team and members of the support team discussed a range of options for the mission, given Kioko's condition. The first option was letting him go with one good knee. This was the preferred option of Bassari Squad. It was not uncommon for squad members to perform with physical injuries. And Bassari Squad had seen Kioko perform admirably under worse circumstances. Even Mama Nicole supported this option with the caveat that Kioko's cast would need some modifications to improve mobility and to provide added support, since the gravitational pull would add stress to the knee. However, this option was voted down by Adio and Fenuku. They pointed out that Kioko's prior performances "under worse circumstances" were not preceded by teleportation. The act of transporting through Chumba cha Usafiri entailed separating matter at the subatomic level and reassembling it at the destination.

As Baba Fenuku put it, "Our use of the device is too new. We do not have enough history to know how well a broken bone would respond to the stress of the stretching that is induced in the transport. If the lives of four VITs weren't on the line, I might be willing to try it. But if we have a viable alternative, I recommend we us it."

The second option was to send one of the members of the Engineering Team in place of Kioko. This option was initially preferred by Bassari Squad, but it was ultimately rejected by everyone else. The reason was that if work had to be done on Chumba cha Usafiri the engineers should not be shorthanded.

Following this last discussion point, the room was quiet until InDuna Taharka asked, "Well are there any other options that anyone would like to raise?"

Up to this point, Kahuthia and Ojore did not contribute to the conversation. So, when he spoke, the thunderous rumble of Ojore's voice caught people off guard, "I am willing to go. More than willing; I am begging to go."

InDuna Taharka, tried to cut him short. "Baba Ojore, I appreciate your willingness, but there is a bigger mission for which you are needed."

Ojore continued, "I have, for many years, trained Vanguardians at Camp Furaha. In fact, I have trained or helped to train nine of the Vanguardians in this room."

As they realized the truth of this statement, the men of Bassari Squad and the Engineering Team smiled and nodded. He had been a hero to these men when they were teenagers. And as the years progressed, and they themselves experienced the hardship of life as Vanguardians, they grew to love and appreciate him even more.

Baba Ojore added, "And training these men is no small matter. In training these men, I am also responsible for training their Mwalimu. This is not a summer job. I do this work seven days a week for fifty-two weeks of the year. So, despite being old…" he paused and looked at InDuna Taharka, "…I am capable of enduring the rigors of a mission."

Baba Ojore was winning the room. The admiration that Bassari Squad and the Engineering Team had for Baba Ojore was permeating the room. Mama Nicole, Baba Adio, and Baba Fenuke were joining them in their enthusiasm for this committed leader.

Baba Ojore concluded, "I am volunteering, not because I am capable, but because four young men were left in my charge, and now they are in danger. I would be a coward to sit idly by, watching other men secure their safety, when that is a charge that was given to me. Let me do the job that I was charged to do."

With that last appeal, Ojore looked at InDuna Taharka. Everyone present followed his gaze. Despite the weight of their stares, Taharka's face remained impassive as he turned to Chiumbo and commanded, "Chiumbo, brief the extraction team."

Dan's Hooey (O'Leary)

Erick observed Dan for much of the day without intervening. However, as the workday ended, Erick stood up and walked around Command Center 2, asking questions of those present. One of the questions he asked was, "What is your area of specialty?" He also asked, "What are you expected to contribute to the team?"

When asking these questions, Erick found that, on at least three occasions, there were two people sharing the same role. The practice of having role duplication was against company protocol as it caused unnecessary conflict. Erick also learned that the three people who were in duplicate roles were added to the team as an afterthought. This, again, was a violation of company protocol.

Erick later asked Dan why the Research Team was so far behind scheduled data collection. Dan smiled, nodded, and went into his "Gee whiz-Aww shucks" routine. He talked about the challenges of a heavy gravitational pull, about the presence of a "hostile" native population, and about a plan for "leveraging native resources." It was all a bunch of hooey. But Erick nodded agreeably. So, to Dan, it seemed that Erick accepted it.

Erick then asked Dan about the qualifications of the Research Team. Again, with more hooey, Dan explained that because the planet was populated with a humanoid species, he had to balance scientific expertise with the expertise of managed confrontation. He went on to explain that the team on the ground had the best mix of those two "imperative" skill sets.

They continued with Erick asking questions and with Dan feeding him hooey. Until finally, Dan gave him the straight story on the militaristic intervention. Here, Dan explained that the research portion of the mission had been hampered by hostile natives. He claimed the Research Team had received support from a second group of natives, and that the two groups were embroiled in conflict, and the Research Team had provided information to the friendlier of the two groups to help their chances of collecting data and getting home safely.

Erick's response was unsettling to Dan. He did not respond in any way that gave Dan an indication of what he thought of Dan's explanation. He simply said, "Thank you. I will see you in the morning." And with that, Erick left CC2.

SECRETS OF THE VANGUARD ORDER

The War Council

The morning of the battle, Kikuyu Squad tried to tell Baba Kahuthia everything that transpired the day prior. He would not let them say too much on that topic, because of time. Instead, he peppered them questions about their movements on the planet. When were they captured? How far had they marched? Were there any distinguishing landforms? At the end of their conversation, he said, "In the next few hours, a tea…" Then, as usual, the transmission became choppy just before ending completely, and they never caught the end of Kahuthia's message.

Shortly after the transmission, Jah-Bil and Gan-Jof came to Kamau and invited Kikuyu Squad to sit with Tado Guh-Dal's War Council. Interpretations were provided by Raymond and Gan-Jof. Tado Guh-Dal wanted to attack the enemy in their own territory. However, to get there, they would need to traverse a mountain range. Without going up and over the mountain, there were two ways to get there. There was a northern pass, which was described as very rocky and the distance of three villages. There was a southern pass, which was not rocky, but it was very windy and wet. It passed through a marshy area and it, too, was the distance of three villages.

Tado Guh-Dal chastised his War Council when, as best as Raymond could explain, they had given him an incomplete report. So, one of the Council Members explained that there was a third pass going through the heart of the mountain. It was the distance of two villages. As this was explained to Tado Guh-Dal, his War Council begged him not to take this path. They explained that it was a very narrow pass, and that, at certain points, only two men could walk abreast. They explained that, if they took that pass, and if the enemy met them at the mouth of the pass, they would not be able to fight, because only one or two men at a time could emerge to confront the enemy.

Hearing this, Alton pronounced to Kikuyu Squad, "He's going to take the narrow path."

Surprised by Alton's pronouncement, Kamau asked, "Why do you say that?"

Alton explained, "His War Council is begging him not to do it. So, the enemy people probably won't expect it."

After allowing his council to deliberate, and hearing all they had to offer, Tado Guh-Dal gave his war plan, "Let those of you who fear truth take the northern pass. Let those of you who fear justice take the southern pass. But as for me and doPotakwe truth bearers and doPotakwe justice bearers, we stand with the God of the doPotakwe and shall take the middle pass."

There was a palpable tension among the members of Tado Guh-Dal's War

Council. Many of his councilors were frustrated that Tado Guh-Dal had chosen the narrow path. In addition to this, there were new concerns. A smaller but more vocal group of councilors questioned Tado Guh -Dal's desire to have Kamau and his friends fight with the doPotakwe. Chief among the dissenters was Goh-Del, Tado Guh-Dal's uncle.

The Vanguardians watched this tension play out from a distance. Raymond was able to provide small bits of insight as he heard and understood snippets of the discussion. However, his input was limited as they were a good distance away, and he could not hear very well. Also, he did not have Gan-Jof to help with the interpretation.

The Battle of NiOutokwe

Jah-Bil marched the doPotakwe to the mountain range that served as a barrier between Potakwe and NiOutokwe. Once there, the doPotakwe were organized into fighting units. Watching this was fascinating for Kikuyu Squad. The doPotakwe were not one unit, but a collection of units, each with its own leader and unique structure.

Jah-Bill commanded the largest fighting force, and a portion of this fighting force was the one that had rescued Kamau and Chandler from the dewa doPotakwe. The doPotakwe in Jah-Bil's fighting unit were much like him. They seemed excited about the prospect of war. Jah-Bil insisted that his force take the front guard, the foremost position. None of the other leaders argued against him.

Tado Guh-Dal did not have a traditional fighting force. He commanded the Tado Guard. So, this relatively small, red-sashed unit positioned themselves in the middle of the column, and Tado Guh-Dal positioned himself in the middle of this unit. Here, he would sit upon a raised scaffold supported by two wahtaka. This platform allowed him to see the entire column. It also allowed the other leaders to see him and follow any commands that he might give.

Gan-Jof did not lead a fighting force, though he was a member to one. His leader was a doPotakwe named Jee-Val. Gan-Jof convinced Jee-Val to allow Kikuyu Squad to fight with his force, and Jee-Val agreed, placing Kikuyu Squad in the middle of his ranks.

Goh-Del also controlled a fighting force, but it was much smaller than Jah-Bil's. Goh-Del's fighting unit was much like him as well. They seemed as though they were willing to go along. But overall, they were disinterested in the prospect of war. Perhaps it was for this reason that Tado Guh-Dal placed them at the very back of the column. If they decided to go home early, they would not interfere with any of the fighting that would be taking place.

As the doPotakwe fighting units were organized, each man selected a weapon to carry. The Tado Guard carried their customary weapons. The leaders of the fighting units carried spears. A few doPotakwe carried the bow and arrows.

Kikuyu Squad was uncertain as to what they should do. They were not very good with weapons combat, and they had no idea who or what they would be fighting. Kamau took two short staffs. Raymond and Chandler each took a bow and quiver of arrows. Alton initially took a short spear, but after considering it, he exchanged it for two short staffs. Kamau had considered taking the short spear. He opted not to, when he was overcome with uncertainty as to whether he could actually kill. He was much more likely to whoop somebody with a stick than to actually run them through with a spear. And he knew this about himself.

As the column was formed, they marched. For the first half of the journey, the doPotakwe sang songs in rhythm with their marching. Although Kikuyu Squad did not know the meaning of the songs, they sounded jubilant, like songs of celebration. But for the second half of the march, Tado Guh-Dal commanded that the singing should cease. He also commanded that the marching should cease. Each man was to walk at his own pace, so there would be no rhythmic sound that might alert the enemy.

In short time, they were near the opening of the pass. However, the movement of the column was stalled.

Vanguard Support (Taharka)

Adio monitored the transmission from the Akofena unit that Ojore carried. With the new unit, it was possible to monitor Akofena the entire time. However, doing so was not wise. Even low-level communication required substantial energy demands. So, to conserve energy, Adio pinged Akofena every thirty minutes. As long as Akofena responded favorably to the ping, Adio would not reach out to Bassari Squad.

Up to this point, the spirits of the Support Team at Udhibiti wa Dhamira were high. Everything was moving along according to their plan. The transmission of the Extraction Team was a success. Using the information provided by Kikuyu Squad, basic tracking techniques and their own wits, the Extraction Team was able to locate Kikuyu Squad.

Once they were about a tenth of a mile from Kikuyu Squad's suspected location, Bassari Squad used Akofena to scan the region and transmitted the results back to Udhibiti wa Dhamira. Within minutes, Adio spoke, "Baba Taharka, I have the report."

Taharka responded, "Transmit audio to Bassari Squad and begin."

With Bassari Squad and the Support Team listening, Adio reported, "There is a mountain range just ahead of you near the dark side of the planet. Kikuyu

Squad is moving away from you through a pass in that mountain range. There is a long line of humanoids. And Kikuyu Squad is in the rear third of the line. They are all together."

Mandla interrupted Adio's report, "How many stand between us and Kikuyu Squad?"

Adio was calculating and responded slowly, "It seems that there are about five to six hundred in the line. So, there would be between one hundred and sixty to two hundred humanoids between you and Kikuyu Squad." After a pause, Adio continued with his report, "There is another group of about three to four hundred humanoids on the other side of the mountain range."

Mandla asked, "Are they at the opening of the pass?"

Adio chuckled slightly, "No, Brother. You won't believe this. Their forces are split. Two thirds are about a klick to the left of the pass and one-third are about a klick to the right of the pass. You've seen this before. They are waiting at the opening of two different passes."

Bassari Squad smiled and looked at one another knowingly. Ojore nodded and said simply, "The Battle of Megiddo."

Adio concluded, "Yurugu's location is about four klicks from the opening of the pass. I've sent the coordinates to Akofena."

After hearing Adio's report, Bassari Squad agreed to follow the line until the alien forces emerged from the pass. Once through the pass, they would identify and secure Kikuyu Squad, bring them back into the pass away from the fighting, and transport home.

About twenty minutes after his report, Adio's most recent ping to Akofena returned a notification. He scrambled to determine what it was. And he reported, "InDuna, Akofena is reading a point-to-point transmission on the planet's surface."

Taharka inquired, "Is Kikuyu Squad's Akofena unit capable of point-to-point communication?"

Adio explained, "Yes, it's capable, but it seems unlikely. They are all together. Who would they communicate with?"

It was Oko Addo, the military tactician, who solved the puzzle. "Brother Adio, open a line of communication with Brother Ojore. Confirm that he did not have any communication through Akofena since your report."

Adio radioed Ojore, "Bassari Squad, this is Udhibiti wa Dhamira. Can you read me?"

Baba Ojore's voice was amplified throughout Udhibiti wa Dhamira, "This is Bassari Squad. Come in."

Adio replied, "Yes, Bassari Squad, we are reading point-to-point communication signals on the planet surface. Have you had any communication through Akofena since our last communication?"

Ojore repeated Adio's question aloud. When he answered, his voice was stilted as he was distracted, "No, we have not…"

At that moment, throughout Udhibiti wa Dhamira could be heard the sound of mayhem, shouting, and cries of anguish.

Then suddenly, Manquoba's voice came through against a backdrop of scuffling and shouting, "Quickly. Pierce the rear and secure Kikuyu Squad!"

Hearing this last transmission, Baba Oko commanded, "Cut the transmission! Have Akofena scan the surface for an outbound communication signal."

Adio began pecking away at his terminal, and he responded in a barely audible tone, "Okkkayyy, but why would there be a… Wow! I found it. How did you…"

Baba Oko interrupted, "Cut that signal."

Adio pecked at his terminal a bit more and punched one last key defiantly. "Done!" He then turned in his chair to face Baba Oko. "How did you know?"

It was Baba Taharka that answered, "The aliens have a traitor in their ranks."

Botched (O'Leary)

As Dan Silverstein opened communication with SEV Fitzroy, he began the status check routine. Dan knew that the status check was a moot point, but he also knew that Erick would be watching closely. So, he decided he had better go by the book. He began with a voice that was full of sunshine and rainbows. He sang to them more than he spoke, "SEV Fitzroy! This is Dan Silverstein. Good morning to you! I want you to know that we are all pulling for your success. Erick Sabbatini, the CEO of TechInnoGen is here in the coordination center with us today. So, your support is coming straight from the top!"

Several of the staff in CC2 grinned with delight at Dan's cheerful presentation. Erick Sabbatini sat stone faced. He was not amused.

Dan continued, "SEV Fitzroy, Health Status. Report."

The gravelly voice of the team leader responded, "Health status, good. All team members are good to go!"

Dan continued spreading his cheer, "Well that's good to hear. Good to hear! Provisions Status. Report."

"Provision Status, good. We are on schedule."

Dan continued, "OK! We are two for two! Habitat status, Report."

Here the team leader seemed to hesitate. "We ar… s…ll ha…ing so… trou… w… …r ant…avity gen…r. … pl… …ing … of… ..n…"

After this last garbled response, the transmission went dead. Dan remained cool. He commanded Cathy Camp, the communications director, to try to re-establish communication. However, after several attempts, she was unable to do so. "Mr. Silverstein, the communications link is fried. There must have been a surge of some sort. It needs to be repaired at the source."

Cathy was, however, able to access the geoplotting server that fed information to SEV Fitzroy. This server provided a low-resolution map of the region surrounding SEV Fitzroy and heat signatures of the crew. As she projected this map on the screen, she explained to everyone what they were looking at and how it was typically used.

Once she brought it up, Cathy regretted that she had. There were hundreds of heat signatures showing on the map. Everyone was astounded by what they saw. Dan asked what many were thinking, "Why are there so many heat signatures? Are those people? We only have a crew of ten."

Still stone-faced, Erick's interest had been piqued. Cathy hesitantly began to explain, "The red circles represent our Research Team. Humans have a higher body temperature than the native population." She stopped.

Erick urged her on, "Catherine, please continue."

She glanced at Dan apologetically and quickly looked away. "This appears to be two different groups of natives. Those nearest to our crew are on the dark side of an extensive mountain range. Their heat signature is blue. Those with a yellow heat signature seem to be moving towards our crew through the mountain range."

Everyone sighed deeply. It appeared that the SEV Fitzroy was the final destination of an advancing army. What is more, this army was twice as large as the one positioned to defend the SEV Fitzroy.

Erick then asked, "Dan, why are there eight red heat signatures advancing with the natives against our Research Team?"

Ojore's Stand

Without hesitation, Bassari Squad ran to the rear of the column. As they approached, they saw fighters of the rear guard attacking the fighting force just ahead of them. Funani scowled, "Traitors!"

Ojore commanded, "Funani and Mandla, attack these traitorous forces here. I will push ahead to secure Kikuyu Squad."

Funani asked, "Baba, how will you get through the line?"

Ojore replied, "Manqoba will make a hole." With that, he and Manqoba engaged the cloaking mechanisms of their uniforms.

Emotion filled Manqoba, and he let out a fierce, blood curdling cry. It was chilling, and, because Manqoba could not be seen, the column froze in confusion. He then forced his way in front of Baba Ojore, and with his massive frame fueled by an intense rush of emotion, he cleared a path. Manqoba ran through the column, widening gaps provided by the doPotakwe and, on occasion, creating his own. As Baba Ojore followed in his wake, he could see Tado Guh-Dal giving commands from his elevated post. He pointed to the rear guard and shouted something incomprehensible. His aides gave signals to the troops below. Engaging their own cloaking devices, Funani and Mandla went to work in the rear, dispensing doPotakwe traitors one by one.

Meanwhile, at the rear of the column, Kamau heard an intense commotion coming from the rear guard. He looked at Raymond and asked desperately, "What is it?"

Raymond's reply came with a tinge of fear, "I don't know!" As he looked towards Gan-Jof for help, he found that Gan-Jof, who was in front of him, had turned to face him, and his face was frigid with fear.

Although Kamau could not understand the commands that were being given, there was no mistaking the sounds of war. He heard spears and sticks crashing against each other and against stone and flesh. He heard the cries of anguish and despair as doPotakwe cried out in pain. When the realization hit Kamau that they were being attacked from behind, he instinctively employed the drill commands that had been hammered into them at Camp Furaha. "Squad, about face. Ready, Arms." And just as instinctively as Kamau gave these commands, Kikuyu Squad followed them. Kikuyu Squad stood in formation with Kamau and Chandler facing the attack first, and Alton and Raymond stood right behind them.

Gan-Jof, who now had his wits about him, informed Raymond that they were being attacked by Goh-Del's forces. Raymond announced this new information to Kikuyu Squad.

Kamau then announced nervously, "Okay. Be more ready." As he stood there waiting for the advancing forces to work their way up the column, he felt a sense of overwhelm with the moment. Here he was, light-years from home. He was about to die in a strange place and among strange people. He would not have the opportunity to say goodbye to his family. He would not be able to apologize to his father for being ungrateful. He was overcome with regret.

Raymond must have sensed that something was wrong. He said, "Kamau, remember our meditations on death. We should always be prepared."

With that, Kamau closed his eyes and imagined his life. He visualized every good thing he could imagine: his loving family, his devoted father, his safe neighborhood, the magnificent food, his friendship with Imani, his brotherhood with Kikuyu Squad, the love and instruction he had received from the Mwalimu.

As he imagined each of these, he also imagined then vanishing. For he understood that nothing was intended to be permanent. His feeling of regret gave way to appreciation for what he had been able to experience. At that moment, Kamau's mind and heart were clear. He spoke to Kikuyu Squad. "Kikuyu Squad, I could have no greater brotherhood in life than I have with you right now."

Alton, Raymond, and Chandler felt a surge of emotion at Kamau's pronouncement. Each of them had, for his own reasons, looked up to Kamau. But none of them had known how devoted he was to them in return.

Kamau began quoting one of their poems, "If we must die, let it not be like hogs... Hunted and penned in an inglorious spot..." Alton, Chandler and Raymond stood taller. Their heads were held high, and they joined Kamau, "Like men, we'll face the murderous, cowardly pack, pressed to the wall, dying, but fighting back!"

Alton, Chandler, and Raymond erupted in a chorus of "Yebo's" and "Umoja's." Just then, the advancing force was in sight. Slowly one by one, the forces of Jee-Val fell, and the forces of Guh-Del grew closer. Chandler readied his bow, while Kamau stood with his left leg forward and his short staffs pointed towards the ground at his side. He noticed that the attackers were fighting with long spears. Jee-Val's men had little opportunity to fight because the distance was too great.

Kamau spoke, "Chandler, when I say 'shoot,' you let it fly at the nearest attacker, then quickly reload." Kamau then took two steps back, forcing Alton and Raymond to push the line back. This created a bit of room.

As soon as the man in front of him fell, he gave the command. Chandler shot. His shot missed as the doPotakwe attacker stepped right to avoid it. But in stepping right, he lowered his long spear, and Kamau rushed towards him. Kamau swung down hard on the attackers left hand, causing him to cry out in anguish. Kamau herd the bone crack as he struck it. He then swung up with his left stick, striking the attacker in the face. The attacker wobbled and fell backwards.

A second attacker quickly took his place. As he worked his way around his fallen partner, he stumbled to find his footing. Kamau crouched low and shouted, "Chandler shoot!" Chandler launched another arrow at the second attacker. This one struck him in the leg. The second attacker was stunned, and his movement was slowed by the arrow protruding from his leg. Kamau took full advantage as he stood and swung his sticks wildly. His first strike knocked the short spear from the hand of the second attacker. His second strike missed his head and came crashing down on the attacker's shoulder. Again, Kamau heard the crunching of bone as he struck. The second attacker crumpled to the ground, grasping at his wounds.

By this time, Chandler, Raymond, and Alton had worked out a system. Chandler and Raymond stood side by side, each ready to launch an arrow at Kamau's command. Alton crouched at their feet ready to join Kamau in the attack, when called to do so.

After the second attacker was disabled, Kamau again crouched low. This time he saw Kikuyu's Squad's fighting formation. He called, "Alton be ready!" Then, "Raymond, shoot!" As soon as Raymond launched his arrow, Alton sprang to replace Kamau. Kamau ran back to a kneeling position just below Raymond and Chandler. Using this system, Alton dispensed the next two attackers. Kikuyu Squad had disabled four attackers in total. Alton and Kamau switched positions again. This time, however, the attackers had grown wise, and they were not attacking one at a time. When Kamau took his attacking position, there were two doPotakwe, each holding long spears, preparing to thrust them at Kamau.

Approaching a break in the column, Ojore could see Kikuyu Squad in the distance, engaged in the battle. He thrust his right hand into his uniform. There was a hidden pocket near his chest. When he removed his hand, it was gloved. He repeated this motion with his left hand. Ojore then disengaged the cloaking mechanism of his uniform as he jumped onto the side wall that enclosed the pass. Springing off the wall with a growl, he cleared Manqoba and three rows of Guh-Del's forces landing in front of Kamau, between Kikuyu Squad and the attackers.

Without a word, he turned to fight, bounded forward and struck the attacker on the right with his gloved fist. That doPotakwe's eyes rolled back in his head, and he collapsed instantly. Blood trickled from his mouth and nose. The attacker on the left thrust his spear and cut a deep gash in the side of Ojore's thigh. Ojore wobbled for a moment. But he spun round, stepping behind the attacker, grabbed his neck, and twisted it quickly. Ojore picked up the spear that had cut him and thrust it at the next attacker. It struck him, throwing him back into the next two rows of would-be attackers.

Kamau and the rest of Kikuyu Squad watched in awe. They had known Baba Ojore as a joyful teacher. He was hard and exacting, but he was filled with joy and compassion for the VITs. Now, they saw that he was also a ruthless and efficient killer of his enemies. He continued to lay waste to the attacking column, destroying every attacking doPotakwe that dared to remain in his presence. As he killed them one by one, and sometimes by twos, he took the weapons that fell and used them to kill others. He was moving through the column so quickly that he was actually pushing back towards the entrance of the pass. Jee-Val's men were emboldened and followed him, waiting for an opportunity to engage.

Bassari Squad had nearly annihilated Guh-Del's forces. Most were being killed by hands they could not see, let alone fight. So, as the pass became littered with corpses, they began to lose their will to fight. Seeing this, Ojore cried out, "Bassari Squad, to the mouth of the pass!"

To Kikuyu Squad's utter amazement, three Vanguardians appeared from nowhere. They moved along the pass, pushing past the remnants of Guh-Del's forces and towards the front of the column. Seeing the figures appear, Jee-Val's forces gasped in awe. They began whispering "Onka ne tahu." Soon they were cheering and chanting, "Onka ne tahu."

Ojore commanded, "Njama. Stay with Manqoba. I will clean up the pass." Manqoba lead Funani, Mandla and Kikuyu Squad to the mouth of the pass. The few doPotakwe who remained in the pass, cleared the way as they approached.

***

When they arrived, they found two rows of doPotakwe fighting in front of the pass, and more were emerging. Bassari Squad fought with forces to the left of the entrance. Baba Funani commanded Kikuyu Squad to stay behind them.

In Kamau's portion of the battlefield, Bassari Squad did most of the fighting. They were fierce and efficient. They fought with weapons left on the battlefield. Kikuyu Squad mostly watched the battle unfold. Periodically, an opposing attacker would get behind the line and a member of Kikuyu Squad, usually Alton or Kamau, would need to debilitate them. In just about twenty minutes or so after the pass was opened, the battle was nearly won by the doPotakwe. As Raymond looked around, he saw Gan-Jof and others in Jee-Val's fighting force, but he did not see Baba Ojore. Raymond yelled over the din, "Baba Manqoba, Baba Ojore is not here!"

Funani looked around and called out, "Bassari Squad! We need to check on Baba Ojore." They ran until they reached an area that was not clear. The path was blocked with the fallen bodies of Goh-Del's forces. They stopped, looked around, and began calling for Baba Ojore.

Suddenly, a figure appeared right at their feet. Baba Ojore sat on the ground, sweating profusely and out of breath. Alton's eyes grew large, and he said in amazement, "Wow! It's like magic!"

Baba Mandla smiled broadly at him, "Baba, these work very well!"

Baba Funani turned to Alton, "No, Little Brother. It's not magic. It's technology. It is a wearable cloaking device, a new tool for the Vanguard Order."

Baba Ojore added, "Funani, when we return, you will report the effectiveness of this tool to InDuna Taharka."

Baba Funani protested, "No, Baba, you should present it."

Baba Ojore gasped as he answered, "I will not be able."

At that moment, they looked closely at Baba Ojore. His left leg was swollen, turning shades of purple, black, and red, and the skin was unnaturally hard and scaly. There was a collective gasp. Mandla said solemnly, "It's infected."

Manqoba said, "Baba, if we go back now, they can heal you. There is still time."

Baba Ojore looked harshly at Manqoba. He struggled to stand, using the jagged rocks that lined the pass to pull himself up. Then, without breaking eye contact with Manqoba, he said sternly, "If we go back now, we will not have completed the mission."

Funani replied respectfully, "Sir, our mission was to secure the VITs."

Ojore smiled slightly, "Funani, our mission is to secure our people."

Manqoba was visibly fighting back tears.

Baba Ojore strained to smile, "Now Vanguardians, we shall finish this mission. Mandla and Manqoba take Chandler and Raymond with you to liberate as much Yurugu technology as you can. Then destroy the rest. Remove any sign that he ever existed on this planet."

Mandla responded, "Yes, sir!"

"Funani, you will stay here with Alton, Kamau, and me."

Funani responded, "Yes, sir!"

Baba Ojore concluded, "We will meet on the doPotakwe side of the pass, and we will transport from there. Let's move!"

Funani, Alton, Kamau, and Baba Ojore walked back to the designated point of transport. While they walked, Funani asked Baba Ojore questions about his experience as a VIT and his time as a young Vanguardian and Bausi. Baba Ojore enjoyed telling these old stories as much as the others enjoyed hearing them. While he shared his experiences, he also shared lessons that he had learned through life.

At one point, Kamau apologized. He felt responsible that Baba Ojore was cut while protecting him. He felt responsible that Kikuyu Squad came to the planet accidentally and that Bassari Squad had to come rescue them.

Baba Ojore asked him, "Kamau if you are hammering a nail with your right hand, and you strike your left thumb, does your left hand blame your right hand?"

Kamau gave an embarrassed chuckle, "No, sir."

He continued, "Njama, we are one unit. When a small toe is hurting, the whole-body swoops down to attend it." He paused as Kamau contemplated the proverb, then asked, "Do you understand?"

Kamau nodded his understanding, "Yes, sir."

They continued sharing stories and lessons. And after a time, they shared their hopes and dreams for the future, for Vanguard, and for the Abantu. When the rest of the group reported, they returned home.

The Return

The Purification

Once Adio received communication from the extraction team, Taharka gave the command, "Prepare for arrival!"

The support team scrambled to action. A medical evaluation team was stationed at Chumba cha Usafiri, along with a portable decontamination chamber, sterile clothing, and two transport vehicles. Living quarters were prepared in a secluded section of Camp Furaha. Human service professionals and psychologists collaborated to assemble a team for psychological evaluation and reacclimation. This team would guide Bassari Squad and Kikuyu Squad through the Purification Ritual.

As the support team bustled about, Baba Adio shouted, "Bausi Ojore is injured!"

With a look of concern Taharka asked, "How bad?"

Adio's mouth dropped as he listened to the communication. He nodded his understanding, "It's bad, sir. He's been cut badly, and it's infected."

Mama Beatrice asked, "How could it be infected so quickly?"

Mama Nicole explained, "It's another planet. It could be that the microorganisms are new, and he doesn't have natural defenses to fight them."

Baba Osei added, "It could be that he was exposed to a poison or toxin that is just presenting as an infection."

Before Taharka could give the command, Mama Nicole jumped to action, "I'm on it!" She grabbed her notebook and satchel, turned to Chiumbo and, with the grace characteristic of a woman of the Abantu, she asked, "Brother Chiumbo, would you mind contacting Dr. Oshi and asking him to send the AMNB12 to B-6?"

Struck by her calmness and the warmth of her voice, Chiumbo's eyes glazed over, and he grinned stupidly as he turned to Taharka. Before he could speak, if indeed he was going to speak, Taharka snapped, "Permission granted."

Chiumbo turned back to Mama Nicole still grinning, "Yes, ma'am."

He then stood there rooted in place until she smiled and gave the warmest and most polite dismissal she could muster, "Thank you!"

On their return, Kikuyu Squad was not permitted to rejoin Mkhosi Kunye. Instead, they were taken to a remote location somewhere at Camp Furaha. They were awakened by the Hwamanda each morning. They received a set of exercises for ritual purification. They completed these each day. They ran and trained in a small, private Ukumbi wa Mapambano.

Each day, Baba Kahuthia came to visit with them three times. When he visited, they met in a facility where he was separated from the squad by a glass wall. On his first visit of the first day, he reviewed the daily Instruction Set in survivalism. These reviews were helpful, but they did not replace the long arduous instruction under the hot sun, the struggle against the boredom of repetition, the bite of insects, or the yelling of the Mwalimu as they barked commands and acted incredulous at every error. They really missed the old Akhet.

On Baba Kahuthia's second visit, he talked to Kikuyu Squad about their journey. He let them know that everything they shared would be recorded for Vanguard scientists to review, but aside from that, he was a curious listener. He asked questions about the doPotakwe, their land, and their customs. He asked questions about Kikuyu Squad, how they felt and what they thought at various points during the adventure. During this visit, he was joined by another man, who was helping to conduct the psychological evaluation. This visit also gave Kikuyu Squad time to ask questions about Mkhosi Kunye. They missed the other VITs and were eager to return. They enjoyed hearing the updates.

On Baba Kahuthia's third visit, they were given a reading assignment. It was a very long book about the history of the medical abuse of Black people. In a way, they were lucky to be secluded. They had a lot of time to read the massive book. They would typically read ahead a few chapters and discuss the reading among themselves in preparation for Baba Kahuthia's visit.

Although Kikuyu Squad could not join Mkhosi Kunye, they were able to spend time in the presence of Bassari Squad. On the second day of the Purification, Kamau learned that Bassari Squad trained each day. He asked if Kikuyu Squad could train with them, and they were happy to oblige. Bassari Squad focused their time with Kikuyu Squad on Combatives Training. They all learned a great deal. Funani taught them to be patient and observant while fighting. He pointed out how to determine an opponent's weak points and vulnerabilities. This lesson was especially valuable for Kamau. He had already begun thinking this way, and Funani helped him to hone and refine his approach.

Baba Manqoba taught them to become stronger. They did this, not by lifting weights or becoming bigger, but by using leverage and angles to their advantage. Chandler especially liked this instruction. After a few days of instruction, Chandler was able to throw Mandla. Of course, Mandla was not fighting back, but he was twice Chandler's size, and this showed that Chandler was using leverage properly. Now, learning to do this during combat was another matter. But only so much could be accomplished in a few days.

Other members of the support team visited Kikuyu Squad each day. They took blood and scraped skin for sweat. They required them to spit and urinate in cups so much that the Squad wondered how they had any fluid left in their bodies. Each day, they were given an extensive array of physical and psychological tests. Their bodies were scanned. They were poked and prodded by doctors who wore hazmat suits. It was exhausting. The only normal contact was their time with each other, with Baba Kahuthia and with Bassari Squad.

Each evening, Kikuyu Squad built a fire and gathered for Group Reflection. Seeing this, Bassari Squad asked if they could join. Kikuyu Squad was happy to have them. Together, they shared their thoughts and feelings about all they had seen.

At the start, Bassari Squad listened as Kikuyu Squad discussed the tragedies of Tado Guh-Dal. They bemoaned the fact that he was subjected to the jealousy of his own people. They lamented that outsiders would travel from so far away to destabilize a whole planet of people simply to steal their natural resources. They were incredulous when reminded of Goh-Del's treachery. How dishonorable it was that he would betray his own people, his own flesh and blood, all in the service of a common enemy.

Hearing the absurdity of Kikuyu Squad's reflection, Manqoba began to breath so heavily that everyone could hear him. Mandla quickly intervened. He said playfully, "Man Cobra! We were young once. Have you forgotten?"

Then he turned to Kamau and Kikuyu Squad, "Can you think of any ways that the history of our people is similar to the condition of the doPotakwe?" With that question, it all came back to them: the fomenting of discord that led to jealousies, the social and cultural destabilization, the theft of natural resources, the treachery. They had read multiple accounts of all these offenses. And they knew full well the impact these offenses had on the Black community. Discussion around this question kept them up late into the evening.

Over the next week, during those Group Reflections, Kikuyu Squad peppered Bassari Squad with questions about their own experiences as VITs, Vanguardians, and as men. They also talked quite extensively about girls. This seemed to be a favorite topic of Vanguardians, young and old.

But it was Alton alone who dared ask the question that every member of Kikuyu Squad wanted to know but feared to ask. And he asked it solemnly, even reverently, "Did Baba Ojore live?"

The Aftermath (O'Leary)

The morning sun shone bright into the conference room. And the way it fell, it warmed the chair and table in the area where Dan sat. Normally, Dan would enjoy a bright summer morning, but today, this accident of nature was eerily ironic because Dan was literally and figuratively in the hot seat.

Dan tried to keep a casual smile on his face. He didn't want to grin too much, but he had to remain optimistic, and open. He was relying on his charm. At this point, that's all he had.

Seated around the table were all the senior level executives of TechInnoGen. Erick Sabbatini stood and walked part-way around the table to address the group. "We all know the recent tragedy that brought us here, so there is no need for introductory remarks. But I do want to keep you apprised of what has transpired these past few days."

The executives sat wooden faced, each looking at Erick. At this point, even Dan managed to maintain eye contact. *And still, he wears that foolish grin,* Dan thought. He then addressed the executives assembled. "First, I received word this morning that TechInnoGen now faces fourteen wrongful death lawsuits. Although there were ten researchers killed, divorce and remarriage has given four of the decedents additional 'immediate family members' who are eligible to sue."

Erick's eyes narrowed to a squint, and he scowled unconsciously each time he looked in Dan's direction. Dan noticed, and it became increasingly difficult for him to maintain his optimistic grin.

"Second, the SEV Fitzroy is destroyed." Erick paused and looked around the room. He wanted to ensure that the message sank in. "You should understand that over the past five years, we have invested $6.2 billion into this project. There is no trace of SEV Fitzroy, which means that we have lost all traces of the physical product in which we have invested. What's worse, once news of this gets out, we will not be able to restart this project. No one will touch it."

Erick's voice was beginning to lose its cool composure and grew louder and angrier with each thought. "No investor will give money. No researcher will lend expertise. No adventurer would dare step foot in the vehicle. No reporter will write a story that is not reminding the world about how we killed ten people!" He slammed his notebook on the conference table. "We'd be lucky to find a janitor who's willing to wash toilets tied to this project!"

Erick breathed deeply, picked up his notebook, and regained his composure. The executives were very uncomfortable, shifting uneasily in their seats. As for Dan's grin, it was completely gone. "Not only is the money that we put into this project gone, but we have also lost the time of many very capable researchers."

Dan attempted to get Erick's attention. However, he was so shaken that his voice came out mousy, "Uhh. Sir, if I can…"

Erick said nothing. But he looked at Dan in such disbelief that Dan would dare open his mouth. Dan quickly sank back in his seat and looked down at the floor. Several of the executives looked at each other in similar disbelief.

Having stared Dan under the table, Erick continued, "Why do I raise this? Losses are a part of doing business. Our job is to provide goods and services that people want. In doing so, we take risks. Sometimes those risks pay off, and we earn money." He was smiling as he gave this lesson in Business 101. "And sometimes, those risks don't pay off, and we lose money. Either way, I am not a person that is opposed to losses. Losses are a part of doing business."

Erick's smile faded, "What I am opposed to is executives that violate company protocol." He turned his gaze towards Dan and continued speaking squarely in his direction. "I am opposed to executives who put their own advancement ahead of the company's well-being." His eyes narrowed, and Dan sank a bit in his chair with each sentence. "I am opposed to executives who put their own advancement ahead of the lives of company employees and customers." Erick then slammed a manila folder on the table right in front of Dan, "I am opposed to executives who wantonly lie!"

As he did this, Erick's assistant passed out copies of manila folders like the one that was given to Dan. The manila folder contained a photocopied image of the original project plan for the second launch of SEV Fitzroy. The copy showed handwritten notes, which indicated that it had been in the possession of someone outside of TechInnoGen. As they examined the file, the executives gasped and stared at Dan in disbelief.

Dan tried to speak, but he was so overcome with shock and shame that nothing coherent came out. Erick ignored his babblings and continued, still staring at Dan, "This file was provided to us yesterday by local police. They recovered it after busting an intellectual property theft consortium." He turned away from Dan, "Here's what I think. I think that some fool had his briefcase stolen. I think this briefcase contained the complete project plan. I think that instead of reporting the theft, this fool rushed TechInnoGen into a mission for which we were unprepared."

Erick stopped speaking, sat down, and stared at Dan. The executives were fit to be tied. There was murmuring, teeth sucking, headshaking, eyerolling… and sinking. Poor Dan was sinking into his chair. After two minutes of this torture, Erick spoke again, "Dan Silverstein, you are dismissed. Your services are no longer needed here."

Embarrassed and ashamed, Dan could not leave quickly enough.

Goodbye, Old Friend (Taharka)

There was little room to move in B-6 as Bassari Squad and Kikuyu Squad stepped out of Chumba cha Usafiri. The flood of medical equipment, medical personnel, and supplies made movement difficult. Everyone except Bassari Squad and Kikuyu Squad wore hazmat suits, so their movement was slow and cumbersome. Mama Nicole, accompanied by Mama Zuri, moved awkwardly to evaluate Baba Ojore. He was very weak but holding on to consciousness as he clung fast to Manqoba. They laid him on a gurney and ran the body scan over him.

The Vanguardians and VITs surrounding him wore looks of heavy-hearted sadness. One by one, he examined their faces, then spoke between gasps. He struggled to project his voice as he had done so many times before, "Vanguardians, if we want to live past our allotted time, will we?"

Smiles slowly crept onto the faces of those surrounding his gurney, Manqoba, Funani, Mandla, Kioko, Kamau, Alton, Raymond, Chandler, even Adio, and Chiumbo. Though they had heard it at different times, and under slightly different circumstances, they had all heard this same lesson. Almost in unison they answered, "No, we will not, Baba."

Baba Ojore gasped, "Brothers… death is inevitable. It is the proper conclusion to life." He breathed heavily and paused to muster his strength. "But I am not dead." He paused gasping between each sentence. "I am a vessel. The war spirit of our ancestors was poured into me. I have poured that spirit into thousands of Vanguardians. You do the same." His voice then became stronger and defiant, "And we will never die!"

Kamau felt a swirl of emotions. He was at once proud, sad, emboldened, and angry.

The medical personnel then whisked Baba Ojore away. Moments later in a medical treatment room, Mama Nicole spoke to InDuna Taharka, "He's not going to make it. The infection has spread too far throughout his body. We can't control it."

Taharka responded, "Very well, Sister. His arrangements have been made." He then looked at Baba Ojore, "Old friend, you have served valiantly. It has been an honor to know you. Would you like to say goodbye to the Warriors?"

Baba Ojore smiled and nodded, "Yes, I would like that very much."

For the next two hours, Mwalimu from throughout the Akhet were brought in groups of two to bid farewell to Baba Ojore. He had trained them all, and they all loved him. The VITs of Mkhosi Kunye were also allowed to see him. They came one squad at a time. Baba Ojore found strength from deep within himself to impart a final bit of wisdom to each. Whether a proverb, a line from a poem, or a prophetic word of what each young man would accomplish in the years to come, he gave them all a final bit of himself.

Once the last man had seen him, he turned to InDuna Taharka and said, "Goodbye, old friend. Asante Sana." And he transitioned.

Notice of Baba Ojore's transition went first to Iya Iyaba and the Elder Council and then to the entire Abantu. There was no community within the Abantu that did not know and respect Baba Ojore. A formal ceremony, or Mazishi, was scheduled. Each community would send a contingent of two to three people to Camp Furaha. Each community would also organize its own Mazishi to be held concurrent with the ceremony at Camp Furaha.

The Mazishi was held at the completion of the Purification Ritual, which was seven days after the return of Kikuyu Squad. There seemed to be thousands in attendance. There was no food, no choir, no floral arrangements, and no eulogy. The funerary rites of the Vanguard Order were notoriously plain and conspicuously simple. As a matter of practice, Vanguardians avoided anything that looked like self-aggrandizement. They shunned pomposity and sneered at self-importance. Their entire existence embodied an unwavering commitment to the whole. Whether that whole be a squad, Mkhosi, Ibutho, or the Vanguard Order itself, they lived for each other, which was seen as a greater good. As in life, so it was in death that they would not countenance a ceremony to praise any one of them.

So, the Mazishi was simple by design. It provided a time for those still living to officially acknowledge that one of their own was no longer with them. All arrangements were made by the decedent, and there were very few. An official historical record of the decedent's life was prepared by the decedent, and it was filed with the records division of the Vanguard Order. This practice was adopted to avoid the messiness of loved ones who, in times of grief, could not keep themselves from sanitizing the life of the departed and confusing history in the process. It was observed early on that mistresses were made into wives, children conceived outside of marriage were thrust into newly created nuclear families, agnostics were transformed into Christians, and those with only a year or two of college were given degrees that they never really earned. All of this was avoided when each Vanguardian documented his own life history.

So, in keeping with the spirit of a Vanguard Mazishi, Baba Ojore's body was washed, rubbed with oils and fragrance, and fitted in his official Vanguard uniform. He was laid in repose for the entire day on a funeral pyre under a round gazebo. His arms were folded across his chest and his fighting gauntlet was laid at his side.

For nearly two hours, as evening fell, Mazishi attendees circulated, greeted one another, and, in small clusters, they shared stories about their experiences with Baba Ojore. They told stories of how they met him, shared adventures, embarrassing moments, funny moments, things they taught him, and things they learned from him. Members of the Elder Council talked about how much he impacted the Abantu. Vanguardians told stories of missions they had with him. These stories, however, were only told among other Vanguardians.

Both Jabari Njama and Rafiki Baharia were in attendance. Kamau was able to speak with both of them briefly. It was at this moment that it became clear to Kamau that his father was a Vanguardian. He learned that his father had a long-standing relationship with Baba Ojore. He also learned that his father was well known and very well regarded among the Vanguard Order. Kamau also introduced his father and Baba Rafiki to Kikuyu Squad.

The Hwamanda sounded and attendees quieted and turned to InDuna Taharka, who stood at the base of the gazebo. InDuna Taharka spoke, "As you may know, it is customary for Vanguardians to plan and maintain current copies of all final arrangements. Bausi Ojore has asked Namazzi Akello to deliver a recitation."

Sister Namazzi was very young. She was only a few years older than Kamau. She had the beauty and energy that came with youth, and she was gifted with a strong voice and a passionate delivery. She stood next to InDuna Taharka and recited, "When Great Trees Fall."

Following that, Baba Taharka recited Bausi Ojore's Oriki. He recited it first in Yoruba and a second time in English.

Finally, Bakari Njeri came forward and sang the Vanguard version of, "A Change Gone Come." He had a smooth, pure baritone voice that reverberated through the night sky. But he sang simply, the way the song was written. There were no flourishes or embellishments. It was, by far, the best rendition of this song that Kamau had ever heard.

As Bakari sang, torches were given to four Vanguardians: Baba Taharka, Kamau, Baba Manqoba, and Baba Kojo. It is customary for the decedent to identify four trusted and, sometimes, close Vanguardians to light the funeral pyre. These men symbolically send the deceased off into the ancestral realm. Kamau was surprised that he was chosen.

Baba Taharka explained, "Baba Ojore asked that you take part on behalf of Kikuyu Squad. He indicated that I represent the past, Baba Kojo and Baba Manqoba represent the present, and it is you and Kikuyu Squad that represent the future."

These four Vanguardians each laid their torch on a different side of the pyre. Taharka laid his on the western side, Kamau laid his on the eastern side, Kojo and Manqoba laid theirs on the northern and southern side respectively. As the pyre and the gazebo burned, the attendees joined Baba Bakari in song.

At the conclusion of their singing, when the fire was fully ablaze, all Vanguardians stood in a circle around the pyre. All VITs from the Akhet stood closest to the pyre. The Mwalimu and Bausi from the Akhet stood immediately behind them. Behind them stood every other Vanguardian in attendance. With arms folded to form the X across their chests, Vanguardians recited, in unison, the Vanguard Creed. Outside the ring, members of the Abantu said a quiet prayers of thanks.

A Bright Future (O'Leary)

Timothy O'Leary sat at the large conference table across from Erick Sabbatini. Erick was almost apologetic as he spoke, "Timothy, I have observed your work for a long time. I value your contribution to the company. I anticipated that this day would come. I just wanted it to come under better circumstances."

Timothy nodded his understanding, "Yes, sir."

He continued, "I would like for you to consider taking Dan's position. By now, I am sure you have heard the circumstances under which he left. There is a lot of cleanup that needs to take place. If you take this position, much of that work would fall on you."

Timothy nodded again, encouraging Mr. Sabbatini, "Yes, sir. I understand."

"I don't see this position as a permanent one for you. I want to re-evaluate your role with the company again in two years. I anticipate that, at that time, we will be able to promote you again. I've had language to that effect included in your contract." Erick paused for a moment, then asked, "Do you have any questions for me?"

Timothy responded, "No, sir. I do not have any questions." He paused as though measuring each utterance. "My answer is yes. And I have a plan that I would like to implement immediately." He slid a report across the table to Erick. "This plan is intended to mitigate the PR damage that we are going to suffer. It also includes a five-year plan to recoup the losses incurred with the loss of the SEV Fitzroy."

For the next hour, Timothy reviewed his plan with Erick, who assented to nearly everything in the plan. Within a week, Timothy brought Anand back to the company with a salary increase and at a higher position. He reached out to Marlene who had left shortly after Dan was fired. She had assumed that, with Dan gone, there would be no place for her. Timothy asked if she would be willing to stay and work with Anand. She agreed enthusiastically.

Timothy revived the intern program that had once brought him to the company. He also extended the program to support a small number of promising high school students. It was noticed by some executives that these high school students were typically African American boys, and they were never available during the summer. But no matter, it was nice to have their youthful energy in the building.

Timothy also maintained contact with Dan, who was having more trouble than he could manage. He was being indicted on charges of fraud and corruption and was facing civil suits from the families of the deceased Research Team as well as TechInnoGen. To complicate matters, Amelia was becoming increasingly incorrigible. She was spending money like it was water and threatening to leave at every turn. She provided no support whatsoever.

Yet, when they met, Timothy always lent a sympathetic ear. He was probably one of the few people that Dan could actually speak to. Encumbered by legal trouble and bleeding money, it was surprising that what bothered Dan most was that Erick had figured out his scheme. This concerned him far more than the death of the Research Team, the loss of the SEV Fitzroy, or even his mounting personal losses. Timothy couldn't understand it. But he didn't need to. He always reassured Dan that the minute he had an opportunity to help Dan back on his feet, he would do it. And this promise pleased Dan. In his mind, Timothy was still his boy.

Know Thyself, The Tenth Virtue

Immediately following the Mazishi, Kikuyu Squad rejoined Mkhosi Kunye. That evening they stayed awake longer than usual. During Group Reflection, the VITs and the Mwalimu discussed recent events. They discussed the Mazishi; why the Mazishi differed from funeral ceremonies they had seen before; the lifestyle and commitment of Vanguardians; the life and death of Baba Ojore; and his supposed successor.

The VITs were never told how Baba Ojore died. This was known only to Kikuyu Squad. They were never told what actually happened to Kikuyu Squad for those eleven days that they had gone missing. And on both counts, Kikuyu Squad was sworn to secrecy. Kamau found it interesting that the Mwalimu never lied about the cause of Baba Ojore's death or the whereabouts of Kikuyu Squad. If asked once, they would simply say, "It's classified." If asked a second time, they would say, "Don't ask again," and the message was crystal clear.

Kamau was in heaven when he was, once again, able to run with the Mkhosi. He had not realized how much he had come to love the routine and how much his mind and body had adapted to the rigor of the training. He had not realized how he had sorely missed the brotherhood. When they returned to the Mkhosi, it was the middle of Week Nine. The virtue was perseverance. The poem they learned was, "See it Through." The survival skill they learned was ropework. And they were reading a book about the role of armed resistance during the Civil Rights Movement. Baba Kojo had taken on the responsibilities of Baba Ojore, much like he had when they were Ginks.

After their adventure, everything had so much more meaning. Kamau had lost all interest in winning the Intersquad Competition. Sure, he would have liked to win, but winning this competition did not drive him. He was driven by a deeper purpose. And this change was visible to others. Kamau was quieter. He was more focused than he had been prior to their adventure. In fact, all of Kikuyu Squad had changed in this way. This deep change had come to the fore in Week Ten.

Week Ten began like all the others. The poem they learned was, "Still I Rise." Kikuyu Squad liked this poem. It reminded them of the challenges they had faced in that other world and how they were able to overcome it. It especially resonated with Chandler, who commented that he might have this poem recited at his own Mazishi.

The survival skill they learned was first aid. They paid especially close attention to these lessons. They asked very insightful, very specific questions. They had all experienced being knocked around by strange, yet stronger, fighters, and they realized that, as good as they might ever be, they might also find someone better or even luckier. This is what happened to Baba Ojore. The way he fought, he could have held off that foreign phalanx for days, even those year-long, alien days. But ultimately, he was done in by an errant spear and alien microbes. No. Bravado was out for Kikuyu Squad. They wanted to know how to patch themselves up under every possible circumstance. Kamau, especially, had come to realize that survival and winning weren't always glamorous. Sometimes, it required doing dirty, inelegant, and boring work.

The book they read that week was all about the internet and how it is dumbing down Americans. This wasn't such a big deal to any of Kikuyu Squad. They didn't have phones or computers or any of those types of devices. In fact, they found it hard to believe that people could spend too much time staring at a computer when there were so many other things that could be done.

The virtue for Week Ten was self-knowledge. "Know Thyself" is what the Mwalimu said throughout the week. This was a strange virtue. The VITs of Mkhosi Kunye understood the other virtues: courage, unity, loyalty, and restraint. These are traits that people might not have, but traits that can be developed with understanding and with effort. But who couldn't know themselves? It didn't make much sense.

As the week progressed, the realization that they would be leaving one another began to set in. There was an air of sadness that pervaded the Mkhosi. They were told there would be a special culmination, a celebratory weekend in which the entire Ibutho would have a joint adventure. This promise lifted their spirits.

On the last Thursday, during Group Reflection, Mkhosi Kunye discussed what they would do once they returned home. The conversation eventually morphed into a discussion of what they would do later in life.

It was during this conversation that Kamau's life came into view. He didn't share it with anyone, but he knew it within himself. He would find and marry a woman who was much like his mother: a caring, nurturing woman who would love him and his children unconditionally. She would be a woman who, by her presence and special touch, was a ray of sunshine in his home. He would, by his force of will and his new friendships, ensure the well-being of his community, no matter how big or how small. He would ensure that all those who lived in this world, his world, would be safe from the injustices that lurked outside. And he would not mind getting his hands dirty in the process. In fact, he believed he would like it. He would ensure the safety and well-being of his children, no matter the cost.

It was at this moment that Kamau came to know himself. He was, indeed, Jabari's son.

Glossary

Abantu: The Abantu is a loosely coordinated group of people who have committed themselves to improving the social condition of African people. The Abantu is comprised of several smaller communities, clustered about geographically throughout the Unites States. It is governed by an Elder Council comprised of representatives from those communities. And it is protected by the Vanguard Order. The Abantu is sometimes referred to as "the Community." (Xhosa)

Akhet: Akhet is the summer camp experience in which young men are trained to become Vanguardians. Founders of the Vanguard Order took the name from the ancient Kemetic name for the first season of the year. Akhet means inundation, for this is the season during which the Nile river flooded, bathing the plains with water and nutrients for the soil. Similarly, the summer camp experience is an inundation into the life of a Vanguardian. (Kemetic)

Akofena: Akofena is the portable control panel used to operate Chumba cha Usafiri. It is named for the Adinkra symbol displayed on the panel. (Twi)

Asante: Asante is a Swahili word meaning "Thank you." (Kiswahili)

Assegai: The assegai is the long spear used by the Maasai. (Arabic)

Camp Furaha: Camp Furaha is the name of the property at which the Akhet takes place. Camp Furaha is the central location of the Vanguard Order, and a prime location for important Vanguard gatherings. Furaha means happiness in Swahili. (Kiswahili)

Chaki: In the Vanguard Order, the word Chaki is used as a strong reproof. It means no. But when used by Vanguardians it is much stronger than no. (Kiswahili)

Chumba cha Usafiri: Chumba cha Usafiri is the transport chamber used by the Vanguard Order for teleportation through space-time. Chumba cha Usafiri works in conjunction with Akofena. Both Chumba cha Usafiri and Akofena were developed by scientists of the Order who drew on time travel research pioneered by a Black university physicist as well as technology appropriated from other sources. (Kiswahili)

Ebe Nyocha: Ebe Nyocha is the primary Research Center of the Vanguard Order. Because it is located at Camp Furaha, it is a safe location. So it also contains many artifacts and serves as a gathering location for the Vanguard Order and members of the Abantu. (Igbo)

Elder Council: The Elder Council provides direction and loosely governs the Abantu. Members of the Elder Council are chosen to represent the various communities that comprise the Abantu. (English)

H-Zone: The H-Zone, or habitable zone, of a planet is the distance around a star in which a planet would be capable of supporting life. It would require a planet to be able to maintain water in a liquid state and to provide sufficient atmospheric pressure. Estimates are that there could be as many as 40 billion earth-sized planets in H-zones in the Milky Way galaxy alone. (English)

Hujambo: Hujambo is a Swahili greeting that is often translated as "Hello." However, the more literal translation is "How are you." Hujambo is used when speaking to one person. When speaking to two or more people, the equivalent term would be hamjambo. (Kiswahili)

Hwamanda: The Hwamanda is a wind instrument usually made from the horn of a kudu. It is used primarily as a signaling device, especially in war and military exercises. (Shona)

Ibutho: Taken from the Zulu, an ibutho is a regiment of Zulu warriors based on age group. For the Vanguard Order an ibutho is a collection of five Mkhosi, their Mwalimu and Bausi. (Zulu)

InDuna: InDuna is the title for the leader of the Vanguard Order. The InDuna is styled after the traditional Zulu and Xhosa role of InDuna. In addition to commanding the Vanguard Order, the Vanguard InDuna has the responsibility of acting as an intermediary between the Vanguard Order and the Abantu. (Zulu and Xhosa)

Iklwa: Short Spear used by the Zulu. (Zulu)

Isfet: Isfet means "disorder." In Kemetic philosophy, "disorder" is much more than untidiness. It is the opposite of Ma'at, which means "order." Ma'at or order is regarded as essential for high quality human life. It connotes desirable ideals such as truth and justice. Isfet is the antithesis of Ma'at. Isfet is associated with injustice, chaos, and violence. For this reason, Vanguardians regard disorder as more than an inconvenience. It is a threat to the quality of human life. (Kemetic)

Iya Iyaba: Iya Iyaba is the title for the head of the Elder Council. The Iya Iyaba is styled after the traditional African role of Queen Mother. The Iya Iyaba is responsible for monitoring the condition of the Abantu, soliciting guidance from the Elder Council on matters that pertain the Abantu as a whole, facilitating the transition of new members onto the Elder Council, and granting the Vanguard Order permission to go to war. Iya Iyaba also appoints the inDuna of the Vanguard Order and is in-turn appointed by the Elder Council. (Yoruba)

Kambi: Kambi is the term for "camp." It is the location where each Mkhosi's tents are pitched, where they sleep, and meet for morning call and group reflection. Each Kambi is named for its Mkhosi. For example, Kambi wa Mkhosi Kunye is the Camp of Mkhosi Kunye. (Kiswahili)

Klick: A klick is another term for a kilometer. It is the equivalent of .62 miles. (English)

Mazishi: Mazishi is the name for funerary services. (Kiswahili)

Mduara ya Heshima: Mduara ya Heshima is the Circle of Honor. During the Akhet, Vanguardians and VITs perform this ritual at the end of each day. The ritual requires participants to share something for which they are grateful. Statements of gratitude are usually affirmed by the group. (Kiswahili)

Mkhosi: Mkhosi is a Xhosa term which means army. For the Vanguard Order an Mkhosi is a collection of five Squads, their Mwalimu and Bausi. (Xhosa)

Mti wa Umoja: Mti wa Umoja is literally translated as the Tree of Unity. During the Akhet, Vanguardians and VITs perform this ritual at the start of each day. The ritual requires participants to share an affirmation. Affirmations are usually affirmed by the group. (Kiswahili)

Mwanangu: A contraction of mwana (which means son) and angu (which means my), mwanangu means "my son." (Kiswahili)

Quarter mate: A quarter mate is a person with whom a VIT shares living quarters. During the Akhet, VITs sleep two to a tent. Wherever possible, VITs also partner with quarter mates during activities.

Sijambo: Sijambo is a Swahili greeting that is translated as "I am fine." It is the common response to the greeting, hujambo. Sijambo is used when one person is responding. When two or more people are responding, the equivalent term would be hatujambo. (Kiswahili)

Udhibiti wa Dhamira: Udhibiti wa Dhamira (also referred to as Mission Control) is the location where Vanguard operations are coordinated and managed. (Kiswahili)

Ukumbi wa Kunye: Ukumbi wa means "hall of" in Swahili. Kunye is the Zulu word for one. The literal translation is "Kunye Hall." This is the gathering hall for Mkhosi Kunye. It is here that the Mkhosi has their meals, evening reading, movie nights, and other indoor gatherings. The gathering halls for the other Mkhosis (i.e. Kubili, Kuthathu, Kune, and Kuhlanu) are similarly named. (Kiswahili and Zulu)

Ukumbi wa Mapambano: The literal translation is "Hall of Struggle." At the Akhet, each Ukumbi wa Mapambano is a Combatives Training hall. Each Mkhosi has their own Ukumbi wa Mapambano. Mkhosi Kunye's is called the "Terrordome." Mkhosi Kubili's is called the "House of Pain." Mkhosi Kuthathu's is called the "War Zone." Mkhosi Kune's is called the "Ring of Fire." And Mkhosi Kuhlanu's is called the "Front Line." (Kiswahili)

Acknowledgments

I extend gratitude to my editor Cindy Prescher for her thoroughness with the text, and her patience with the author. I also thank Sienna Arts for her excellent cover design and professionalism.

I give special thanks to my beta readers (who, as irony would have it, are all Alpha Males), Bradford Lewis, Sr., Oje Aboyade, Jelani Kush, and Mwalimu Baruti. Their insight, critique and encouragement has helped to strengthen my retelling of Kamau's story, and given me confidence in sharing this story with the world.

I am especially grateful for my family. First, because the tedious task of writing was not only mine. They too have been understanding and supportive enough to endure long hours of my absence as I sat at the computer. Second, because, in the course of life, they have also introduced me to their many friends, co-workers, schoolmates and other acquaintances. Exposure to so many different people and personalities has helped me to better represent the various members of the Vanguard Order and the Abantu.

Finally, I am most appreciative of Kamau, Old Cyrus, and those members of the Elder Council who have patiently helped me to understand the workings of the Vanguard Order and the Abantu.

Author Biography

Jomo W. Mutegi has jumped from a plane at over the Velds of South Africa, braved the rushing rapids of the Cheat River, raced down the slopes of Colorado mountains, and explored monuments on the Giza Plateau. Yet his greatest adventure is that of a husband, father and educator.

A professor of science education, Jomo studies how children learn science. He founded Black Kids Read to develop children's book and curriculum materials that tackle challenging, social and science-related topics. He currently lives in Hampton Roads, Virginia with his wife and their youngest son. Learn more at www.es2rp.org and https://blackkidsread.org/.

Call to Action

LEARN MORE ABOUT THE VANGUARD ORDER

Join Kamau and Kikuyu Squad in their ongoing quest to learn more about the Vanguard Order. Click the QR code below to find more detail on the Abantu, the Akhet, the technology of the Vanguard Order, and the planet Potakwe. Lesson plans and other instructional material are available here.

BRING OTHERS INTO THE ABANTU

Write a review of the book. I'm not asking for an empty five-star review. I would rather have an honest review that lets me and potential readers know how the book impacted you.

Tell us your likes and dislikes. Tell us what you learned and what you want to know more about. You can leave a review on the Black Kids Read website, Goodreads, or Amazon. Learn more by clicking the QR code.

STAY CONNECTED TO THE MKHOSI

Sign up to the Black Kids Read email list. Through the email list, I provide resources, information, and updates on this and other Black Kids Read titles.

Follow Black Kids Read on social media. Find us on X and Facebook by snapping the QR Code.

ORGANIZE YOUR OWN GROUP REFLECTION

I conduct in-person or virtual author visits with book clubs, school groups, or other community organizations. Snap the QR code to schedule a visit

https://blackkidsread.org/pages/secrets-of-the-vanguard-order

www.ingramcontent.com/pod-product-compliance
Lightning Source LLC
Chambersburg PA
CBHW030354310726
48979CB00001B/306